CAMELOT
DEPARTED

Published under licence by Brown Dog Books and
The Self-Publishing Partnership, 7 Green Park Station, Bath BA1 1JB

www.selfpublishingpartnership.co.uk

ISBN printed book: 978-1-83952-194-2

Cover design by Kevin Rylands
Internal design by Andrew Easton

Printed and bound in the UK

This book is printed on FSC certified paper

CAMELOT DEPARTED

THE TRAVAILS OF A CATHOLIC
PREP SCHOOL HEADMASTER

JONATHAN WHITE

BROWN
DOG
BOOKS

Acknowledgments

I would like to dedicate this book to my wife Marion
and my four children who have always supported me in this
endeavour as in all others. The idea of this story was that of
my eldest son Toby. In many ways this is his book
is much as mine. Special thanks to friends who gave
so much help and support – especially Ivan, Rosemary,
Harry, Dominic, Matthew, Giles, Catherine, Wayne,
and Toby Ross.

Dramatis Personae.
Camelot Departed.

William Jones	The Headmaster
Mary Jones	The Headmaster's wife
Francis Jones, James Jones, Charlie Jones, Flora Jones	
	The Jones children
Gethin Jones	William's father
Dilys Jones	William's mother
Owen, Carwyn Glynis	William Jones siblings
Tom Bruce	Glynis Australian husband
Ernest Becker	Mary Jones's father
Mr Owen Evans	William's teacher
Bob James	College friend of William's
Edwin Morris	Gethin's Masonic friend
Gavin Cronin	Bully at William's grammar school

Clergy

Rev Gareth Powell	Baptist minister
Father Thomas Father Columba	Dominican Friars

CAMELOT DEPARTED

Father Sean O'Connor	London Parish Priest
Prior Anselm	Parkies St Wilfred's Priory
Father Brendan O'Rourke	Parkies Parish Priest
Canon Basil Paine	Parkies School Founder.
Dom Osmund Ward	Parkies Downside

St Oliver Plunkett

Roy Childs	Chair
Mrs Lucy Thornley	Secretary/Bursar
Gary Prendergast	Staff

Parkies

Jonathan and Celia Carpenter	Chair and wife
James Thwaite	Jonathan Carpenter's friend
Lancelot and Geraldine Waters	Former head and wife
Thomas and Sarah Brown	Governor and wife
Margaret and Roland McKenzie	Governor and husband
Gerald and Tracey Grimes	Governor and wife
Barbara and David Watson	Governor and husband
Nigel Denton	Governor
Lord Robert Castle	Governor
The Hon Clementine Volkov	Lord Robert's sister
Viscountess Agnes Grey	Parent
Earl of Faversham	Lady Grey's father-in-law
Sir Reginald Godwin	Lady Grey's father
Kate and Robin Bell	Deputy Head and husband
Brian and Ludmila Varga	Staff

CAMELOT DEPARTED

Martin Pugh	Staff
Nathalie Harris	Staff
Graham Warner	Second Bursar
Janet Chester	Headmaster's secretary
Piers and Isabelle Dalton	Staff
Noah Bradley	Staff
John and Karen Lipman	Staff
St John and Angela de Vere	Staff
Elsie Tickle	Staff
Major George Hardy	First Bursar
Jenny and Jade matrons	Staff
James Waters	Staff
Evelyn Morley	Staff
Calvin E. Bauer	Psychotherapist and friend
Richard Perry	Appraiser
Tarun	Disturbed Pupil
Lord Gervase Tremane	Parent
Ambrose Hudson	Parent
Sam Graeme	Abused child
Persephone Grey	Pupil
Chief Inspector Patton	Senior policeman
Irina	Ludmila Varga's mother
Rory McKenzie	Pupil
Oliver Burns	Pupil

Finally, the headmaster's best friend: Alan Howarth

Contents

Camelot Departed.

Preface

CAMELOT DEPARTED

This novel is what might be best described as semi-autobiographical. Perhaps all first novels are to some extent so; I suspect incidentally this will be my first and last! It concerns the prep school world as it existed in the last two decades of the 20th century and one man, William Jones's, experience of it.

I lived in that world during that time. Clearly the character of William Jones has more than some passing similarity to me. However, it is not meant to be a pen portrait. Much of what is best about William is certainly not true of me. Whether or not I was as ingenuous and naive as him, I can only let others judge. Pride makes me think that was not so.

The schools which are characterised are Roman Catholic foundations. The schools I ran were also Roman Catholic. An important subplot of this book is an examination of the Catholic social scene with its numerous variations and how it related to the wider community during that time.

What William Jones was experiencing was a dramatic change in the Catholic community and its schools. These changes have further accelerated in recent decades. The distinction between convert recusant and Irish Catholics is much less significant now than it was even then.

At that time these labels were haphazard and probably even to Catholics increasingly meaningless.

However, the various prejudices and snobberies that then existed in that community were of course mirrored throughout the whole of English society, as I believe it still is. I hope that the focus on Catholics, and what may still be seen by some as their very peculiar ways will not make this story inaccessible to those who are not of this faith. I trust and believe that it will not.

Much of the culture of English prep schools was not in any way specifically Catholic. The origins of such institutions were firmly grounded in the English Anglican establishment; Catholics in the main simply borrowed their clothes. This was, I think, true equally of all independent schools of other religious traditions, or none.

I try and address in one chapter the issue of sexual abuse in boarding schools. This has become a much more live question in recent years. I have avoided the issue of clerical sexual abuse. This is not because I do not consider it as important. It is a particularly shameful issue.

The trouble is that I was hardly personally aware of it. Recently, exposures at schools like Downside, Ampleforth and Stonyhurst have shown that terrible things were happening whilst I was in situ as head of a feeder Catholic prep school.

The vast majority of the priests I have known were, however, I believe, good men untainted by this particular vice. I know of no children who were sexually abused by Catholic priests. This doesn't deny it happened; it probably simply illustrates my lack of awareness and intuition. The abuse circumstances I describe are entirely fictional. They are loosely based on a particular situation I did encounter. I have tried to deal honestly with an appreciation of the likely consequences of such behaviour as I witnessed and experienced it. I hope this narrative also partly addresses the very mixed motivations schools often had then when dealing with these problems.

I believe William Jones dealt with these issues honestly and with some integrity. However, looking at this through contemporary eyes, there is much in his approach which would now be quite reasonably criticised. One must look at situations in real time and on this question we have moved on. The way these matters would now be addressed is much altered. In the present milieu William Jones would no doubt have acted very differently.

The other characters sometimes have depictions that do refer at least obliquely to people I knew. However the characters are at most an amalgam of those with whom I was acquainted.

No single character is in any way related to anyone living or dead. They are essentially fictional constructs. With all such constructs they will depend on the author's imagination. The process of imagining will by necessity draw together both fantasy and memory.

I have, moreover, tried, at least at one level, to develop a kind of morality tale. This by definition involves good versus evil. One consequence of this has meant that some of my rather black and white characterisations have produced some individuals who are often much nicer than anyone I ever remember. Some are far worse. I recognise that situations are never quite as clear-cut as I describe in this story. Motivations are more complex than I sometimes suggest. However, this gives my story some structure which is my justification for it.

Parkies is an entirely fictional conceit. Obviously, it has elements within it which are similar to the boarding school I served at as headmaster. However, I never worked in Suffolk and as far as I know no such school exists or has ever existed in that county. St Oliver Plunkett school in London is also an imaginary construction. No such establishment exists or has ever existed. It is true that I was head of a London preparatory school and I cannot deny that I have drawn much from my memories of that time. I hope, nevertheless, that this story adds some perspective about the tale of the English Catholic preparatory school in that tumultuous and changing time. It is of course simply my perspective, my truth firmly bounded in a cloak of fiction.

I have always loved the Arthurian story. This story of a noble doomed endeavour to construct and enhance a truly utopian kingdom is one that I have repeatedly been drawn to. In my first years of married life I took my long-suffering wife on many holidays to places associated with that character. I tried to place William's quite different tale in that broad, romantic, nostalgic context. Sir Thomas Malory's fable is essentially the story of an unrealistic dream always impossible to achieve. Yet it was an ideal, ultimately destroyed by the naivety and malice of the main players as well as the implicit limitations of that venture. Perhaps what gives the story its timeless aura of calamity and disaster are the many defects of the people involved. As well as the mixed, sometimes unconscious nature of their motivations. This was the core of this tragedy – thus my justification for the name of this book.

I believe now, as I have all my life, that to be involved in education is one of the noblest of all callings. I count myself privileged to have spent much of my life within the educational world. I don't think I was as idealistic or indeed as unworldly as William Jones and certainly not as courageous as he was. What his humane, liberal vision of what schools should be about is one with which I entirely concur.

In this book William's romantic, unrealistic, lofty dream ultimately failed . It failed mostly because of William's innate limitations. It was bound to fail because as a fantasy it was simply unrealisable anyway. It also challenged too many of the prevailing shibboleths of its time and probably our time, too.

Whether William really understood that is a moot point. These probably are the only really important tenuous links to Sir Thomas Malory's tale.

I hope you enjoy reading this. In the end I trust it might provide an insight into the extraordinary world I once inhabited, which for good or ill is largely no more.

Camelot Departed:
The Travails of a Catholic
Prep School Headmaster

Chapter One

THE RETURN

In the early spring of 2019 the Jones family made a final pilgrimage to Suffolk. William and Mary Jones hadn't really wanted to go. They suspected that it was their now adult children who really needed to make this journey. William and Mary had been so loath to return, it was only to please them that had finally persuaded them.

They needed to finally draw a veil over such rarely spoken of memories that still so often enthralled or even haunted them. William had once been headmaster of the now defunct St Dogmael's prep school, the site of which they were now revisiting. It was an experience that hadn't ended well. It was the time, they felt, to finally address this.

William was now, he would very reluctantly admit, an old man. Older, he reflected, than his father had been when he had died thirty-four years previously. He looked at the driving mirror and a vision of an unfamiliar septuagenarian's wrinkled, blotchy face stared back.

He could hardly believe that this elderly visage could really be his. It was a thought that increasingly obsessed him. As he glanced at the ominously quiet, tight-lipped Mary he realised that she felt just as nervous and uncertain as him. She, too, was an elderly lady, although perhaps somewhat better preserved than him.

She retained a natural grace and pose, dressed in slacks and colourful jumper set off with a bright, floral silk scarf, she didn't look her sixty-nine years. Her normally lively, mobile features were firmly set in a steely attitude of uncertain, even dreaded expectations.

This rather forced, jovial family banter and increasingly unsuccessful attempts at recounting amusing reminiscences that had dominated much of the journey from London abruptly ceased as the people carrier car they had hired turned into the familiar gates of St Dogmael's.

William scanned the rather tense faces of his adult children and realised with a jolt that they, too, were just as anxious and uncertain as him and Mary. They hadn't talked much about the significance of this journey, but even so, as the car drove through the pretty, familiar countryside still filled with the last blooms of spring, he intuitively knew that they couldn't quite imagine how to decipher this both very familiar landscape with so many happy memories, and what still remained a strange, threatening, foreboding place redolent of past injury and unresolved regret.

It had been nearly two decades since they had last seen these rather austerely laced, wrought-iron gates that some local Victorian smith had conceived as the epitome of style and sophistication. Not for the first time William considered that the attempt was somewhat flawed. These gates had then been riddled with rust and flaking black paint. Now every swirl and mythical beast was picked out in a medley of a lurid and vivid palette of clashing colours.

What they now saw beyond this barrier was entirely unrecognisable. Long gone was the potholed, weed-infested, run-down country house avenue. It had been replaced by a much wider, well-maintained, tarmacked, suburban-like thoroughfare.

The former playing fields and tennis courts had long disappeared. In their place were avenues of elegant Neo-Georgian dwellings.

Each house was surrounded by manicured lawns and monotonous, regimented flower beds all neatly planted with a medley of garden centre favourites. Criss-crossing the site were the streets and cul-de-sacs redolent of a well-heeled, smug, suburban England.

Each had a familiar name. Mary saw that there was a Carpenter Road, a Paine Close, even a Denton Drive and a Waters Avenue. Hardly remembered names were now reified in neat, retrospective Gothic script. It was as though a theme park of an imagined counterfeit English respectability had somehow been relocated into the more naturally diverse landscape of the rolling hills of the West Suffolk countryside.

As they approached the old Victorian mansion, they noticed how that, too, had been entirely transformed. New gates even more tawdry than the paradigm they had just passed now enclosed some modestly sized gardens.

Scattered around the lawns were garden seats intended, or so it seemed, to be occupied by the elderly and infirm. A large sign confirmed that this was now 'St Dogmael's Rest Home for the Elderly'. They noticed the absence of the familiar massed ranks of terrapin buildings that once surrounded this house like tatty, unloved sentinels.

There was nothing shabby about this building anymore. Shorn of its ugly appendages, it was again the impeccably smart country house its Victorian builders had once envisaged, though now entirely lacking the wide, pastoral prospect that had been such an essential component of this once rural Arcadia.

These views were now replaced by restrained, oblique glimpses into those geometrically arranged commuter terraces and semi-detached dream houses of the newly affluent, aspirational, mostly metropolitan middle classes. The old house looked rather like an elderly swan, surrounding herself with a bevy of unloved, certainly pristine, but very ugly signets.

The newly spruced, smoothly tarmacked, but still winding drive terminated at the former stables where a large sign announced: 'Parklands' Stables Holiday Lets'. This was an exclusive complex of bijou apartments let out to wealthy holidaymakers, who wanted, so the sign further explained: 'Easy Access to Glorious Suffolk and the Norfolk Broads'.

The Jones children noticed that the ragged, untidy woods in which they had once played their games of tag, built their dens, and swung from the ropes of a rudimentary assault course, were no more.

They couldn't even conjure up an accurate vision of their beloved former teacher, Noah Bradley, who they most associated with this place.

The old outdoor swimming pool had long disappeared under the foundations of the 'Parklands' Community Centre', a rather unsuccessful architectural parody. It was a contemporary attempt to echo the old house's Neo-Gothic style. They even noticed that the dilapidated yard, a former kitchen garden that had once been pretentiously misnamed the cloisters, was now neatly repaved and enclosed by a huge, ugly conservatory. No longer was there the familiar, shrill chatter of children. It was now the domain of the elderly, near lifeless residents. There they sat contemplating their imminent and often much-desired demise.

Most of the characters who had been associated with this place in the days when it had been a school were long gone. Even the 'St Dogmael's Former Pupils Association' only barely limped on since the death five years ago of its long-time chair Jonathan Carpenter. It would not be very long before even the living echo that a school even existed would dissipate, remaining only as the petrified memory of a plaque on a wall.

William's name was commemorated nowhere. It was as though he had never existed. Perhaps no one wished to recall the thirteen years he had served as headmaster.

Were they too embarrassed to commemorate a person whose tenure had ended in failure so traumatically nearly twenty years before?

William hoped that he might remain a little longer in the minds and hearts of some of the children, whose lives he hoped they had influenced. If that was so, far better than having an estate road named after you. It brought to William's mind a quotation from his beloved Thomas Malory:

The sweetness of love is short-lived, but the pain endures.

Even after they had left St Dogmael's prep school, they like everyone else had come to affectionately designate it as Parkies. This landscape and the memories it evoked had continued to cast a huge shadow over the rest of all their lives.

This had been somewhere that had given them great joy and intense sadness. It had been the place where William and Mary had watched their children grow up with all its inherent joy and sadness. To William, it had been the pinnacle of all his dreams and the depths of his nightmares.

To all of the Jones family it had at one time been something more: it had been home. It felt important to have returned once again, if only to try and lay to rest the many ghosts they associated with this place. In some ways it was not so painful an experience as William had feared. What he saw now was a so different and unfamiliar alien world. It was something else transformed and diminished simultaneously in their eyes; a pastiche perhaps, but not real, at least to them.

Their Suffolk idyll was finally irrevocably over. Although they often felt as though it was just yesterday, they would finally fully understand both in their hearts as well as their minds that this world had truly gone. This visit would simply bury it for good.

It had all seemed so much more positive and optimistic over thirty years before, when they had first driven down the then so dilapidated driveway. William and Mary were young, enthusiastic, and full of optimistic anticipation then. They had travelled to Suffolk from London, for an interview at the then St Dogmael's Preparatory School. They hoped that this opportunity might, if they were successful, represent an exciting new beginning for them.

They didn't then really believe that they had any realistic chance of being appointed. Even the experience of seeing this new, unfamiliar world was an adventure. They knew with absolute certainty that if the unbelievable happened they were going to transform and renew this fading institution. It never occurred to them that a venture like this could be other than a roaring success.

That confidence and hubristic optimism were so palpable as they drove through the gates of Parkies in 1987. The rolling acres of West Suffolk had then seemed the ideal place to bring up their young family of three little boys: a new beginning pregnant with possibilities.

Chapter Two

LET THEM EAT CAKE

The cake, as always was excellent. A huge chocolate concoction with cherries on top took pride of place, with a delicious strawberry cheesecake and scones for those who would like an even greater variety.

Jonathan Carpenter looked at this sumptuous spread with some cynical amusement. He was chairman of the governors of St Dogmael's Prep School for boys, Parklands. Today the board of governors were to meet, and as usual no expense was spared in preparing the lavish tea that was always spread before them.

This was the preliminary to an extraordinary governors' meeting called on this especially gloomy February afternoon in 1987. Today they were to select a new headmaster. Present in this room together with Jonathan Carpenter, were the other school governors: Mrs Margaret McKenzie, Lord Robert Castle, Mr Gerald Grimes, Mr Thomas Brown, Prior Anselm, and Father Brendan O'Rourke. It was certainly going to be an interesting, perhaps, Jonathan mused, even an enlightening meeting.

Jonathan nevertheless allowed himself a quiet chuckle at the ironic nature of the milieu in which they were meeting. The room the governors were using had once been the epitome of Victorian wealth and excess. Oak and leather-lined walls with magnificent fireplaces made for a very luxurious, prestigious setting.

However, that was the past. If you looked carefully you could see the many subtle, and not so subtle, signs of decay and dissolution. The opulent, gilded, Spanish tooled-leather wallcovering was in many places faded and ripped. The ornate wooden skirting board was scuffed and in places inexpertly repaired. The fireplaces, filled with their now largely chipped and discoloured De Morgan tiles, had not been used in years, despite the bitingly cold Suffolk winter.

This afternoon was especially chilly and the ancient, inefficient night storage heaters did little to modify the sense of a damp, glacial, anaesthetised miasma that pervaded this room. This seemed to him to be an atmosphere wholly appropriate for the task in hand. The pompous, wealthy Victorian grandees that had once resided here were long gone. Parkies had taken their place and that, too, was in terminal eclipse.

It had once been a very grand prep school in the glory days of its revered founder, the eccentric former Anglican, latterly Catholic priest, Canon Basil Paine. It had been one of the smartest Catholic prep schools, dominating the scholarship lists of the greater Catholic public schools, with even the occasional boy, like Jonathan, moving on to Eton, Winchester, Uppingham or Oundle.

In those days when diplomats, administrators and soldiers were spread all over the dying empire and needed to offload their snotty-nosed striplings to someplace where they could often forget about them, Parkies had flourished. Now the empire was finally dead and the rich gentry no longer wished to send their sons to a crumbling pile in the middle of nowhere. Parkies was dying.

Yet, Jonathan knew there was little understanding within this room of this sad direction of travel. Most governors remained convinced that, despite the overwhelming evidence to the contrary, this world of ostentatious, if now faded, privilege was still somehow retrievable. Perhaps the culinary extravagance in which they were indulging went some way to soothe their ever-niggling fears and anxieties.

Jonathan turned to look at his colleagues on the board; many were loudly quarrelling as usual. Some were, he mischievously reflected, the mix of people that Parkies so definitely now deserved.

His eye alighted on the three most energetically engaged in the lively exchange of views on the virtues, or otherwise, of the candidates with whom they were about to soon be personally acquainted: the tweedy, rather too well proportioned, middle-aged Mrs Margaret McKenzie; the bull-necked, red-faced and seemingly perpetually angry Mr Gerald Grimes; and the elderly, tall, somewhat rumpled, plump figure of Lord Robert Castle. They seemed particularly exercised by the small pile of papers in front of them: the curricula vitae of those candidates they were about to meet.

All the members of the governing board were present on this important day. Prior Anselm the charming, elderly, graciously and appropriately attired monk, in a well-tailored, crisply ironed Augustinian black monastic habit. This frail, somewhat ethereal priest was the former Prior of St Wilfried's Augustinian house in Ipswich. Sitting beside him was the endearingly vague, dishevelled Father Brendan O'Rourke, the Irish parish priest and custodian of the hideously Art Deco Catholic parish church of St Patrick in the nearby town. His earthy, rather shabby, tattily uncared-for appearance contrasted sharply with the elegantly manicured, spruce monk.

Jonathan realised that these two priests were no longer going to be key in deciding who would be the next headmaster. There were fewer Catholic children now and the influence of the clergy was therefore waning. This was a fact that Prior Anselm in particular refused to accept. "You know, Jonathan, we must absolutely respect the wishes of the founder," a sentiment he frequently enthusiastically expressed.

The trouble was that with barely a quarter of the school pupils Catholic, the reality was that this now only represented a minority interest. This could no longer be the only, or even predominant, consideration in planning for the future.

Jonathan hoped that a newly appointed governor, present at his first meeting, was going to play a more significant role. He was the smartly dressed, business-suited, seemingly rather bemused local industrialist, who was perched on a somewhat rickety, allegedly antique Chippendale chair at the very edge of the proceedings.

Thomas Brown looked for all the world as though he felt he had strayed into a strange, bizarre menagerie and was considering any means of escape. The problem was no one really noticed this obvious outsider; a fish out of water so removed from this natural habitat that no one other than Jonathan could understand quite why he was there.

Thomas was anxiously reflecting how it was possible that he could have been foolish enough to have allowed himself to have been persuaded by Jonathan Carpenter to accept a place on the board of governors and thus join this curiously eccentric group of people. He realised that he had become the victim of Jonathan's beguiling charm and subtle flattery.

He wasn't even a Catholic, and when he looked at the idiosyncratically attired Lord Castle and the frankly peculiar, positivity retro-medieval figure of Prior Anselm, he was jolly glad he wasn't!

A year ago his little boy Marcus had joined the Nursery. They had chosen the school for entirely geographical reasons. It was situated quite close to a recently acquired home. Parkies' Catholic tradition was a serious detriment rather than a positive encouragement in their decision-making.

He reassured himself somewhat with the last words Jonathan had addressed to him before he had accepted his offer: "Really, Thomas, don't be too alarmed by the oddities of some of the other governors. It is your common sense that we need; Protestant or otherwise," he added with his customary winsome smile.

He therefore presumed that Jonathan Carpenter had invited him onto the board because of a reputation for supposed business acumen. He couldn't think of any other obvious reason. To be frank, he and his wife Sarah barely knew the Carpenters. They were part of the grand Suffolk set the Browns had not the slightest wish or desire to be included within. The pretentious sense of social entitlement which he associated with so many members was something he truly loathed. The feeling, he guessed, was mutual.

Thomas, with his very obvious Suffolk burr and déclassé demeanour, was in the eyes of many of his neighbours a parvenu, a person of little consequence. Wealthy certainly but lacking in the essential social gravitas essential to be truly acceptable.

Yet Thomas, now he was here, was determined to do his best to attempt to inject a bit of his hard-headed pragmatic view of the world into this odd, and as he was now increasingly perceiving it, curious, outlandish realm of the Suffolk prep school.

He didn't rate highly his chances, but he smiled wryly when he thought that he was not entirely unfamiliar with such difficult challenges. Judging from the previous half an hour or so, Parkies was going to be an especially interesting and demanding one.

The board were now trying to decide on one of three candidates for the position, and the discussion was getting heated: "Are these really the best three people we could find?" keenly questioned Mrs McKenzie, looking as always for reassurance to Lord Castle, who gave her, in Jonathan's opinion, a rather vacuous, half-irritated smile. "Of course not, my dear," sneered an aggressive and somewhat exasperated Grimes with all of his customary blunt, sarcastic rudeness. "We have, after all, the headmasters of Eton and Harrow and the Vice-Chancellor of the University of Oxford all waiting patiently as our second choices. We just thought we'd waste everyone's time before making the real decision." Mrs McKenzie opened her mouth, presumably, Jonathan impishly imagined, to remark, "Thank goodness, why don't you show them in."

In growing frustration Grimes then started to growl. "Of course they are the best people we could find in fact they are the only people who applied!" Whilst this was not strictly accurate, it was close enough to the truth to be of real concern. In fact there had been six applicants, in what Jonathan Carpenter especially regarded as an appallingly weak field.

Grimes then raised his eyes in his trademark gesture of supercilious contempt; the stupidity of some of the board, he told himself, never ceased to amaze him.

This pose of an obviously counterfeit patronising superiority might have aided Grimes's sense of his own self-importance, it rarely convinced others.

Most of his fellow governors thought of him as boorish and ill-mannered. Grimes's stentorian outburst did, however, have the effect of finally drawing Prior Anselm out of his postprandial stupor: "Can't we find a decent Catholic? Surely someone from the right family must be interested?"

Prior Anselm still imagined that the world of posh Catholic recusant families still trod their way to the Parkies' portals, and a lesser sprig must surely be interested in the privilege of being the future headmaster. He had failed to notice that only one such parent still remained. Given the fact that Sir Robert Despenser was on his third marriage following two messy divorces; the recusant or any Catholic connection was tenuous at best.

St Dogmael's ironically was located in the area of the kingdom with one of the smallest proportion of Catholics. When old Canon Paine had founded the place and the school consisted entirely of boarders, that seemed hardly to matter. With the now more local Protestant and secular clientele, most current families, like the Browns, thought of these papist traditions as a colourful eccentricity at best, a harmful distraction at worst.

This had long ceased to be a 'marketing tool' to use the corporate speak that few governors understood or approved.

To all the people in the room the applicants were, to put it kindly, less than stellar. Percival Haggerston appeared the best, from a social and probably, from Prior Anselm's perspective, a religious one, too.

The Haggerstons were a family who could trace an unbroken Catholic recusant lineage right back to the Reformation.

There was no obvious sign that Percy took this hereditary religion very seriously. His attendance at Mass was, for example, very irregular to say the least. Nevertheless, he could claim to be the sprig of a family of unimpeachable Catholic orthodoxy, as well as incidentally containing two gruesomely martyred saints. One way or another most of the spectacularly ineptly organised papist plots of the 16th and 17th centuries had a Haggerston thumbprint on them: a family heritage Percy was usually less keen to crow about. On this occasion he took a somewhat less coy attitude!

Even his wife Miranda's firmly Protestant roots could claim a tenuous, elite recusant link: a great-great-grandfather had been the first Catholic allowed into the Indian Civil Service in the glory days of Empire.

This gave even her background a tincture of the swish Catholic upper class, for which so many governors assiduously yearned. They did, therefore, tick quite a few boxes!

Unfortunately, Percy had singularly failed to live up to this distinguished, if somewhat contested, heritage. Not only had his parents failed to educate him at a Catholic school, so he had therefore little experience of their distinct ethos, and only the most rudimentary understanding of the faith they promulgated. Moreover, it was well known that he had acquired, whilst at Oxford, a somewhat raffish reputation.

Fifteen years earlier, the popular press was full of reports of the most recent outrageous example of the loutish behaviour of the notorious Bullingdon Club. This involved, amongst other things, the debagging of an unsuspecting innocent local greengrocer. Percy had been an active, possibly the leading participant in this appalling violation, involving as it did an entirely novel use of a leek. Not, it must be said, in any way related to a vegetable stew!

This had resulted in a night in the police cells, a sizeable fine, as well as being bound over to keep the peace. His riotous reprobate behaviours were an important factor in his securing a mere third in his finals.

A few considered that he was extremely fortunate not to be sent down. This did not initially detract from his appointment soon after as a master in a well-known, if not Catholic, public school.

His greatest and ultimately fatal weakness was that he had to resign rather suddenly from his current position as housemaster for 'inappropriate contact with the boys'. Such a live accusation, although not yet tested in the courts, or indeed ever likely to be, had convinced a few of the governors that he was a totally unsuitable candidate for any school, particularly one largely consisting of many vulnerable boarders. However, this was not yet the settled view of the board as a whole. Social connections so often trumped moral turpitude in the outraged opinion of Thomas Brown and Father Brendan especially.

The fact he was being interviewed at all, Jonathan also believed, other than the sparsity of other candidates, was largely due to his good looks and charm, which had so influenced many of the females he had come into contact with. This was especially so with Mrs McKenzie, who had firmly insisted on his inclusion and was therefore his greatest advocate.

His charm was nevertheless compelling. The result perhaps of a life of always getting his own way, and an only slightly blemished record (at least in his view), if not one of notable success.

His career was one of adequate, perhaps somewhat pedestrian, professional progression. His background of leading public school, Oxford and numerous high-profile, if not especially prestigious jobs all in illustrious, non-Catholic independent schools gave his application a certain specious credibility. Before his recent resignation, the only real surprise was that a man of such impeccable credentials would be applying to such an obvious dump like St Dogmael's.

The second applicant was the favoured choice of the previous headmaster and had home advantage. John Lipman had been deputy headmaster of Parkies for ten years. He had followed the retiring head Lancelot Waters, in the view of many, into the abyss of dissipated decay and decrepitude, rather like, Jonathan acerbically considered, a well-trained Labrador. Unfortunately 'Sipper', as he was known by all those connected with the school, was a drinker.

In fact, Sipper could, it was said, outdrink anyone in the Common Room, a not insignificant feat as most of Parkies staff were, in Jonathan's view, the most unrepentant and persistent dipsomaniacs he had ever had the misfortune to come across.

In Parkies the beer, spirits and wine flowed freely, be it day, night or, indeed, especially on Prize Day. The honoured guest at the last such occasion, the local Conservative MP and former butcher Charles Harvey, had been amazed to discover a bacchanalian carousel fully in play almost before he had completed the process of prize-giving.

The MP, not a man usually easily dumbfounded, given his many well-publicised affairs and propensity for insider dealing and luxurious taxpayer-funded foreign junkets, was apparently so shocked by these events that he later described the school to a friend and local notable as St Drunkens of Brahms and Liszt. This label had sadly and predictably stuck.

The widespread scandal this had caused was rumoured to be a significant factor in Jonathan Carpenter's decision to finally insist on the retirement of the present head. Despite all this, John Lipman felt that, as he had served the school for over twenty years, this fact alone made the headship a right which he had both earned and fully deserved.

Self-examination and reflection were not talents that John Lipman possessed in any abundance. Worst of all he had only the faintest notion of the part his behaviour had contributed to the school's present perilous situation.

Finally there was the outside candidate. William Jones was the current head of some insignificant London day school that few from the lofty heights of Parkies had ever heard of. He was a nobody, moderately successful and apparently fairly competent.

Jonathan Carpenter had taken the trouble to visit William Jones's London school some weeks before. He remained ambiguous about certain aspects of this candidate's background. Certainly, he would be an unusual choice for any boarding prep school. He had, however, in his own mind already decided that he was the only possible realistic option available.

He was acutely aware that Jones's present school would not remotely be considered an institution that most of the other governors would ever have regarded as an appropriate launch pad for a future headmaster of St Dogmael's. He was also conscious that most of the other governors hated the very thought of him and were bemused by Jonathan's insistence that he should be shortlisted.

A tradesman son, a grammar schoolboy, without a decent degree, and worst of all his voice betrayed a faint Welsh lilt. He was, as far as they could tell, a practising Catholic convert.

One of his referees was Father O'Connor his parish priest, who had spoken very warmly of the Jones family. This religious enthusiasm hardly detracted from a sense of his déclassé plebeian social inferiority in the opinion of most.

Whilst theoretically the head of Parkies should be Catholic, nobody on the board really cared, except for Prior Anselm, Father O'Rourke and perhaps, surprisingly, Jonathan Carpenter who, despite the vicissitudes of his life, retained a modicum of his mother's faith.

Even Prior Anselm was as much bothered by the kind of Catholic who was appointed. Preferably posh and English, not convert if it could be helped: definitely not Irish! Jones, to his mind, was not satisfactory on any of these points, although Prior Anselm might just reluctantly concede that being Welsh was marginally better than Irish. Father Brendan was far more inclusive and tolerant. He just wanted a believer. He thought that perhaps in William Jones they had found one!

Jonathan had also quickly detected a certain artless naivety in William Jones's character. He would not understand the role Jonathan had clandestinely designated for him. Quite simply, Jonathan was convinced that they were appointing the last headmaster of this school.

Despite a keenness and a somewhat endearing enthusiasm, it was obvious, too, that the titles and the ersatz gentility of Parkies had quite bowled Jones over.

This was something that could, Jonathan was ashamed to admit, be exploited. This was just the sort of chap, he considered, who would be the perfect nominee for leading Parkies into its final inevitable demise. This could be spun, if necessary, as a consequence of his obvious limitations. The perfect 'plausible deniability' should any hint of blame on behalf of the board and of him in particular be remotely suggested. A secret part of the chairman's darker psyche was already celebrating the fact he had found the perfect candidate. Now to arrange it just so...

Jonathan now decided it was time to open proceedings. "Ladies and gentlemen, welcome. I trust you all had no difficulty getting down here for this interview?" The assembled interviewees nodded their heads.

"We will commence interviewing you individually in alphabetical order in just a moment. Before we do I would like to give you the opportunity to exchange a bit of small talk with the board and refresh yourselves before we begin." Jonathan smiled. "Would anyone care for a drink?"

Half an hour later things had progressed as Jonathan had anticipated. 'Sipper' Lipman had immediately taken up the offer and proceeded to serve himself and Percy the typical Parkies gin and tonic. He could never understand why the 'and tonic' bit was included in the title, as tonic water constituted no more than a splash into this lethal concoction.

William Jones and his wife, on the other hand, were being conspicuously ignored by Lipman. He was, as Jonathan knew, at heart, a terrible snob, as well as predictably and coincidentally being horribly socially insecure.

John Lipman felt insulted that Jones had even have been offered an interview. Lipman had a very precise view of who would, or who would not, be a suitable headmaster. Blind certainly to his own limitations, he believed that any candidate would at the very least have some experience within the boarding prep school world.

As far as he could tell, Jones definitely did not. He had observed the previous evening to his wife Karen: "I simply don't understand why this man Jones is being interviewed. No class, no contacts, no experience: what could he possibly have to offer?"

Sadly, it seemed obvious that Lipman thought the job was in the bag. That alone, Jonathan observed, was going to make the situation more complicated.

His rather obvious rude, dismissive attitude to another candidate was not, however, helping his case. The Jones couple were standing uncomfortably on the margins of the group. Partly because of all this, Jonathan thought it better if he served Jones and his wife. He was very careful to offer a far more restrained tipple to them than the other candidates were currently quaffing.

The existing headmaster, Lancelot Waters, was someone who had seemed quite content in recent years to use his position to increase, or perhaps more realistically, maintain his social standing, at the same time allowing the school to crumble around his ears.

In fairness his understanding of the prep school market had fossilised at least a decade before. He believed that the privilege was in allowing parents to choose St Dogmael's, not the other way round. To him the question was essentially one of tone. If he maintained the right unchangeable *ne plus ultra* atmosphere of the traditional prep school mores, all, he assumed, would be well. This was an attitude that he had engraved on the psyche of his impressionable protégé John Lipman.

He had finally, with considerable and much resented persuasion from Jonathan, agreed to go. He had once been something of the young lion of the prep school world. Thirty years of copious gins, professional disappointments and a growing if yet not fully understood sense of the imminent demise of the world he aspired to belong. This had contributed to a frequently tipsy, curmudgeonly, usually irrational, and grumpy approach to most staff and parent relationships.

To him the demise of his career was largely explained by a mix of inexplicable misfortune and personal malice. "I simply don't understand Carpenter's attitude," he had opined to his wife Geraldine the previous evening. "He was educated in the system, he has even sent his lad to Parkies, yet inexplicably he seems not really to believe in any of it. I wonder whether he really wants this place to survive at all." Geraldine, who was much more prescient about the bleak realities of the prep school world, simply replied distractedly: "Of course, dear, if you say so."

Waters, a former athlete, who had once played fly-half for Scotland, had once been a fine figure of a man. Now his copious tummy was the first thing that seemed to heave into view. His once handsome face was now lined with the burst blood vessels that was the telltale sign of a heavy drinker.

He had perfected the art of greasy and insincere charm. This was something he regarded as the core attribute of a successful prep school head. Jonathan knew he had really lost interest in taking any significant role in the management of the school. Much of this task had been left to John Lipman, who was a highly effective administrator as well as being an impressive teacher. Charm, insincere or otherwise, was something Lipman conspicuously lacked.

Lancelot Waters's attire was that of the shabby country gent: quality clothes that had seen better times. His close friendship with Margaret McKenzie and her husband Roland had rather encouraged him to buy into their delusional views of the status and future prospects of the school.

Deep in his psyche, he half-understood it would not be in his best interests to hang around for Parkies' last death throes. The auditors might finally be called in and more closely examine the gross financial ineptitude and organisational drift that had characterised recent times. No, that wouldn't do at all. Better, he sometimes reluctantly accepted, to let a new man take the heat. At least, he happily reflected, now that he was merely the bagman, any decision would not be his.

Each candidate was invited into the school drawing room, accompanied by their wives. The first in alphabetical order was William Jones and his wife Mary. If William was somewhat problematic from the perspective of much of the board, Mary was even more so.

Mrs McKenzie and Lord Castle in particular had a clear idea of the role of the headmaster's wife: dull and subservient being the two operative words. Mary did not conform to any of this.

Most of the board would probably have conceded that she was pretty, in a rather boring, suburban way: her piercing green eyes certainly suggested some intelligence and character.

Her background of solid working-class, upwardly mobile endeavour did not appeal. "My God," Mrs McKenzie proclaimed, "I think she might even be a feminist." Gerald Grimes looked for a moment as though he would have a seizure.

Worse, too, in the eyes of many, Mary was dressed in a smart trouser suit rather than the more acceptable and conventional skirt, blouse and jacket. "So common," opined Mrs McKenzie. "Even her shoes are M&S!"

Father O'Rourke lifted his hands into a steeple and appeared to be deep in prayer. This was a pose he often affected when he didn't really approve. In this case, which would have much surprised some of his fellow governors, it was Mrs McKenzie's appalling and overt snobbery and prejudice of which he definitely didn't approve.

Despite a wobbly start when Mary had asked to use the toilet, Lord Castle was heard to mutter: "Doesn't she even know it is called a lavatory?!" The interview was not, however, a disaster.

William was able to answer the questions, albeit diffidently, but probably adequately. Jonathan's encouraging air certainly irritated and confused other panel members. Many had considered Jones as merely the outside fill-in candidate. They didn't understand why the chair had to be so friendly and encouraging to him.

Jonathan had even managed successfully to draw the shy, nervous William out. In this endeavour he was assisted by Father O'Rourke and the newcomer Thomas Brown. Thomas might not understand the intricacies of the prep school marketplace. He recognised that William probably did. The answers Jones gave were certainly not inspiring, but they at least didn't entirely scupper his chances.

Whilst there was still little genuine enthusiasm for his appointment, most board members judged him now to be a faint possibility, if of course there was absolutely no other alternative.

John Lipman was of a known quantity. Lipman considered this to be his trump card. Unfortunately, this was very much a mixed blessing. Everyone on the panel had at least as clear an inkling of his weaknesses as of his supposed strengths.

Gerald Grimes made a gallant attempt to steer the questions away from the drinking culture of the Common Room, and of him in particular. Jonathan had not, however, forgiven or forgotten the incidents of the last Prize Day.

This was not helped by a nickname he had acquired in the county: 'Jonathan Canned of St Drunkens'. He was damned if his previous efforts to save this school were to be crowned with social ostracism and ridicule.

In his most soft-spoken, reasonable and, to those who knew him well, dangerous voice, he enquired whether it was true that he and the present headmaster regularly shared a whole bottle of sherry with Lipman at lunchtime.

Lipman responded with obvious discomfiture and embarrassment. He hadn't even imagined that Carpenter knew about this. He was not the first to underestimate this polite, charming, somewhat smooth, but very grounded country gentleman and industrial tycoon.

Despite Grimes attempts to make light of this, with the hearty observation that boys will be boys, this one question was the Exocet missile which shattered poor Lipman chances. Even with his obvious virtues of loyalty and pedagogical competence most of the board recognised that an alcoholic might not be the best potential candidate.

The final interview was with Percy Haggerston and it started extraordinarily well. He strode into the drawing room as though the job was his already. He was beautifully kitted out in the most *du jour*, elegant, sophisticated Savile Row suit.

He looked the very image of the successful head. His wife Miranda was fashionable and refined. Her ensemble had touches of Leander in Henley, on regatta day. She scrutinised her handsome husband with just the right mix of awe and deference; the perfect wifely submissiveness. There wasn't even a hint of M&S in a single item of her attire. Mrs McKenzie simpered in evident pleasure and delight.

Prior Anselm looked like a cat who had glimpsed the cream, in his case the authentic image of the true Catholic gentleman. When he described, with such manifest pleasure, the many social contacts he and his wife had acquired at their smart Clarendon school, Lord Castle was not the only one who glimpsed the possible, much-desired, social renaissance of Parkies.

Percy even hinted of his wife's somewhat tangential aristocratic connections. Her grandmother had been one of the many mistresses of the late Duke of Kent. It was rumoured he had been the father of her equally disreputable mother; perhaps not entirely respectable, but enough to impress most of the board.

It was left to the doughty Father O'Rourke to ask the one question that Haggerston and his main ally Mrs McKenzie dreaded. "What was the nature of the inappropriate contact with the boys?"

Obviously, Percy had expected this, and before he could frame a reply his feisty wife interjected: "It was a complete fabrication." Percy lamely tried to calm what was increasingly becoming an embarrassing, possibly catastrophic riposte. Miranda Haggerston continued: "The boys involved were lying and worse still, they and their ghastly parents were plotting to destroy my husband's career."

The apparently rather bumbling, shambolic Father O'Rourke to the surprise of some persisted. Looking directly at Percy, he asked: "If that was so, why did it require your immediate resignation?"

Percy decided to play the 'virtue card'. "I resigned," he stated rather pompously and unconvincingly, "because it was the honourable thing to do. I wanted to protect the reputation of the school." Gerald Grimes barely audibly muttered, "And yours, too!"

There were lots of further questions about school finances, the independent school market, recent educational trends, as well as much else. To be fair, Percy dealt with these with aplomb and much charm, as well as a considerable fund of know-how and intuitive understanding.

Father O'Rourke's interjection had fatally undermined his application. Jonathan felt that, despite the persistent, somewhat contrived, stilted coquettishness of the obviously besotted Margaret McKenzie, it was clear that the board no longer trusted his assurances. "Too damned smooth by half," was the acerbic comment of Gerald Grimes over his gin and tonic after the meeting. For once he seemed to be expressing the views of nearly everyone.

With the eventual departure of the candidates, the board reconvened to consider their decision. They sat in a rather disconsolate, demoralised circle to weigh their thoughts. Mrs McKenzie and Gerald Grimes might just have reluctantly conceded that their particular favoured candidate hadn't quite cut the mustard.

However, the thought that they might be lumbered with this rather plebeian, entirely unknown man Jones was entirely anathema to both of them. Prior Anselm enquired tentatively whether it would be better to simply re-advertise. He was sure that somewhere there was just the right man. It was only necessary to have some faith. He even ingenuously suggested prayer as one possible option. Grimes guffawed in his usual churlish manner. On this occasion, too, he again unwittingly reflected the sense of the meeting; even Mrs McKenzie could not suppress a reluctant smirk.

It was left to the newly appointed Thomas Brown to insert a modicum of realism. "Despite weeks of advertisements in every publication we can think of, at considerable expense, might I remind you, we have only received ten enquiries and six applications. The three we rejected were either illiterate, entirely unsuitable, or both!" He continued. "The people we interviewed today are the only possibilities: whether we like it or not, it has, in my opinion, to be one of them."

In the final analysis it wasn't then so much who was best, but rather who was least worst in the minds of most. Two gins into the meeting and Lord Castle summed up the situation in the pithy phrase: "It comes down to an alcoholic, a paedophile or a social inadequate." That night Jonathan Carpenter telephoned a rather surprised William Jones and offered him the post of Headmaster of St Dogmael's School.

Chapter Three

CANON PAINE'S FAILING DREAM

Parklands House had not emerged unscathed from a wartime occupation by the rumbustious airman of the USAF. This evidence of neglect and damage occasioned by the more outrageous japes of its young, increasingly bored inhabitants was enough to discombobulate the most uncritical potential purchaser.

It was, however, extraordinarily cheap for so large a house that might house a school. That single fact was its main attraction when Canon Basil Paine purchased this property and then subsequently opened St Dogmael's preparatory school in the freezing winter of 1947.

Most of his friends and fellow priests thought he had taken leave of his senses. A friend who had served with him as an Army chaplain during the war was so perturbed by this decision he commented: "Basil, this is quite mad. Mr Attlee is in the process in dismantling the Empire, the aristocracy and removing wealth from anyone who might remotely afford school fees: who do you imagine will attend your school?"

Canon Paine was a man of considerable independent means and gargantuan self-assurance. Some might have called it stupendous obstinacy. This admonition did not dissuade him from sinking most of his fortune into this ugly Victorian mansion. He could now fulfil his lifelong dream of providing a Catholic education for those boys who had formerly attended the smarter Protestant alternatives.

Canon Basil, who converted to the faith in the heady atmosphere of 1930s Oxford, was determined to provide the kind of elite education for Catholic boys he himself had experienced at the robustly Anglican Ludgrove School in Wokingham. Whatever Mr Attlee was up to, Canon Paine was sure there would still be plenty of potential takers. As it turned out, he was absolutely right.

In the twenty-three years in which he served as the charismatic and, in opinion of many, legendary headmaster the school managed to attain the heights of academic and social prestige. Canon Paine was a naturally urbane patrician. As such he was wholly immersed in English elite culture. It amused him sometimes to announce that his father was a Bishop. Having waited for the frisson of shock such an announcement produced in Catholic circles, he would add mischievously that he was of course an Anglican Bishop. His father held the Irish see of Connor.

This had given him an insight from his earliest childhood into the strange, indecipherable Roman Catholic world of Ireland. He supposed that many Irish Catholics would have considered him a fully paid-up member of the Anglo-Irish Protestant Ascendancy: not always a good start in developing a positive relationship with his Hibernian neighbours. The fact that his maternal grandfather owned 5,000 acres in Kerry, as well as the distinction of having his house burnt down by the Fenians in 1921, would have surely confirmed such a suspicion.

It was certainly true he wasn't always entirely enamoured by what he saw of the Irish Church. This was reinforced in his mind by the two years he had to spend in an Irish seminary after his conversion. At the very least this was an enormous cultural shock, especially after his time at Christ Church Oxford and a spell at the Anglo-Catholic St Stephen's Theological College: better known to its former students as 'Staggers'. Whilst he didn't always care for some Irish practices, it left him with a fascination: horror mingled with some lingering affection for the Irish Church.

This was a surprising if not always fully understood component in his former conversion. Jokingly he sometimes used to comment: "The greatest cross the Church in England has to bear is that of Ireland." Given his many Irish friends, no one ever believed he really meant this.

Despite this background, or perhaps partly because of it, he was very socially secure and this meant most of all he didn't much esteem the various fake hierarchies beloved by so many of his class. To him the Catholic ideal was a world of faith and charity, together with a sense of the possibilities that Divine Grace provided hope for a common flawed humanity. This always easily trumped the narrow snobberies of class and status.

His vision of community and shared values, something he had witnessed as a boy in Ireland, had often meant that he was willing to finance many disadvantaged families who he thought might benefit from his school. If this offended some of his snooty, more pretentious parents, so be it: he simply didn't much care.

When he retired in 1970, despite, perhaps even because of, his holistic vision of what education might be for everyone, Parkies had become the preferred choice for many aspirational Catholic as well as other non-Catholic families. Unfortunately, the following seventeen years became a time of inexorable decline.

This had clouded his few remaining years of retirement at St Wilfred's Priory. He had mourned what he perceived to be the end of his dream and the ruin of his life's work.

This had been an important factor in persuading him to finally approach one of the most successful of his old boys, Jonathan Carpenter, to take over as Chairman of the Board.

The little eight-year-old, who had trembled with fear and anxiety at the door of his newly opened school thirty years before, had become one of the elderly Canon's closest and most esteemed friends. He hoped that his Midas touch would work its magic on his crumbling school and fading dream.

Jonathan Carpenter was now a tall, bespectacled, rather dapper, middle-aged man. When he was a young undergraduate at Pembroke College Oxford he had something of a reputation with the ladies. He had rowed for his college, and to the very few women then residing in the university he was seen as a god. Certainly he never lacked for female company, or even more so, it was salaciously reported.

Blond, muscular, with that languid confidence and wit that was the mark of a true Etonian, he looked the very image of the patrician *beau monde*. Even at the age of forty-seven, he was thought of by some of the younger female teachers at Parkies as a dish.

This was the result in part of his relatively abstemious diet, as well as his employment of a personal trainer and his propensity for energetic riding. Regularly out with the West Suffolks, he could still show these youngbloods a thing or so.

Dressed as he was on this day of the interview, in his customary hacking jacket and cavalry twill trousers, he looked the very image of an English country gentleman. His appearance was not in any way ostentatious, a thought that would have absolutely horrified him. He took great pains to avoid such an impression. This even went as far as his choice of an originally expensive, but now a very discreetly unpretentious 1965 Jaguar Mark 2 saloon car. He nevertheless took some quite justified pride in his wealth and status. He had become one of Suffolk's most respected landed gentlemen.

His pile, Walton House, had, it was reputed, being designed by the lesser-known architect Joseph Pickford. It was his only excursion into a neo-Palladian style and, as such, was not regarded highly. It had once been described as 'lumpenly Venetian, more at home in Bradford than Vicenza, a poor imitation of Stowe'. Yet Jonathan loved it. The estate had been acquired by an entrepreneurial ironmaster great-grandfather at the zenith of his Victorian affluence.

Two generations of incompetent, dissolute, and profligate forebears had by the outbreak of the last war reduced it to near bankruptcy. His delightfully complaisant impractical father had inadvertently made things infinitely worse by getting himself killed in Arras in 1940, when he as a young Grenadier Guards officer had mistaken an advancing German Obergefreiter for his batman returning to the trench with a mug of sweet tea.

His demise, Jonathan often reflected, was a sad testament to his whole life, a pointless end after an unproductive existence. It also meant that death duties removed most of what was left of the family wealth. When he considered his father's melancholy end three months before his own birth, he often thought it was the only genuine productive thing he had ever achieved.

Oscar Wilde's aphorism, "Alas, I am dying beyond my means", came to his mind as a truly appropriate epitaph for someone who with all their limitations he truly revered. Walton Hall, like Parklands, was let out to the Americans during the war and later still became an approved school. Within a decade or so the buildings and estate were in a ruinous condition.

Jonathan's mother had perished when he was just eight, during his first term at St Dogmael's prep school. She had become a rather needy hypochondriac, who had never recovered from the tragedy of her husband's early death and spent the rest of her short life largely confined to her boudoir, convinced of various imagined ailments, some of which were eventually revealed as genuine.

Her death did not perhaps impinge on her son as much as might be imagined. The warm, wonderfully loving, gentle housekeeper Ivy White doted on this little, blond, sad waif. She had cared for him during most subsequent holidays and had provided the young Jonathan with some much-needed emotional security. Forty years later she still held a place in his heart and was provided with a house on his estate. If Jonathan had ever had a mother, Ivy was the nearest he could claim.

His holidays spent in her modest cottage had acted as a judicious antidote to the snooty illusions which prep school and Eton might have engendered in this vulnerable, impressionable child. It was the reason for his grounded, unpretentious attitude to life and provided him with a continuing concern and sympathy for the lives of ordinary people.

Jonathan was sent to Parkies just before his mother's demise. He was one of the first pupils at this school founded a year before. The extraordinarily kind Canon Father Paine became another important seminal influence on the young Jonathan. Nothing was too much trouble for Father Basil in his quest to encourage and develop the little boy's fragile confidence and self-esteem.

At thirteen he arrived in Eton College. Eton was his father's old school, the main reason he was sent. He was the first boy from Parkies to enter the portals of that illustrious establishment. Later, after a spell at Oxford and during National Service in the Rifle Brigade, he became, to his surprise, but not to his colleagues', a formidable businessman.

He made a fortune in the nascent information technology industry. Whilst he could be ruthless and sometimes unsparing with his staff and colleagues, he prided himself on never being entirely unscrupulous: a difficult balance in the 'loads of money' culture of Thatcher's London.

Most people who knew him would have credited his extraordinary charm as the key to his success. Yet, despite the appearance of an apparently effortless, patrician assumption of privilege, he was at heart a modest and generous person who quietly supported many county charities – including Parkies.

This newly acquired wealth had allowed him to restore Walton Hall and its grounds to something like their former glory. This was an achievement of which he was immensely proud. The fact that his wealth derived almost entirely from grubby commerce was, he knew, a fact that still grated with some of his snootier, pretentious and jealous neighbours.

Back in 1977, shortly before his death, Canon Paine had finally persuaded the reluctant Jonathan to take over as Chairman of the Board at Parkies. Even then and on subsequent reflection, Jonathan could see that, in trying to please the elderly Canon, he had allowed himself to be burdened with a poisoned chalice.

He had agreed because he loved the old priest, who had become a kind of surrogate father to the newly orphaned boy. Now ten years later Jonathan thought the time had come to finally drink up. Ultimately he was a realist: whatever happened today would not, in his opinion, change the stars for Parkies. He was now absolutely convinced that sooner or later the school would close. His task, he was sure, was to find the candidate who could make that as painless as possible.

Lord Castle, also present on that afternoon, was an ageing aristocrat with a liking for practical jokes. Technically he, too, was a Catholic; that is certainly how he labelled himself.

His rather eccentric, spendthrift, sexually incontinent father, Frederick, had married the younger sister of a Catholic Irish peer. As a result of this he had reluctantly converted. It was rumoured that he had been rather friendly with Evelyn Waugh. Certainly, they had both led rather notoriously dissolute lives in the world of 1920s Oxford.

To be honest, many considered his conversion to have been essentially a cynical, convenient means of entrapping a girl who was thought by many to be one of the great beauties of the time. Sadly, for her at least, it had done little to restrain his roving eye; as a result, the marriage had not lasted.

Religion had not therefore been especially important for him, even less so for his son Robert. Robert Castle had that quintessential appearance of faded chic so beloved of the English upper classes.

His once smart tweed suit was showing signs of wear and tear, not helped by numerous stains, evidence of a gargantuan appetite, as well as a failure to always judge the distance from plate to mouth. He sat gobbling away at his third cream scone. Much of the remains of this repast was evidenced scattered down his waistcoat, a garment straining to contain his ever-expanding tummy.

His veiny, red, bulbous nose and rubicund, bloodshot eyes revealed his delight in the more than occasional tipple. This was the reason why he could no longer drive. His most recent conviction for driving under the influence was occasioned by a late-night lift he had given to Prior Anselm, which had resulted in a breathalyser test at the very gates of St Wilfred's. Jonathan ruminated on the thought that it gave a new meaning to the term 'Holy Spirit'.

Lord Castle's hilarious jape of opening a trapdoor at his spectacularly tatty country pile, under the designated chair of any dinner guest whom he considered to be especially conceited or overbearing, was still the talk of the county. A few years ago, the particularly bumptious, swaggering, lesser sprig of a formerly grand, now somewhat diminished aristocratic lineage was invited to dinner.

The Honourable Charles Fitzgibbon had not been amused to find himself spreadeagled in the cellar suffering from a broken wrist and much-reduced self-respect. This was only seconds after being served his third enormous brandy. The subsequent court case and hefty damages were also part of the reason Lord Castle did not now have more than a couple of pennies to rub together.

His financial situation was further damaged by a combination of enthusiastic, if unlucky, gambling, as well as an obsession with medieval siege engines. He delighted in lobbing whole cows, already dead, one hoped, hundreds of yards, thrown on a trebuchet of his own design and manufacture. The annual school outing to witness this remarkable extravaganza had become something of the highlight of the summer term.

The consequences of his pride in being a Lloyd's name, and the substantial losses in recent years this implied, had been the final straw in ensuring his near ruin. He was, nevertheless, the most socially prestigious person Jonathan could persuade to join the board – at the price of the ongoing risk of serious injury at Haddon Park, or, worse still, the possibility of being bored to death in numerous late-night, boozy expositions of the virtues of particular racehorses that seemed, to him, uniformly to fall at the first fence.

The best you could say of Mrs Margaret McKenzie, the only lady present on the interview panel, was that she had married well. She had no particular intelligence or beauty, but rather a driving, obsessive determination to crawl up the greasy pole that was Suffolk's social ladder.

Once a petite, prettyish brunette, years of too many dinner parties and indulgent puddings, as well as her partiality for the large biscuit tin, hidden discreetly in her drawing room, had meant that her charms had rather blossomed.

Her tweed jacket, tartan skirt and sensible, brown country shoes marked, in her mind at least, her status as a leading lumina within the county. Her efforts to fit her expanding frame into this rather compact ensemble forced her rather ample bosoms so far forward that meant that at some angles she appeared almost physically deformed.

Some of the pupils had mischievously dubbed her as melons. This was a label that had stuck far beyond the grubby imaginings of Parkies schoolboys. Margaret McKenzie would have been mortified if she had known the wicked amusement this epithet occasioned in so many county drawing rooms.

Not everyone, least of all Jonathan, would have recognised her social pretensions. Indeed to many she was viewed as a faintly preposterous caricature. This was a sentiment she would have never recognised, even though its veracity was so patently obvious.

The truth of her background, which she kept firmly concealed, was that she was the offspring of a self-made hotelier and grandson of a Scottish crofter and his wife, the younger daughter of an impecunious Shropshire squire.

She was a Catholic in the rather limited sense that she attended St Patrick's Church every Easter and Christmas. However, this colour-wash of a half-hearted religious adherence did not in any significant way influence her life, and still less that of her husband or children.

Roland, her husband, had made a small fortune in the criminal law. He had defended, usually successfully, many of the worst villains of the last twenty years. His reputation of being rather too friendly with some of the more significant members of this criminal fraternity had probably been the key factor in his failure thus far to achieve promotion to the judicial bench.

Mrs McKenzie had no inkling of why this honour had so far eluded him. Yet she lusted for this more than anything else in her rather empty, rudderless life and increasingly arid, unsatisfactory marriage. The lack of the title of 'lady' that would have gone automatically with her husband's promotion was one of the very worst frustrations of her life.

This was second only to her growing realisation that Roland's secretary Marcia was rather more embedded in her husband's life than she could bear, or as yet really accept.

One of her children attended the school and she was convinced that this 'gifted' son was being educated in the best prep school in England.

The fact that Parkies was a world away from being that, and the young Rory McKenzie was not the genius his mother supposed, did not deter her fanatical determination that he was or should be an unrecognised genius.

Mrs McKenzie enjoyed playing the Lady more than anyone Jonathan had ever met. Whilst few took her pretensions seriously, to openly mock would be unwise, for this lady had talons! Jonathan certainly recognised Margaret McKenzie's limitations, but tolerated them albeit reluctantly. She might not be quite as genteel as she supposed, but her influence, such as it was, had, he felt, some value.

With the exception of Lord Castle, whom she treated with a grovelling obsequiousness, her approach to everyone else was that of haughty, detached disdain. Those she considered well beneath her she described as 'fish and chips shop owners'.

This included all the staff at the school and the vast majority of her fellow parents, as well as 99% of the rest of the entire population, including of course the 'tradesman' Jonathan, an attitude he found amusing and irritating by turn.

The third member of this rather odd triumvirate who that afternoon were to be so critical in deciding Parkies' fate was Gerald Grimes. He was, most of his contemporaries considered, a bully. He was a large, middle-aged man whose once impressive physique had run to fat and blubber. This was clearly evidenced in his formidable double chin, huge belly and fat, stubby hands. He was dressed that afternoon in his newly acquired, imagined country gentleman's apparel which he considered appropriate for what he deludedly believed was a prestigious meeting.

Gerald Grimes, it had to said, had only the very haziest idea of what any illustrious gathering might look like. He was rarely invited anywhere in the locality, a source of his growing alienation and bruised self-esteem. He naively imagined that membership of the St Dogmael's board might afford him some small access into the elusive Suffolk county world.

His attire consisted of a rather too loud three-piece, Prince of Wales check, suit. A farmer by trade, his present get-up made him appear rather more like a cross between a prosperous sanitary engineer and Mr Toad. This was a perception which, if he had known, would have seriously disconcerted him.

He tended to use his physical bulk and known propensity for sharp practice and intimidation to get what he wanted. This was a fact that rather confused his present aspirations and certainly detracted from his social ambitions. Most of the time he didn't know what he wanted, except to make everyone else's lives miserable and to acquire lots of money. He had become one of the least popular persons in this part of the county. Lord Castle, in particular, thought him a truly obnoxious oik. "Why have we got to have that loathsome scoundrel on the board?" he bemoaned to Jonathan some weeks before.

Nevertheless, a combination of graft, cunning and dubious practices had made Grimes rich. This was of course the only reason Jonathan had invited him to join them. Not that Gerald really cared about popularity of course. He rather luxuriated in his malign reputation.

Yet ironically, he also yearned for some social acceptability, if only for the rather spoilt son who attended the school, and was rapidly becoming a clone of his father, thuggish and menacing. He deludedly expected that membership of the board might be a way of providing increased social opportunities for this boy. To be fair, he had secretly, if reluctantly, accepted that it was too late for him.

He would often roll his eyes in meetings, whilst parading an apparently effortless display of commercial understanding and competence. This combined with a sulky and somewhat baleful curl of his ample lips, ensured that this menacing, intimidating façade was rarely challenged.

It meant, too, that he could pretend an expertise, whilst little actually existed! Such an approach had numerous advantages. Today he and his colleagues had to make a decision of some importance, rather than the usual trivialities. Grimes felt, not for the first time, out of his depth, an emotion he covered with his customary bluster.

Jonathan's only son Tobias had attended the school, having left two years before. It had not, he considered, been an entirely happy experience. This institution had indeed maintained a few strengths, he would concede. If it wasn't for his strong sense of loyalty to the place, he didn't think he would have freely chosen it.

The fact that he had was considered by many of his friends and colleagues as another example of a peculiar and unexpected eccentricity on his part. "The Dragon, Ludgrove, or Summer Fields, or even Cothill, would suit much better and you would be absolutely sure of a place at Eton," his friend James Thwaite had observed. "Why choose a place which cannot remotely guarantee any of this?"

It is true that whilst Tobias had barely scraped into Eton, Jonathan was not convinced that this achievement had much to do with Parkies. Probably, he considered, it was in spite of it. Tobias was not a scholar and suffered from exclusion from the scholarship set.

It wasn't just the excessive drinking that concerned him. Rather it was rather the unrealistic illusion, that seemed to be prevalent amongst most of the staff and the headmaster in particular, that the school had a status and a quality it simply didn't possess.

In his opinion the headmaster Lancelot Waters had developed into an absolute liability. Jonathan had always known that Waters could not hold a candle to dear old Father Paine. Perhaps he loyally considered no one ever could. Yet over his time at the school, he had slowly and insidiously dismantled the founders' civilising tradition of humane Christian child formation.

It had been replaced by a rather superficial, snooty expectation of social entitlement. This Waters judged was more appealing to the new, largely arriviste clientele.

Jonathan simply didn't believe the comment made in a recent edition of *The Good Schools Guide* that Parkies 'was probably the best Catholic prep school in the country'. He assumed rather cynically that such an observation was a further indication of a growing Freemasonry within this narrow, self-obsessed independent school world, which simply refused to accept some basic new realities. One of the lessons he had learned in business was that one simply had to face the truth, however painful that might be. He was determined to ensure that one way or another Parkies would experience that epiphany.

Jonathan was hoping, too, that the new man Thomas Brown would be ideal for assisting him in making that happen. He believed that Thomas, the self-made, successful, but rather déclassé mechanical, was just the man to make the difference.

Thomas Brown had never attended any university, least of all the English Ivy League of Oxford and Cambridge. He was not public school educated and his voice retained something of the cadence of his native Staffordshire combined now with a distinctive Suffolk burr.

Thomas and his wife Sarah might have considered themselves Christian in a somewhat semi-detached way. Catholicism, especially the fey variety of smells, bells and over-ornate vestments that dominated the imagination of some of the governors of Parkies, left them both coldly unmoved.

Jonathan remembered with some amusement when he had proposed Thomas's name to the other board members at the previous meeting. Margaret McKenzie's face had taken on the appearance of someone who had recently smelt an especially noxious odour. Later she observed with some disgust to her friend Lady Grey: "Do you know, I might have even detected evidence of engine oil under his fingernails. Jonathan Carpenter is truly scraping the barrel in inviting him onto the board."

Prior Anselm had exclaimed, "But Jonathan, this man isn't even Catholic, do you really think he is even from the right background to govern a school of this quality?" Jonathan thought he was exactly the right person. Despite some half-hearted opposition and much nose-holding, he was eventually voted on.

Chapter Four

CATHOLIC OBSESSIONS

What was it that had brought William and Mary Jones to West Suffolk on that cold winter afternoon? William believed he had applied for the post of headmaster of St Dogmael's because of a burning desire to work again in a Catholic boarding school. He sometimes recognised his motivations were not as simple or uncomplicated as this.

They had spent five years living in this world, when William had secured the position as a lay housemaster in a Catholic senior school, before they had decamped to London. Two of their boys had been born there and they remembered it as a very happy, fulfilled time in their lives.

Both William and Mary had loved the experience of being involved in a community that wholly reflected their twin passions of education and religion. William had come to believe that the inclusive experience of boarding school life truly enhanced the life chances of pupils under his charge. He truly yearned to return to this life.

This application was more William's idea than Mary's. In the end she was reluctantly prepared to accede to this because she believed that William needed the challenge and she would anyway always support him.

Whilst she realised, as had Jonathan Carpenter, that the exclusive, if fake, values of Parkies were at least subconsciously attractive to her husband, she accepted that was not the predominant motive in William's mind.

Rather she believed that William's restless energy needed a project; without this focus she feared that his rather fragile self-esteem might implode. Like William, she had reservations about life in the materially obsessed world of North London. She was keen to find a milieu that could offer a more wholesome environment for her young family. If St Dogmael's could offer this, she would be well satisfied.

The frustration William had experienced when he served as a housemaster was common amongst lay teachers in clerically run schools at that time. Power was held entirely by the clergy. Shortage of available and appropriately qualified clergy demanded that these schools reluctantly appointed more layman, sometimes even laywomen. However, there were few clerically run establishments where the views of the laity were ever taken very seriously.

It was also true that communities of celibate men were by no means always as peaceful, fastidious, and devotional as William had once supposed. The power politics of a religious community were, William had slowly discovered, often as red in tooth and claw as any in the secular world.

Although the laity were rarely even consulted about important, or indeed less important, issues, William still wanted to work in a Catholic environment. He was even sufficiently ambitious to want to run his own show.

When he reflected about it, he considered that he had probably not entirely lost his own deep-seated Protestant anti-clericalism, in his case further informed by his own somewhat flawed experience in working with the clergy.

This prejudice was perhaps not very surprising given his years of attendance at his local Baptist chapel. There were aspects of this experience William treasured all his life. He loved the enthusiasm so many members of the congregation showed, not only in their hymn singing, but also in the determination of so many to follow in the path of their saviour in absolute integrity.

During his adolescence, his attendance at chapel became sporadic, and finally at about the age of fourteen ceased altogether. He often reflected why this had happened. Some of it had to do with his deteriorating relationship with his father who was, after all, still a chapel elder. Most of all it was the adolescent angst which found the whole experience irrelevant compared to the new discovered delights of sexual fantasy, pop music, and the forbidden fruits of cigarettes and cider.

There was something about the sense of respectable exclusivity that emanated from some of the church members that grated. They often had that firm, unassailable sense of their own virtue and superiority compared to those lesser unbeliever mortals who were not devotees. This was an attitude that seriously discombobulated him.

There seemed to be in that mindset a remnant of the old Calvinist notion of predestination. William simply didn't believe that chapel-goers were better than everyone else. This was especially so when he so often witnessed the gap between the high-sounding moral exhortations promulgated within the confines of the chapel community and the reality of much of the congregation's behaviour outside.

William was looking for something that seemed to him more authentic. This led to various half-hearted erratic involvements in politics. This mostly consisting of pointless demonstrations and endless rather boring committees where the details of the Marxist dialectic seemed to be picked apart in an increasingly tiresome examination of irrelevant obscurity.

This left him in his later teens and early twenties with a growing sense of ennui and vacuity. This was made worse by debilitating attacks of anxiety, which he suspected, and later confirmed, were related, at least in part, to his dysfunctional relationship with his father.

Seventeen years before, at the age of twenty-two William Jones had found his new Catholic religious enthusiasm following a visit to the Dominican Friars in Oxford. Ironically, he had only reluctantly attended a weekend retreat with a friend Bob James as an afterthought. "You will find it really interesting Will," Bob had insisted. "They are not remotely like you imagine Catholic priests are."

He decided to join Bob, when the unappealing prospect of an especially boring, lonely few days in his shabby bedsit, located within a grotty artisan cottage in the unattractive, narrow, neglected streets of St Paul's neighbourhood in Cheltenham, had somewhat palled.

To his surprise and the bemused amazement of Bob, his erstwhile mentor, he had converted in a frenzy of devotion. This led Mary in the same direction a few years later. Bob, whatever his initial enchantment, didn't follow the same road and couldn't quite understand William's newfound passion which he had inadvertently closeted.

William thought that here he had found the authenticity that he had for long been searching for. In the kindly friars he met he discovered that for the first time in his life he was taken seriously. He quickly discovered that the stultifying, pious conformity he had experienced in Usk was not so highly prized in the more inclusive congregations of the Catholic parishes.

This fact was well illustrated when he and Mary attended Mass at Blackfriars one Sunday. Mary had noticed an elderly, somewhat disreputable, shabby old man helping himself to the money on the plate. In shocked outrage she had approached one of the friars to report this abomination. His rather surprising response was: "Surely he needs it more than we do." On reflection she realised that of course he probably did.

At that time Blackfriars Priory had a reputation as a hothouse of liberation theology and radical Catholic thinking. It was a place that buzzed with excitement and profound religious and political ardour.

William had never before come across men quite like the friars he came to know there. It was a revelation as different as it could be to anything he had ever experienced before. It reinforced in his mind the need to escape the boring provincialism of his Welsh narrow Chapel focussed home and gave a new purpose and focus to his life.

The friars were a fascinating group of often eccentric but also passionately engaged people, many of whom became for him role models and mentors. The experience was, for him, an extraordinary personal liberation. For the first time in his life he really believed in something beyond himself.

Prayer, religious practice, even self-control were not for him easily acquired. For William, in his somewhat flawed attempts to become a better man, this gave him an aspiration and meaning which often brought him intense joy and purpose.

Father Thomas, his instructor and confessor, was a gentle scholar who spent much of his time in the Bodleian Library working his way through the most obscure medieval Latin texts. He was determined to attribute various texts more accurately previously supposed to be the work of his namesake Thomas Aquinas. This was a project he eventually completed.

Despite his modest, humble, self-effacing demeanour, he was a formidable scholar with an international reputation, for admittedly his rather obscure, even perhaps somewhat obtuse expertise.

Father Thomas also had a wicked, playful sense of humour. He was an excellent mimic and was able to caricature the rather pompous Prior Ethelred and gave a pretty competent impression of the newly acquired, probably slightly fake, Irish brogue of the loud, forceful, and often insufferable Father Columba.

For six months William travelled from Cheltenham to Blackfriars weekly for instruction. These sessions truly inspired him, although he had to admit that some of Father Thomas's perorations into the more obscure doctrinal issues, sometimes required him to rub spittle on his eyelids to keep awake. Even so, Father Thomas seemed to consider his rather superficial, half-baked notions as worthwhile contributions.

He felt that the brothers thought he had a brain and a modicum of intelligence, and this realisation entirely revived and regenerated his sense of self-worth. Sometimes he was invited for lunch. The friars took it in turns to prepare the meal. Some of their concoctions were dreadful: entirely colourless, inedible mush.

William remembered one occasion where Father Thomas nudged him before he was served some grey, lumpy, particularly noxious-smelling soup with the words: "Don't touch it, Will, it might poison you: Brother Cyril made it."

The experience of religious conversion, and the new friendships he made with some of these extraordinary men, transformed his life. Later he could not be sure which was of more importance, whether it was a newfound faith, or his fascination and admiration for these friars and their way of life.

William came to believe that Father Thomas was one of the best men he had ever known. He could never remember an unkind or thoughtless thing he ever did – an observation that Father Thomas would certainly not have agreed with.

Later, when William was teaching in a comprehensive school near Oxford, he sometimes took Thomas out for a meal. This was something that the good friar always accepted with alacrity. When William asked where he would like to dine, Thomas once replied, with a twinkle in his eye: "Anywhere which doesn't involve any of my brothers helping out in the kitchen."

On one occasion Father Thomas even agreed to chat to some of William's rather challenging fifteen-year-olds pupils about his life in a religious community. They looked at him in some awe and trepidation as he strode into the classroom in his full black and white regalia.

This was a sight none of them had ever witnessed before. Whether it was their bemusement or a genuine respect, they quizzed him politely for perhaps half an hour showing genuine interest in what they must have considered part of a bizarre pageant. One of the boys enquired of him later: "Do you have fights in your monastery?"

Thomas responded with the wry comment: "Only with our tongues, never with our fists." It was an honest response which did not attempt to patronise or diminish the lad who had asked it. That very obviously impressed his rather rumbustious as well as confused audience.

Later, Father Thomas became terminally ill when only in his fifties. He faced his final illness and his end with a touching, ennobling faith, as well as fortitude, dignity and pose. This happened just before the interview at Parkies in 1987. William and Mary mourned their beloved friend and sage for many months. They missed him still.

In William's reception ceremony in 1971 his mother Dilys persuaded his very reluctant, suspicious father Gethin to attend the service. On the journey from Usk to Oxford, she kept repeating the same comforting mantra to a disconsolate Gethin. He was hugely angry and disappointed by his son's incomprehensible conversion.

Gethin, who was seeped in the culture of Welsh nonconformity, could not understand why his son had taken this path. "The boy has entirely gone off his head." "It is really all right, Gethin, these Catholics are not like they used to be," Dilys tried somewhat unconvincingly to reassure him on the long journey to Oxford.

By the time they arrived his father was at least partly assuaged. He had come to half-accept that the Catholic Church was not quite the den of iniquity and treason he had once supposed. Unfortunately, as he walked into the lobby of the church, he immediately spied a huge poster proclaiming, 'Support Sinn Féin', the work of the enthusiastically pro-Irish Republican Friar Father Columba. Not the best introduction William supposed that his parents might have had to his newfound faith.

This incident entirely convinced William's father that he had been right after all. "You see," he whispered to Dilys, "it is as I have always supposed: this idiot boy has got himself mixed up with a load of skirted terrorists. I always told you he would come to no good!" For the rest of his life he could never be persuaded that his son had not joined a nest of potential traitors and fanatics.

Dilys sometimes thought that William was rather like a large cuckoo who had somehow appeared in the Joneses' nest. He had never, it seemed to her, really fitted in. What made matters worse was that he seemed inexplicably to spend much of his time mischievously tweaking his father's proverbial nose.

Nor must it be said Gethin much cared for his wayward son. This new Catholic adventure simply reinforced and confirmed in him his overwhelming sense of disappointment and despondency with the antics of his obstreperous offspring. On the rare occasions he later referred to his son's conversion, he would simply comment: "The Catholics have got Will."

The Sinn Féin poster was the work of a friar, more eccentric than most, who had become an enthusiastic supporter of Irish Republicanism. Father Columbia's fervour for this somewhat dubious cause led him often into rather unwise ardour.

To be fair these were in the days before the IRA terrorist campaign had truly got into its stride. It spoke volumes of the principle that intelligence and common sense are often rather contrary notions.

The most obvious expression of this was when he preached what became his standard theme. Northern Ireland was Palestine, the Protestants were the Sadducees, the Catholics the Pharisees, the IRA, the Zealots, and predictably the British were the Romans. Father Columba was a remarkably intelligent, internationally acclaimed theologian. On the few occasions William attended talks by him, his depth of intellectual insight and wide range of knowledge were awe-inspiring. Usually William had real difficulties remotely following the complexity of his thought.

When William married Mary in Abingdon in 1973, Father Thomas presided, and many of the guests were kitted out in the black hoods and white habits of the Dominican Order. It was not a sight that William's father much enjoyed or appreciated. "Is this a bloody wedding or a special meeting of the Inquisition?" he was heard to irritably mutter.

William's friend Bob James was his best man. During the service he played a lovely especially composed song on his banjo. It was a very special touch and had the additional virtue of detracting from the slightly monastic feel of the whole event.

Mary's very grounded down-to-earth mother was so provoked by the sight of all the monastic habits, she at one point made the whispered comment: "I wonder why he didn't become a monk, rather than marry my daughter!" William, when he heard this, wasn't quite sure whether it was just an observation, or perhaps an earnest desire.

In the years that followed William's conversion, soon to be followed by Mary, Father Thomas became a close friend. He baptised their eldest son Francis and on numerous occasions came to stay with them when William served as a housemaster.

Father Thomas grew very fond of the Joneses. He recognised that William was certainly no scholar. He sometimes playfully reminded him of the occasions during his instruction when he had nearly fallen asleep. He never patronised or in any way put him down; even on the many occasions when William could be insufferably pompous and self-opinionated.

Once when Thomas was staying with them and William was doing his dormitory rounds, he unexpectedly turned to Mary and said: "I worry that William overidealises me. I realise, too, that his conversion has driven a further wedge into his family. In the end both of you need to understand that faith is about trust in God, not in individuals. I don't think William yet has quite grasped that."

Quite soon afterwards, Mary realised that Father Thomas knew, or at least suspected, that he was seriously ill. After he died some years later, she remembered this conversation and appreciated that the good friar was trying to start the process of goodbye in the most gentle way he knew how. A reflection, she thought, of a profoundly good, decent, and thoughtful person.

William had come to believe that he had a genuine vocation to teach and, given his newfound faith, it seemed appropriate to choose Catholic schools. This therefore was the essential underlying reason for applying to St Dogmael's.

Yet he was undeniably attracted by the swanky atmosphere of Parkies as Jonathan Carpenter had so intuitively understood. William loved the romantic stories of recusant aristocrats, doomed Catholic risings, and courageous martyrdom. In a way St Dogmael's reminded him of all this. They were still by no means sure they would be able to fit into such alien surroundings. William also realised that the opportunities to run a Catholic boarding school were few and far between. He was nearly thirty-nine years old and he recognised that the chances of breaking into this world were diminishing fast.

William was as aware as many of the Parkies governors that his curriculum vitae was hardly an ideal starting point for such an ambition.

St Dogmael's with all its obviously limitations, was an opportunity he could not let slip.

He might even be able to change the school in a way that conformed closer to his ideals. William Jones was confident or, more likely, deluded enough to believe that this was a challenge he could handle. Mary was yet to be convinced. Only time would tell.

Chapter Five

APPOINTMENT

William hadn't expected the call. When the telephone rang he and Mary were in the throes of putting their three little boys to bed.

They had arrived home quite late, and as a result the children were unusually fractious and demanding. This might have been the result of their fraught journey back to their modest, if somewhat shabby, terraced house in Friern Barnet.

William and Mary had never experienced anything remotely like St Dogmael's before. Mary remarked as they drove home down the MII; "It was extraordinary, William. I cannot really find adequate adjectives to describe it. Grand, shabby, antiquated, pretentious are the ones that first come to mind. Do we really want it, Will?"

"I don't think they will look at us, darling, but oddly enough if they did offer it, I would be tempted," a thoughtful William replied.

They were simply perplexed by the whole experience; it was a world they had not supposed even existed beyond the novels of P.G. Woodhouse or Evelyn Waugh. William hardly dared yet admit, even to himself and certainly not Mary, that this bizarre cosmos rather attracted him.

Mary kept her counsel, but Parkies was not a place she really wanted anything further to do with. She would just await developments and earnestly hope that William's pessimism was justified.

This sense of a confused, anxious mix of excitement and dread was not to be diminished by their decision to stop off in Watford to discuss matters with their old friend and mentor Alan Howarth.

Alan an old college friend, had many increasing difficulties understanding the odd and frankly inexplicable obsessions of his chum William. The Joneses imagined that the confession they were about to make would not help in scaling back Alan's growing sense of exasperation with some of their antics.

Their unannounced visit was simply because Alan was their closest friend and they needed to experience a smidgeon of his wisdom. Not, Mary reflected, that the pig-headed William would be likely to take any notice whatsoever.

Years before, they worked together in their earnest, if naive, quest for the socialist utopia that seemed about to manifest itself in England in the midst of the miners' strikes and political mayhem of the early 70s. They had joined many demonstrations: the political slogan, 'Margaret Thatcher, Milk Snatcher', was engraved on their psyche and their lips in those years.

William had been, at that time, at least as enthusiastic a student rebel as had been Alan. Yet Alan had never entirely lost the faith. Possibly as a reflection of this he still sported a Che Guevara moustache and beard. He worked as a youth leader in this less salubrious part of Watford. William suspected that almost everyone he had just met at St Dogmael's would consider everything about Watford as insalubrious.

A thought he and Mary kept to themselves as they drank coffee from chipped mugs in Alan's shabby, untidy little flat.

Alan had originated from Buckinghamshire. A bright lad, he had been the only boy from the notorious council estate in which he hailed to achieve a place at the prestigious Royal Grammar School in High Wycombe. Partly as a result of this, things had not worked out. Being one of the few working-class boys in this rather precious, middle-class establishment had left him permanently afflicted with the feeling of being an outsider who needed to buck the system.

His tendency to wear his school tie as a kind of waist-high fashion accessory, and his refusal to accept the regulation school shoes, opting instead for some truly ostentatious winkle-pickers, had marked him out at an early stage as trouble. When he left school at fifteen and took up a job as a machine hand in one of the local furniture factories, most of the grammar school staff breathed a sigh of immense relief.

He had kicked over the traces as a teenager and had predictably got into trouble with the police. His appearance in the local magistrates' court on the charge of affray meant he was bound over. It also ensured that it lost him his apprenticeship, but it had not cowed his spirit.

The comment made by the rather stuck-up, overbearing chairman of the court, that he was "the worst kind of hooligan, a disgrace to his neighbourhood, his former school and his family," had further fuelled Alan's anger, resentments, and rebellious spirit.

Alan was one of most passionate, angry, but also intelligent and caring people William had ever met. His enthusiasms and refusal to be bludgeoned by what he thought were silly or unnecessary rules were something that William greatly admired and feared by turns. He was both courageous and reckless: one could never be absolutely sure in which direction he would go. He was one of those personalities people either loved, hated, or feared, or perhaps all three at the same time.

William remembered a jape which had almost ensured their expulsion from the training college. Student representatives were chosen by election, having been first authorised by the Principal. This meant in William and Alan's admittedly somewhat paranoiac view that the whole thing was a fix.

The candidates were in their opinion a collection of rather creepy, obsequious people who always followed the establishment line. The two of them resolved to disrupt the election. Alan rugby-tackled the teller, and William ran off with the box of votes.

They were lucky to escape without expulsion and on reflection even these two comic crusaders realised it was a very silly and in the end pointless gesture. However, it perfectly illustrated their rather naive, anarchistic frame of mind at the time.

Alan always looked a scruff and even in his now semi-respectable phase, his jacket and jeans appeared as though he had acquired them in the local charity shop. His round, rather powerful spectacles firmly placed on his rather long, strong nose added a certain intensity to his gaze. In repose his face possessed a rather serious, thoughtful quizzical expression. When he smiled his visage was transformed into one of infectious joy and bonhomie.

He was someone with little guile; his feelings were not easily masked. Anger and elation were emotions always plain to see. He was a faithful friend, but it has to be said a dangerous enemy.

Over the years he had developed into an exceptionally gifted youth leader and had managed to acquire and maintain an extraordinary relationship with some very difficult, often damaged boys. He could find amusement and dark comedy out of the most tragic and traumatic of circumstances.

It was his anarchistic sense of humour which, William believed, kept him sane. It certainly staved off the bouts of melancholy to which he was prone.

He had none of that middle-class sentimentality and fear of confrontation that so often afflicted William. He had absolutely no time for those whom he considered 'do-gooders' more interested, in his mind, in displaying their virtue, rather than any genuine attempt to transform the lives of their charges.

To begin with, William thought he was a bit of a despot in his relationship with his youth club members. His combination of strict, easy to understand rules and the fair, sometimes harsh, but always ultimately compassionate enforcement, worked a treat. There was none of the false, informal bonhomie that so afflicted much of youth work during that period. Alan was, for example, always Mr Howarth to his charges.

Yet the boys recognised in him something special, a person who originated in the same kind of chaotic, underclass, delinquent background that many of them had, or were experiencing. He had overcome this and as such became for them a wonderful role model, and in some cases, William believed, a kind of hero.

Alan's principles were firmly rooted in the working-class culture from which he had sprung. He had, he would probably admit, somewhat idealised his less than respectable past. From it had derived a passionate conviction in the virtues of community cohesion and fairness.

He might not be religious in a formal sense. He was one of the most truly Christian people William knew.

Both William and Mary loved their eccentric, honest, decent, and sometimes dangerously unpredictable friend. They thought some of his ideas were bonkers, but he had the same opinion of some of theirs. They just laughed at each other.

For a time Alan and William had become somewhat estranged by William's new religious passion. To Alan, Catholicism represented the knee-trembling wing of Fascist authoritarianism. Even when William had explained that the Dominicans were one of the few English religious orders that had not supported Franco in the Spanish Civil War, Alan had retorted: "The point is, Will, most did, and the Church legitimised Spanish Fascism as they did in many other places. Just think about Ireland and that obnoxious clerical Fascist de Valera."

William conceded Alan had a point, but this did not detract from his personal experience of the intelligent, civilised and tolerant friars he had met in Oxford, or convinced him he had made a mistake to convert.

Despite their widening, often diametrically opposed visions of the world, the two men had remained close friends: William valued Alan's opinions, even if he rarely accepted them. He hadn't yet admitted that he had made the Parkies application. He was simply too embarrassed to reveal it. He even wondered whether Father Thomas, if he was still around, would have approved either. Posh private schools were not something that he much cared for either. A thought that William earnestly tried to suppress!

Even given the very unlikely prospect that now arose that he might be appointed persuaded William it was time to come clean. He imagined, as it turned out, correctly that Alan had no inkling of what he was about to announce. He trusted that Alan would understand, if of course entirely disapprove of, what he had done. It was important to him that whilst he might not understand, he would not condemn him for it. William always yearned for Alan's approbation.

At root, Alan felt William's religious obsession had led him into a betrayal of what he considered then, and still half-believed, was the straight path to secular salvation. He feared, too, that the petty snobbery that was increasingly the meat and drink of William's professional life had somehow corrupted someone he considered was still a person of progressive instincts. Now sadly somewhat obscured.

This unexpected and uninvited visitation was, he imagined, occasioned by what was likely to be yet another bizarre declaration. His one hope was that whatever it was, the more grounded Mary would dissuade the credulous William from any further lunacies.

A nervous, apprehensive William then described the day's events. As he did so, Alan's sense of dread magnified. He had never heard of St Dogmael's. Frankly, from what William had told him, he was awfully glad of that.

There was a name he thought he knew. Was Mrs McKenzie's lawyer husband the insufferably conceited barrister who had represented a lad from his youth club? This had not been one of McKenzie's triumphs, and Darren the unfortunate boy had gone down for four years. He sensed that this preening popinjay hadn't cared a damn or tried very hard to save him.

McKenzie's arrogant disavowing of any responsibility for this and his haughty disregard for the feelings and interests of this boy, or his disadvantaged underclass family, represented everything he hated about the supposed ruling elite. Seared into Alan's memory was the dismissive and arrogant way McKenzie had treated the boy's distressed mother after the trial. Alan thought he might have shown more kindness to a dog. Could he be somehow connected with the McKenzie woman William had mentioned?

As William outlined what he considered was a disastrous showing at the interview, Alan hoped that this might portend failure or rather, from his perspective, salvation. At any rate Alan knew enough of the malign reputation of boarding prep schools, to seriously question his friend's sanity in allowing himself to be so deluded as to apply to lead one.

Anger and indignation bubbled up and his parting shot as William and Mary left his tiny flat was an enraged bellow: "Why are you really so determined to lick the arses of the ruling fucking class, you stupid prat!?" It made him feel better, but it did little to further cement their relationship. A downcast William retreated from Alan's flat, convinced not only that he wouldn't get this fantasy job, but also that he had possibly sacrificed an important friendship in the quixotic attempt to do so.

He secretly suspected that Mary probably sympathised with Alan's view more than she let on. This made it an even more bitter pill to swallow.

By the time William and Mary had picked up their boys from the childminder, they had both convinced themselves that London life wasn't too bad after all. William's dream of corduroy trousers and sports jacket in some distant country mansion, playing the role of a kind of budget Mr Chips, was just, that an unobtainable dream: probably better for remaining so. Then the telephone rang.

"This is Jonathan Carpenter; can I speak to William Jones?" "This is he." The polished, suave vowels of Jonathan's disembowelled voice then announced: "The Governors of St Dogmael's school would like to offer you the post of headmaster." William was dumbfounded. How could this be, given his lamentable performance earlier that day? Mary was listening in. She seemed even more surprised.

The silence seemed interminable. Jonathan feared that he hadn't been heard; it had after all been a long day. "Can I call you William?" he finally interjected with a touch of irritation. "Yes, of course," came the delayed reply. "Would you travel to my place, Walton House in Suffolk, to discuss your package?"

Finally, William's brain kicked into gear. "Thank you, Mr Carpenter, I think I would very much like the job, but I cannot justify another trip to Suffolk, I have already missed two days at school." "Fine," came the reply. "I suggest we meet at my club next Wednesday evening. It is the Stirrup Club in St James's, 7:00 pm sharp on Wednesday, then." William could only manage a strangled "Yes." The phone went dead.

The following Wednesday, William returned from school early and carefully dressed in his best light grey lounge suit and, sporting his prized OU tie, made his way to Arnos Grove tube station en route for the Stirrup Club. This was situated in a grand mansion abutting The Mall with, he later discovered, exclusive views over St James's Park. It was also reputed that the rear of Whitehall and Horse Guards could be glimpsed from its elegant dining room, something that was sadly not visible on this dark, early spring evening.

William had hardly considered that such places even existed. They were as far from his experience as was the Roman Curia from that of his Welsh nonconformist father. He had no idea what the correct dress code was, or indeed any clear idea where the building was. This was made more problematic by the fact that London clubs do not generally advertise themselves. The smarter the club, the less the outward display.

The only indication that such a place existed was the gorgeously attired porter, replete in top hat and white gloves, who paraded self-importantly outside. The only certain proof that this was really the right place was a brass plaque discreetly placed next to the front door. To read this it was necessary to walk past the porter and peer.

This immediately exposed William to the attentions of this humourless, implacably supercilious functionary, who enquired, with just the right mix of courtesy and contempt, what he was doing. William replied with more than a touch of submissiveness, panic, and an overwhelming conviction that the porter knew exactly his true, rather lowly status: "I have an appointment with Mr Carpenter," he spluttered. The porter now seemed to lose interest. "Wait in the lobby, Sir." William felt that the sir should have been spelt *cur* – it certainly sounded like it.

For ten minutes he watched the great and the good parade past him. Some he had seen on TV, more often than not, were greeted by the obsequious "Good evening, my Lord."

He became aware of the total inappropriateness of his dress. Everyone seemed attired in well-cut charcoal grey suits. His ill-fitting, light grey Debenhams outfit and brown Oxfords, he immediately realised, made him look like a down-at-heel bookmaker.

His pathetic attempt to give himself status by wearing his OU tie made him, he now appreciated, seem needy, pretentious, and ridiculous. Those ten minutes were those of absolute humiliation: he even considered flight!

"Good evening, William," a familiar voice intoned from behind him. He was greeted by a charming, friendly Jonathan Carpenter. "Let's have some champagne to celebrate the occasion." They found themselves sitting in a beautiful anteroom. There were portraits of bewhiskered former politicians and proconsuls of Empire. These were interspersed, as one would expect given the club's name, with Stubbs-like studies of exquisitely bred racehorses.

Gorgeous antique furniture adorned every corner of the room. The sense of wealth and power this place exhibited took William's breath away: as was the point, of course.

Jonathan, whatever he thought of William's appearance – to be frank when he first saw him in the lobby, he feared he had made a ghastly mistake – was all charm and graciousness. He often reflected that his time at Eton had schooled him well in this beguiling insincerity. Sometimes he had mischievously wondered whether this was the only skill worth paying school fees for.

The business was easily concluded. The salary was most satisfactory and the position was offered on a year's probation. There would be a headmaster's three-bedroomed flat and reduced school fees for William's children. It all sounded very agreeable: William had never remotely earned anything like this before.

They dined in the elegant dining room. The twinkling lights of Whitehall and Buckingham Palace could just be perceived in the growing twilight. Occasionally other club members greeted Jonathan.

Neither did Jonathan introduce him, nor did they seem vaguely interested in him, so he was able to hide behind the mask of anonymity.

This had both given him a sense of relief, but also confirmed a growing insight that he was a fish entirely out of water, and probably he feared always would be. The meal ended and William returned to the far less imposing environs of his former artisan cottage home in Friern Barnet.

Chapter Six

INTO THE JAWS

A few days later a recorded delivery bulky letter, postmarked Suffolk, landed on William and Mary's doorstep. It confirmed his appointment, as well as the details he had previously gleaned from Jonathan Carpenter. It also invited Mary and him to Suffolk two weeks hence to meet the other governors and the staff of St Dogmael's.

It was suggested that they stay with the retiring headmaster. Mary convinced William this was not a great idea. "I didn't much care for him," she averred. "You absolutely need to radically change that stuffy institution: you will have precious little chance, if you are immediately seen to be in his pocket."

They both therefore decided to make a weekend of it, finding a nice hotel, as well as bringing William's mum to mind the children during the welcoming reception. The following day the whole family would have a chance to look around the school and view the proposed headmaster's flat.

In preparation for this trip Mary and William took the boys on a rather expensive shopping trip. Traditional shorts, new shoes and muted coloured jumpers were purchased. William splashed out on a new charcoal grey suit, and Mary spent hours in John Lewis looking for an appropriate outfit.

The children and William's mum, who had volunteered to child mind, were deposited in a local, nice, if modest, hotel, and William and Mary dressed in their new, hopefully presentable finery made their way to the school.

Dusk was falling as they drove up the long, potholed drive. The dark shape of Parklands slowly emerged out of the gloom of a drizzle-soaked Suffolk March evening. Both William and Mary felt a huge weight of anxiety bear down on their tummies.

Mary thought it was a bit like that opening scene in Alfred Hitchcock's film *Rebecca*, when the camera followed the drive up to the great house Manderley. She half-expected to see the twisted, bitter face of Mrs Danvers staring out of one of the windows. William had this irrational fear that the increasing nausea he felt would lead to a devastating explosion at just the wrong moment. The import of the decision they had made slowly manifested itself with the emerging shape of the huge, ungainly building.

It occurred to William that the architect that had designed the Gothic fantasy of Parklands was the selfsame fellow responsible for the Victorian lunatic asylum at Colney Hatch, the enormous, soon to be closed, mental institution which dominated the landscape of Friern Barnet. He trusted this was not an omen!

The reception took place in the school drawing room, in which the interviews of two weeks before had taken place. It was not difficult to identify this location in the semi-darkened bulk of country house, converted stables and terrapin buildings. All the noise and most of the light were coming from this one window. It sounded incongruously as though a party was in full swing. Neither William nor Mary felt much in partying mood.

Awaiting to welcome them at the front door was Lancelot Waters, the retiring head. He stood in the doorway with a glass in his hand. "Good evening and welcome, Mr and Mrs Jones," he politely intoned. His eyes, however, suggested that it was neither a good evening, nor that the Joneses were welcome in any sense at all. Lancelot Waters thought that the governors had made a catastrophic mistake.

A few days before, he and his wife Geraldine had been invited to the McKenzies for dinner. Lancelot's fears had been articulated perfectly by Roland McKenzie when he opined: "This man Jones runs a dreadful little school in an equally horrid part of North London. I have made a few enquiries: half his clientele appear to be prosperous Asian shopkeepers; the other half, persons I seem to meet rather too often in the criminal courts."

He continued with a growing sense of haughty foreboding: "The Joneses are the progenitors of the new money-grubbing, common, vulgar hoi polloi, who will soon dominate Suffolk, God help us. I checked his background," McKenzie sneeringly continued. "His father was a shopkeeper in Newport, his grandfather nothing more than a coal miner: hardly the heritage we might expect from a future Parkies headmaster." Actually, Roland McKenzie was somewhat misinformed. William's upbringing was not quite as modest as he had suggested. Nevertheless, the reality was unimpressive enough.

Geraldine Waters was especially exercised by this dreadful intelligence: "I simply don't understand how they could replace you with such an obvious little oik like William Jones. Parkies depends on its social cachet. He will simply finish it off: can you imagine anyone wanting to come to his appallingly naff, reconstructed dame school? I don't think so!"

Lancelot ironically was a convert himself: although Radley, Exeter College Oxford, a few years in the Lancers as well as a spell as a housemaster at the Oratory School, was certainly a far more prestigious, and in Lancelot's opinion more appropriate, pedigree than that of his successor. He knew that he had not left Parkies in remotely the state he should. Somehow irrationally in his mind, his failure had become in some way correlated to the Joneses' appointment. Indeed it was perhaps a confirmation of it.

The hubbub of noise in the drawing room started to die away; this seemed to be the signal for the start of more formal proceedings. Both William and Mary were offered a drink. They decided to opt for a small sherry, rather than the large gin and tonics which were generally more *de rigueur.*

The tension in the room was unbearable, and the bonhomie was at best superficial, but seemed to both William and Mary rather more menacing than friendly. It was certainly anything but reassuring!

Jonathan Carpenter made a brief speech of welcome. He ended with the words: "William and Mary, Parkies has always been a friendly, welcoming place. We all earnestly hope that you William and Mary and your family will be very happy here." The little William knew of Jonathan probably meant that these words were genuinely felt. However, his warmth did little to melt the chilly, stand-offish atmosphere that still overwhelmingly pervaded the room.

This drawing room was full of people – in truth it was somewhat overcrowded. Given the fact that there was no evidence of any other form of heating, this at least was a blessing. William recognised a few people from the interview. Jonathan was there and, as on cue after his warm words, he walked over, hand outstretched, exuding his most charming smile. They were introduced to his elegant, extraordinarily lovely wife Celia.

Margaret McKenzie and her husband Roland managed a subdued, underwhelmed greeting. Mary was sure she could detect the cold wind of icy reproach in their attitude.

Thomas Brown and his wife Sarah, on the other hand, appeared to exude a genuine warmth and welcome. Sarah made a special effort to make Mary comfortable. She chatted happily away about their children. For the first time that evening Mary felt genuinely appreciated.

Father O'Rourke, dressed in a rather shabby cassock, looked almost as uncomfortable as William and Mary felt. He hated events like this; they, he considered, reminded him of American beauty contests, all false bonhomie and knife-like cordiality.

Prior Anselm was standing rather flustered and disconsolate at the edge of the proceedings. He, too, was very wary of this appointment. He noticed how the Joneses seemed not to be at all comfortable in this milieu. William Jones's self-deprecating and ingratiating manner made him seem more like a promising potential butler than a future headmaster of a well-regarded preparatory school.

Like Lancelot Waters, he judged that the appointment was a ghastly mistake. "Social confidence is about self-belief and the ability to display that in appropriate situations. In my opinion William Jones has none of that," he had opined to Lord Castle a few days later. "His deficiencies will be exposed very quickly: this will be a disaster for the school."

William feared that Mary and he had just entered the lion enclosure, and many present, having agreed they were the menu, were simply deciding which course to start first. Perhaps Mary thought that Jonathan Carpenter's suggestion that Parkies was welcoming was more in the sense that a lion welcomed a gazelle.

The evening was not going well. When William glanced at the rather strained face of Jonathan Carpenter, he sensed that he was not the only one who perceived this.

Later when Celia was preparing for bed, she turned to Jonathan, her face unusually sombre. "Did we do the right thing, darling, persuading the Joneses to decamp to Suffolk? I felt so sorry for them, they seemed entirely unprepared for this particular bearpit. At the risk of mixing my metaphors, they reminded me of one of those scenes in a biblical epic: two Christians waiting for the lions."

Jonathan merely nodded. "I am not sure," he briefly, if rather shamefacedly replied.

Perhaps the most problematic encounter William and Mary had was with John Lipman and his wife Karen. Mary particularly felt a real empathy for the dejected, defeated air both exuded. John had already drunk rather more than he should. Whilst he was not exactly hostile, William recognised he was best avoided. His manner was something of Vesuvius the day before Pompeii. Surprisingly, on what was actually supposed to be a showcase occasion, it was soon obvious it wasn't just Lipman who was the worse for wear.

The History and English man Martin Pugh approached William in a most friendly, ebullient way. His words were slurred and he radiated a miasma of alcoholic malodour.

He seemed, William thought, a very amiable if, he guessed, inwardly rather woebegone, sad man. He was tipsy certainly, but rather than any impression of truculence, there was about him an overwhelming impression of extreme vulnerability and wounded dignity. At the very least it was clear that he had not bought into snooty, judgmental negativity that was being so ostentatiously paraded by so many of the leading players within that room.

William later discovered that he had a first-class reputation as a fine teacher as well as a man with genuine and profound intellectual interests. He had, William discovered, one of the finest libraries of rare first editions in the county.

Heaving over the horizon was the enormous bearded figure of Noah Bradley, cradling his signature glass of Special Brew. William later learned he was the legendary science teacher. The children referred to him as 'Bangs'. His lessons, he was told, rarely missed a denotation of one kind or another.

The children, as William was soon to find out, loved this gentle giant, and at weekends his old pickup truck was often loaded with boarders on an endless search through the junkyards of East Anglia for materials to blow up. William immediately liked him and thought his straightforward, unpretentious guilelessness was a refreshing antidote to the atmosphere of toxic conviviality that pervaded the room.

In one corner of the drawing room was a gaggle of young men and women who hardly looked old enough to have left school. Most of them were dressed quite casually. One of them had clearly been unable to change and was still kitted out in a tracksuit.

They were happily engaged in an enthusiastic examination of recent rugby results. That very afternoon the school team had beaten a local rival, the source of considerable, even gleeful satisfaction. They did not seem terribly interested in who or who was not to be the new head.

Their attitude of detached indifference was at least honest and uncomplicated, two virtues somewhat lacking in this pressure cooker atmosphere within the room of false cordiality.

Standing together quite separately was a rather tall, superior-looking chap with a dumpy, querulous tight-mouthed, seemingly somewhat tetchy woman. William assumed she was his wife. He was introduced to him as St John de Vere, a senior teacher responsible for Classics. He stood grasping tightly his wine glass at the same staring at them with an air of bemused and hostile bafflement.

Mary felt that he was observing them in the way Kurtz, the character in Conrad's book *Heart of Darkness*, might have done when first being introduced to an exotic member of a Congo tribe. He didn't much care for what he saw and was imagining ways in which he might steal their ivory.

To the de Veres, it wasn't just that they disapproved of William's appointment; the Joneses were another species. They might indeed have even originated from the Congo River. Everything about them was inexplicable and entirely alien. De Vere simply believed that the governors must have been bewitched to have found such unsuitable people.

The various meaningful grimaces he made in the direction of John Lipman suggested neither of them were at all pleased to welcome any new head – this one in particular! His dumpy wife Angela was on her umpteenth gin and tonic and had an air of barely suppressed antagonism.

This did not, William suspected, bode well for the future. De Vere was determined to be as chilly as minimum politeness would allow. Actually it seemed to William that even this constraint was somewhat transitory. He would not wish to test its permanence.

A rather gushing middle-aged man and his pretty foreign wife made a beeline for William. He introduced himself as Piers Dalton. William noticed the slight grimace, momentarily evident on Lancelot Waters's face. It was obvious that there was no love lost between him and the retiring head.

In a rather confidential, oily manner, he started to outline in a rather hushed, clandestine voice some of the obvious deficiencies of some of his colleagues and the unfairness with which he and his wife were treated by the retiring head.

He ended his quiet invective with a rather loudly and insincerely expressed compliment: "We are so pleased that you and Mary are joining us, we are sure you will make a huge difference." It was obvious that he was doing his very best to discomfort Lancelot Waters. This was not a conversation William welcomed or encouraged.

It made him feel incredibly uncomfortable; he didn't quite know how to terminate it without offending an unpleasant but potentially influential member of staff.

He was further annoyed that somehow this man was trying to involve him in what was clearly a long-standing clash with the existing authorities. He instinctively disliked the fawning insincerity that was so overtly manifest in this person. He tried extremely hard to hide this animosity.

William was now sure that his relationships with many of his colleagues were going to be highly very problematic. He certainly didn't wish to provoke any antagonism before he had to. In truth his feelings were not as simple or as straightforward as this. He was quite simply starting to experience a sense of pure panic.

What, he asked himself, had he got himself into? Whatever it was it didn't fill him with confidence. The worm of self-doubt had, he realised, entered his soul. He feared that his gargantuan self-assurance was merely insubstantial hubris. For the moment at least he kept such dark thoughts to himself, even from Mary. She, of course, was not fooled!

This was confirmed when Mary commented later as they drove back to the hotel. "I had the impression that few liked us, or even wanted to see us. To be honest, William, the atmosphere rather frightened me. It felt tonight like the anteroom to Purgatory."

The evening ended in what William and Mary were soon to discover was the usual Parkies fashion with large numbers of rather tipsy people. As the drink flowed, inhibitions weakened and the atmosphere of barely concealed hostility proliferated. Both William and Mary now fully, if reluctantly, realised this was going to be an immensely difficult and challenging job. In contemplation of this, they escaped back to their hotel as soon as they could politely absent themselves.

They returned the following morning with their children in tow. It was clear that the move to this isolated, rather bleak location was to also be very challenging for two of their boys. Francis, their eldest, seemed to increasingly view the move with unmitigated horror. As they walked around the building, Francis descended into a silent, anxious, fearful apprehension. William's mother Dilys was almost open-mouthed. The shabby grandeur of the place reminded her of those visits her husband

Gethin and she had made to various National Trust houses. Parklands, to her, had that same air of formaldehydric preservation.

It seemed lifeless, an inert, sterile milieu she now associated with those old country houses. A historic heritage chimera, where the substance had long gone and what was left was now wholly peripheral, unreal, lifeless, and arid.

She wondered, with some anxiety, how on earth William and Mary were going to breathe life into this particular corpse. It reminded her of the first time she had visited Blackfriars, at her son's reception into the Catholic Church. To her then the vision of all those white-clad friars and a sense of revisiting the medieval world had entirely discombobulated her. She felt at least as uneasy about his new fixation.

She was getting used to William's strange fantasies and extraordinary enthusiasms. She simply hoped that this one would not completely overwhelm him. She feared that it would, with very mixed feelings, and a sense William now reluctantly accepted that just maybe his friend Alan might have been right after all. The Jones family returned to London in something of a funk. They all feared the worst but hoped for the best.

Chapter Seven

LONDON MEMORIES

The few months that now elapsed between appointment and arrival at Parkies were frenetic and profoundly uplifting as well as demoralising, almost by turns. William and Mary were surprised and delighted to have sold their house so quickly, at a surprisingly good price.

It became increasingly obvious, and something of a surprise and joy, that so many of their colleagues and friends would seem to genuinely miss them. William was astonished and very touched that so many people seemed genuinely fond of them. Barely acquainted parents would wander up to both him and Mary, expressing apparently sincere regrets about their leaving.

They had not expected to be so affected by their departure. Whatever William's feelings about the *nouveau riche* environs of North London, he increasingly wondered whether he had been a little unfair in his harsh judgments of many of the school's parents. He was also rather proud of what he had achieved at St Oliver Plunkett's School.

It was true that its modest buildings and small playground didn't compare with the sweeping acres and huge country house of Parkies.

When William had been appointed five years before, the school had been on the verge of dissolution. He often laughed at the fact that between his appointment in 1982 and his arrival three months later, the numbers had dropped by one-quarter. "They must have heard of my coming."

Yet William had been very lucky. The NUT had decided to target the primary schools in Mrs Thatcher's constituency with a series of wildcat strikes. St Oliver Plunkett's sat geographically right on the edge of that. Suddenly, his school had become the flavour of the month. Desperate parents seemed almost to line up at the school gates, determined to secure any uninterrupted education that local primary schools could no longer guarantee.

By the time he had left in 1987, the largest single ethnic group within the school was Asian. They represented 40% of the total school roll, mostly Hindu and Sikh families. Oddly enough, that didn't really present a problem in a Catholic school. These families simply added the Trinity and pantheon of Catholic saints to their already very extensive ensemble of Gods.

The older Sikh boys were even provided with a regulation school turban, with the school badge prominently displayed at the front. The logo contained the Latin words: *Accipe Daque Fidem*. This translated loosely to 'keep and accept the faith'. It didn't, however, specify which faith!

The parents or children didn't seem to mind at all. It caused William great amusement. He rather admired these families' willingness to be so tolerant and inclusive. Jewish and Muslim families had been understandably less attracted to the institution.

This was partly, William thought, because they had plenty of choices of schools of their own denomination. Also, critically, the overtly

Catholic nature of St Oliver Plunkett's was a much bigger problem for them to cope with.

There were, however, some Jewish children, all of the liberal tradition. One morning the local rabbi was invited in to take the morning assembly. As he walked into the hall the children sang out: "Good morning, Father." As quick as a flash he replied with a winning smile, "Thank you, children, I am definitely someone's father."

The school, when William arrived, had literally no competitive games on offer. The man responsible for games, such as they were, was a chain-smoking, very scruffy-looking, uncouth Lancastrian, Gary Prendergast. When not using a medley of very vulgar words he wandered around the rough field that masqueraded as a football pitch, smoking copiously, dressed not in a tracksuit, but rather in a tatty sports jacket. He was organising, if that was the correct term, the odd desultory soccer kick-about.

Cricket didn't exist, and when girls were first introduced in his second year, there were neither any proper games, nor even facilities on which they could play. A financial arrangement with the local cash-strapped comprehensive school meant that St Oliver's were able to secure a limited use of their playing fields and sports facilities.

Eventually, netball and tennis were introduced: netball for the girls and tennis for both sexes. William even managed to organise a rudimentary programme of competitive games.

Part of the cellar in the main school building was converted into some extremely basic changing rooms. To begin with, soccer matches were lost with cricket-type scorelines. Gary Prendergast didn't always help matters by expressing rather forcibly and colourfully his views of opposing coaches and the more enthusiastic parents.

Luckily the chain-smoking Lancastrian finally departed. This was after many attempts by William at encouraging him to apply elsewhere. William, to oil the process, gave him a splendid, if entirely fictional references.

Unfortunately on one occasion when he had applied as Deputy Head to a small convent primary school, the very perspicacious nun headmistress telephoned him. "Would you appoint Mr Prendergast as Deputy Head of your school, Mr Jones?" she enquired.

This was immediately after William had spent the previous ten minutes singing Gary's rather fantasy praises. William couldn't lie anymore. "No, you see, I don't have such a post, Sister," he rather lamely responded. The exasperated nun then brusquely demanded, "What if you did, Mr Jones?" William was cornered. "No, I am afraid not, Sister."

This conversation thus ended, as did Gary's chances. Finally, after many more attempts and a fair amount of further falsifications on William's part, a desperate, if not very discerning school appointed him. William was finally able to employ a more suitably qualified and agreeable PE teacher.

This man, a Northern Irish former seminarian, might not be the most impressive games player, but at least he wore a tracksuit and his presence was not foreshadowed by a miasma of tobacco smoke.

At much the same time, William introduced cricket. Virtually the only coaching was undertaken by him in that first season. He was a totally useless coach, having hardly played the game himself. In truth he had hardly played any games whatsoever! It was quite literally the blind leading the blind.

Embarrassingly, in one of their first matches, the school was beaten by a local rival prep school with the final score for the home team, all out for three, and the visitors were two hundred and twenty for no wicket. Things did slowly get better: they couldn't really have got much worse! The employment of a part-time cricket coach of course helped.

By the time William left, the school remained still very weak in cricket, but had become quite strong in soccer. The girls had even won a netball match.

One of William's key objectives was to secure membership of IAPS (Independent Association of Preparatory Schools) for St Oliver Plunkett's School. This he finally achieved at the end of his third year.

Membership of this organisation was seen as a kitemark of quality. Without it the school would be stuck with its rather dubious status as a glorified dame establishment.

There were various standards the school was required to reach to achieve this. This was partly about teaching standards, but it included further issues of basic facilities, an adequate curriculum range, as well as much else. When William was appointed a whole swathe of these standards were not yet adhered to. Eventually with the help of a wonderful friendly and helpful HMI, he was able to bring the school up to these minimum requirements.

This gave the place, he thought, a vital bit of added prestige and would perhaps encourage a few more traditional middle-class families to send their children to him. This was something that did not in fact materialise.

William was keen to encourage parental participation. He set up a parents' association, who in the first year formed work parties to assist

William in his painting programme. The chocolate and cream school decor was soon replaced by a more colourful and child-friendly palette of colours, albeit rather amateurishly executed.

The chair lady was a large, blousey, attractive, warm-hearted woman. She was married to a chap who was subsequently arrested for armed robbery.

As a way of thanking this group William and Mary threw a party at their house. During the dancing that followed the buffet, very much in the traditions of 1980s entertaining, William found himself unintentionally in a cheek-to-cheek smoochy dance with this lady. In the semi-darkness, she then placed William's hands on her ample bosom. He was transfixed by an impulse of total, unmitigated terror.

This was not helped by the fact that her formidable, steely husband was only yards away. William found himself in a difficult, rather delicate quandary. If he squeezed he might encourage her, which he certainly didn't want. If he quickly took his hands away, he might mortally offend and thus lose her two children from the depleted school roll.

In the end he stood paralysed like a frozen rabbit. Finally, after her husband went to prison, she took up with another member of the local mafia. William felt he had had a very lucky escape, certainly morally and, given the circumstances probably physically, too.

Every year the school organised a rather grand, if somewhat pretentious parents' ball. The Dorchester hotel was a favoured venue. The then Chairman of the governors, Roy Childs, a rather modest, gentle, bespectacled local solicitor, decided to invite a colleague.

His friend, a lawyer who worked in criminal law, kept nudging him, whispering: "Roy, I know that fellow." The list of familiar faces was rather a long one. This lawyer tended to prosecute offenders rather than defend them. He was therefore not likely to be very popular. They both decided to cut their evening somewhat short.

What it did show was that William's encounter with his parent gangster was by no means unique. He quickly came to realise that some of the most ostentatiously wealthy parents were by no means necessarily operating on the right side of the law.

The few spare funds he had he used to paint and restore the rather cramped, dilapidated buildings. During a number of summer holidays, he had even taken to a spot amateurish classroom painting, thus adding to the improvements his parental work parties had already achieved.

He even got a jobbing builder to encase one of the huts in brick. The school started to look quite attractive and the classrooms were now beautifully equipped with all the most modern teaching equipment he could afford. He went around various school fire sales buying furniture.

He acquired an ice cream machine from a former Sacred Heart Brothers school in Highgate. The sale of ice creams took place after lunch and was an especially useful way of paying for extra equipment and helping with the costs of a part-time gardener to cut the grass and maintain the flower beds, something which the diocese had not budgeted for.

William reflected at the time that there must be few, if any, headmasters acting as the Mr Whippy man. Perhaps not something that added greatly to the children's healthy-eating options! Mary was amazed that parents were not in arms, marching up to William's door with legitimate complaints that the school was actively promoting obesity.

Nevertheless, the exercise was very profitable as well as, from

William's perspective, extremely enjoyable. Given his cavalier attitude to basic hygiene, Mary thought it was wholly remarkable the school did not suffer a bout of serious salmonella poisoning!

Within three years pupil numbers had more than doubled. The school desperately needed new facilities. There was after all only so much that could be done with gallons of brightly coloured paint; or indeed litres of soft ice cream.

Back in 1982, when he was appointed, the diocese had promised to act as guarantor for a bank loan to build a new classroom block, if an increase in numbers justified this. It soon became obvious that the diocese had made this promise when they had assumed the school had no real future. These were empty words, probably said to encourage William to accept the job.

It became clear had they had never expected or intended to have to honour them. The NUT had unintentionally rather scuppered this and made it a tad more difficult for them to back out.

In recent months they had very obviously gone rather cool on this assurance. Always the optimist, William tried to force their hand. He had plans drawn up and even prepared a planning application. The diocesan finance office reacted to this initiative firstly with irritation, then with fury, and later with ominous silence.

Eventually, William and his chair of governors Roy Child were summoned to Archbishop's House in Westminster for a dressing-down from the finance officer. This gentleman, immaculately clad in a tailored pinstripe suit, had a disconcerting technique of peering through his half-moon glasses as though William and Roy were errant servants who had inexplicably dipped their hands into the family piggy bank.

He explained in words of one syllable that they should understand where power derived – not, they were given to understand, with them. There were in addition various pious admonitions about the greater wisdom of Mother Church and the need to respect that. They must bear in mind the relative status of lowly lackeys such as them, compared with truly important persons presumably such as himself. Roy, with unusual and out-of-character heat, angrily responded by pointing out that we were simply following through on previous promises. This cut no ice with this pompous poohbah.

They were arbitrarily dismissed, apparently because, as this functionary explained, he had a more important meeting with a significant clerical person. They assumed he meant the Cardinal, which their extremely impertinent presence had regrettably delayed.

The meeting ended supposedly inconclusively, the matter being left theoretically in the air, although actually there was little doubt about the real direction of travel.

William increasingly assumed, as it turned out correctly, they were preparing to renege on this promise. They had probably forgotten they had given it in the first place. This was one important reason why he decided to look for another position.

Some of the local Gujarati parents invited them both to a leaving feast at a superb Indian vegetarian restaurant in Finchley. They were all teetotallers, but insisted, with their customary hospitality, that William and Mary drank the most expensive malt whisky with their meal. This was an offer it would have been churlish to decline. It was very ironic, William reflected later, that they should end an evening with a group of vegetarian teetotallers as drunk as lords.

William's long-suffering secretary/administrator, the elderly Mrs Lucy Thornley, actually cried when they said their farewells: "I wish you all the luck in the world – come back and see us when you can." She didn't know that within a year the school, as she had known it for over thirty years, would not still exist. Her inoperable cancer was a secret that she shared with no one, and quite soon afterwards she died.

Yet when William thought about his London years, he considered he had been quite successful, as well of course as very lucky. Before the interview in Suffolk, Jonathan Carpenter decided to visit his school, to check him out. He was impressed by the way William escorted him around the place with obvious pride in his achievements.

When he returned home to Suffolk, he was chatting over the experience with his wife Celia. "It was the most extraordinary place, a bit like Bombay meets Dublin. There were all these Sikh children with Catholic insignia on their turbans. Most of the buildings were dollied-up terrapins, but beautifully decorated and actually rather surprisingly most attractive." Jonathan then laughed. "You know, darling, I even saw this chap Jones, dishing out ice creams from his Mr Whippy machine. It was totally bizarre. Jones is either going to be a roaring success if we appoint him, or he will convert Parkies into a Suffolk Gurdwara. I wouldn't want to guess which!"

Whilst this visit had left Jonathan Carpenter with some reservations, he couldn't deny that he possessed considerable reserves of energy and imagination. The question he asked himself was whether William's eclectic style would go down well in the shires. Truthfully, he still remained rather doubtful. Celia, on the other hand, thought that this fellow might be just the thing that was needed in the stuffy world of West Suffolk.

Father Sean O'Connor, their gentle, kindly, very Hibernian local parish priest, and the new chairman of the governors, since Roy Child resigned in frustration at the attitude of the diocese, even tried to dissuade the Joneses from going. "What the hell do you think you are doing, dear Will?" he said. "You are chasing a ridiculous fantasy. It is just an unrealistic dream: surely you can see that people really care about you here. You can see the great job you have done in London."

He concluded, "They will, in my opinion, simply use you, then spit you out in that posh outfit up there." He then pointed out, with his customary wisdom and empathetic understanding of William and his family, that he believed that they didn't understand the real deal being offered. He was sure it just wasn't as they supposed! He feared that the naively enthusiastic William was going to be used then discarded by these stuck-up English ingrates.

William put a lot of this down to Father O'Connor's ingrained hostility to all things English. Like many Irish priests he knew, he distrusted the old English Catholic gentry, at least as much as his overtly Protestant neighbours: "At least you know where the blow is coming from, but these buggers smile sweetly whilst stilettoing you from behind," he commented in one of their last conversations.

William didn't know it then, but his departure was the only excuse the diocese really needed to sell St Oliver Plunkett's. It was one of their few remaining independent schools. The buyers were some American educational entrepreneurs. This feat they succeeded in achieving within months of his departure. Father Sean suspected this would happen and hated the very thought of it. Yet he never once, even later, harboured any resentment, at least not to William.

For the Jones children the move was even more difficult. Childhood friendships are so precious and they were not only leaving their friends, but also about to inhabit a world a million miles from the diverse and, for all its faults, vibrant world of North London.

Suffolk might as well have been on the moon; there was no way back. Francis, the eldest, left his best friend Raj. The other children, though less affected, were also losing long-standing friends and their familiar surroundings. It felt for Francis like the end of the world. If their dad felt like a fish out of water, Francis feared he was about to be grilled. Francis only fully shared his feelings of those times years later, when he did finally clearly express the extent of the trauma he was then facing. William, on the other hand, thought that Parkies offered a real opportunity for his children.

Francis passionately disagreed, but felt unable to really express what he felt, for fear largely of upsetting his beloved dad. It took years for him to fully recover from what had happened, or indeed entirely forgive his father for putting him through it all. This was something William hadn't appreciated at all, and Mary only dimly at this stage.

Chapter Eight

WELSH IDYLL

This journey to a new life, William kept telling himself, provided opportunities for novel experiences and exciting possibilities. This at least was a belief he tried to cling onto. The traumatic departure from London was more wearing and upsetting than either William or Mary had ever imagined. In Mary's mind the Suffolk future seemed rather more threatening than exciting.

The neat terrace in Friern Barnet from which for so many years William had yearned to escape, suddenly seemed unexpectedly alluring. When he last viewed this familiar landscape he was surprised by the intensity of feeling of an acute loss and melancholy. It was in this confused frame of mind that the family finally decamped at the end of the summer term to William's mother's draughty, old Victorian villa on the outskirts of Usk in Monmouthshire.

William's dad had died two years previously. His widowed mum was delighted to have the family staying with her whilst their flat in Parkies was being prepared.

Gargantuan qualities of food had been bought in, as though Granny thought that she was about to be invaded by the barbarian hordes. The family wealth, such as it was, consisted of three rather old-fashioned ironmonger's shops in the Newport area. William's brothers Owen and Carwyn now managed the business.

The growth of out-of-town shopping malls, and the ongoing decay of traditional Welsh heavy industry accelerated Jones's Ironmongery's inexorable decline. It was felt by Owen in particular, that the advent of Mrs Thatcher's market-driven ideas had made matters infinitely worse. This had not, however, dissuaded him from retaining his membership of the local Conservative Party.

This had hit the family firm very hard. "It is so bloody difficult, Will," Carwyn declared: "We can't compete on location or price, it is only a matter of time." Carwyn had that uniquely Welsh pessimistic vision of the world. Even in the best of times, his naturally drooping, bull terrier-like facial features exuded a sense of a revelatory gloom of 'the end is nigh' variety.

This William thought was probably partly the result of generations of apocalyptic chapel orations, together, William imagined rather spitefully, with the painful haemorrhoids induced perhaps by the peculiarly uncomfortable benches on which the chapel congregation were expected to sit, sometimes for many hours.

Carwyn was still an Elder of the local Baptist chapel, a congregation much diminished in size and influence in recent years, whilst he continued to mouth the apparent doctrinal certainties of his nonconformist Faith. William rather supposed that these days his status as Past-Master of the Usk Masonic lodge was of greater import in his life.

When their father had first applied to join the lodge in the late-

1950s he had barely reached the minimum bar of the required social respectability. He had to wait six long years for the privilege of an invite to the lodge. When he was accepted he thought he had finally arrived socially, and lodge meetings became the essential, not to be missed occasions: a mark of a newly discovered respectability. Now, of course, membership was less a matter of gentility conferred, but rather a scrabble for any possible inductee.

This was a fact that neither son was willing to acknowledge, or rarely to contemplate. Moreover, both Carwyn and Owen had followed their father in furtive visits to the far less respectable Newport Spiritualist Church. They sought the guidance of long-dead relatives and in recent years that of their father in particular.

However, on this visit William thought Carwyn's gloom might have a point, as William drove his family's Citroën past one of the branches located in a row of scruffy shops on the edge of Newport, most of them empty. The Jones's Ironmongery façade was much in need of a coat of fresh paint and customers seemed very sparse indeed.

William usually had very mixed feelings when he returned to Wales. He always felt a frisson of excitement when they crossed the Severn Bridge and they passed the sign 'Welcome to Wales'. This was, after all, his country and he was proud to be a Welshman, especially when he could wave the dragon flag and annoy what he often considered were the rather pompous, entitled English at Twickenham.

It produced in him, when he stayed for any time, a strange, claustrophobic sense of being enclosed, unable to get out. He imagined that this was in some ways connected with the fire and brimstone preachers that still occasionally visited their local chapel in his childhood.

He was coming back to a community that was hemmed in physically between the mountains and the Bristol Channel, and psychologically by the long South Walian experience of decline and decay. It was as though the people around were in constant expectation of disaster.

They had somehow made a comforting shibboleth of a fantasy Welsh heritage identity, of choirs, funny hats, and rugby at The Arms Park.

Escapees like William didn't always feel entirely welcome when they returned. There was possibly a residue envy for those who had had the nous to leave. These emotions were now returning. He was quickly aware of a sense of stifling enclosure, matched, of course, by the excited joy in returning home.

William, as the eldest son, had been expected to join the family business. To his father Gethin the shops were the source of most of his pride and sense of social and personal worth. Every member of the Jones family were expected to indulge fully that passion. William's small contribution to that ironmongery phantasm was that he was required, when still a schoolboy, to spend his Saturdays as an errand boy delivering parcels of tools, rope, emulsion paint and much else around the more prosperous houses of Newport.

He had hated this; he was bored by this whole world of DIY and the obsessions with appearances and respectability that it seemed to imply. Later, when he served in one of his father's shops, he felt mostly foolish and ignorant. He was never was able to answer customer questions.

This was in part because he was physically very impractical, as Mary was later to find out to her chagrin. He was bored silly by the whole experience, and nor did he have the wit to hide this.

This might also have been a negative, rebellious reaction to the family expectation of having to take an active part in their obsessive preoccupation with painting and decorating the shops and family home. For William this usually meant holding the bottom of the ladder for hours on end, whilst his more dexterous and interested father and siblings were enthusiastically slapping on paint.

Thus, the sheer boredom and ennui of small-town Welsh life were a huge factor in his decision never to join the family firm and later to escape from the suffocating routines and rituals of this petty bourgeois Cambrian existence.

This all proved a huge disappointment to his father. Gethin judged that William was the epitome of ingratitude and selfishness, and simply couldn't understand why anyone would thumb their nose at such a golden opportunity. This had been the source of many adolescent spats and bitter arguments, ultimately to lead William to a period of nihilistic, unfocussed, and often destructive antagonism. Gethin reacted by desperate attempts to contain and control his son's antisocial behaviour. These included fruitless attempts to restrict his freedoms and deny his other limited privileges.

On many occasions William had simply decamped from the family home in ultimately pointless attempts to run away. Often this ended with the arrival of a dishevelled, upset teenager at his kindly aunt's little cottage in Roath in Cardiff. Auntie Blod was actually his father's first cousin. She simply accepted the wayward boy and often defended him against the incandescent rage of his father.

These were contributory causes, William thought, to his catastrophic showing in his 'O' level examinations. At school, despite his physical bulk, he was a rather shy, nervous, disengaged boy. A memory of some of his more enthusiastic teammates pushing him into an imaginary scrum and eagerly kicking him as a kind of replacement ball, was one he would not easily forget.

His grammar school wasn't, he felt, really very interested in the joy of learning for the sake of learning. Most of the classes were focussed on the mechanics of dry, factual recall.

When he later recalled his experience of life in his school, he often thought that the Dickensian figure of Thomas Gradgrind from *Hard Times* was still alive and well, at least there.

This perception was to be an enormous influence on William's subsequent educational thinking. He spent his whole career resisting what he feared was a reappearance within the school curriculum of the Gradgrind principle: namely that of the sterile utilitarianism of factual content, divorced from imagination and real empathy.

The one person who so inspired him was a gifted, enthralling, talkative, little North Walian History teacher, Mr Owen Evans. He was a little whippet of a man, with a large, balding head and vivid green eyes enlarged by his round national health spectacles. This often gave him the look of a slightly petulant Turkey. He always wore a faded academic gown which he used as a dramatic prop thus further added to the impression of a bird trying but failing to launch himself into the firmament.

His imaginative, often theatrical perorations into the minutiae of past events, frequently accompanied by the rather dramatic device of jumping into a waste-paper bin and enacting a character from the past, that had entirely enthralled him.

Mr Evans was an obsessive enthusiast, particularly about the whole contested story of the Dark Ages, and especially the Arthurian myth.

Arthur was for him a real historical figure: a true Welsh hero.

One year his class visited Glastonbury and they all struggled up to the top of the tor. Owen Evans was almost dancing with joy, describing in great detail the topology of Dark Ages Somerset. This one experience also nurtured in the young William a fascination for the whole Joseph of Arimathea fable, and the supposed grave of Arthur and Guinevere. Even Owen Evans considered these stories as rather fantastical. To William they were rich nourishment for his romantic soul.

This teacher's greatest enthusiasms were for each and every event that had somehow embarrassed the English, whom he insisted on calling the *Saesneg,* and displayed them in what Mr Evans believed was their true malignant colours. He so admired every example of the most forlorn of Welsh resistance, with a special affection for the Rebecca rioters, the revered local Gwent exemplars. This all stoked William's sense of a proud Welsh identity.

Arthur was of course the greatest of his heroes. It wasn't just Arthur who Mr Evans was sure had existed. The whole pantheon of Malory's *Morte d'Arthur* cast of characters were to him entirely real.

He developed the strange notion that Sir Kay had been a resident of nearby Caerleon. He was sure, for example, that the Gwent King Meurig was Arthur's father, a somewhat dubious assertion, as William was later to discover.

William most vividly remembered his lesson about Llewelyn ap Griffith and his courageous resistance against the obnoxious brutal English King Edward I, Longshanks. This had inspired him then, and he still remembered wistfully and fondly the little, bald-headed, bespectacled birdlike teacher tearfully describing Llewelyn's last stand, at the same time waving his begowned arms in an enthusiastic even rather believable impression of the final death blow.

This man had captivated his curiosity and cultivated in him a romantic, passionate love for history which had never left him, as well as encouraging him later to become a teacher himself. Between leaving school and ultimately securing a place at training college, William had undertaken many rather boring clerking jobs. Whilst at evening classes, he worked hard to remedy his lack of qualifications. He had then left the family home as quickly as he could.

Gethin was the apogee of the self-made man. He had married the pretty, if rather mouselike Dilys in his late-thirties, whilst she was still a teenager. Gethin delighted and exulted in the role of paternal martinet. Gethin demanded total subservience from all his children.

Outside the family many colleagues and Masonic and chapel friends saw him as an amusing and likeable raconteur: "Such an amusing, delightful man, a pillar of the community, with such a lovely, supportive family," the Rev Gareth Powell, the somewhat unctuous Baptist minister, commented to a parishioner after one lengthy Sunday service. When the polished brass and newly painted front door of the family house was closed to the outside world, Gethin often, in fact, developed into a terrifying ogre, where the slightest resistance or opposition to his will provoked verbal and sometimes physical abuse.

When he was in a particularly ugly mood, retaliation did not even require much provocation. His children were never quite sure whether when he returned from work, he would be the genial dad or the avenging angel. What the Rev Powell assumed was the supportive love from Gethin's children was in reality often one of abject terror.

William conceded that all fathers damage their sons; Gethin had truly excelled in this art. William had not been alone in experiencing the growing ire of an intimidating, irrational, inconsistent father.

Owen and Carwyn were the products of years of verbal and physical bullying. Carwyn suffered from a debilitating stutter, which William attributed largely to the frequent humiliations he had suffered at the hands of their father. Owen, too, lacked any confidence, or the ability for independent thought. Since his father's demise, it seemed to William he had been in a permanent funk of angst and dejection.

The limitations and damaged psyches of these offspring were certainly a factor in the decay of the family enterprise and would, William believed, probably ultimately lead to its demise. Yet both sons had virtually canonised their dead father. Nothing detrimental could be said about him.

This myth was reinforced by the shrine that the family home had become. Every nook and cranny were festooned with memorabilia of Gethin's many perceived triumphs: as Mayor, as Magistrate, Borough Councillor, Masonic Provincial Grandmaster and Chapel Elder.

William had frankly detested his father, an emotion that had done much to define the rest of his life and increasingly and particularly his dysfunctional relationships with his extended family.

Since Mary had arrived on the scene fourteen years before, there had been less and less reason to return to Wales. They had met at Cheltenham when Mary had attended St Mary's and William, St Paul's Training Colleges. The fact that William had decided on this college, rather than a more local or Welsh institution was in itself a further sign of his growing rejection of his Joneses' Cambrian heritage.

Mary's dad still lived in Goring; her mother having died a few years previously. Goring had always been a more convenient location, especially as most of their jobs had thus far been in the London area. Consequently they saw much more of Mary's widower father Ernest.

Mary's sparky, opinionated personality had not fitted with Gethin's vision of ideal womanhood. In that regard he had much in common with some of the governors at Parkies! Mary, when faced with the especially grumpy ironmonger, refused to take these moods very seriously.

Whether it was true or not, Gethin thought Mary had a rather supercilious attitude; this rather defined his opinion of her.

"Nothing but a rather snooty bluestocking," he opined to Dilys after William had taken Mary to the railway station on one of her visits. Gethin had acted as virtual matchmaker in directing who would be appropriate wives for Owen and Carwyn.

These were compliant shop girls, who were in awe of the large, portly ironmonger and pillar of the local establishment. The great advantage of this arrangement from Gethin's point of view was that these daughters-in-law rarely expressed an opinion, or indeed complained when he frequently pinched their bottoms, or placed his large, hairy hands on their breasts.

Gethin was terrified of Mary. For a start she was educated and had often inexplicably disputed his antediluvian views and attitudes. "I really don't think black people are as bad as that," she confidently asserted in one such heated debate. On another occasion she suggested that "the trade unionists do have a point; my dad is a shop steward and he is no radical Marxist." He confessed to Dilys after the first time Mary had challenged him: "I can't stand opinionated women with a rather overblown opinion of their own intellect." Worst of all he blamed her for William's conversion to Catholicism.

Catholicism remained in Gethin's mind a malignant creed, dominated by continental ideas, treasonous designs and, worst of all, its Irish adherents. When Mary observed, "Even the Marquess of Bute was a Catholic," he almost had an apoplexy.

In his central assertion he was wrong: William's conversion had nothing to do with Mary and happened long before he met her. The real agent for the event, Mary believed, was Gethin himself. In the Church, and especially in the gentle Dominican Friar Father Thomas who had instructed him, Mary felt he had discovered an alternative, kinder father.

William, ironically, was the only one of his children to be given an English name, the consequence of the ironmonger's passion for Chepstow Castle, the venue for many childhood outings. It was William Marshal who had built it – hence the name!

This appellation had somehow defined William's role within the family. He was the odd one out, the source, too, of huge and growing embarrassment to Gethin from chapel and Masonic friends alike. Gethin's Masonic friend Edwin Morris once said in William's hearing: "Catholics are an abomination. Should one be accepted into the lodge I would be the first to resign, that includes your boy, too, Gethin."

William's Catholic amour was of course the visible expression of his rejection of everything Jones' Ironmongery and the narrow Welsh petty bourgeois world stood for. The fact that Gethin dimly understood this, at least at a subconscious level, further tore into their lingering increasingly toxic association.

Despite the veneer of respectability that Gethin assiduously promoted, Mary knew that was merely a front. She saw the lascivious looks and wandering hands that defined much of the relationship between her father-in-law and his deferential, naive Welsh Valley shop girls.

Whilst Gethin was far too intimidated to try the same behaviour with her, she witnessed the bullying, and the cruel, sarcastic, barbed, often vicious comments directed at William and to a lesser extent his brothers. She knew, too, that William had not been immune from his father's wandering hands. At Gethin's funeral, much had been made of his generosity and service to the various local youth groups: Boy Scouts and Boys' Brigade in particular. The thought of what she suspected was his real motivation left her with a distaste, abhorrence, and shame.

Yet William adored his mother Dilys, an emotion he was sure was fully reciprocated. She was the daughter of a mine manager who had died suddenly of cancer when she was a child of only five.

Her mother Elen then survived on a very modest pension, enough for only the essential basics necessary for maintaining an illusion of respectability in the economically depressed mining valleys of 1930s South Wales.

Dilys childhood life had consequently been one of relative, if genteel, poverty and emotional neglect. Her mother was somewhat disappointed in her. She had none of her mother's dark, sultry, seductive good looks.

She was not an especially attractive girl, rather too tall, somewhat angular with long, thin legs and a rather flat chest. Her pretty face was spoilt, in her mother's view, by a long, thin nose.

Cruelly her mother would sometimes joke that in time her pointed chin would meet with her equally long prominent nose. These were facts and opinions her increasingly embittered, unhappy mother was rarely slow to point out.

Dilys did not attract a raft of suitors, at least those acceptable to her formidably ambitious mother. As time went on she developed into a rather shy, withdrawn, timid girl. She was, however, bright, who for a few years had attended the Rhondda Girls High School.

She left at fourteen when the money ran out, to work as a clerk in the Llanwern Steel Mills.

She had met her future husband at a YMCA shindig in Newport. Gethin was just about socially acceptable to her mother, certainly much better than the probable alternative of a rough local miner. She was therefore happy to accept, if not exactly promote, the match. When Dilys announced her engagement Elen reluctantly agreed and, as was required given her daughter's age, she gave formal permission for the wedding.

However, she couldn't resist the caustic comment: "Rather a boring, unattractive man, dear, but beggars can't be choosers." She herself sadly only survived three months into her daughter's marriage, dying like her husband quickly of cancer at the age of only forty-two.

Dilys was thus married at the very tender age of seventeen. This meant that she was thrown entirely onto her own limited resources; this whilst she was hardly more than a child. She had therefore literally no support, other than from her newly acquired, demanding, and controlling, much older husband.

William was born a year later. William angrily thought his father had used her as a skivvy and worse. She worked in the shops, did the accounts, brought up her children and was still required to provide a hot dinner at 1:00 pm sharp. In the first ten years of her marriage, she was pregnant nine times, only four of which resulted in a live baby. Yet inexplicably she seemed to still adore Gethin.

In many ways, she remained the naive valley girl, who had found a father figure and seemed able to ignore the intimidation, powerlessness and sexual deviance that seemed to be part of the deal. Even now five years after his death, she treated his memory with an extraordinary reverence. William felt this was undeserved and totally mystifying.

Even now she was doing her best to protect his legacy. Jones' Ironmongery was certainly struggling, but it was largely down to Dilys's efforts and intuitive talent that it survived at all.

This was a fact generally unrecognised and ignored by his two brothers. Dilys always maintained a protective shield over these two sons. They were allowed, even encouraged by her, to imagine that they were entirely responsible for any business success that was achieved.

Any failures were always the fault of others. This delusion bred in them an unrealistic, if probably fragile, confidence in their own competence and self-importance.

It also encouraged them to regard William and Glynis, the family escapees, as somehow morally deficient, in turning their backs on their world of small-town respectability. William did not believe that his mother's leniency was of much benefit to either of them in the long run.

William had therefore together with his sister Glynis escaped the Gwent curse. Neither saw their mother as often as she wanted, or as they should. Glynis was by far the most successful of his siblings: she had a post in finance in London and was on the fast track to success. She lived a life of what too much of her family seemed the epitome of metropolitan sophistication and prosperity. This was even, in some ways, more confusing for her brothers than William's increasing oddities.

Her feisty shell masked an equal dislike for the boring provincial life of Monmouthshire. The youngest of the family, she, too, had suffered from Gethin's merciless tongue. She seemed more able to sidestep and largely ignore the nastiness. Gethin had died when she was in the sixth form. That probably ensured that his malign influence on her life was rather more limited.

William was sure it was Glynis that Dilys loved most of all. Perhaps an ultimate subconscious revenge on her exacting husband. Was this just a fantasy? He couldn't tell. In the end he just believed it was so.

Even with Gethin no longer around, family relationships were sometimes rather fraught. Part of the problem was that the horizons of the Jones family were firmly defined by the Wye and the Taff. William's successful application to Parkies was a source of much perplexed and confused hostility. His brothers had vaguely heard of Monmouth School and Christ's Brecon, but that was the limit of their knowledge of the posh independent school world to which their increasingly peculiar brother now seemed to aspire to belong.

Dilys had made a few trips to London and had even attended one of St Oliver Plunkett School's Prize Days. Father O'Connor had pulled on every ounce of his considerable Irish charm, and Dilys had decided, albeit somewhat reluctantly, that some Catholic priests weren't too bad after all.

On one grey, late-November Sunday William has persuaded her to attend Mass with him at St Elthelreda's in Central London, on the Feast of Christ the King.

The congregation were treated to a sermon by an extraordinary clerical French eccentric, Jean-Marie Charles-Roux, on the surprising theme of 'The Royal Martyrs'.

The congregation even sang the national anthem after the homily which, William reflected, would not have shamed Archbishop Laud. Whilst all the smells and bells did not appeal to Dilys's nonconformist soul, she still found them somewhat foreign and entirely inexplicable.

She was, however, rather taken by the atmosphere of loyal, patriotic conformity. She no longer thought of Catholicism as Gethin had. Yet she remained sceptical and still considered it fundamentally as an alien, mystifying creed.

She could understand the basic ethos of a school like St Oliver Plunkett's which seemed rather similar to the modest, little, private primary school in Newport where she had sent her own children. Most of the pupils at Oliver Plunkett's weren't even Catholic. She did not feel quite the same about this apparently rather grand place, Parkies.

This would separate him from the only world she really knew or understood. She feared not for the first time that she was about to lose much of her family.

William's brothers' attitudes were in some respects less complicated. During the many adolescent battles their elder brother had fought with their father, they had almost always sided with their dad. Sometimes they had even joined in his various humiliating games he excelled at initiating. Over the years, they had bought entirely into Gethin's view that William was a troublesome nuisance or worse and that his rebellious attitude was entirely reprehensible.

William who had seen the way they, too, were both bullied by their burly ironmonger father, assumed that they were displacing their own fears by joining the perpetrator. The bullied boy who becomes part of the gang and behaves worse than initiator is a common theme in the school playground and the world of institutional and national politics.

Since their father's death they had simply ignored him. They increasingly viewed his attitudes and career as proof positive of his irredeemable eccentricity and peculiarity.

Owen's opening gambit when he first met William on this visit was to sneeringly observe: "On holiday again: do you teachers ever do a decent day's work?" Was this attitude the result of jealousy or contempt? He couldn't tell.

Mary, on the other hand, was to them an entirely unknown quantity; like their father they were slightly frightened by her. Their wives saw her as a rather dangerous, exotic creature, best to be avoided if possible.

William and Mary's failure to show the vaguest interest in the Jones's Ironmongery empire was considered perhaps the ultimate betrayal.

When William considered his brother's attitude to him, he remembered Evelyn Waugh's observation in his very apposite novel *Decline and Fall*. "Never get mixed up in a Welsh wrangle. It doesn't end in blows like an Irish one but goes on forever." It was a quotation that often seemed so appropriate in the ongoing saga of the Jones family.

Mischievously, and certainly unwisely, William couldn't resist jokes about rolled-up trouser legs and strange handshakes. Masonry was, to his brothers, beyond humour. It was the source of most of what they really cared about.

It was the core of their vision of respectability and status, as well as the centre of their rather narrow, humdrum social life. The local, ugly little Masonic Hall was their own authentic temple, the place that fed their sense of worth, perhaps even their very *raison d'être*.

On the other hand, they thought of William's new religion as little more than a mishmash of peculiar doctrines and even odder practices. They had, after all, years of being told just this by their now deceased dad.

Carwyn remembered one of his father's most telling jibes: "The trouble with you, William, is you were born in the wrong country in the wrong class in the wrong century." This had become part of the holy writ of Gethin memorabilia.

The Parkies announcement seemed to fully confirm much of the authenticity and truth of this comment. William, they felt, had always been pretentious and rather stuck up. This new job was just going to make him even worse.

They wouldn't even admit this to themselves, but there was perhaps just a frisson of jealousy. They were, they believed, stuck, working their hides off, maintaining the never-to-be-admitted, declining family firm, whilst their uppity elder brother was swanning around with the aristos.

Owen summed all this up one evening when he joked: "I do hope that you won't tire of the quails and caviar, but you know, as we do, they will soon find you out, and understand that you are really just a bit of overdone Welsh rarebit."

Despite the negative undertones, the visit was a rare opportunity to spend some time with Mum. One day they made a valedictory visit to Chepstow Castle. The site was now much tidier than William remembered all those years before. He still didn't really fully understand why William Marshal had exerted such a hold on his dad's imagination.

It might even, he considered, represent an extraordinary contradiction in his personality. Somewhere in the depths of Gethin's

Welsh soul, he was desperate to escape the confines in which he had placed himself. William Marshal, the dominant national figure through three Plantagenet reigns, was one of the most important historical figures associated with Monmouthshire.

Perhaps Gethin had in some subconscious way envied this great man who had a real national reputation and pre-eminence that overshadowed and expanded beyond the small provincial world so familiar and suffocating to him.

In the end William Marshal had escaped this provincial claustrophobia, something that Gethin probably deep down wanted to do as well.

William thought that if he had been called Emrys, his mother's preferred choice, he doubted whether with such an obviously Welsh Christian name he would even have been interviewed for Parkies. In a strange way his father had done him a favour. Or perhaps it was his ultimate revenge!

The time came to make the long journey to Suffolk. Unusually his rather non-demonstrative mum gave them all a hug; William thought he might even have detected a small tear. Francis clung to her as though he would never let go. He more than anyone had the greatest fear in moving to this alien world. For all the world he would have much preferred to stay in Monmouthshire with his beloved henfam.

As they drove away, Dilys carried on waving until she could see them no longer. She always hated the moments of departure on their all too infrequent visits. On this occasion it was much worse. William and Mary had only the remotest idea of what awaited them. It was quite clear that the rest of the Jones family had an even fainter conception of the challenges that lay ahead.

Dilys feared that her somewhat pliable, rather unworldly elder son would be eaten alive by the sophisticates of this unfamiliar privileged English world. She was filled with a sense of foreboding.

William's new surroundings were those that she could only vaguely imagine from the pages of P. G. Wodehouse and the recently televised *Brideshead Revisited*. This process of departure had itself been especially harrowing for the children and remained so for Francis in particular. The time had come to move into their new flat and take over the mantle of Parkies.

Chapter Nine

A SHAKY START

The first day of term arrived remarkably quickly. In the few weeks preceding, William and Mary had experienced an incredibly swift, but by no means obstacle-free learning experience. The main pressing difficulty was in completing the conversion of their flat. Major Hardy, the bursar, seemed to regard the project as one of extremely low priority. He was, moreover, determined to complete it at the absolute minimum expense.

Mary eventually took rather a strong line. She was regularly seen at Major Hardy's door cajoling and pleading by turns. This seemed eventually to work, but it did not make her very popular, at least with the good Major. "That bloody woman is a harridan," Hardy angrily declared when explaining the situation to Lancelot Waters, when they met later at the local golf club: "She never gives up and seems to expect expensive 'ideal home' fittings everywhere: who the hell does she think she is?" he finally exploded. "The Duchess of Builth Wells, I suppose."

The flat that was eventually completed was quite comfortable in a rather shabby, down-at-heel sense. The large rooms were designed for big, now unfashionable Victorian furniture.

They had scoured the second-hand stores and auction houses of

East Anglia for what should probably be admitted was often cheap, hideous, Victorian bric-a-brac to provide what they hoped was an acceptable gentility to their surroundings.

The boys had acquired new uniforms, copious shorts which almost reached down beyond their knees to long socks tipped in the school colours of green and gold. The other main parts of the uniform ensemble were the Eton collar jumpers and extraordinarily itchy, grey woollen shirts, which all the boys complained bitterly about. James, the middle one, was especially animated on the subject; for some time he simply refused to wear it. William kitted himself out in what he thought was the correct attire of sports jacket and mud-coloured cords. Mary was dressed top to toe in what she hoped was a sufficiently fashionable and restrained Laura Ashley combination. She hoped this would satisfy even her most virulent critic.

Francis, their eldest boy, was still truly dreading his introduction to life in a new school. He expressed this trepidation when he wrote to his former school friend Raj. "We had been taken to Harrods where I have been dressed in what I considered to be the most ridiculous kit I had ever seen in my life. I had to wear these pair of baggy shorts that stretched to well beyond my knees, a horridly itchy grey shirt and green jumper which my mum had told him had an 'Eton' collar. When she said 'Eton' it really confirmed that I most definitely was not in Friern Barnet anymore. Had anyone turned up at Gladstone Place dressed like this; it would not have gone well for them: I felt like a fool. I will miss you and London so very much."

The previous regime had operated a staffing policy, which William now understood was not untypical of some of the supposedly 'smarter' prep schools. Most of the heavy lifting was undertaken by a group of young, enthusiastic 'stooges' largely unqualified and paid only a pittance. In exchange they had the run of a large estate and the use of a bar which opened everyday immediately before lunch. They were generally a jolly crowd, who in the main did an excellent job, entertaining the often rather vulnerable, homesick, and frightened young boarders.

They were also required to teach, which was usually a rather less satisfactory arrangement. The most glaringly problematic example of this was James Waters, the young nephew of the former head, who taught Geography. His charges usually sat in his classroom copying from a somewhat out-of-date textbook. This was whilst he occupied himself cutting the grass on the pitches on his swish new mower.

The other difficulty was that his only qualification for this was a single 'O' level in Geography. Mary commented when she heard of this: "Well, at least it was the right subject, imagine if it were Serbo-Croat." The smooth, oily, middle-aged fellow Piers Dalton, who had pounced on him back in March, assisted his wife in the teaching of French. Neither had any formal qualifications.

She was, however, remarkably talented; he, on the other hand, despite an elevated opinion of his abilities, was not. It soon transpired, as William had suspected, that his gentlemanly airs masked a remorseless sense of victimhood and resentment. He was someone who couldn't understand why the world did not judge him at his own estimation.

William soon discovered that his junior French lessons very largely consisted of a detailed examination of various engineering phenomena; notably bridges, a passion the children exploited mercilessly in a desperate attempt to distract him from the usual tedium of his classes.

There were some quite superb teachers. When William first looked around the school the one room which immediately overwhelmed and impressed in its stunning profligacy of colour was the small area dedicated to art.

Nathalie Harris, the Art teacher, usually clad in a smock festooned with the remnants of various paints, bits of clay and blobs of glue, did an extraordinary job in drawing out every child's natural creativity. Every inch of her cramped space was covered in paintings, mobiles, pieces of pottery and much else besides.

Nathalie was beloved by all; she always encouraged her charges and no child, she considered, was without talent. They responded by producing the most amazing pieces of artwork. Perhaps less importantly, she was able to secure a raft of art scholarships. William was astonished by what she was able to achieve with the few resources and a wholly inadequate space in which to work. Luckily for the Jones family, it turned out that James was a talented and enthusiastic artist. He hugely benefited from the encouragement he received from Nathalie. In this respect he was one of many fortunate children.

Martin Pugh who taught History, some English and much Drama was, as William realised, an alcoholic. To be fair this rarely affected his teaching. Perhaps ironically it might even have enhanced it. His wonderful eccentricity and dramatic elucidations were often actually facilitated by his semi-drunken state. He was a fellow Welshman, although, William thought, reflecting on his mother's background, much more mine owner than mineworker.

Martin had a somewhat tramp-like quality to his appearance. On one occasion a visiting grandparent during a school dramatic production Martin was directing actually thought he was a vagrant when he found him drunkenly snoring in his classroom during the intermission. It took some time for William to persuade them otherwise. Nor did he think they were overly impressed, at least in a positive sense!

What made Martin so special was his love of knowledge: he was exceptionally well read, who also in his spare time wrote mournful and lyrical verse in honour perhaps of his love of Wales as well as a reflection of his tortured Celtic soul.

His truly authentic, sincere solicitousness for the interest of his boys and his genuine warmth towards them meant that this was usually fully reciprocated by his charges. They might recoil at his beery breath and woeful personal hygiene. They knew he was on their side, a superb teacher, and a true scholar. He was always straightforward and never false.

Despite his own difficulties, his struggles with the demon drink and his persistent problems with depression, he was always positive and encouraging to them. Some of the poetry the children produced under his tutelage was extraordinary.

He was able to draw from some quite modestly talented pupils work of astonishing insight and perception which William considered would not have shamed many a sixth-former.

In the final analysis he was a tragic reflection of a particular strand of the Welsh psyche. His pessimism and depressive melancholy were the mirror image of his brother Carwyn and perhaps William, too, if it had not been for Mary, as well perhaps the Grace of God .

John Lipman, despite his growing alienation and drink problems, was another exceptional teacher. He had a talent, unusual in Mathematics teachers, in William's experience, to make the subject both interesting and accessible.

He didn't inspire the affection that Martin did, yet he was nevertheless highly respected. For years, as deputy head, he had essentially run the place during the growing incapacity of Lancelot Waters. John was an excellent administrator, but he lacked the talent to inspire. Like William he wasn't quite 'it' socially. Mrs McKenzie at one of her soirées had commented even before the February interviews: "I would forgive Lipman his drinking, if he was not so sullenly boring and married to a domestic." So typical of Margaret's acerbic, snobby wit, this perfectly illustrated John's present dilemma.

It was true that in his early days at Parkies he had married Karen, a young junior matron. Over the years she had graduated into the most efficient housekeeper.

He had served the school faithfully for most of his career, and had virtually been promised the prize, which had been snatched from him and given to a person who, he considered, neither wanted it as much as him, but certainly, he believed, didn't deserve it as much.

He had been very attached to the urbane Lancelot Waters. Occasionally a thought crossed his mind, though swiftly suppressed, that Waters had used him, and the promises he had made were not meant genuinely, merely a ploy to ensure loyalty and relieve him of onerous work.

He could hardly bear to be in the same room as William; the only way he could cope was to drink yet more copious amounts of gin. This crushing, unbearable sense of loss and bitterness was very rapidly destroying him. He was becoming compelled, almost driven, to lead the opposition to the new regime. All his hatred, disappointment and sense of thwarted ambition were now focussed on William.

It has to be said his late-night drinking sessions at the Royal Oak with de Vere, Dalton and Gerald Grimes did not help. The long, manipulative expositions by Dalton and Grimes about the injustice of it all, listing Jones's real and imagined deficiencies, added fuel, as was of course intended, to his righteous anger and growing rage. He knew, at least at one level, that he was being manipulated and exploited. Yet he had ceased to care. All he wanted to do was destroy William; if others wanted the same thing that was all to the good.

St John de Vere was a man who absolutely believed in his star. He taught Classics and was, it has to be admitted, the main buttress of Parkies' enviable scholarship record. In every respect bar one, his establishment background thoroughly trumped that of William.

He was a former scholar both at Eton and at Cambridge. He had rather blotted his copybook by his rather unwise, hasty marriage to the dumpy Angela. In his view he would have made a far better headmaster than any other likely alternative; especially the present incumbent. His only significant weakness, he imagined, was that he wasn't a Catholic.

He had enquired of Jonathan Carpenter whether this would be an insurmountable obstacle in his application for the headship. He was, to his great surprise, inexplicably informed that it would be.

The central snag of which he only dimly guessed, but couldn't wholly admit, was his wife. It wasn't just the fact that she was of displaced Kenyan settler stock, it was her oft-uttered, harshly gutturally vowelled, strident opinions on the state of the world. Her standpoint was rooted in a colonialist frontier prejudice and included a detestation for all Blacks, Asians, and any group that she perceived as a lesser breed.

When tipsy, as she frequently was, she would pour forth racist venom which made even Gerald Grimes and Mrs McKenzie blanch.

Lord Castle remonstrated when Jonathan shared with him the prospect of de Vere's application: "My God, with that woman around, the few remaining pupils that still inexplicably lingered here would be wearing Hitler Youth uniforms and we would be greeting each other with Mosley salutes."

De Vere, who was now desperately searching for alternative employment, could hardly bear the prospect that William and Mary now represented. The fact that this obviously plebeian, unsophisticated person had been appointed over him confirmed his growing sense of the fundamental injustice of the world.

He erupted after he and Angela had toddled back after the March shindig. "What an insufferable oik that fellow Jones is; his ghastly, simpering wife is only marginally better. You know, Angela, they will simply convert this place into a fucking coeducational knocking shop for the great London unwashed."

Ironically, he was closer to the truth than he imagined. Coeducation was a central plank of William's future strategy. He imagined that Mary was socially smarter than her vulgar, Welsh, philistine husband. "Don't like her much, but she has a bit more class than her awful Welsh husband."

Neither William nor Mary had the courage to admit that Mary was not a product of a Thames-side villa as the de Veres had assumed, but rather a council house in one of the least reputable parts of Berkshire.

Except for Art, which by definition was open to all, it was this very small, talented group of teachers whose efforts were focussed almost entirely on the bright scholarship boys. Lancelot Waters had prided himself on Parkies' scholarship record. Indeed the year before William arrived, two boys secured academic awards at Eton, another at Oundle. There were minor scholarships, usually referred to as exhibitions, to Downside, Haverhill and Uppingham. This achievement was impressive and formed the core of the school's reputation.

The problem was that the non-scholarship boys were often taught by the unqualified and crucially often far less competent staff. Outside London, entry to most public schools was in truth not very challenging. It was therefore easy to secure places on very mediocre Common Entrance results.

This fact was to be reinforced for William when in his second year James Waters, the unqualified teacher of Geography, managed to teach the whole Common Entrance cadre the wrong syllabus. Every boy spectacularly failed. Even so, every single boy secured a place in their first-choice public schools.

In effect this meant that the school's resources were being focussed on a tiny minority of able boys at the expense of everyone else. Apart from the obvious issues of justice and fairness, that often became an important question when a borderline candidate for the scholarship group wasn't picked.

One of the first examples of such a case William had to deal with was Rory McKenzie, someone his mother believed was destined for high academic achievement. That was not his opinion, or the view of any of the staff at Parkies. William saw Rory as a rather mediocre, lacklustre pupil whose main difficulty was an overbearing and unrealistic mother.

When that September he was placed into the also-ran Common Entrance class, rather than the elite scholarship group, she was incandescent with rage. Mrs McKenzie quickly appeared at the door of his study demanding an immediate reappraisal. It seemed to her that Rory's talents were not being adequately recognised.

Every weapon in her considerable arsenal was deployed, not least her status as a governor. William did reluctantly change Rory's designation, under intense pressure rather than any conviction.

However, William quickly ensured the way the academic structure was organised was less divisive and fairer. Fewer resources were put into this scholarship group at the very moment Rory McKenzie had secured his place.

Mrs McKenzie felt passionately that her son had been betrayed, as well as Lancelot Waters's legacy vindictively destroyed. Certainly, Parkies did afterwards secure fewer academic scholarships, although William believed that the quality of education for most of the children was immeasurably improved.

Rory McKenzie didn't succeed in procuring the yearned-for prize and wouldn't have done whatever structure was in place. This was not something that the McKenzies accepted. Their vocal and oft-expressed annoyance at what they perceived as the failure of the school was to be further grist to the mill for William's critics.

On that first day of the new academic term on a sunny, warm September afternoon William and Mary located themselves in the panelled front hall waiting for the apprehensive new boarders and their nervous, anxious parents to arrive.

In the past there would have been perhaps thirty predominately seven- and eight-year-old new sprogs appearing. Those times were long gone, and only ten new boarders that September were introduced to their unfamiliar world of lumpy ex-hospital beds and lockers in austere, shabby, uncarpeted, unadorned dormitories. Not surprisingly many of the children were somewhat disconsolate.

William had never himself been a young boarder, but he could imagine what a seven-year-old dragged from a comfortable London home might feel when faced with prospect of months living in the large, barren, barely heated spaces they were now obliged to consider as their new abode. To sweeten the pill, at least for the parents, the school provided a 'posh tea' similar to one available at governors' meetings. This was a combination of lashings of cake, sandwiches and an especially gorgeous, chocolate, gluey biscuit which William believed was entirely unique to Parkies.

The school employed an army of domestics. Every morning the school minibuses appeared in the largest council estate in the local town and picked up a gaggle of cheerful ladies who gossiped their way every morning to the former servants' entrance at the rear of the country house.

Many of these ladies had worked in the school for many years. One of them, Elsie Tickle, was the doyenne of the group. She had more than twenty years service under her copious belt. She had her own scullery and it was there that food was transferred to the children's refectory. It was also from there that the children went to eat their slab cake and sweetened tea most afternoons.

On high days like this, her job was to transfer the enormous beanfeast into the more splendiferous surroundings of the panelled hall. Elsie looked as though she had escaped from an episode of *Last of the Summer Wine*. She wore a flowery apron over a grey, shapeless skirt. Her stockings were usually twisted which meant, at least to William, that she resembled the character Nora Batty from that sitcom. She spoke in that wonderful Suffolk sing-song, interspersed with the occasional oath or expletive, depending on her mood.

On this particular afternoon she was suffering from something of a sulk. Elsie did not like change. The man who throughout most of her time working in the school had stood at the front door welcoming parents was her beloved Mr Waters accompanied by his fat Labrador Retriever Buster.

Now there was this strange beanpole of a man, accompanied by an especially ugly, scraggy mongrel named Bobby. He looked, she thought, as though he was half-expecting to be devoured. Not only that, but he also insisted on being friendly. Elsie preferred to be ignored. His bonhomie rather forced her to respond in an agreeable manner: Elsie did not do friendly!

The bursar, a former Army paymaster, who had struck up an acquaintanceship with Lancelot Waters when they had messed together whilst both serving in Germany during their National Service, had similar feelings to Elsie about the change of regime. The new man had this irritating habit of calling him George. Despite years of mutual familiarity Major George Hardy and Lancelot had never been on first-name terms. This might partly be because their relationship was defined by George's Pay Corps background and Lancelot's more prestigious Cavalry and public school history. Everything had always been very formal; that is how he much preferred it.

Now he was faced with this new, rather common fellow with his strange Welsh intonation trying to be all matey. That was not even to mention his ghastly, opinionated, demanding wife. Not only that, he also had lots of plans. Plans meant money; George did not like spending.

He had expressed his concerns to Gerald Grimes: "This new man wants to do up the dorms, he wants to improve the classroom equipment. How does he think we are going to pay for this? From a bloody Welsh money tree?" He was relieved that he only had a year to serve before a well-deserved retirement. It could not come too quickly!

Finally after hours of trying to comfort crying mums and distressed boys, William and Mary decamped into their flat for a much-needed drink. The gin bottle looked on this occasion immensely appealing.

At that very moment, a small, distressed, weeping boy appeared at their door. Mary chatted and cuddled him and then escorted him back to the dorm.

Whilst she was away, William reflected on a story he had heard from another prep school. The headmaster's wife, having consumed three swift gins after a very stressful first day, was required to attend to a distressed lad in this dormitory.

After perhaps half an hour the little boy had calmed down. He turned to the headmaster's wife and murmured: "Thank you so much, you smell just like my mummy." Mary returned after about an hour. William was glad she didn't have time for her little tipple, so the same thing could be said of her.

Both of them could hear a lively party fully underway in the Common Room. They were both concerned that the young boarders might not be able to sleep. However, when William did his rounds a little later, it was clear that his fears were groundless. Even the little boy who had been so upset an hour or so earlier was sleeping peacefully cuddled up to an enormous teddy bear.

It was also obvious that the party had hindered many, or indeed any, staff from visiting the dorms. The young boarders had been left largely alone. This drinking culture William increasingly understood was going to have to be his first priority and most pressing headache.

William had decided right from the outset that he and Mary were going to be very high-profile. Every morning they ate breakfast with the boarders. It was a perfect time to judge how the young ones were doing.

It was amazing how quickly the smallest, apparently fragile, seven-year-old got used to this new life and the strange, confusing regime.

The boarding area was directly supervised by a few of the younger stooges. The nitty-gritty of bed changing, supervising bath time, hair washing and teeth cleaning was undertaken by young girls designated with the rather grand title of matron.

In the main the relationship these young women had with the children was that of kindly big sister. Mary was responsible for supervising them, and it was they who reported any problems of homesickness or isolation that might be occurring.

Perhaps the most extraordinary part of the boarding domain was the bathroom. This consisted of perhaps sixteen serried rows of identical tubs. Twice a week the boys would don their bathrobes and have a bath. There was no privacy of course, but this didn't bother these scamps.

Although technically not allowed, these mass bathing experiences involved much splashing and the occasional bowling practice in lobbing bars of coal tar soap.

These young matrons sometimes were inadvertently hit by one of these flying objects, a source of much hilarity from the bathers, but not, it has to be said, from the girls themselves.

Another one of Mary's myriad duties was that of medicines supervisor. In this she was assisted by the school doctor, a kindly somewhat curmudgeonly local GP who wisely considered least was best, as far as the doling out of pills and lotions.

The youngest boarders were only seven. For a short time they had one little boarder who was just six. Sometimes when their parents lived abroad, boarding was the only possible option. This was especially so when their fathers were soldiers.

At the time of the first Gulf War half a dozen children had fathers directly involved in this military action. There were huge anxieties at the time of the dangers of chemical weapons and the like. Part of the job was to reassure nervous children and to avoid newspapers and the BBC news if that was possible.

There was also a dying tradition amongst some of the smarter families to send their children away to boarding school at seven or eight. However, this tradition was in free fall.

Those young children who did arrive were often the products of broken homes and/or uninterested, unassociated parents.

An increasing problem was the exponential growth in divorces and family breakup. This was an especially trying situation for children away at school, who suddenly found their family circumstances transformed.

On one occasion a little nine-year-old was informed rather casually by telephone that Mummy and Daddy were splitting up. It took them two further weeks to bother to visit their child and explain to him personally.

William and Mary were not unfamiliar with the often traumatic effects of family breakup in their day school in London, or indeed when William had been a housemaster beforehand. However, William felt that with these young boarding children it was often a far worse experience.

This was partly because they were away from home, which might have protected them from the visual experience of family conflict. The fact they only knew of these things in a second-hand way often seemed to amplify their suffering and anxiety.

An especially memorable example in these early years was that of rather gentle nine-year-old Harry. His mother and father broke up. His father wanted to maintain contact. In fairness, it seemed that the father was the guilty party. Mother was so bitter about the situation and what she, probably rightly, considered was the result of her husband's perfidy that she fought a long battle to stop Father receiving Harry's reports. Legally, she hadn't a leg to stand on, but the fact that William didn't comply with her wishes meant that much of her ire was therefore directed at him.

Harry, a rather fey, gentle lad who hated games, as well as being rather quiet and introspective, was eventually sent to a rather brutal colonial public school in Zimbabwe, a country his mother had originated from. Predictably Harry was entirely destroyed by this experience.

On another occasion a mother arrived with her new lover to remove her children and take them to Ireland. Unfortunately, they were met by the rather thuggish-looking, baseball bat-wielding employees of her husband, a local builder and developer, who had got wind of her intentions. This situation occurred on a Friday lunchtime just as the

Nursery children were being taken home.

It was as though the Chicago mob had just arrived in Kensington Gardens. As though someone had pulled out a Tommy gun in the middle of a Royal Garden Party. The young mothers and their infant children looked as though they had inadvertently become extras in a gangster film.

At any moment, William supposed a full-scale battle was about to take place right in front of the school mansion. He immediately got in touch with the local constabulary, who helpfully, if initially rather reluctantly, sent two police cars to prevent a violent altercation.

This was not, it has to be admitted, a very usual assignment for rural bobbies in a posh private school. Luckily, they arrived just before violence was about to kick off. When they did turn up, the situation had escalated to the point where various large men were shouting abuse. The threatening language that was being used was somewhat fruity and certainly not what one might expect at the portal of any school, least of all one claiming to be the abode of the well-mannered middle-class families.

At least this was still a situation of posturing threats, rather than actual physical violence. It soon transpired that a judge in chambers was required to decide whether to allow the children to be removed from the country. The local bobbies took the very sensible decision that the hostile parties should be separated.

Over lunch most of the rooms in the headmaster's flat were converted into separate dining rooms. Each room was guarded by a constable in order to avoid any further trouble. Everyone ate a fish and chips lunch, followed by ice cream and chocolate sauce. This seemed to have a very beneficial effect on the tense atmosphere. William flitted from room to room, trying to chat away in a friendly manner to the various possible combatants and hopefully ease tensions. All afternoon the stand-off continued while everyone awaited the judge's decision.

Finally, at about 5:00 pm the rotund local police sergeant took William discreetly aside. "I have a problem, sir," he earnestly announced in his broad Suffolk brogue. "If the judge doesn't decide by 5:30 tonight, I have to put the children in a place of safety. The only place of safety I have is in the police cells.

If you would agree I will make your flat an extension of the cells for a night so the children could stay here." William readily assented. However, almost as he finished speaking a motorcycle courier arrived with the judge's ruling that the children were not to be taken out of the country. The three little waifs involved returned home without their mother, having been part of a most humiliating and public display of family estrangement.

William wondered with some trepidation what the long-term effects of this would be on these children's psyches. Mary once described this aspect of their job as "Social Services for the Middle Classes". Mary kept aside a selection of jumpers, socks, and trousers so that she could reclothe some of the often posher children, who would sometimes turn up at school dressed like ragged tramps. She described such families, William thought pretty accurately as "The gipsy gentry".

The evenings were, however, a very jolly time and on every such occasion the various age groups had a story read to them. It became even nicer later when carpets were laid and the heating system was improved. William provided beanbags on which the boys could snuggle up.

These formerly expansive, chilly spaces became positively homely. Reading stories was an activity that both William and Mary loved. In fairness they had many years' experience in reading to their own boys. They both later remembered with pleasure the little lads clad in their dressing gowns, often clutching a beloved teddy bear, listening with evident pleasure to the various tales. Frequently, before they had finished, the little ones had a thumb firmly embedded in their mouths and had dozed off and had to be gently carried back to their beds.

This task greatly assisted in their own understanding of and the range of contemporary children's literature they realised was available. Privately, William still really preferred the traditional Oscar Wilde stories, especially 'The Happy Prince' and 'The Selfish Giant'. He even hoped that some of the children felt the same!

Chapter Ten

JOHN LIPMAN

Often cocoa was served after prep: this was the moment when quite suddenly the building somehow ceased to be a school and transformed into something else. It was the time of the day when the children wandered around in their pyjamas chatting, and in the case of the older ones playing board games and even occasionally watching television.

In these early days William and Mary were very happy to spend most evenings in the dormitories. This was no great chore and anyway two of their own boys lived in them. They didn't feel that Francis and James could continue to enjoy the privileges of day boys whilst living in the same building as the other boarders. Charlie was still a bit too little for this particular experience; Mary did not appear until he had drifted off to sleep.

When they had one of their two evenings off a week, or if they were often away visiting a potential senior school, this task was undertaken by John Lipman as their deputy. However, so worried was William about John Lipman's state of mind that he usually made sure that he popped upstairs to ensure all was well after lights were out.

Sadly, the bitterness and hurt that dominated John's increasingly nihilistic frame of mind often bubbled over in unfocussed anger and rage. A very typical encounter occurred a few weeks into this first term. As William entered the duty study, he immediately realised that John was aggressively drunk: "Why don't you go away?" he slurred. "I have been doing this job for years and I don't need you to nursemaid me." As his exposition blossomed and his resentments deepened, he added: "If you spent more time doing your job instead of presiding over this fucking catastrophe, this school might just survive the disaster of your headship." This was not, it has to said, great for William's morale.

For John Lipman, his experience of life in this period was truly awful. He was in the midst of his own personal dissolution. He had been at Parkies ever since he had left university twenty years before. He had never known anywhere else since his childhood home. He loved this school with an intense passion. He was not entirely unaware, at least in his more perspicacious moments, of his limitations or those of the school.

He fervently believed, however, that in essentials little needed to change. He was not a public school man himself, and his marriage to Karen had made him even less acceptable to some of the snooty clientele as a result. Yet John had grown to be very fond of Lancelot Waters.

He had become a kind of father figure to the young Lipman. John had lost his own father whilst he was at primary school and his mother ten years later. Quite literally Parkies became absolutely everything to him.

His invitations to dinner with the Waters, and his ultimate promotion to deputy head, gave him a spurious status, as well as flattering his rather fragile ego to boot. John came to believe that he was an important cog in a significant elite boarding prep school. He had in recent months come to increasingly imagine that the Joneses had some kind of a malign agenda which he was absolutely determined to resist.

He had of course never worked in another school. His judgments were therefore necessarily partial and somewhat skewed. He totally bought into what he perceived to be the Waterses' view of the standing of Parkies.

Indeed, partly because of this lack of experience, or indeed because he had not been educated in the independent school system, his essentially uncritical rosy view of Parkies was one that even Lancelot Waters no longer really believed.

His one overriding passion was to protect what he loyally conceived as the Waterses' legacy. Quite literally, that meant for him little or no change. A tradition preserved in stone. The school should, he believed, continue to focus on maintaining its scholarship record as well as keeping its robust, austere, traditional boarding environment.

His bitter disappointment at not being offered the post of headmaster synthesised with his growing detestation for Jones. He was convinced that William was someone who would destroy that legacy.

This raw, peevish sense of injustice and feeling of naked betrayal, fuelled by a growing dependence on gin, was increasingly manipulated by the more subtle opponents of the Joneses. John Lipman was, although he didn't yet understand this, becoming a victim twice over.

William's perspective was that, whilst John Lipman's behaviour and attitude were becoming increasingly intolerable, there was little he could do. This was until John did something totally outrageous. He was untouchable, protected by his friendship with Lancelot Waters, who still lived at the bottom of the school drive, as well as his long-standing relationships with many of the teaching staff.

It was clear, as William slowly came to understand, that Waters frequently shared his own sense of resentment with the downcast Lipman, as well as some of the disenchanted governors and most of the senior members of the Common Room.

In the first few weeks William had tried to develop some kind of *modus operandi* with John. It was clear quite soon that such an arrangement was doomed. Unfortunately in making the effort, it reinforced in John Lipman's mind that William was weak and ingratiating. His delusional sense blossomed, encouraged by others, that William would be an easy target to destroy. This was an idea that John Lipman clung onto with the tenacity of desperation.

In November William and Mary attended an open day at one of the local minor public schools, Haverhill College. Contacts with potential successor schools were a vital part of William's job, made especially pressing by his near-total ignorance of the non-metropolitan public school scene.

Haverhill, in its Victorian Gothic complex of fake gentility, had long since lost any real claim to academic or social pre-eminence. It was somewhere, despite long protestations of its splendid academic and sporting traditions that would now in fact take virtually anyone.

As such it represented an essential backstop for any prep school head looking for alternative options for their weaker candidates. The classic sales line in such circumstances was: "I think your boy needs a smaller, more caring establishment." Remarkably, William thought, some parents still bought this.

When they arrived back from their jolly, pandemonium and chaos pervaded the school. A white-faced young matron greeted them with a tale of woe. "Mr Lipman has gone entirely off his head," she wailed.

"During the rugby tea, he was drunk as a skunk and was really abusive to the other school's coach. He then staggered around prep bellowing at the children." She went on: "He so frightened little Oliver Burns that he burst in tears. He then shouted at him again and then told him to shut up and stop behaving like a silly baby. Later, he was staggering into the dorms and was again yelling at the children: they were all terrified. Eventually," she blubbered, "I was able to get hold of one of the teachers and with great difficulty he was persuaded to go home."

The moment of decision had eventually arrived. William knew that this was the time when he had to make a stand. He was of course on very strong ground. Yet in the end this didn't matter . William had, he considered, no real choice.

John's growing erratic behaviour had become an open secret with the parents. Already John's frequent drunkenness was a source of much gossip.

To be fair, this was not a new development. It had become even more obvious in recent weeks. There seemed to be a reasonable and growing expectation amongst many parents that William's new regime would deal with this. It was, therefore, only a matter of time, if not addressed, before this whole issue blew up into a real, devastating scandal.

Prevarication was one of William's greatest weaknesses. However, even he could no longer think of any excuses for not grasping the nettle, even after his long talk with Mary. That night sleep largely eluded him as he worried how he was going to address this particularly spiky weed.

Mary had got to know Karen Lipman, and whilst her grumpy, maudlin, resentful, often obstructive attitude was a problem, she understood and sympathised with Karen's impossible situation and realised that as they occupied a school cottage, if John lost his position the whole family could be homeless.

She was moreover, good at her job, and didn't deserve the penury, if William persuaded the governors to dismiss her husband. Perhaps they both hoped there was a way of dealing with this without actually getting rid of him.

She and William therefore talked late into the night. By the time they finally retired to bed, they hoped they had what they thought might just be a workable plan.

First thing in the morning William contacted Jonathan Carpenter, Thomas Brown, and Father O'Rourke who he thought might be the most reasonable governors and most inclined to be receptive to his ideas. The easy bit was his demand that John be suspended until the next full governors' meeting designated for a week later.

Given the severity of the incident, both Jonathan and Thomas were happy to concur with this, Father O'Rourke less so. William then suggested that they meet again to discuss options. Thomas Brown offered his boardroom adjacent to his factory in Ipswich as a venue far enough away so as not to elicit unwanted gossip.

John Lipman knew he was in trouble. He admitted as much to Karen the morning after. He realised that he must have been very drunk, mainly because his memory of the events was so vague.

The central question in his mind was how Jones was likely to react. Given what he considered to be his simpering, amiable, inadequate personality, John believed that the worst that might happen was a slap across the wrist. He didn't suppose that Jones would dare take matters further.

It was a nasty and unexpected surprise when immediately after breakfast the headmaster's secretary telephoned him to demand his immediate presence in William's study. John Lipman arrived ten minutes later. It has to be said his demeanour left no hint of the alcoholic bender of less than twelve hours before. He walked into the study with apparently absolutely no sense of contrition, or even, it seemed, a recognition of the gravity of his situation. Indeed, his attitude was one of almost devil-may-care. He didn't take William Jones seriously and was still not unduly concerned.

His tactic seemed to be to bluff it out. William outlined the circumstances of the previous day as summarised by the young matron, whom he had interviewed the previous evening.

John denied that he was drunk; he also claimed that as he was a senior member of staff and as such he demanded to be believed ahead of "a hysterical and not very bright domestic". His attitude was one of provocative belligerence. His lack of respect and virulent dislike for the headmaster, he no longer attempted to mask. His visage displayed an attitude of vitriolic, contemptuous disdain.

It was the moment of truth and both men knew it. William steeled himself for this decisive and necessary denouement. "Whatever you say, John, you need to understand that I do actually believe Jade."

He then added, "I would like you to remove yourself immediately from the school premises. The governors' decision on your future will be conveyed to you after their next meeting." This was more than a bit pompous, as William knew; however, he couldn't think of any other way of putting it.

At this point the room detonated. John immediately stood up, walked rapidly towards William's desk, then he placed his puce, angry, distorted face inches away from the headmaster's nose. William could now clearly smell the noxious odour of yesterday's gin.

"I don't give a shit, you haven't got the balls to get rid of me." He then continued with a growing uncontrolled passion: "Do you really think anyone will take a blind bit of notice of a pathetic Welsh pipsqueak like you? I am going to destroy you, Jones, you just wait and see."

With this he stormed out of the room. However, to his relief William noticed a few hours later that he was no longer on the premises.

Jones had surprised John Lipman. It seemed now that the headmaster might have more balls than he supposed. This weakling even had the nerve and the audacity to actually order him off the premises.

Lipman needed to find out what was actually going on: he didn't believe that Jones could have thought this up on his own. He couldn't fathom who might be behind this. He had always believed that Mary had more about her than her husband. Perhaps it was her who put him up to this, he mused: he could think of no one else. It was important, however, to be sure of that if he could.

He telephoned Lancelot Waters. "Lancelot, I may have done something pretty stupid," he insinuated. Lancelot suspected he had a pretty good idea what.

"I had rather too much to drink last night and Jones has suspended me. Would you credit it?" John tentatively and ironically suggested. To be frank, Lancelot considered, he was getting rather annoyed by the regular accounts of Lipman's drunken escapades.

"What exactly happened?" He then received a somewhat edited version of the events of the previous evening. Waters had no problems with drinking per se. After all, ever since his days years ago in the officers' mess he had prided himself on his ability to consume gargantuan quantities of gin.

However, the mark of a gentleman was, in Lancelot's opinion, the ability to hold one's drink. Clearly that was becoming an increasing problem for Lipman. Actually, as he reflected about it, this had always been Lipman's basic weakness.

Furthermore, he disliked the way in which Lipman's excesses were being in some sense associated with him. The story of the shared sherry bottle had somehow spread throughout the county.

He wondered whether this was the result of Lipman's maudlin confidences, although on balance he considered the most likely sources were Jones and his allies. "You had better come and see me," he ordered, and then put down the telephone.

The following day William arrived at Brown and Sons factory and offices in Ipswich. Thomas's firm was doing something high-tech, which few people other than Thomas Brown seemed to understand. Yet the factory complex was authentically Victorian. It was a former brewery and the boardroom was so furnished it felt as though the original revered Victorian brewer might walk in at any moment. William sat opposite Thomas, Jonathan, and Father O'Rourke at the end of the long, beautifully polished boardroom table.

The Victorian faces peering from the portraits on the walls were not the aristocratic faces of the Stirrup anteroom. These were those of the hard-faced, more grounded entrepreneurs of which Thomas Brown was their linear successor.

They appeared, it seemed to William, to look down on this little anxious party of men with just a smidgen of disapproval and supercilious disdain. Their hard eyes and bushy beards suggested that they would demand a more austere, unforgiving approach to this problem.

"A bit of a dog's breakfast isn't it William?" commented Jonathan. This was a problem Jonathan didn't want to face and assumed anyway it was William's fault.

Thomas injected: "If it is, Jonathan, it is one of our making. We must have known this was bound to happen, this was catastrophe which was largely cooked in our kitchen, not by William. The question is what are we going to do about it now that it has happened?"

This seemed the right moment for Jones to make his pitch. This was the proposal he had worked through with Mary late the previous night. He tried to pretend a confidence he didn't really feel; nevertheless, it seemed to him that he had reasonably successfully concealed his unease. He thus with a considerable sense of fear and apprehension launched into his argument.

"As I see it, John Lipman is more victim than perpetrator; he has given his life to Parkies and ultimately, at least from his point of view, has been betrayed." "I am not at all sure about that," Jonathan spluttered somewhat indignantly.

"Let the man finish," interrupted Father Brendan. "The point I want to make," continued the nervous William, "is that he is one of our best teachers. Frankly, we don't have too many of those; he is also popular amongst many parents and most of the Common Room."

He continued. "We certainly have the grounds to fire him, but there may be many unfortunate unforeseen consequences in doing that." William was conscious that his voice was now wavering with tension and emotion as he proceeded to outline his proposal: "Can I suggest that we remove his status as deputy head, stop him using the school bar after classes, and at the same time make some significant changes to the school's drinking culture?"

"What changes?" enquired Brown. "We separate the bar from the Common Room, and do not open it until after supper. At the same time we make sure that Lipman understands that this is really his last chance. We even suggest that it might be a good time to start looking around for something else. Then at least we haven't totally destroyed his career."

Finally, after what seemed an ocean of silence, all the governors present agreed to William's proposals, albeit in the case of Brendan and Jonathan with some reluctance.

Father Brendan expressed this when he commented: "Whilst on the face of it your solution seems elegant, even fair and moderate, have you considered, William, that by demoting John you will simply further fuel his resentments and thus make his ultimate destruction inevitable."

William had considered this, but countered it with the observation, "Of course you have a good point, Father, but in the end the decision whether or not to accept this is John Lipman's. If we do less than this we are handing him a victory and my position would effectively then become untenable."

Yet even as William enunciated this, he recognised the truth of Father Brendan's observation. Whether Lipman accepted this or not, there was little chance this could have good outcome. William knew of course that his motivation in all this was essentially self-interested; in pretending otherwise was entirely disingenuous.

As always, Father Brendan had exposed this central truth. Jonathan's parting shot was: "We may agree this, but I won't put money on anyone else buying it."

Father O'Rourke walked back with William to the car they had shared. "I know you are having a rough time, Will, but John is not a bad fella, you know, I am going to see them this evening, pastoral duty and a bit of a crack. It might help."

John Lipman arrived later that day at Lancelot Waters's house. He was accompanied by St John de Vere. Waters had reluctantly telephoned Gerald Grimes and suggested he attend, too. Grimes, Waters believed, was Lipman's closest ally on the board: his opinion might be very apposite in these difficult circumstances. Lipman was forced, under pressure, to confess to an unedited version of the previous day's events. This showed that the situation was rather more serious than Waters had initially supposed. De Vere tried gallantly to make light of the situation: "Look, Lancelot," he posited, "it is surely no worse than that situation with the shooting club last year."

This was not an incident that Lancelot ever wished again to be reminded of. De Vere was referring to an occasion when after a rather large liquid lunch, Lancelot was showing some prospective parents around the school. As they approached the hall where the air rifle shooting club was taking place, his formidable wife Geraldine had stood in front of him and said: "You may go no farther, Lancelot." "Look," he irritably responded, "I am the headmaster after all. I may go anywhere I wish."

Eventually Geraldine got him with some difficulty to understand that Martin Pugh, who was supervising this club, was so drunk that he had fallen asleep on the stage whilst the boys had been playing chicken with their air rifles. He had therefore barely avoided an enormous, possibly catastrophic scandal. He did not remotely consider this a trivial incident; as an afterthought he reluctantly accepted it might have prematurely ended his career. It might even have injured one of the boys.

Nor did he believe that the Lipman incident was any less serious. He clearly owed John Lipman much. He and his wife Karen had effectively run the school for the last three years at the very least. This was a difficult fact for Lancelot to accept, which in reality he only did intermittently. He further believed he had, by supporting Lipman's application for the headship, fully honoured that debt. Moreover, he increasingly deplored Lipman's excessive and uncontrolled boozing.

Whilst he was acutely aware that he owed him this measure of loyalty, it was high time, he now considered, for some serious candour. "You have been a bloody idiot," Lancelot angrily opined. "You have just given Jones the perfect weapon to hit you with it won't be a question of merely suspending you for a few days. How do you really seriously imagine he will use it: what would you do in his shoes?"

Gerald Grimes who had been thunderous in his silence up to this moment, suddenly exploded in exasperation: "What the fuck do you think you were doing, Lipman. I stuck my neck out for you. Your behaviour has not only stuffed yourself, it has also made me look a bloody fool as much as you. I grant you that Jones is a cretin, but even he would not be so stupid as not to get rid of you now."

At the governors' meeting four days later, not a special extraordinary meeting, but rather the usual termly affair that punctuated the yearly cycle, there were many items on the agenda. It was the first such meeting of William's tenure.

At 2 in the afternoon, the governors trooped into the school's drawing room. All had been formally informed as to the situation with John Lipman. However, that did not in any sense detract from the tsunami of gossip and speculation that had dominated many of the governor telephone lines during the previous five days.

As a result the atmosphere was one that was tense and expectant. Some governors arrived with belligerence written all over their faces.

Since the meeting in the Waterses' house, Gerald Grimes had, together with Margaret McKenzie, visited Lipman in his little cottage two days prior to the meeting. Whether that was strictly ethical was something that did not overconcern either individual.

Neither Mrs McKenzie nor Mr Grimes had ever previously associated in any situation, either business or social. Their alliance this time seemed to be centred on the dictum, "My enemies' enemy is my friend".

Nor had either of them actually ever before entered the somewhat shabby little house the Lipmans occupied. The meeting was theoretically a confidential one, but nothing in a small community like Parkies could ever stay secret for long. The two sat in Lipman's parlour, whilst Karen served them tea. "Well," began Grimes, "as I said the other day you have been a very silly boy." The shamefaced Lipman nodded his assent. "He may have been," Mrs McKenzie suggested, "but surely the situation is retrievable?"

"The trouble is, Margaret," began Grimes, being addressed by her Christian name was not something Mrs McKenzie normally sanctioned, and most certainly didn't encourage from a person such as him. However, this was a serious and unique situation, which necessitated unusual and surprising civilities. Grimes then continued. "We have seriously underestimated Jones; he has got John totally over a barrel."

"But" Margaret sputtered, "Parkies has always been a very hospitable place. John had a few too many, that surely is all that this is about."

"Look, John." Grimes directed his comment pointedly at Lipman. "The issue is, as Jones is presenting it, that you were drunk whilst supervising the boys."

The silent, previously apparently unengaged Lipman then quite suddenly and unexpectedly spoke with real passion and anger. "I was drinking, that is true, but all that Jones has on me is the word of a silly girl. Having a drink and being drunk are two quite different things."

His voice rose to a crescendo of desperate, agonised misery. "This is not about drink; it is about Jones deliberately entrapping me. He is," Lipman's visage evolved into a new wrathful animation, "a pathetic little worm. If you Governors face him down and tell him you simply won't accept my suspension and demotion, it won't happen. I have been here for decades; the staff and parents absolutely won't stomach it."

Almost tearfully he continued to plead: "For Christ's sake you owe me this, Gerald!" After perhaps an hour of listening to John Lipman's increasingly desperate polemic, Margaret McKenzie and Gerald Grimes left.

"Certainly, we should try and pull Lipman's irons out of the fire," opined Mrs McKenzie, "but if he raves in front of the others, as he did tonight, the omens don't look promising. In the end it depends on Carpenter." "I agree," concurred Grimes. Neither of them returned home with any great confidence that with this issue Jonathan Carpenter was in any way reliable.

The various routine items on the governors' agenda went through quite rapidly. Then Jonathan outlined what he considered to be the salient points over the Lipman issue. "Essentially, it comes down to one issue: was he drunk on duty or not?"

Grimes immediately interposed: "I don't think it does, in my opinion. Lipman has been deliberately entrapped by the headmaster. Having a drink is what the staff at Parkies do. That does not mean John Lipman was incapable of undertaking his duties. It is obvious that William Jones wanted him out the way and now he thinks he has succeeded."

"I fully agree," added a somewhat theatrically piqued Margaret McKenzie. "John Lipman is absolutely essential to the well-being of this school. This misdemeanour should be accepted as just that: and no more!"

William now laid out his case. When he mentioned the young matron, Grimes sneered. "Is that your evidence, some snotty-nosed teenager?" It was then agreed that John Lipman could talk to the governors himself. William reluctantly left the meeting; what then occurred was relayed to him later by Thomas Brown and Father Brendan. Lipman was apparently belligerent and pleading by turns. It seemed that he was determined to ram home the nonsensical notion that this was an incident engineered by William to secure his removal.

This argument was rather undermined by Jonathan's announcement that William hadn't requested his removal, merely his demotion. Moreover, William has done some homework.

He had managed to get a statement from the other school coach, who described in the most graphic way Lipman's terribly rude abusive behaviour at tea. It seemed that when this young teacher had remonstrated with him, he had been told in front of shocked parents from both schools, "Why don't you go and fuck yourself?"

Even with somewhere with Parkies' boozy reputation, this kind of incident was unheard of in the ersatz gentility of the prep school world. Even Grimes and McKenzie could see it further seriously damaged the school's reputation.

With considerable courage another junior matron had stepped forward to make a statement supporting her friend Jade. Grimes and McKenzie were now effectively scuppered. When the final vote was taken, they followed Jonathan Carpenter's lead and voted for the Lipmans' demotion, which was all William had actually requested.

They also agreed to support the head's decision to restrict the bar's opening times and to move it out of the Common Room in the immediate future. As Thomas Brown commented after the meeting to William: "Game, set and match to you and sucks to Grimes and McKenzie." Despite a worrying sense that it still all might go wrong, William couldn't have put it better himself.

This was not quite how Grimes and McKenzie saw matters when they talked things over later. "I don't understand Gerald," Margaret McKenzie observed, using his Christian name for the first time. "Why did Jones satisfy himself with a mere demotion? He had him on the run, this proves to me that at the very least he lacks the killer instinct. I am sure that this softness may in the end be his greatest weakness."

Grimes thoughtfully replied, "That may give us our opportunity, all we need now to ensure is that idiot Lipman keeps his bloody nose clean. Sooner or later Jones will make a mistake and then we will have him."

When Father O'Rourke visited John and Karen later that evening the advice to avoid further trouble was in part his message, too. The good priest hoped that John might accept the justice of what had been agreed. Father Brendan worked hard to get John to understand his real situation.

As a final gambit the good priest suggested: "Why don't you work with William, John? You know you are really on the same side. William is not a bad bloke: with your combined talents, you could really make Parkies special." Whilst John mumbled assent, his eyes gave out a contrary message.

At a staff meeting before chapel the following morning, William made his two bombshell announcements. The first concerning Lipman's suspension was not a secret.

Indeed it is fair to say that it had been virtually the only Common Room conversation for nearly two days. Dalton and de Vere sat in a thunderous silence. Their aura of disapproval and common cause was almost touchable in its power and malignant impulse.

Yet this view did not seem to be by any means the consensus within the room. Whilst the younger teachers may have had some sympathy for Lipman's predicament, they had rather more for the young matron Jade. Her reputation, intellectual prowess, integrity and much else had been rubbished by Lipman and his cronies.

The second part of the head's message was more difficult to sell. "We cannot supervise children and drink copious amounts of gin at the same time. Moreover, our performance in afternoon and evening school is not enhanced by our imbibing before the end of prep. Therefore, from today, the bar will remain closed until 7:00 pm. Furthermore, during the Christmas holidays, contractors will be employed to build a new bar in the east wing."

There was a gasp of surprise and incredulity. A puce, incandescent de Vere stood up, intending obviously to make a contrary, mutinous statement. The deed had, however, been done and William walked back to his study before further discussion could ensue.

When he sat down and was joined by Mary, she noticed that his hands were shaking. Yet, deep inside he had a kind of inner glow of satisfaction. He felt that he had finally taken control.

Later, William had a telephone call from Father Brendan. "It is going to be very difficult, Will. But I do really think I might have got that 'eejit' to understand that this is really his last chance." William earnestly hoped that Father Brendan was right: although in his heart he knew he wasn't.

The trouble remained, as many of his friends as well as his enemies had appreciated, that whilst John could no longer prop up the staff bar as he once had, he remained a malign influence. Sitting in often drunken isolation in his cottage, he became an increasing focus of discontent.

The problem of John Lipman had not gone away. William came to realise all he had ultimately succeeded in doing was to bury it. Even this he wondered if he had done very effectively. It was a problem that was inevitably going to end up "biting him in his arse", as dear Brendan might have said.

Chapter Eleven

THE BITING TRUTH

The bar was moved and the drinking culture was at least modified. Thus with the demotion of Lipman as well as Father O'Rourke's benign influence, things for the time being seemed to have improved. The atmosphere was less tense, especially in the evenings when John Lipman was out of the way. This meant that his closest allies also tended to avoid socialising within the school precincts. It was now even possible for William and Mary to take coffee in the Common Room without feeling as though they were pariahs.

There remained many ongoing problems, not least the unresolved Lipman issue. One immediate challenge was the result of some of the many antics of the Joneses' little dog Bobby. He had been rescued a few months before they had arrived at Parkies from a pound in South Mimms in Hertfordshire.

He was an ugly little mongrel. He was a sort of cross between a whippet and a very small Alsatian. However, his translation to Suffolk had revealed some very serious character flaws.

He was always affectionate with the children and with most women. He disliked men in general and anyone rich and powerful in particular.

How he could detect a burgeoning bank account was a total mystery.

Perhaps this was because when he was a puppy he had been hit by an iron bar. This was presumably wielded by a large, vicious man. It was therefore easy to understand why he especially hated males. It was less clear why he should pick on them only if they were wearing expensive suits.

Perhaps his tormentor had been smartly dressed in one! It was almost as though he could smell out such people. Jonathan Carpenter and Lord Castle were near the top of his hate list. It was only by luck that he hadn't taken a chunk out of either of them. The male staff used the shower in the Joneses' flat after games. Some of the men had a few close shaves. They had come to treat Bobby with considerable respect.

Given Bobby's preference for the rich and well-heeled, the Joneses called him their 'Old Labour Dog'. It was touch-and-go as to the final choice of epithet they would use. 'Engel Footie' or 'Neil' were other popular options.

One afternoon late in that first term Gerald Grimes arrived for one of his very frequent moaning sessions. He and his wife chose usually the most trivial issues of which to make a fuss. Today there was the question of the missing shoe liner in his son's trainer. It was mystery that Mary thought might even tax the legendary Sherlock Holmes. The previous day Mrs Grimes had appeared in the changing rooms searching for this lost item. When it was obvious that it had disappeared she had in her usual belligerent way collared Mary. "This is not the first thing to go missing, Mrs Jones. I feel sure that children's possessions should be better looked after than this."

It seems not to have occurred to Tracey Grimes that her son might have a smidgeon of responsibility for this. Mary had not found it or indeed telephoned Tracey with what she considered was the appropriate creeping apology.

This had provoked her husband to appear at the school to add his two pennyworth to his wife's grievance. Mary always felt rather sorry for Tracey Grimes. She suspected that she was horribly bullied by her aggressive, assertive husband. Most of her complaining, she thought, was really Tracey desperately trying to placate an increasingly irascible spouse.

Gerald Grimes was now waiting outside William's flat wearing his usual expression of a grumpy, rather edgy impatience. William's secretary was away that afternoon, and anyway, Grimes did not have an appointment.

This was not something that ever overly concerned him. He was standing outside the Joneses' flat examining his watch and tapping his foot with obvious irritation. Most parents understood that Bobby regarded the headmaster's flat as his own private domain. This was somewhere which he would defend come what may.

For this reason, mainly of self-preservation, few took the risk of entering uninvited. The flat was supposed to be private all the parents were discouraged from entering without invitation. Even Lancelot Waters had previously insisted upon this.

Gerald Grimes was, however, now becoming increasingly annoyed by not seeing William immediately. He, moreover, saw himself as far too important to obey any of these trivial rules. He expected to observe him beavering away at his desk. Most of all he required that Jones would always be at the Grimes's beck and call. It was quite a simple issue in his mind.

The large school fees he paid demanded an appropriately subservient approach. Gerald Grimes was not good at understanding notions of collaboration. To him William Jones was essentially his servant and he was the master. Eventually increasingly frustrated and annoyed by the wait, he opened the door of the flat and marched authoritatively in.

Bobby was not as fierce as he appeared. Mr Grimes didn't know that. He was also reluctant to admit he was rather nervous of dogs. Bobby could never quite grip the polished wooden floor and so his approach was preceded by various scrapes and slides as he attempted to get his footing. This noise was well known to the male staff. They quickly exited the flat when they heard it.

Gerald Grimes either did not hear the noise, or more likely hadn't realised its import. The grumpy governor thus carried on regardless. Perhaps, too, the self-important Grimes would not exit for anyone, least of all a little mongrel dog. Gerald Grimes did not retreat despite the obvious potential threat and thus carried on marching purposely towards the Joneses' kitchen, calling out in his usual peremptory way for the required instant attention. Rather like William remembered a certain sort of rather superior customer at his father's ironmonger shop had insisted on shouting "Shop!" when they were not immediately served.

Then in a moment of horror Gerald Grimes first witnessed this fierce little animal bearing down on him. Bobby, whilst quite small with his teeth bared in attack mode, was, to be fair to Gerald Grimes, quite an awesome sight. Worse still, this part of the hall was carpeted so the little creature now had perfect grip. Growling and snarling he gained speed, readying for the attack.

What Grimes should have done was to keep perfectly still and the dog would have simply made a lot of harmless noise. Bobby was at least as frightened as Grimes. Sadly, he didn't.

The first thing Mary saw as she rounded the main school corridor into the flat was Grimes in full, panicky flight and Bobby in extreme hue and cry. The overweight Grimes, not noted for his athletic skill, ran as though the hounds of Hell were in hot pursuit.

Finally after an epic chase Gerald Grimes was able to find a hiding place in the games store cupboard in the cellar. Bobby was standing guard, snarling, growling and barking loudly outside. Mr Grimes was predictably not amused. In fact he was absolutely incandescent with rage and humiliation. The staff and boys who witnessed the incident thought it the best comedy show they had ever seen.

Their laughter seared his soul: Gerald Grimes could not ever endure humiliation. He and his son were not at all popular and a few wags quickly coined the phrase, "Bobby the hero dog, the Grimes destroyer". William, when the incident was described to him, thought it was pure Buster Keaton.

Grimes did not view it in any way comic. Indeed anything that touched his dignity was never even remotely funny. He swiftly wrote abusive letters of outraged pride to both William and Jonathan Carpenter, demanding amongst other things the summary execution of the hound.

He claimed that the school and specifically the headmaster were tolerating the presence of its own version of *The Hound of the Baskervilles*. Bobby, who was about the size of a smallish terrier, was an unlikely substitute for any hound from Hell.

It was, Jonathan thought, wholly hilarious. When he described what had happened to his wife Celia she was so entertained that the tears actually started to roll down her cheeks. "Not a very nice dog but an absolute treasure with a thug like that around. Next time I see Bobby I will give him a biscuit." Nevertheless, Jonathan still advised William that it would be wise if Bobby was sent away.

In the end William reluctantly thought it best to rehome him with his mother after her Christmas visit. Bobby spent the remaining years of his life living his days sitting in a basket next to Dilys in the company offices in canine seventh heaven. There he was able to terrorise numerous reps and tradesman as well as being fed copious quantities of biscuits and assorted treats.

William thought that the 'flight of Grimes' was the comic highlight in his life so far at Parkies. There were at this point few challengers.

The trouble was, of course, that Gerald Grimes with his total lack of a sense of humour and naturally nasty, unforgiving, vengeful nature now came to believe that William had deliberately allowed his dog loose on him.

Much more seriously yet, he even had the audacity and gall to laugh and make fun of him. He was even more determined to get his own back. No one he allowed could humiliate him and get away with it. As he said later to his wife Tracey: "If that bastard Jones thinks he has got one over on me, he will be sadly disabused." The problem that Grimes had not yet fully appreciated was that many, perhaps most, people within the school thought William already had.

The Christmas holidays had come and Dilys, William's mother, was to join the family for a traditional Suffolk Yuletide. Driving her from Monmouthshire it was increasingly clear to William that Dilys was worried and distracted. Normally he would have expected her to be bubbling over with excitement at the prospect of seeing her grandsons. Christmas was always her favourite time of the year.

On this occasion she sat in a mournful, pregnant silence. She was never someone to display her emotions. When something was bothering her she normally tried to paper over these anxieties. William thought this was very typical of her generation: it was certainly true of her.

This tactic was usually employed very successfully and had served her remarkably well in the years of her marriage to Gethin. Her mind tended to compartmentalise issues so that each individual worry was firmly contained separately in her mind and thus rendered innocuous or at least less threatening.

She never escaped the business concerns of making ends meet in the challenging world of Welsh ironmongery. William sensed there was much more on this occasion. As they drove through the darkening world of north Hertfordshire just before a meal break they planned to take at Royston, William turned to his mother.

"What is the problem, Mum, are you all right?" He was shocked to suddenly realise that Dilys was crying. She was inconsolable with this grief. He could only remember one other occasion in his whole childhood when he witnessed her weeping. Even then it had none of the abject, uninhibited despair that he now thought he witnessed.

He was shocked and rather shaken. Even men of forty-one expect their mothers to be rocks of fortitude. William was of course no exception!

He stopped the car and did something he had always found exceedingly difficult. He put his arm around her. The odd thing was he could never remember doing that in his childhood: they had never been a very touchy-feely family. Mum had never done overt displays of affection. William knew she felt things very deeply. She had never quite overcome a profoundly nonconformist suspicion of sentiment as shameful self-indulgence.

William imagined that there was a volcano of emotion being held in check by his mum's iron restraint. "Something terrible has happened!" she wailed. "The day before yesterday a policeman turned up unexpectedly at the house. I asked him in and he then announced to me that one of the Boy Scouts had accused your dad of something awful."

William dreaded what was coming. Dilys continued. "He said your dad had interfered with one of the boys. This is a terrible calumny and Dad is not even around to defend himself." William realised that this was a problem even she couldn't compartmentalise. It attacked the very root of her being.

Her whole life had been about protecting and nurturing her difficult but also beloved husband. If this accusation was true it rendered the central purpose of her life meaningless.

The problem William had was that he knew, or at least strongly suspected, that such an accusation was in fact probably entirely accurate. For a short time when William was a young adolescent Gethin had anyway done the same to him. An incident in the family's camper van was a memory that still tormented him more than a quarter of a century later. To his knowledge Dilys neither knew this nor even suspected it. "Dad really liked these young lads. He did so much for them and all they now do is betray him when he can't answer back." They sat together in the Little Chef for nearly an hour. Finally Dilys had recovered something of her customary equilibrium.

William had this ridiculous compulsion to share his shameful secret with his mum. In these circumstances it was neither appropriate nor even remotely possible. Probably he reflected, it never would be.

The rest of the journey took place in a fraught and tense silence. Christmas under these circumstances was somewhat more gloomy than William and Mary had expected or hoped.

Dilys didn't share any more of her feelings but it was clear from her frequent distracted and anxious gazes that the prospect of disgrace and the dissolution of her world was never far from her mind.

Dilys had always had a very clear, unambiguous view on child abuse. She had often expressed the attitude that men involved in such heinous activities should be very severely punished, castration or worse being her preferred options. The thought that Gethin was one of them was totally unthinkable.

William had often wondered what she imagined was her husband's motivation for surrounding himself with so many little pretty boys for all those years. Obviously, Dilys had blanked out any suspicions. He thought maybe that was another factor in her present distress. The fear that there might even be some truth in this.

Despite this there were compensations. Outside their flat was a huge Christmas tree, a leftover from the children's end-of-term party. The fire which had not been lit for decades was brought back into use after the chimney had been relined. This was an expense that had definitely not pleased the grumpy bursar.

This gave the place a very festive feel. Mary had pulled out all the stops. The five days they were all together became a gargantuan feast of turkey, goose, Christmas pudding and lots of chocolate. There was a day trip to the coast at Southwold, and a visit to the pantomime in Norwich.

The trip to the seaside took place on what was one of those bitter, East Anglian winter days where there was a biting wind that seemed to come all the way from the Ural Mountains. When they returned home Dilys looked as though she was about to peg out with hypothermia. However, it was a great opportunity to try a spot of kite-flying and to let their little dog Bobby have a day of ball chasing and digging on the beach.

The good news was that the presence of Granny cheered up the children and especially Francis. William suspected that he had shared his growing unhappiness with his grandmother.

The love that Dilys felt for her favourite grandchild did something to repair his fragile morale. William came over these few days to increasingly appreciate that Francis's wretchedness added yet a further dimension to Dilys's feelings of despondency and dejection.

The holidays ended with another long journey back to Usk, this time with a rather disconsolate Bobby in tow. This was an ideal opportunity for William to elicit a little more information from Dilys about the police visitation.

It seemed that the complaint originated from a lad that had once had a Saturday job as a delivery boy. This young man had described one incident that had taken place in the warehouse. He was a Boy Scout and it was through Dad's contacts with the Scouts that he was initially offered the job. Dad had always a small coterie of boys that helped out at the weekend. William thought he could remember the lad as a rather pretty young fellow who was the latest favourite of his father about the time he had first become a housemaster ten years previously.

The evening after they arrived in Monmouthshire, Dilys immediately called a family conference. His two brothers were predictably indignant.

They both thought the boy was little more than a gold-digger and believed that the accusation was basically motivated by pecuniary considerations. Carwyn commented, "If the little shit wants £500 that can be no doubt arranged. Hopefully, that will be the end to this nonsense and Dad's reputation won't suffer too much."

Owen was much more circumspect: "If we pay him off we are effectively accepting that the old man was guilty. What happens if it gets out as it probably will in this little community? This could destroy our reputation and probably the business with it."

William knew it was a provocative and probably an unwise thing to say but he couldn't resist it. "Have you considered the boy might be telling the truth?" It was as though he had just lobbed an exploding grenade into the conversation. "What are you saying, William?" a rather hurt Dilys coldly enquired. "I am saying," William hesitantly replied, "that in my experience children usually tell the truth." "If that is so," Dilys said, now bristling with barely suppressed, wounded rage, "you are saying in effect that your dad was a pervert. How could you even think that?" William decided to back off and left the question hanging in the air. However, he knew that he had failed the ultimate test of family loyalty. Nothing, he thought, would be quite the same again.

The new term began. The first priority was to find a new deputy head. That person would have to be an outsider. There was no one suitable or, more precisely, sufficiently trusted or with sufficient appropriate experience on the staff.

Luckily for him, most of the governors concurred with this. The only possible internal candidate was de Vere, and if they appointed him they would have to continue to tolerate the insufferable Angela. That was too much even for Gerald Grimes or Margaret McKenzie. The list of candidates was not a long one. In the person of Brian Varga who was eventually appointed, William was sure he had found the ideal person.

Brian had had a fascinating career. He had taught in comprehensive schools, a prep school, and recently in an international college in Kiev. He had a wide range of skills. He could teach a whole range of subjects and was in addition fully qualified.

He had an extremely good degree from TCD in classics. He even ticked the Mrs McKenzie socially acceptability box, having been educated in a public school, albeit only a minor one! As his name implied, his background was middle-European. His father was a wartime refugee with strong socialist credentials. He was somewhat less forthcoming about this aspect of his past.

He would take up his post the following September. For the time being William had to cope as best he could. He was so pleased that he could at least finally see a way forward. He considered himself to have been very lucky to have at last found someone he felt he could work with and trust. In the grim maelstrom of the Parkies Common Room over the previous six months that possibility in itself would make a welcome change.

Chapter Twelve

A TERRIBLE SECRET

William was of course vaguely aware that sex abuse was not unknown in preparatory schools. He had, however, never been personally aware of it until now. The term before he had arrived at Parkies he had a telephone call from Lancelot Waters. Waters had then explained that he had dismissed a master for inappropriate touching.

William had not gained the impression that this was terribly serious and assumed that it had been fully dealt with. He should have perhaps asked more searching questions. The former head had gone to great lengths in this initial telephone call to reassure him that this was indeed the case, that this was simply a one-off piece of stupidity. He then said, "I have known this chap for years. It is clear to me that this was an unfortunate aberration. I don't think any real harm has been done."

It later turned out this was not exactly the case. It was also true that this was an issue that had occurred before William's time, and was he was relieved to accept was not therefore immediately his responsibility.

Given his own personal experience it was perhaps too hot a potato. It was therefore easier for him to let others to deal with it. Not an entirely creditable attitude but given the many issues on his desk in those first few months, it was at least an understandable one.

It had now become abundantly obvious that Francis was being bullied. However much William had tried to ignore it, this was under the combined pressure of his mother and wife no longer possible. Mary was becoming increasingly worried and anxious about her eldest son's state of mind. Francis was becoming more isolated and disassociated from both the other pupils and even from his own siblings.

William could not therefore procrastinate any longer. He didn't have a sufficiently strong or trusted senior member of staff to deal with the issue. He therefore decided to attempt to resolve matters by seeing the main suspect informally. This was, he knew, a very risky strategy but he couldn't bear to see his son's obvious distress anymore and hoped that he could at least partly resolve matters by making this lad see sense.

Sam, the main suspect, knocked on his study door just after prep one dark, cold, miserable January evening. He was a large, rather taciturn boy.

He arrived soon after the end of games and his appearance was one of jumbled, panicky chaos. His tousled blond hair needed a brush and his knees betrayed the surviving mud of the rugby field.

Sam seemed extremely nervous, understandably perhaps, given the fact that he had just been summoned to the head's study. Yet his anxiety seemed of a different order than William had expected. Sam was not someone whom William thought was so easily intimidated. He had even now not entirely lost his swaggering, challenging gait that William knew so intimidated Francis.

There was also something painfully vulnerable about him. It was as though in this moment much of his natural assertiveness had started to simply wither away. He couldn't look the headmaster in the eye and he fiddled nervously with a tassel on the arm of his chair. There was even a sheen of sweat visible on his face. This could have been the result of rushing to William's room, but it looked more like the consequence of an anxious and inexplicable panic.

William saw again what he had occasionally recognised before in this boy: a very fragile self-confidence. This was a very thin skin hidden behind an apparently assured, pugnacious strut.

The tactic William employed was to be informal and friendly, and essentially to enquire into what appeared to be an academic underperformance on Sam's part. Sam was a very able boy, a potential scholar, and his present performance was unlikely to be enough for him to achieve the prize. Some of the staff had commented that he wasn't really focussing on his work and should be doing a great deal better. Martin Pugh with his customary perception observed that Sam had become very distracted and often absent-minded.

"He is a talented writer and some of his prose and poetry had once been of an exceptional standard. Recently, this is not the case." Martin then said, "Sam's performance has been in free fall for over a year or more. His written work is scrappy and rushed, and he doesn't seem vaguely interested anymore." Others confirmed his growing lack of concentration, as well as a tendency to fly off the handle whenever challenged. William hoped this chat might help address some of these difficulties and even lead to a discussion of Sam's relationships with the other boys. This might allow him eventually to talk about Francis.

As it turned out, the conversation went entirely haywire when William's sympathetic approach elicited rather more information than he had ever expected. William had simply asked, "Is there anything worrying you, Sam?"

The boy's first disengaged response was to reply unconvincingly, "No, sir, I am fine." William remembered the conversation he had with Lancelot Waters about a 'minor' issue of a teacher 'fiddling' with boys the term before he arrived. He recollected that he thought Sam might have been one of the boys involved.

It was only when William started to delve into this as a possible reason for his lack of concentration that unexpectedly the dam burst. Sam in obvious increasing distress started to talk about the abusive experiences he had had with the former, now dismissed, teacher in the previous year. Sam then broke down and sobbed as though he would never stop. The unexpected nature of this extreme reaction was such that it entirely shocked and rather disempowered the headmaster.

It was a situation that William had not the remotest idea how to deal with. It was only when William called for Mary and the lad buried his head in her bosom that the hysteria started to be slowly controlled. It had become increasingly obvious that what Sam had clearly experienced amounted to very significant sexual interference. Worse still, it transpired that it had taken place regularly over an appreciable period. As Sam recounted what had happened he started to slowly calm down. It was as though once the initial emotional storm had passed, what now appeared was the calmer waters of a more profound, extended, dejected misery.

William unexpectedly found himself dealing as compassionately as far as he was able with a terribly traumatised lad when he had originally assumed that this was largely a disciplinary issue. The trouble was that, as William swiftly appreciated, he had absolutely no experience of dealing with something like this. Nor did he have the remotest idea how widespread these problems were in the boarding prep school world in which he was now involved.

William finally asked him whether his parents knew. "I suppose so, sir." William then asked, "Why do you say suppose so?" He assumed they knew. They were rather buttoned-up people who William thought might find this difficult to talk about. William hoped that by making this suggestion it might provide him with a justification to contact them. "Well, sir," Sam started to cry again, "no one has ever talked to me, my parents have never mentioned it, and I am far too embarrassed to ask them." Eventually it became clear that Sam didn't know if they knew. Even if they did, it seemed to William a good idea to approach them. At the very least it might encourage a collaborative approach to Sam's obvious difficulties. "Shall we ask them?" Sam reluctantly agreed.

It was obvious from Sam's testimony that there were quite a few other boys in this group involved.

Frankly, he really didn't know how he was going to even start dealing with this. Mary, as always, stiffened his resolve and reminded him that this was an issue he couldn't escape from. "William, what has happened is literally diabolical. Unless you try and deal with it as honestly and courageously as you can, all you will do is make matters worse. This is your responsibility and that ultimately, darling, is what you are paid to do."

Over the next few days, seven children one after another appeared in his study. Their stories were dreadful, in some cases worse than even Sam's. One boy, a lad called Hugo, described what had happened with the kind of clarity only a child could muster. "He came into my dormitory every week, sir, sometimes more often. It started when he felt my willie, then he asked me to do the same to him." "Didn't the other boys see, Hugo?" "Well, it was always after lights out and he was very quiet. The boys were asleep and I am sure didn't see what was happening."

William subsequently discovered that Hugo was mistaken and at least one other boy had seen what was going on. "How long did it go on for?" William enquired. "For at least a year." By this stage Hugo cried as though he would never stop. It wasn't only normal childhood distress; it was as though a dam had burst and this lad was in the process of being drowned by his own shame and distress.

He seemed most worried that William was somehow judging him. He kept asking for reassurance. "It wasn't my fault, was it, sir?" Hugo was after all only ten years of age and some even younger when these monstrous events took place. These children had been in many cases exposed to virtually the whole gamut of possible and inappropriate sexual behaviour. The fact that so many of these young lads thought it might be their fault seemed to make the situation immeasurably more disgusting and unforgivable.

Extraordinarily, it became obvious that no one in the school had ever really talked to these boys. They had been left to cope with this nightmare virtually unaided. An assumption had been made as William's initial conversation with Lancelot Waters had illustrated these were relatively trivial one-off incidents. No serious investigation ever took place.

One boy commented, "It was as though we had done something terrible no one wanted to know. I think we all blamed ourselves." One lad courageously and honestly confessed, "We all thought he was wonderful: we were his favourites and that made us feel really special." He then added shamefully, "Sometimes, sir, I enjoyed it, so surely it must have been my fault." However hard William tried to reassure him, he didn't think the boy was in any way convinced.

William even imagined that in this admission the lad felt an additional sense of guilt for having somehow betrayed the adult who had abused him. The dynamics that had existed between the abuser and the abused was more complex than William had previously imagined. If of course he had really thought about it enough, he should have appreciated this from his own more limited personal experience.

All that had actually happened when the molestation was discovered was a cursory physical examination by the elderly school doctor who was far too embarrassed to ask more than some improvised superficial questions. He clearly believed that these were relatively trivial incidents. Perhaps in fairness the kindly view was taken by some that to talk about it would only make matters worse. It was obvious that his Waters hadn't the vaguest idea how to offer these children appropriate support, even if he had appreciated that they had needed it. This was something William doubted.

William could barely imagine the terrible confusion and distress these children had and were still suffering. He thought angrily of the superior, disdainful attitude that Lancelot Waters and so many in the independent school world had taken to what they thought of as the lesser breed of state school. Nothing, he considered, so scandalously inept and casually cruel could ever have happened in any state school of his acquaintance.

Worse still, it soon became abundantly clear that no one, least of all the school, had even told the boys' parents. William then looked at the former teacher's file: there was literally nothing it. Such a scandal could easily destroy Parkies. This self-interested thought was not, he shamefully admitted, far from his consciousness.

Understandably perhaps, most of the boys he had interviewed had an underlying contempt for authority and a cynicism about the motives of adults the like of which William had rarely witnessed so blatantly and directly before. They might go through the ritual of "Yes, sir, three bags full, sir." Their eyes, and especially those of Sam and Hugo, were full of distrust and the certain expectation of further betrayal. By sticking together even in their negativity and cruel coercion of others, they were acting out that notion they were probably vaguely aware from their Latin classes, *contra mundum*.

It protected them from the evil and careless behaviour that had been so much of their experience of all the adults at Parkies. Except perhaps ironically the unsophisticated, rarely considered eighteen-year-old junior matron Jenny who had eventually courageously blown the whistle. She was one of the few people who ever offered these children even the most rudimentary emotional support.

William came to rather admire these lads whilst hating the effect it had on his son Francis. In an odd sense William realised that Francis was a victim of this awful man, too. Even in the challenging comprehensive school in which he had first worked he had rarely encountered such damaged children, although with a prep school genteel accent and superficial social gloss. The bullying of his son was clearly related to this. Now, however, he steeled himself for his first duty which was to telephone the parents and support the boys as best he could.

The conversations were to put it mildly difficult. The first was with Sam's mother. "Good evening, Mrs Graeme, could you spare a few minutes of your time?" "What do you want, Mr Jones? Is there a problem with Sam?" came back the polished, if slightly anxious, intonation of Mrs Graeme's Home Counties cadence. After a few initial courtesies William falteringly declared, "Are you aware that Sam has suffered sexual abuse whilst a pupil at St Dogmael's?" After what seemed decades she answered coldly and deliberately, "Could you explain exactly what you mean, Mr Jones?"

For perhaps ten minutes William described what he knew. He didn't hide anything or indeed try to excuse or justify the many obvious failures of the school. He was fully aware it was much easier for him than it might have been if he were in situ whilst these abuses were happening.

Whilst he strenuously avoided blaming his predecessor, that thought clearly hung in the air which was something else he felt uncomfortable about. It seemed rather unchivalrous to even imply blame when the person was unable to defend themselves. The conversation ended with an agreed time for Mr and Mrs Graeme to come into the school to discuss matters more fully with him in the next few days.

He made this call or something very like it seven more times over the next few days. The most challenging conversation was with a mother whose son had not actually been physically touched. He had witnessed some of the events and reported this to his mother. Hugo didn't know, but the abuse he had suffered had actually been witnessed on many occasions.

When she approached Lancelot, whom she much respected,

she had been fobbed off with the comment, "Little boys have vivid imaginations, I have come across this frequently. Your son is, I believe, simply imagining something. Perhaps in a bad dream of some kind. It is never wise to believe everything children say."

This lady entirely trusted this man's word and professional integrity. Indeed, he was the main reason she had chosen the school. A profoundly bitter sense of betrayal was now her governing emotion.

This boy was therefore understandably immediately taken away. As William escorted this lady to the front door she turned to him and in a tone of indignant anger and distress commented, "You know, Mr Jones, I think that schools like St Dogmael's are the absolute dregs. They make these highfaluting claims that they care and are interested in their charges, but in the end the children are merely the unwitting, innocent tools for the egotism and perversion of the adults who are supposed to care and look out for them." The other parents decided, albeit William suspected, in many cases very reluctantly, to leave their children at the school.

There was one rather eccentric dad who announced that he intended to drive down immediately. This was a fellow currently married to his third wife. Henry the victim's mother was his second wife. William had first got in touch with her. She said when she was told, "Look headmaster, I genuinely honestly believe you are doing your best for Henry. I personally would prefer to leave matters as they are. However, I can tell you my ex-husband truly loves litigation. He will be so angry; I suspect this is the route he will take. To my certain knowledge he has three cases outstanding at the moment. In my humble opinion you and the school are in real trouble. He will definitely sue you."

When William heard that this father was on his way he uneasily assumed that all hell would break out when he arrived. He had only been at Parkies for six months. It might, he thought, be the shortest headship in history!

This was a long drive: the family estate was over two hundred miles away in Cumbria. William supposed that this meant the lad was to be summarily removed. He was anticipating at the very least a difficult and painful scene. The sports car tyres screeched up to the front of the house and Dad summarily instructed his son Henry to get in. William expected this was the last they would see of him. At least before the inevitable court appearance.

An hour later a lady, a resident from the local village, telephoned describing in the most outraged, indignant and shocked terms what she thought of the sight of a little boy in the Parkies school uniform of Eton collar jumper and short trousers, drunk as a lord in the middle of the afternoon outside the village pub. Her parting shot was: "Headmaster, what sort of school do you think you are running?" William thought later on reflection that was a jolly good question! He had no clear answer. If only he really knew.

Ten minutes later father and son reappeared. "We shared a bottle of champagne," the rather tipsy and now quite friendly father explained. "He has told me everything, I believe that means everything will be all right." Dad left, and William sneaked Henry up to the flat where Mary put him to bed in their sons' bedroom to sleep it off.

Years later this chap sent his younger children to the school. William was flattered by his trust. He was immensely grateful for this. Something he didn't consider that he had really earned.

The offending teacher, he discovered, had been dismissed; more accurately encouraged to resign some months before William's appointment. To be fair, the school had insisted that he should not continue to teach. William believed that he had subsequently honoured that commitment.

This in itself was, he later discovered, an unusual mode of operation at that time. William came to realise that prep schools more often than not ensured that such perverts were given good references and moved to other schools post-haste.

The various scandals in children's homes and boarding schools which resulted from this practice had recently reluctantly persuaded the government to pass the Children Act.

This was to come into practice within a few months. What disturbed William, as much as anything, was that there was absolutely no paperwork on this erring schoolmaster. He supposed that records were not kept. Although an unworthy suspicion did occur to him that they might have been removed or even deliberately destroyed.

This single fact stopped William from automatically adding him to List 99 (a list of pervert teachers excluded from schools). To achieve this, further evidence would be required. In these circumstances by necessity that would have to be acquired from the abused children.

William knew that there was no way parents were going to agree to their children being interviewed by social workers or the police. Nor were they going to risk the prospect of a ghastly court appearance should this man – as he was advised by the school solicitor he was likely to do – challenge the veracity of these accusations. The only evidence would after all be the children's testimonials.

The damage such a process would do to these already victimised children would he thought be potentially horrendous, if not worse than the initial abuse or at least something very like it. He knew that the parents would not tolerate this. In their position William believed he would have precisely taken this position.

It was, however, clear that as this man was no longer a teacher, probably the future risk to children was slight. This might have been wishful thinking! William was uncomfortable about his decision not to take matters further. As the Children Act was not yet in force he was therefore allowed more leeway than he subsequently would be allowed.

Was he motivated by a concern to protect the school? This certainly existed. He hoped it wasn't his primary reason. He wasn't sure that he was being entirely honest with himself. He contacted and then discussed the issue with the local Director of Social Services. This man virtually demanded that William agree to the children being interviewed by his staff. In the end after a somewhat tense meeting, they had to agree to disagree. The governors supported his approach, although in reality they probably had little choice.

Lancelot Waters had not formally shared the details of the original accusations with the board. Some were rather more aware of the situation than they cared to admit. It was the question of the School's reputation that was foremost in many of their minds. Most of them were governors at the time. Was the possible damage to own reputations and interests not that far from their thoughts, too? He could hardly claim that he was entirely innocent of these considerations.

Long after William left Parkies some of these boys, now men about to enter middle age, reported all this to the police. It turned out that children had been abused by him in two other schools prior to his appointment at Parkies. Apparently nothing of the kind had happened subsequent to the incidents at St Dogmael's. William belatedly gave evidence and finally the errant teacher was sent to prison for eight years.

These terrible abuses confirmed that great changes needed to be made. This had been initially discovered by the most junior of teenage matrons. The boozy atmosphere engendered by the bar and the endless gins had meant that the actions of a predatory adult were barely noticed.

This particular behaviour had gone unobserved for a year or more. The children were entirely vulnerable once the lights of the dormitory were turned out. William needed to introduce a proper structure of pastoral care, and quickly.

He and Mary would have to be even more directly involved in this. For many months he would sit in the corridor outside the dormitories after lights out in the pose of protector or policeman, despite the fact that no danger really existed anymore.

On the positive side Francis no longer seemed to be the target of bullying. He still didn't make many friends but at least he wasn't being persecuted. In helping to resolve this outrage, ironically and coincidentally William had lanced the boil which had so warped the atmosphere of the boarding house and of this dormitory in particular.

This man had targeted particular kinds of boys. They were physically attractive, in a pretty, childlike way. They were all imaginative, intelligent, and sensitive. In short, they were precisely the kind of boys who would be most damaged by this brutal, abusive behaviour. The fact they had all initially admired him was used by him as the pitiless means of ultimately entrapping them.

When William asked Lancelot Waters some weeks later why he hadn't contacted the police at the time, the wounded, outraged response was, "I wasn't entirely sure I believed it anyway. He was after all at school with my son. I had known him and his family for many years. I know his mother would never have forgiven me for involving the police. She even expected I should give him a second chance and not even dismiss him. Do you realise when I insisted he resign that she hasn't talked to me since. I believe I did everything I could or indeed should."

He also pointed out that he had contacted the headmaster of one of the local public schools who had advised him to do precisely what he did. He angrily concluded, "What, William, gives you the right to judge me? I don't believe in these circumstances you would have behaved any differently."

William reluctantly admitted Lancelot Waters was right. Could he be absolutely sure he wouldn't have reacted exactly the same if the circumstances had been alike? This dilemma was to be a consistent feature of every school scandal in preceding and subsequent years. Parkies was by no means unique in its cowardly, self-interested approach. Lancelot's belief that it was reasonable to trust someone he had known for years didn't seem entirely unreasonable.

These were attitudes not to be found just in schools. William was acutely aware that his father Gethin's behaviour was being addressed in a remarkably similar way back in Usk. Later, too, William was to understand that even the Church was not immune from such behaviour. Indeed future clerical scandals might suggest its behaviour was often worse.

News was sparse from Usk. Since William's declaration after

Christmas there had been little contact. William then had a telephone call from his brother Carwyn.

He explained in the most cold, chilly tones that the police now regarded the issue of their father as closed. His sibling seemed to feel vindicated and therefore he spoke in the most righteously virtuous terms.

William could hear the suppressed rage in his brother's voice. He had certainly not forgiven William for the implied acknowledgment of their dad's guilt earlier. It was better William judged to leave matters there, at least for the time being.

Whether this outcome was arrived at through lack of evidence or more duplicitous means William didn't know. Yet he suspected in the closed world of small-town chapel and lodge this boy's version of the events would never be taken very seriously.

Dilys came up to Suffolk for a visit that Easter. To begin with there was certainly an atmosphere of tension and mistrust. Yet the mutual love they felt for each other soon thawed any remaining icicles. On the journey home again from Usk, William realised with a growing conviction that no relationships were entirely open and frank. The love he felt for his mother could still, he hoped, withstand a few undiscovered or unacknowledged secrets.

Chapter Thirteen

PARADISE POSTPONED

There was still something truly wonderful about working in a boarding school. With the younger children he came to realise that you knew immediately whether they were happy or sad. Most were incapable of any artifice. Their faces generally were a book that was very easy to read.

Every morning when William joined the boys for breakfast he loved chatting away to them and listening to their little triumphs and usually their still smaller woes. "I really don't like kippers," one the young boarders reluctantly opined. William was able to ensure that he didn't have to have them. He knew he wasn't too keen on them either.

With such small concessions it was possible to enhance the morale of even the most susceptible child. This nurturing relationship with the boarders was often what made his job such an infinite pleasure. He suspected not for the first time that the children gave back far more than they received.

He knew by now he was never going to win round the hardcore of staff or governor opposition. Lipman, de Vere, Dalton, Grimes, and McKenzie were sworn enemies and he could do little to change that. He recognised that most of his staff were committed, cooperative and above all often impressively good teachers.

The hours of work they put in were extraordinary. There was never a shortage of volunteers for a whole range of activities. They never complained, and as far as William could tell, really enjoyed the experience of being so involved. The younger teachers, and especially the stooges, lived in their rather cramped, shabby bedsits, the former maids' rooms in the eves of the old mansion. They had few comforts of any kind but seemed wholly unconcerned by this.

They had a wonderful sense of camaraderie and a great awareness of the ridiculous. Given their long hours, poor living conditions and minuscule salaries humour and laughter was never far from their evening socials. William thought they probably needed these opportunities to let off steam.

Few seemed to buy into the rather precious social delusions of some of their senior colleagues. When William was a child he once spent a week at Butlins holiday camp.

In some ways these young people reminded him of the Yellow-coats he had met then. He mischievously thought he might start the day with a 'Hi-de-Hi' followed by a sing-song. He might even be a reasonably competent entertainment manager!

Amongst many staff and some governors, there was a growing recognition that William had handled the abuse issue quite well. The school had escaped a devastating scandal and there had been no mass exodus of children.

Even those staff who had opposed the delayed opening of the school bar were starting to realise that this was now essential. Lancelot Waters's influence was waning significantly. There was a widespread recognition that the abuse issue had exposed the worst excesses of his recent mismanagement. Whatever William Jones's limitations were, most of the staff could no longer realistically yearn for 'the good old days'.

Despite the fear in some minds that William wanted to annihilate the Waterses' tradition that was never true. There was much about the rather liberal, permissive, child-centred approach of Parkies that William loved and wished to enhance not to demolish.

Foremost amongst these was a genuine sense of freedom when the children were encouraged to explore not only the world of knowledge and ideas, but also the opportunity to develop a self-confident and fearless approach to life. It was this question of character development which was implicit in all that the school stood for.

The children had free access to the woods. This rather scrappy wilderness became an encampment of corrugated iron, scrap wood and earthen hovels where the boys tried to make little personal spaces from any detritus they could find.

The place eventually, Mary thought, looked a bit like a refugee camp. You took your life in your hands walking through. This was especially so if you were silly enough to attempt this when it was dark. These constructions were like so many elephant traps. You were, however, just as likely to see a ruffled-haired, mud-speckled, little boy appear unexpectedly out of a hole and be cheerfully greeted in William's case with "Whato sir, do you want to look at my den?"

On summer weekends the happy diggers were summoned for tea when the 'bellboy' walked around the house and the immediate environs whilst ringing his large bell. So small was this lad that it sometimes appeared that the bell was larger than him.

One almost expected him to tip over with the effort of ringing it. This was a job that was highly sought after, partly because it came with a weekly allowance from the tuck shop.

The situation became rather more complicated when the school acquired two pigs. They were soon named Ham and Eggs. Every morning before breakfast a gaggle of children would plod down to the woods to feed these pets with the remains of the previous day's leftovers. Later some chickens were added and those who looked after them could claim their freshly laid eggs. There were, it has to be said, no shortage of volunteers for this task.

The car club was another very popular activity. The members painted an elderly, clapped-out Austin Allegro in the most bizarre psychedelic colours. It almost looked as if it had driven out of the Sgt. Pepper album sleeve. The car was theoretically under the supervision of a young male stooge. More often than not some mechanical failure meant that a gaggle of little boys would be crawling over this vehicle in a desperate attempt to get it running again. When they succeeded it would zoom around the fields with an army of little boys in enthusiastic hot pursuit.

The frightening abandon with which this old jalopy skidded over the fields belching out a billowing cloud of black smoke with a blatant disregard for any health and safety rules sometimes even made William feel slightly queasy about the possible perilous consequences.

This all was, William believed, evidence of truly astonishing educative possibilities. This was to him the very essence of what prep schools were or should be all about. Mary used to describe it to Dilys back in Usk as "swallows and amazons in Suffolk".

If you added the midnight swims, camping by the lake, barbecues, boating, assault course canoeing, fishing, and lots more William thought this little world would make Arthur Ransome rather proud. He hoped all this encouraged self-reliance, teamwork, and a *joie de vivre* which William was sure was the essential *raison d'être* of the school.

He noticed, too, that Noah Bradley, Nathalie Harris, and Martin Pugh were clearly distancing themselves from the litany of grouching and remorseless sarcasm that emulated from the Lipman crew. They had become assiduously friendly and positive to both him and Mary.

They no longer seemed to believe he threatened the essence of what they really cared about. It was particularly rewarding to witness and experience the enthusiasm and positive attitude of so many of his young staff. He increasingly believed that the basic infrastructure of success existed. It just needed to be nurtured and developed.

There were moments of great hilarity that often lightened his life, as well as amusing his friends and family. On a wet afternoon in February in this, his first year, he decided to take a group of the younger boarders on a walk in the nearby woods at Kings Forest beyond the school gates. As dusk descended he realised that together with the twenty children and two dogs he was totally lost. Eventually, Elsie Tickle realised that large numbers of children had not turned up for tea.

Mary and James Waters organised a search party which was instantly dispatched. Eventually, the two school minibuses found the bedraggled party walking in entirely the wrong direction through the forest. This was the cause of much amusement in the Common Room.

The consensus was that geography and map-reading were subjects he should avoid teaching. Every four weeks the children were given a 'Studies Card' which indicated their progress in the various subject areas.

One was provided for William where his limitations were amusingly revealed. Nathalie Harris even produced a wonderful cartoon of the confused headmaster lumbering around the woods which had pride of place in the following year's school magazine.

William was gaining something of a reputation for some of his idiosyncratic ways. This reputation for odd eccentricity had rather followed him from school to school.

Many of the younger teachers seemed to quite like William's guileless approach to his job and relationships. Nathalie Harris even produced another cartoon of a collapsing chair incident at his previous school in the following year's school magazine.

It was of course also true that many of the more sniffy staff and quite a few governors strongly disapproved of William's anarchistic and self-lampooning tendencies. As Margaret McKenzie later caustically observed, "This man has absolutely no sense of decorum. I expect a headmaster of a school of this status to behave with dignity, not to play the clown. William Jones is a man entirely without gravitas." She had a point; William might have occasionally and reluctantly conceded. He knew there was quite a strong element of the self-publicist in his nature!

Elsie Tickle, long-serving domestic, had an amazing relationship with the children. Teatime always consisted of a mug of sweet tea and a slab of cake. The children trooped into her scullery for this repast. They stood there with a cup in one hand and the cake in the other. There were sometimes as many as sixty children in this small, cramped space.

She ruled her domain with a rod of iron and woe betide any child who misbehaved. Yet, if you wanted to know which child was unhappy or being bullied, Elsie was the best person to ask. If you wanted information you would simply go and ask 'Tick', the name all the children called Elsie.

If during the holidays the children spied Elsie in the local town they would often shout out with joyful abandoned, "Whato, Tick!" She would wave back with a brilliant smile and a face suffused with joy and pleasure. Rather different, it has to be said, from the rather grumpy pose she often affected in her own scullery.

A few weeks later in that summer term, William was escorting some rather posh, titled, potential parents around the building. He did not feel that things were going very well. They seemed rather cold and uninterested.

Not for the first time potential parents were not overly impressed with the rather limited and even spartan facilities on offer. At the precise moment they passed the scullery stuffed with children, their voices chirping with excitement. Elsie Tickle bellowed out in her most distinctive Suffolk brogue, "You watch it, you little buggers, I've got eyes in my arse."

Amazingly this incident provoked the first hint of amusement and warmth in these rather dour adults. It even appeared to have possibly persuaded or at least not dissuaded these parents from sending their children to Parkies. You see, William told himself, prep schools could still be great fun. If you weren't being eaten alive by difficult parents, stroppy staff, and grumpy governors.

Thus, by the end of the first academic year William had managed with quite a lot of resistance to persuade the governors to start paying the staff properly. This he considered was a moral obligation but also ensured that there was a real fillip to morale.

This did not please Major Hardy, the retiring bursar, who saw this as the obvious start of the ruin of the school. "My God, this man is determined to bankrupt us," he complained to Gerald Grimes after one especially fraught governor's' meeting.

As George Hardy was about to go, his opposition could be largely discounted. Grimes's attitude had not changed. He fully maintained his pose of grumpy indignation. He had failed to grasp or perhaps care that the domestic staff were currently being paid at a miserly rate half the average for the county as well as considerably less than he paid his own cleaners.

In his mind the criticism of irresponsible spendthrift was now to added to the list of William's apparent other deficiencies. Grimes commented to Margaret McKenzie the following day, "I don't see why we should pay these council house wallah domestics anymore. We bus them in and feed them, don't we? What more do they bloody well want?" There was of course an answer to this, not one that Gerald Grimes would have wished to hear.

For the moment William's position seemed to have become much stronger and secure. That is not to say that his problems had gone away. John Lipman remained a ticking time bomb. He was aware that this could go off at any moment. William was under few illusions about either de Vere or Dalton. However, they seemed now to be in a minority in the Common Room.

He had even heard that de Vere might be moving on. William tended to dismiss Piers Dalton as a puffed-up, silly man of no significant threat. William even at this stage had rather underestimated the influence of his wife Isabelle.

A key weakness he possessed was in being very susceptible to a pretty face and a simpering tone. Both of these Isabelle possessed in spades, but it didn't reflect her real character. William had not yet grasped this.

Mary had and tried to warn her somewhat bedazzled husband of the danger this couple represented when one evening she commented. "Look, Will, Piers and Isabelle don't like you. He is not such a fool as you think and she is not the fluffy French charmer you imagine." Not for the first time she discovered that when William had a fixed idea he was often immovable.

The key to headmasterly success in independent schools had always been ensuring growing numbers and Parkies' numbers were rocketing. Staff morale was generally high, probably mostly the result of the recent generous pay increase.

Elsie Tickle's modest remuneration almost doubled within a little over a year. She seemed now to consider the new head as not such a bad fellow after all!

The other important change that he was able to accomplish was that it was finally decided that the following September, this bastion of male privilege would finally take girls. Not, it had to be said, a universally popular decision!

"My God," a rather tipsy Lancelot Waters proclaimed when drinking his fourth gin and tonic on a marathon boozy binge with a group of friends including St John de Vere and John Lipman early in the summer term soon after this announcement. "That bloody man is going to truly convert Parkies into a third-rate dame school. Our sporting tradition all those scholarships and our special, unique atmosphere will all disappear like Scotch mist." Sadly, he knew that whatever he and his chums might think of this, there was little they could do. "So bloody frustrating," Waters opined as he toddled off to bed with Geraldine after his guests had left for home.

Chapter Fourteen

THE FIRST PRIZE DAY

Prize Day always took place on the last Saturday in June. It was the main occasion when Parkies as indeed any independent school put its best foot forward. Not only was the whole building spruced up: classrooms were also transformed into magical locations where each subject teacher would festoon their rooms with colourful displays and the very best of the children's work.

It has to be said that the Geography and junior French areas were somewhat sparse in this department. This was something that was a source of much irritation to the highly nervous and on this occasion particularly anxious William. He knew that a good showing at the Prize Day was essential to the reputation of the school as well as himself. This was something which, not for the first time, he called the 'whited sepulchre' technique.

The grounds became a tented encampment bedecked in bunting and flags in preparation for the school fête that followed the main event. Rather large and expensive cars were parked everywhere.

Elegantly dressed parents were unloading hampers in preparation for their sumptuous picnics. Panama-hatted and blazer-clad men and ladies in flowery dresses paraded pridefully through the school gardens and grounds. Everyone was kitted out in their best bib and tucker.

Even the usually scruffy Martin Pugh, whilst perhaps not entirely pristine in appearance, looked quite respectable in collar and tie and a suit that looked like it might have even recently visited the dry-cleaners. In short, the scene was one of an idealised English summer paradise. It might only have been spoilt if Miss Marple wandered in to find a body in the library.

This was the end of William's first academic year, concluding, as they always did, with this Prize Day extravaganza. Prior Anselm, the school governor and resident of St Wilfred's, was that year's guest of honour. William had judged it politic to invite him partly because he knew he was no fan of him personally. It was therefore a possible way of repairing a rather fragile relationship. It might reinforce in the mind of the parent body the still strong Catholic tradition of the place. Before the main event Prior Anselm concelebrated the Founders' Mass with Father Brendan O'Rourke.

William over the year had increasingly come to appreciate Father Brendan's many hidden and not so hidden virtues. Both over the Lipman issue and later the abuse question he had been a rock of support. Every Sunday evening he attended the school to say evening Mass followed by supper with the head and his wife.

It was an occasion both William and Mary always looked forward to. He was always slightly late, and to ensure that things started promptly two little boys were deputed as sacristans. They laid out his vestments carefully in such a way that he could be ready in less than a minute. This was a very sought-after role probably because, as of a mark of his gratitude, Brendan made sure they were well rewarded with Maltesers, the priest's favourite confectionery. Extraordinarily even when there were only seconds to spare he never looked flustered.

Brendan was much more perceptive about the school's situation and prospects that many supposed. This was certainly true of most of his fellow governors. Perhaps his only real vice was a prodigiously insatiable appetite. He loved food and particularly the special 'posh' supper which was always provided after Sunday Mass. He munched his way through this beanfeast with much aplomb, enthusiasm, and genuine pleasure.

William could never understand how he remained so skinny and emaciated-looking. He must have had the most extraordinary metabolism. It has to be said that he didn't look very impressive.

Not only was he painfully thin, but also the remains of his rapidly disappearing hair had reverted in recent years to a salt-and-pepper rim of a rather untidily barbered half-moon. He usually wore a shabby Roman soutane. There was sometimes just a hint of former repasts dappled down the front of his gown.

He was a very heavy smoker, so his presence was easily heralded by a strong whiff of tobacco. Indeed from a distance his arrival was usually signalled by a thick plume of smoke. "Like the appearance of a rather grubby, beloved, old steam engine," Mary laughingly suggested. His feet were usually shod in what can only be described as a pair of neglected, Army-style boots. His beaten-up Polonez Polish car also presaged his arrival as it backfired its way up the school drive. William sometimes thought it was held together with more rust than rivets.

Father Brendan despised most material things and lived in a genuine holy poverty, although a fondness for his single malt Jameson and a love of large, sweet puddings were small vices in the scheme of things.

He always seemed to avoid judging others and, most importantly, obvious displays of his own piety. For these reasons, whilst most of parents regarded him as irredeemably odd, he was often held by many in much affection and even awe. If a family was in trouble, and with most of the want-to-be and actual local Catholic gentry this usually involved some kind of marital infidelity, the rumble and backfiring of Father Brendan's old car up the drive of their country house would portend the arrival of help. Mary thought he was the best marriage adviser and counsellor in the Kingdom and he was free to boot!

William was sure he didn't really approve of the privileged world that to him St Dogmael's represented. This was a point of view he rarely openly expressed. Nevertheless, on the few occasions when the priest was annoyed and frustrated he was not averse to referring to some of the most self-regarding, pretentious and hoity-toity of his posh parishioners as "feckin' eejits".

Like Father Sean in London, William thought, he didn't really much care for these rather snooty English Catholics. Unlike him, he thought that they might just be redeemable, although being English that might of course be somewhat debatable. These days of course even these swish Catholics were a small minority in the school.

Most parents had little religious faith and rather less interest. This was a fact that Brendan very much regretted. It left a kind of sadness and regret that could sometimes be seen in his large, often slightly mournful brown eyes.

On this morning, the chapel was packed. The school choir always pulled out all the stops. There were motets by Palestrina and Byrd. This was always a great attraction not necessarily for the quality of the music but because most of the children were involved one way or another as members of the choir or as servers, ushers and musicians. Proud parents and grandparents sat simpering at this display of the musical and other talents of their offspring.

At least as much a pull was the homily provided by Father O'Rourke. There was always a frisson of anticipation about what imaginative interpretation he would take to Church doctrine. Sometimes, such as when he called Dante's vision of Hell, an obscenity it resulted in a rather tense subsequent interview with the local Bishop. When he wasn't straying into unorthodoxy or even, some would say, heresy, he always managed to provoke his congregation with a combination of earthy wisdom, impish humour and just a touch of gentle Irish scorn for the oddities of so many strange English conventions. These even after thirty years he neither fully understood, nor would privately admit, often much liked.

Prior Anselm, who was just about to enter his seventieth year was a tall rather spindly chap. Years before after school at the Oratory, university at Sidney Sussex at Cambridge (a college he now avoided mentioning, with its embarrassing Cromwellian connections). He had joined the Augustinian Order. His career had included a spell in Rome as well as a time as parish priest in an ultrafashionable South Kensington parish.

Most of his life had been spent in the hallowed precincts of his beloved St Wilfred's. Despite his perhaps slightly manufactured, gentry-like appearance his background was relatively modest. His father had been a regional manager on Southern Railways.

He seemed to fit easily into this posh Catholic world. His background was respectable if hardly pre-eminent or especially high-born. This was something he avoided mentioning. It was not so much that he was ashamed, rather that he had forgotten these inconvenient near plebeian roots in a lifetime of nurtured gentility. He had a full head of milky-white hair, and on his nose perched half-moon spectacles. These only added to his lordly, patrician air.

A few years before he had given up as Prior of St Wilfred's after eight years in the role. He still retained the honorary title of Prior. He was in his own way a rather handsome man.

Vanity was perhaps one of his abiding faults. Despite an apparently rather unfeigned impression of monkish humility, there was something of the strutting peacock about Prior Anselm. Clerical dress, liturgical vestments, monastic habit – all had to be immaculate in every detail. Today was no exception. He was determined to express in every minutia of his appearance his belief in the pre-eminence of the clerical caste.

Outside the monastery as on this occasion he usually dressed in the most elegant, black, expensively tailored clerical suit. He shoes were black, mirror-polished Oxfords, and his collar was definitely not the nasty piece of white plastic so *de rigueur* amongst the lesser and even – God forbid – many senior clergy these days.

He wore rather his preferred traditional, fully laundered Roman collar so redolent in his mind of a more elegant and gracious past. His regalia from a distance gave him ironically, thought Father Brendan, a strange passing resemblance to Ian Paisley or at least some other firmly anti-papist Northern Ireland Protestant clergyman. This observation would have absolutely horrified the good monk. He was ultramontane to the tips of his elegantly manicured fingernails. He may not have much cared for the peculiarities of Irish Catholicism but the harsh-toned anti-papism of Northern Irish nonconformity were entirely anathema to his sensitive soul.

He was firmly of the opinion, as his appearance on this day fully illustrated, that the priestly caste was or at least should be considered the pinnacle of all social and intellectual distinction. It was the very apex of human perfectibility. Prior Anselm would rather that the Reformation had not happened. Since it had he considered that old Catholic aristocracy of England represented the best, indeed the only significant quality that still remained.

His imagined world was that of *Brideshead* without, William mischievously thought, the less than orthodox figures of Lord Sebastian Flyte and Charles Ryder. Sadly that world had long since disappeared, if indeed it ever really existed.

Prior Anselm could not yet accept the new post-Vatican II realities. This included the Mass in English as well as those dreadful trendy hymns, guitars, and religious folk music. He hated the altar being placed in the middle of the nave.

Most of all those appalling, newly assertive woman were all totally baleful to him. They represented for him the collapse of all essential civilised values. Father Brendan, as far as Prior Anselm was concerned often, played up to these ridiculous and destructive shibboleths.

These were notions he firmly believed would disappear once Catholics of quality and discernment were truly back in control.

Prior Anselm didn't therefore have the salty charm of Father

Brendan. If one were unkind one might even suggest he was just a touch prim with an impression of effortless superiority in his condescending, commanding, patrician tone.

When it was announced that he was to give the Prize Day oration William could almost detect a groan of despondency from much of the assembled body of parents. As Father O'Rourke teasingly suggested before the event, "The trouble is he cannot resist saying ten words when only two would do. Boredom is bad enough, but grandiloquent English tedium is truly the pits!"

Prior Anselm's bible, William sometimes imagined, was Dom Bede Camm's famous tome *Forgotten Shrines*, an early 20th-century celebration of the recusant martyr traditions of Catholic England. He wasn't a snob in the sense that Mrs McKenzie was. He simply didn't understand the 'hoi polloi'. Whilst he might sometimes reluctantly acknowledge his own relatively humble beginnings, a lifetime of public school, Oxford and a smart monastery had ensured he now epitomised the very image of the supercilious cleric.

William Jones was definitely not his cup of tea. Jones, in his opinion, wasn't just plebeian; the real problem was that he positively gloried in that dubious status. He also seemed to have even retained a peculiarly disagreeable Protestant inclination to question priestly wisdom.

Mary Jones was even less appropriately deferential. William Jones rarely dressed in the way Prior Anselm thought appropriate in a headmaster. His accent was not only Welsh, but he also insisted on using plebeian terms like 'toilet', 'lounge' and worst of all 'settee' when everyone knew it should be 'sofa'.

He seemed not to understand or vaguely appreciate what was

required in the demeanour and appearance essential in a headmaster of a school of St Dogmael's quality. He was therefore surprised to be invited. Perhaps he thought William Jones was making a genuine effort to be more agreeable. Or he might have even finally understood the veracity of Prior Anselm's superior vision. Humility and tolerance of other opinions were not part of Anselm's lexicon.

Mary Jones was, Prior Anselm considered, very much worse than her husband. Her real problem was she epitomised in his mind those dreadful, pushy women he so disliked and feared.

She was, he considered, far too inclined to express her own opinions which in his view often veered to the edge of heresy or worse. Prior Anselm essentially thought that women, like children, were best seen and not heard.

On one occasion he remembered when he had been invited to supper with the Joneses she even had the gall to defend birth control. "Don't you think women have some rights over their own body?" she had impertinently asserted. William thought that the goodly monk was about to choke on his lasagne. This was not incidentally a dish he enjoyed or indeed thought should be served in decent, respectable houses.

Prior Anselm considered Mary was everything he detested most in modern women. The most appropriate role of women in the Church was one of flower arranging, cake-baking and tea-making. Most of all they should be appropriately deferential to all priests and to him in particular. Yet on this day he was determined to try and give even this dreadful woman the benefit of the doubt. Anselm still yearned for the return of the days when the West Suffolks had assembled at the front of Parkies as he had watched the scarlet-clad huntsmen gallop their way across the park pursuing some poor, unsuspecting fox. This was an unlikely future prospect, he realised, with Jones as headmaster or the opinionated Mary in situ.

He loved the litany of ancient and noble names that were once the pride of English Catholicism. He was of course in denial. The future he still stubbornly refused to acknowledge was that of persons just like William and Mary Jones. Too liberally inclined, irredeemably common, and deeply misguided as they undoubtedly were. The world he passionately believed was going to the dogs. Despite his determination on this day to be polite and agreeable he was still convinced that William and Mary Jones represented in his mind the worst of these canine excesses.

His Prize Day oration reflected these obsessive fantasies. There were endless references to the smarter Catholic martyrs, a stout defence of all the most unpopular Catholic moral teaching, as well as an entirely illusionary reverie about what he supposed was the illustrious status of the now sadly declining Catholic public schools. He lamented the fact that only two boys that year were moving on to such places.

Most embarrassingly from William's perspective he made an impassioned plea for St Dogmael's to remain a single-sex school. This had immediately followed William's headmaster's report where he had made the contrary announcement of the beginning of coeducation that September. A rather confused and perplexed body of parents thus left the hall.

Prize-Giving was followed by drinks in the quad. Actually, William reflected it wasn't really a quad, rather a tatty courtyard. Lancelot Waters had named it so. It gave a kind of false, pretentious antiquity to the place, as well as feeding into a delusion of elite grandeur.

Such delusions reminded William of Sir Henry Newbolt, the poet, who in a similar obsessive fantasy had imagined his recently established public school, Clifton College, as an ancient, ivy-clad establishment when he had penned the words, "there's a breathless hush in the Close to-night."

He reflected it was a common feature of such places to assume high status and antiquity or, if not immediately available, simply to invent it. Perhaps he considered this was actually a peculiarly English conceit!

Elsie Tickle and her crew of domestics were lined up behind trestle tables with plates of cheap nibbles, inferior South African sherry, and vinegary wine. As the parents assembled, William was faintly aware of a commotion.

He recognised Dr Hudson, a local GP, who was for some odd reason standing on the balcony immediately outside Mary and William's bedroom. He was a celebrated practical joker as well as being rather an eccentric, much-loved local character. Ambrose Hudson was a very supportive parent who had over the past year become something of a friend. He was known to be a very compassionate doctor who always put the interests of his patients ahead of any targets or rules emanating from what he viewed as the hated NHS bureaucracy. Perhaps this was the main reason he was so loved.

Ambrose Hudson bore a faint resemblance to William. Ambrose was dressed, he belatedly dimly discerned, in his pyjamas. Whilst all this was being processed in his mind William heard a voice, which sounded rather familiar, shouting out, "Are you buggers really here already?"

He was a brilliant mimic. It was, he slowly understood, his voice, and the crowd immediately dissolved into raucous laughter. Even

Prior Anselm seemed to find it funny and discreetly chuckled. Father Brendan was laughing so uproariously he inadvertently spat out his mouthful of cheap Shiraz. It just missed a rather po-faced, predictably unamused Mrs McKenzie. She stared at the burbling priest with a look of unmitigated disgust as well as astonished vexation.

She whispered to her equally appalled husband Roland, "The Irish clergy are the absolute pits: this man O'Rourke is just a peasant with a grubby dog collar." Roland, who did not even subscribe to his wife's semi-detached Catholicism, "what do you expect when you give Irish clodhoppers and Welsh subversives any authority you can always expect them to behave badly."

Despite the sourness of the McKenzies, most of the laughter seemed genuinely affectionate rather than mocking. It occurred to William that, thanks partly to Ambrose Hudson, he might tentatively hope to be finally accepted.

At this moment of minor triumph a more threatening image hove into sight. The swaying figure of John Lipman burst into the assembly. William realised that he was absolutely sloshed. He was dishevelled, red-faced and very obviously belligerent. He was now going to make a scene. This was a thought that filled William with abject terror. Parents were already peering querulously in his direction. Quite suddenly and inexplicably he seemed to change direction. William could not see why. Then he noticed the huge shape of Noah Bradley who with a calm but very firm forbearance was whispering something in Lipman's ear. Holding John Lipman's arm Noah led him gently away. The crisis was over: Noah had saved the day!

The afternoon was the occasion of the annual school fête. Parkies converted itself into a mini-country fayre, all wax jackets, peaked caps, corduroy trousers, jodhpurs, and Labrador Retrievers. The staff had worked extraordinarily hard setting up a beer tent, tea tent, cake stall, pony rides, stalls selling school memorabilia, second-hand uniforms and posher bric-a-brac sometimes masquerading as 'antiques', as well as the obligatory ice creams, pop and burgers.

A 'wash-the-beak' attraction was the highlight of what was on offer. Stocks were set up which gave boys and their parents the opportunity to throw sponges at a teacher in exchange for a small, but increasing charge depending on the status of the victim. As the afternoon progressed each member of the Parkies teaching staff stood in the stocks offering themselves to long queues of little boys determined on revenge for some long-remembered and unforgiven slight. Or perhaps it was just a unique opportunity to tweak the noses of those who usually governed their lives.

There were especially long queues of little boys armed with especially wet, grubby sponges awaiting William when it was finally his turn. The experience became more challenging when some of the burly, fast-bowling farmer dads got into the act. Then it could be jolly painful.

The price was doubled for the privilege of soaking the head. Even so, demand was always exceptionally high for this prerogative. This year the queue seemed especially long. The best tactic was to grin and bear it and think of all the money the school was making, and at the same time pray that no one had inserted any gravel into the sponges.

There was, to William's relief, at first no sign of John Lipman. Then with apprehensive dismay William spied him propping up the bar on the other side of the beer tent sitting next to St John de Vere. De Vere was leaving at the end of term having just been appointed to a new post at a rival school.

It was not an especially senior one which had further soured his crepuscular mood and gave him yet more reasons for resentment, imagined victimhood and ire. Over the months this had been increasingly directed, William knew, at him.

His sneering, bitter, brazenly hostile mindset was, after a few drinks, fully and obviously engraved on his facial features. This more than anything alerted William to the looming crisis.

Whilst de Vere was tipsy himself it was not to the same extent that Lipman was. De Vere was clearly controlling things. He was the ringmaster and organising genius of what he hoped would be his venomous final masterstroke. William observed that de Vere was buying Lipman many drinks and at the same time whispering what he supposed must be a trickling malevolence into his ear.

John was visibly becoming more and more antagonistic. The growing anger was etched onto his drunken, lugubrious features. It was clear from his frequent gawps in William's direction who was to be the likely target. William had already entered the tent; there was no easy escape. He was greeted cheerfully by a few of the drinkers, mostly parents. Whilst he was chatting to a rather horsy-looking, tweed-clad wife of a local garden centre proprietor, Lipman staggered towards him. His slurred voice intoned, "I hope you are having a good day, Headmaster."

This banal phrase did not in any way convey the menace and enmity that the tone and malignant, bloodshot stare actually transmitted. William could see the languid, smug figure of de Vere seemingly to egg

Lipman on. "You know that this should by rights have been my day, don't you, Mr Jones?"

The inauthentic, apparent politeness of the initial utterance had now entirely disappeared. He articulated these words with an animus and searing hatred that took William's breath away. Now he was a man finally expressing his real, very genuine, lacerated feelings and mounting volcanic fury.

De Vere, William now appreciated, was the real villain here. He knew what was about to happen and had fully orchestrated it. Now he was leaving St Dogmael's he had absolutely nothing to lose.

Further into the tent William noticed Angela de Vere. She had neither the subtlety of wit to dissimulate, nor indeed any particular wish to do so. Her face was a frightening mask of venom and rage. If de Vere was the Director, Angela was certainly his willing collaborator.

De Vere might be the ringmaster of this pantomime, but William now realised it was Angela who was the malignant sprite who was feeding his rancour. Lipman was of course merely de Vere's patsy. He was being exploited to provide the classicist and his wife with some voyeuristic, vindictive pleasure. Lipman, on the other hand, had literally everything on the line. It was obvious that de Vere was enjoying the spectacle, sitting as he was in an apparently languid, relaxed pose with an expression of sheer delighted, spiteful exaltation.

By this point the garden centre's proprietor's wife had very sensibly made herself scarce. William knew he should not let this get out of hand, although in reality he knew it already had. "What do you want, John?" William politely enquired. "I want my fucking job, Jones, the one you stole!" He was now shouting very loudly.

Desperate to appease and calm things down, William responded, "Do you imagine, John, this is the way to achieve that? Please go to bed and sleep it off." With this, in what he hoped was a quiet, meek slap-down which he delivered in his best headmasterly tone, John Lipman lurched towards him. How could you not feel pity for the open wound of anguished despair that everything about John conveyed? More immediately William feared that he would physically lash out at him.

At that moment, a white-faced Karen Lipman entered the tent. "Come home, darling," she said. Her dignity and pose were impressive and William had to respect this, even though he was having difficulty controlling his own feelings. Two figures then sidled up to John. Noah Bradley and Martin Pugh, who himself looked a little the worse for wear, gently put their arms around his shoulders and with great discretion, tact and kindness walked him out of the tent.

William knew that everyone there and in its environs was mesmerised by this little drama. As best he could with his hands involuntarily shaking and his heart thumping he attempted to make polite conversation with some of the remaining parents and guests.

Father Brendan walked over. He had seen the look of shocked, angry, distressed misery on William's face. He had heard of the altercation. No one at the fête had not.

Mary was organising the tea tent so there had been no opportunity for William to talk to her. Something that usually helped calm him down. The priest understood that he must do something. "Come on, Willie, my lad, time to make ourselves scarce, methinks." He then kindly added, "You must know they are all feckin' eejits, for Christ's sake don't rise to it, old chap."

The priest and the headmaster sat together in his study both cradling glasses of Brendan's favourite tipple of Jameson malt. The fête was over. The parents had gone home. It was time, Brendan thought, for a chinwag. "The trouble with you, Willie, is you don't really believe in all this bollocks, do you?"

"What do you mean?" William murmured. "In my opinion, boyo, you are a bit of a disrupter. I know this because I am, too." "Go on, Father." "Despite present appearances I was once marked out for something more than a rural parish in the middle of nowhere. After a spell at UCD and Maynooth I ended up in the Irish College in Rome. I was one of those silly buggers swanning around the eternal city dressed like a bloody penguin." William remembered seeing those columns of fresh-faced, rather pious-looking young men when he had last visited Rome.

It was hard to believe looking at this scruffy, elderly, down-at-heel priest that he might once have been one of them. 'Some even thought I was a high-flier. See, in different circumstances you might have been calling me my Lord." Brendan smiled at his own self-deprecating joke.

"The trouble is I don't tend to do what I am supposed or even what the Bishop thinks I am allowed to do. You, on the other hand, Willie, appear to be a very compliant sort of fellow but that is not true, is it?" He continued. "Then you don't do what you are supposed to do either." "I don't quite understand what you mean, Brendan," replied a slightly offended William.

"Let me put it this way, John Lipman is a true believer, God help him. He has utterly bought into this ridiculous, elite, independent Catholic school rubbish in a way you haven't. The drinking, I believe, is partly about suppressing the nagging doubt it might all be garbage after all."

Brendan then continued. "You, on the other hand, are a convert.

That is supposed to mean that you are on your feckin knees all the time. I haven't noticed that there is much knee trembling with you. I am not sure this papist thing is that deep within you. Sometimes I wonder why you converted in the first place. I don't think it had much to do an enthusiastic devotion to the Holy See."

"I do know that somewhere inside you there is a true romantic: any decent nonconformist Welshman who gives all his children Scottish Jacobite names has got to be a bit loopy in the romantic department.

However, in the end, dear fella, you are pretty ambitious and I judge, in the right circumstances, can be ruthless, too. You are determined to get your own way, and one of your greatest weapons, and you know it, is that most people underestimate you."

William knew that Brendan liked him, and his judgments were therefore particularly important to him. As Father Brendan left, his parting shot was, "I know that Lipman has to go after today, but he is the victim not the perpetrator. The system has truly stuffed him; it will probably do to you in the end." As he walked through the door his last comment was: "Don't be fooled by their gentlemanly ways. My countryman will tell you that these posh English scoundrels can be more ruthless than the feckin Gestapo. The bloody English just crush you very politely but no less callously for that. Watch what they have done and will do to John Lipman. Goodnight, dear Will." With that the elderly priest walked out, got into his beaten-up jalopy, and meandered his way home.

Of course, William knew, Brendan was right about John Lipman. By the end of term Jonathan Carpenter had agreed to 'let Lipman go'. A compromise agreement was arranged and the Lipmans soon departed.

It was a very nasty business which was fully reflected in the governors' meeting that had finally brought matters to a close.

He wasn't convinced by whatever deeper meaning Father Brendan might discern from these events. In the end John Lipman had been the orchestrator of his own downfall. William was not displeased that Lipman was going.

From William's point of view this was the removal of a serious impediment to his plans. If that meant that he possessed an innate ruthlessness, perhaps it was so.

The trouble was that William liked always to appear virtuous. He was not entirely comfortable with what appeared to be his leading role in the destruction of someone else. This was something that seriously troubled his conscience.

However, it wasn't just John Lipman and his family who had, from the perspective of some of the governors, been humbled. Gerald Grimes and Margaret McKenzie had both been badly wrong-footed by William Jones, someone they had once held in utter contempt but now increasingly viewed as dangerous as well as obnoxious. Even Mrs McKenzie was forced to admit to her husband Roland, "My basic opinion of William Jones will never change but I have to admit that he is a tougher nut than I imagined. We have got to be more subtle in future."

If Grimes and McKenzie had been William's enemies they were now doubly so. Once having viewed William as something of a namby-pamby walkover, he was at least now regarded with a smidgen of respect.

Yet this new judgment and what they considered was the humiliating denouement that had just taken place meant that in future battles they could not afford to make the same mistakes again.

Gerald Grimes and Margaret McKenzie had simply resolved, although at this stage not openly acknowledged, that the only possible solution was to utterly destroy Jones. The longer he remained at Parkies, the less there would be to retrieve of the traditional prep school they believed St Dogmael's was and should be again. They no longer believed that this could be done without using every weapon available to them. They ceased to care how that was achieved, only that it was done and quickly. They would not rest until this had been achieved.

Chapter Fifteen

FEET UNDER THE TABLE

William and Mary had thus passed their first anniversary at Parkies. Now that both de Vere and Lipman had disappeared or were about to do so, it did seem that their situation was yet more improved. William was still very conscious that he was not exactly popular with many of the governors.

At this stage he had no real notion how he was truly loathed. He was now really excited about the imminent arrival of Brian Varga. He felt that at last he had someone who could share his burden. This added greatly to his sense of optimism.

Jonathan Carpenter and Thomas Brown both thought that Lipman's removal was absolutely necessary and further considered that it might even end up being of long-term benefit to the school, although they were also concerned that Parkies was losing a fine teacher.

Only Brendan O'Rourke both recognised the necessity but truly regretted the obvious damage this had done to both John and Karen Lipman. He thought, too, that the whole farrago had done some harm to William and Mary as well.

Father Brendan liked John Lipman. He enjoyed his dry humour

and his talent for mimicking others. He never told William but one of John's best was of him. He entirely captured the William Jones mix of apologetic self-effacement and rather preachy high-mindedness.

In different circumstances he thought they might even have been friends. They had, he considered, much in common. In a strange way they were both idealists. Their ideals were different and often diametrically opposed. The fact that they had them gave them both a basic integrity.

He was sure that John Lipman was the victim and that should be financially recognised. It was he more than any other who pushed Jonathan into providing a generous settlement. To be fair, Jonathan did not need much pushing: he thought much the same as Father O'Rourke.

Lord Castle was, however, vitriolic; William imagined that if he could bring back the stocks he would do so. "The man is a total bounder: he has let us all down. To think we might even have appointed him headmaster," he angrily asserted. "I have just been talking to Lancelot: he cannot understand what possessed him to behave as he has. Lancelot's view is that he deserves nothing."

The fantasy and malice we are all capable of are mind-boggling, reflected William. Lancelot Waters had the lion's share of the culpability for what had happened to the Lipman family. Now he was quite happy to throw them under the nearest bus. That conversation he had had with Brendan O'Rourke after Prize-Giving came into his mind. It didn't fill him with much confidence for his own future prospects. He started to wonder again whether Alan's bleak analysis of his future situation was possibly correct after all.

That summer the Lipman family decamped from their school flat to a little house they had recently acquired in the enchanting resort of Southwold. At least William could walk past that pretty cottage without fearing a confrontation. This was some small consolation.

De Vere had also disappeared and was soon to be working at the Craven Preparatory School in Cambridgeshire. His parting gift, if that was the correct phrase, was to assiduously put about the same story Grimes was to promote in the following governors' meeting.

This was that John Lipman had been deliberately entrapped by the devious and ambitious Jones. He suggested that somehow Lipman's unfortunate behaviour was occasioned by a campaign of intimidation, fabrication, and misinformation.

This narrative suggested that Jones had systematically invented the story of John Lipman's drinking problems, by so doing ironically ensuring that the extra stress engendered by this calumny ended up by driving a desperate Lipman into the arms of the same demon drink that Jones had insinuated he was in thrall to in the first place. This version of events became the convenient gospel truth in the minds of Gerald Grimes and Margaret McKenzie and in many of the drawing rooms the latter frequented. William could do nothing to counter this, despite feeling very hurt when he first heard of what was being said just before the end of term. It was Father O'Rourke who later commented, "The worst fandango of malice, mendacity and imaginative fiction I have ever heard."

The trouble was that quite a few ingenuous, credulous, dupable people unfortunately believed it. Even if they didn't it was a particularly useful weapon. As such it did a great deal of harm to William's reputation. "I suppose," William hopefully commented, "it rather depends whether they like me, doesn't it?"

That was only partly true. Human nature often prefers to believe the worst of others. It was patently obvious that William needed to get rid of John Lipman. The fact that this was ultimately achieved fed into this conspiracy. If William had a plan – which he didn't – Lipman had fallen into every elephant trap that had ever been prepared.

The fact all this was a tissue of fanciful nonsense in the end probably didn't really matter. Ironically, William's stock rose amongst some for probably the wrong reasons. He would not be challenged for some time quite so directly again.

One evening during the summer holidays whilst he was musing about all this, William had a surprise telephone call from Father Sean O'Connor, his former parish priest in London. His message was a sad one. He reported the unexpected death, at least to William, of Lucy Thornley.

She had served in his old school St Oliver Plunkett's for over thirty years and latterly as William's secretary and bursar. She had also become a very loyal and good friend. When the diocese had decided to sell the school, Mrs Thornley was not part of the arrangement between the diocese and the new owners. She was therefore offered retirement.

No thanks were offered for her lifetime of service whatsoever. It was as though Father Sean felt she was simply thrown out like an old carpet. What no one knew of course was that she was already gravely ill.

Lucy was not someone to make a fuss and had left without a word. She was not a Catholic and not being so perhaps would not have expected any recognition for all those years of loyal service.

Father Sean didn't believe that should be the case and had asked the bishop if she be given a Papal Benemerenti medal. This was the most modest award he could award for services to the Church.

His request was, however, simply ignored. A few months later Lucy sadly died. Father Sean was really very upset about this. "You know, William, there are times when the lack of generosity and the basic human decency of the hierarchy is mind-boggling. I am sometimes embarrassed to be a priest. I often feel some of the Bishops just use people, then discard them as they did with poor Lucy."

As was his wont, this humorous priest could rarely resist a funny story even when it occurred in melancholy circumstances. He brought William up to speed on the subsequent sad sale of the school. "When these Americans took over St Oliver Plunkett's – now called, by the way, the North London International Independent College – their boss arrived in his posh, top-of-the-range BMW for a meeting with all the parents. I knew it was going to be difficult and I wasn't looking forward to chairing it.

"I told this smooth, horribly insincere, Armani-suited individual that he needed to reassure the Catholic parents that he would respect the right for their children to continue to receive Catholic RE. You remember, Will, we used the Veritas RE programme.

"To reassure the Catholic parents I persuaded him to allow this to still be used and then coached him to use the right words so as to provide some comfort for them.

"The meeting started with this fellow explaining that he was just a simple schoolteacher who merely wanted to do the best he could for all their children. His smooth, counterfeit appearance and weasel words, together with his expensive car, rather gave the lie to that assertion.

"You might remember Mrs Murphy. She asked precisely this key question about the Veritas scheme at the meeting. Amazingly he replied that he didn't know what she was talking about." Father Sean simply couldn't understand why the diocese had allowed itself to be conned by this obvious charlatan. In his heart he would rather the school had been closed than prostituted in this way."

Father Sean then explained how the diocese had sent this elderly Monsignor to represent the diocese. "More of a bloody posh, clerical stool-pigeon, I think. After Mrs Murphy's question and the American's wholly inadequate response the parents were directing their ire onto him. The atmosphere was thick with a palpable almost electric sense of imminent detonation. The Monsignor looked for a moment positively relieved. He relaxed back into his seat and was obviously pretty happy about this. He thought mistakenly that he might even escape now the fire was being directed elsewhere."

Then Father Sean described what happened next. "The head of our local primary school, Francis Kelly, then stood up and angrily announced that it was absolutely clear this lot were just a group of money-grabbing shysters. He addressed the Monsignor directly and asked him what the hell was the diocese doing selling the future of 100 Catholic children to people who were certainly not Catholic nor probably even Christian? It was, William, as though he had lobbed a proverbial grenade into the meeting."

By this time Father Sean was in full flow. "The old Monsignor looked as though he had swallowed his glasses. His face shaded to much the same colour as the magnolia paint of the walls of the school hall. The old fellow's Adam's apple started to do a St. Vitus' dance. I thought he might have a seizure. I even felt a bit sorry for him."

Father Sean continued with growing pleasure. "The hall then erupted into glorious chaos with all the parents shouting, "We want the Cardinal!" again and again. Later, Jimmy Quinn, young Patrick's granddaddy, sent a leather purse to him with thirty silver shillings in it. I tell you they were all bloody furious about that at Archbishop's House." Father Sean left the best bit to the end. "When we escaped from the hall, barely avoiding being lynched that old Monsignor turned to me and said in his best establishment English voice, "It didn't go too badly, don't you think, Sean?" I had difficulty not laughing out loud. Do you know, Will, I was really proud of those people in the hall, but intensely ashamed of Church functionaries that had brought it about." He then added, "How are we priests supposed to preach the Gospel when the bastards in charge treat the faithful like shit?"

William then told the priest the essence of his experiences of the previous year. He couldn't see the priest's face but if he had he imagined he would have been slack-mouthed with amazement. Father Sean's Irish seminary and London parish had not really prepared him for some of the goings-on in swanky English Suffolk.

"Bloody hell, Will, I don't know how you have survived. I told you what I thought it would be like. I never, though, imagined it would be quite as challenging as this. It sounds like a snooty English *Peyton Place*." He then added, and William was not sure whether it was an afterthought plea or a rescue mission, "There is a primary school headship going up here, if you fancy coming back?" A tempting idea, but not a runner, at least not yet, thought William.

Despite the unsettling nature of his chat with Father Sean, William believed that it seemed possible he and Mary might be becoming more accepted in what Sean so aptly described as Peyton Place. For a time they were even invited to various social functions at some of the grander local residences.

In later years they were inclined to politely decline such inducements. There was a charity luncheon at Ashley Park that October. The great and the good of the county were all there. Because it was a luncheon not a dinner, less important and significant families, and those persons not fully acceptable in politer society were also invited.

This meant that even the Joneses and the Grimes family were included. The Earl of Faversham's infant four-year-old granddaughter Persephone, usually called Percy, was the youngest of Viscount and Viscountess Grey's four children.

She had rather taken a shine to the eight-year-old Charlie who had accompanied them. She insisted on sitting with the Jones family. Not, it has to be said, a popular decision with her mother, evidenced by the rather stony look of stern disapproval imprinted on Lady Grey's prim, censorious face.

After a time Percy asked Charlie to accompany her to the Nursery. William thought he had better escort the children. When they arrived there her two elder brothers were watching a video. The last person they wanted to meet was their headmaster.

William made his embarrassed apologies and walked back to the ballroom with the two children. On the way they passed the exotically dressed Earl sporting as usual a strange medley of Indian and Western attire. The elderly earl peered closely at William and enquired pre-emptively, "Who are you?" William was about to explain when the peer interjected. "Oh you must be the new nanny." He then toddled off down the corridor. William thought he might be many things, but nanny was unlikely. He wasn't even wearing a skirt!"

They were even invited on a few occasions to dinner at some of the posher or perhaps more accurately often rather arriviste residences. William hated these occasions. Firstly he had to squeeze into his rather ill-fitting, elderly dinner suit.

You couldn't even wear ready-made tied bows which were seen as totally *de rigueur*. William found it nearly impossible to tie with his very clumsy all-thumbs and no-fingers hands.

Worse, the bow always looked a dog's breakfast often at a thirty-degree angle to his collar. Secondly he had to attempt polite conversation with people he often found quirky, pretentious, and certainly incomprehensible. Most of what they were interested in bored him profoundly.

He instinctively realised of course that they were equally bored by him. Chatting about the latest county scandal, the many limitations of Mrs Thatcher, the rise in house prices and of course, most importantly, the remarkable achievements of their offspring seemed to him the equivalent of watching grass grow.

William was not good at hiding his tedium. It also reinforced in his mind his status as an outsider. He had in recent years secretly become rather an admirer of Mrs Thatcher. At the very least, he thought, she was impressively courageous. The venom with which she was regarded by virtually the whole county set rather perplexed him.

He could understand his friend Alan's hostile view. He had a genuine ideological objection to all she stood for. However, most of the venom he heard came from those who were basking in a prosperity which was largely the result of her policies.

One lunchtime he was chatting to Thomas Brown who was no great fan of any Tory, least of all Thatcher. His comment was very enlightening. "I dislike this woman because of the brutal effects of some her policies. I thought her treatment of the miners was appalling. These people have a different perspective. Not only is she not of their class, but she also refuses to go along with many of their prejudices. She is so obviously a rather prissy, middle-class housewife. That, in my opinion, is the real source of their hatred. It is essentially simple snobbery!"

William also knew that after a few drinks, he was inclined to be indiscreet. He even wondered whether that was the main reason for the invitations. He was always on tenterhooks should he say something he shouldn't. William knew that he found it almost impossible to hide his emotions as well as an intemperate, foolish inclination to spill the beans. He enjoyed telling what he hoped were amusing stories. Often he imagined them to be rather charmingly self-deprecating.

When he shared some of what he considered were funny accounts of his former life, it probably confirmed in the minds of some his unsuitability for his present role. Frequently he did often say exactly what he shouldn't: this was especially to Mary's chagrin and embarrassment.

Mary loathed the requirement on so many occasions to 'withdraw'. This antediluvian tradition was still maintained in some houses in the vicinity. Some saw it as the mark of distinction and some kind of peculiar elite, social ritual. Mary regarded it simply as pretentious and probably in reality the mark of the flaunting parvenu. She was offended, too, by the assumption that the womenfolk were only good to chat about inconsequential issues, whilst the important and interesting questions were entirely the domain of the men.

At one house, the home of a somewhat notorious, sexually liberated, trendy, avant-garde couple, William and Mary sat down for dinner, with a lasciviously posed oil painting of the naked hostess hung on the wall at the head of the table. The portrait left absolutely nothing to the imagination. William found that it was exceedingly difficult to keep focussed on the conversation or indeed on the now fully clothed hostess sitting opposite him. She was a very beautiful and rather sexy lady.

All William's petit bourgeois inhibitions were fully exposed. He didn't know either where to look or what to say. He was also very embarrassed to discover that he found the picture rather alluring. He suspected that he even blushed when he looked at it. The hostess seemed hugely amused by his confusion.

Mary dealt with this situation with far more panache. In her mind the painting, the coy, malicious hostess and the general air of pretend licentiousness was just a silly game intended to embarrass and discombobulate. It should therefore be treated with contempt. As they left she remarked to this somewhat smirking lady, "What nice legs you used to have." This comment was not well received, as of course she intended. It was perhaps the reason for no further invitations!

Early in the following term he visited Eton College. It was a place which at first he couldn't quite eschew an initial aversion. He swiftly overcame these prejudices. Eton wasn't so much a public school; it quite literally was **the school.** The more he visited, he came to slowly realise what an extraordinary place it was. In the end he finally understood it was quite simply the finest school he knew.

It was of course the establishment personified. Precisely because of that it didn't need to prove anything as so many other replica places needed to do. It was this that made it so special from William's perspective. The facilities were extraordinary. What other school, he reflected, was really an entire town? The middle of the high street was the venue for daily pupil tutorials, for example.

There was an atmosphere of learning and a kind of discreet confidence about the place. Different, in every respect, from the more brittle swagger he often perceived in less august establishments.

William secured an interview with the then headmaster. This took place in his huge study. He thought its size would not have disgraced Mussolini. 'Palatial' hardly described it. The walls were covered with fine portraits and the furniture was all discreetly antique. The head was an extraordinarily kind, informal man who immediately put him at his ease.

This was partly achieved in offering tea made by him in his own little kitchenette secretly hidden at the end of the room. "What is it like in Suffolk?" he enquired. "It is rather like being the second footman." "No, you have it all wrong," came the amused response. "You are the curate."

That very wise insight, William reflected, was exactly his real position. He was at the very bottom of what could be remotely considered respectable, a notch up from the servant class. It sometimes felt that the world he had inadvertently strayed into was straight out of the novels of Jane Austen.

There were far fewer aristocratic families with children in the school. William had never even met someone titled before his sojourn at Parkies. To be honest there weren't too many of those around Newport or Usk or indeed at his training college. It was probably true that he had most of the prejudices one might expect from a person of his modest background. He once joked to Mary, "The trouble is I don't know whether to creep around them or shoot them."

Lord and Lady Gervase Tremane, amongst the most significant of Catholic aristocratic families, were booked into lunch one day. They were going to have a look around with a view to possibly sending their two boys to Parkies. William and Mary were frankly terrified by the prospect. This, he thought, might be the ultimate test of social acceptability. As this had all been arranged by Lancelot Waters, it probably was! William and Mary feared, indeed eventually became convinced, that they would fail the test.

As it turned out they were some of the most delightful people they met during their whole time in the school. Completely open and unpretentious, they seemed to appreciate instinctively the Joneses' anxieties and easily assuaged them.

After lunch William took them on a tour of the school. As they walked through the gardens, the ancient school gardener Bert was assiduously weeding one of his flower beds. As soon as the two men approached he turned to William, touched his forelock, and said, "Afternoon, headmaster." Lord Tremane laughed uproariously and then commented, "You know William, my buggers don't do that."

Years later, William and Mary were invited to lunch at the rather imposing Tremane country house. After the meal they were taken to the family archive and were shown the death warrant of one of Lord Tremane's ancestors. Gervase with a twinkle in his eye laughingly commented, "I play golf every day with a successor of one of those fellows who signed this warrant. He is actually a very good chap but I never cease to remind him of it." This man had a great sense of humour and proportion that wasn't always evident in some of the other Parkies parents. Hoorah for the real toffs, William thought, as they drove home after that lunch.

Their sons arrived the following term and they were absolutely delightful. Mary's observation said it all: "If you are at the top of the tree, you don't need to put others down." This was clearly absolutely true: most of the problem parents were amongst what Brian Varga was to describe as the 'old vicarage brigade'.

People who sometimes did not possess the secure pose and innate sense of right behaviour which to those like the Tremanes seemed to come so naturally. This, William supposed, was because they were still climbing the greasy pole and therefore had to kick hard at those following them too closely behind.

William often reflected on the difference between Suffolk parents and those in North London. Status in London was almost entirely related to wealth and the ostentatious displays of it. If you had money, you flaunted it. In Suffolk it was different: you could arrive in the most beaten-up wreck of a car and you could still belong to one of the most prestigious and respected families in the county.

It was all much more nuanced and subtle. Ultimately, it still came down to money, he supposed. However, issues of family lineage, whether you were at school at Eton or at Haverhill or, worse still, the local comprehensive, were important. As was which university you attended and even which adjectives you preferred to use. They all came into play. Often, when describing his life and the people he was associated with here to his old friends, it often seemed as though he was trying to elicit from them an understanding of Louis XIV's court as though they were Frenchmen who had never left Nancy.

William was starting slowly to gain a slight insight into the gradations of the establishment world that few of his background were privileged or perhaps unfortunate enough to experience.

Alan Howarth spent a few days staying with them during the summer holidays. Alan still found it difficult to believe some of William's more extraordinary stories. He imagined his friend had massively exaggerated things for effect.

Despite himself he was fascinated, nevertheless. "Will," he commented in one of their many telephone conversations, "what you seem to have stumbled into is a curious fantasy of power and wannabe power that most people we know have no idea actually exists." Whilst all this still baffled and confused him, William's escapades confirmed for Alan the oddity and essential madness of his friend's new surroundings. "It's a bloody madhouse: are you sure it's not an annex to Colney Hatch Lunatic Asylum?" William laughingly replied, "No Alan, it is merely Northanger Abbey meets the Clockwork Orange."

One evening during that visit, the two men went down to Pakenham for a swift drink in The Fox. They had hoped that they would be able to do so without being noticed. Unfortunately, they bumped into Roland and Margaret McKenzie.

"Good evening, headmaster," Margaret McKenzie politely, if icily, greeted him. The look of aversion that overcame Mrs McKenzie's profligately made-up and pouty, petulant face entirely revealed what she actually felt. She was not particularly good at hiding her more intense feelings. Her intense focus was much more on Alan than William.

Both men were clad in jeans, sweatshirts, and trainers. Alan's grubby, beatnik appearance seemed to the McKenzies to be far more reprehensible. Worse, too, from both Margaret and Roland's perspective, the headmaster's friend was sporting a typical, disagreeable, social worker-type beard. The greatest outrage was emblazoned across his chest was the flanged image of Mrs Thatcher labelled 'Milk Snatcher', a souvenir of his 70s radicalism. Alan in a flash of recognition realised that McKenzie was the fellow he remembered in the County Court all those years before.

Roland McKenzie's face exhibited a sneer of disgust, which even with his gift for dissemination he could not entirely hide. He might not much care for the Iron Lady himself. Indeed he rather hoped that the current plots to remove her that were rumoured to be maturing succeeded. She was infinitely better than the lefty, long-haired, pot-smoking, pseudo-intellectual clodhopper he judged this fellow to be.

This creature with the beard reminded Roland of all that was worst about those ghastly, entitled social workers and professional do-gooders who polluted so much of his professional life.

When he bought his Suffolk manor house he had hoped that in this expensively manicured Suffolk village one could escape from such ghastly proles. This was, after all, his bolt-hole from London's pandemonium into the seductiveness of this exquisite piece of manicured rural England.

Even here he could not dodge the very image of the hoi polloi swaggering proprietorially along their lanes. That the headmaster of St Dogmael's, his own son's preparatory school, was associated with this outrageous, coarse lowlife was truly appalling and wholly intolerable.

To cap it all, this cove standing next to Jones was staring at him in the most direct, insolent, and impertinent way. Alan, having recognised Roland McKenzie, was appraising the barrister on his home turf. He didn't much care for what he saw. Roland was attired in the uniform: elitist country-wear, well-cut corduroy trousers, a Barbour jumper over a check shirt, immaculately polished brown brogues, all set off with obligatory peaked cap.

As Alan observed him he thought that there was something slightly shifty about his appearance. Alan considered that the get-up suggested something fake and insincere. This man was trying too hard, he thought.

Roland McKenzie was pretending a preening, fabricated, false illusion of rural refinement and class. It was, he thought, an artifice designed to shroud the truth of what Alan knew were McKenzie's money-grubbing and dissolute motivations.

He couldn't hold Alan's gaze and his obvious dislike and distaste of him were openly emblazoned all over his chubby features. Alan enjoyed the impression that his presence was making Roland McKenzie feel extremely uncomfortable. Alan concluded that his initial judgment of him, when he had seen him at Watford Crown Court, was wholly accurate.

For the McKenzies this incident confirmed, if any confirmation was really necessary, that Jones and all his obnoxious plebeian hangers-on were so removed from what they saw as acceptable in a schoolmaster functionary, he must go. The sooner the better!

When William and Alan returned to Parkies Alan was rather quiet and thoughtful. "It was silly of me to go around sporting this provocative tee shirt. I can sometimes behave like a class war blockhead."

He then turned to his friend and, with his customary intense stare and a particularly anxious expression, stated, "Those people are really dangerous, Will." "I don't think so," William light-heartedly responded. "The McKenzies are just slightly ridiculous, that is all. She is simply a parvenu social climber I don't think many people take her seriously."

Alan then countered, "The trouble with you, old friend, is you don't see them for what they are. Of course they are ridiculous, but I saw the way that woman looked at you: it was pure, unadulterated poison. At the very least she is desperate to hurt you even if she does not in the end succeed. Not that she liked me any better, but they can't touch me, thank God. Please, old chum, make sure they don't touch you either."

Alan knew his friend would not listen. He sometimes wondered what planet he had landed on. William had this naive assumption that everyone was fundamentally well motivated, or sometimes, like the McKenzies, just silly.

He simply couldn't understand real malice. He seemed never to see nastiness even when it stared him in the face. If he had experienced the vicious infighting in Alan's local Labour Party he would know exactly how people could behave. It wasn't very pretty.

William simply didn't seem to understand this political imperative. It was not a good idea, Alan reflected, to so underestimate poisonous and vindictive people like this. "Remember you have a family to protect," was his final comment.

Alan's observations were in the end to be fully vindicated. Yet at this stage William seemed untouchable. It was remarkable that so much had been achieved in little over a year. Higher numbers, better-paid staff, coeducation, and even some minor improvements to classrooms and dormitories. William was trying much the same approach as he had once employed in London. Improvements on the cheap.

After the incidents at Prize-Giving at the end of the summer term the governors had decided inevitably, in some cases reluctantly, to finally dismiss John Lipman. He was given a generous payout, financed in the main by Jonathan Carpenter, as suggested by Father Brendan.

The unsavoury nature of the debate that had preceded this decision had fully drawn the battle lines for future confrontations. Gerald Grimes suggested that Lipman had been treated grossly unfairly. He had even hinted at the rumour, as well as assiduously spreading it, that Lipman's demise was the result of the malice and Machiavellian plotting of William Jones.

Mrs McKenzie had heartily disliked the often blunt and socially awkward Lipman. She detested Jones much, much more and wholeheartedly concurred with Grimes, making sure that she, too, spun the same story to her drawing room acquaintances.

This was especially so after the incident in Pakenham. When they had returned from meeting the detestable Jones and his even more repulsive friend, Roland McKenzie was quiet and thoughtful. He hadn't told Margaret but he had also recognised Alan Howarth.

He remembered a few years before when this man had challenged him in the most aggressive and offensive manner after a case in Watford Crown Court. His manner was then extremely and intolerably insolent. He had suggested that somehow Roland was to blame when one of his cases hadn't gone well. As a senior QC, this was something Roland was not used to or in any way appreciated.

This man had such distinctive, rat-like features, as well as the impenetrable cloak of the proletarian class warrior which made him entirely unforgettable. Roland McKenzie simply couldn't understand what he was doing with Jones.

It made no sense in his mind for such an unpleasant desperado to have any kind of relationship with any respectable prep school headmaster. He thus decided that he would use his contacts to try and discover the precise nature of that association.

The really important event of that September was the arrival of the girls. It was strange to see these children parading around in their Black Watch kilts, a uniform design suggested by Mary. Whilst William didn't pretend he had had a sudden conversion to the virtues of coeducation, he had to admit that their appearance had a softening influence on the boys. It was an observation he kept to himself; even Mary would have been annoyed to have coeducation justified in such patronising, male-centred terms.

Nevertheless the core motive for doing this, he accepted, was financial. So many schools pretended otherwise but at least William didn't make up fanciful nonsense about a sudden conversion to its virtues. Initially most of these girls at this stage appeared in the pre-prep. In the first term there were only three female boarders.

However, this did provide an opportunity to improve all the existing dormitories. A rudimentary heating system was installed. Carpets were laid, pictures appeared on the walls, and curtains in the windows.

A lot of pastel colours chosen by Mary replaced the institutional cream of the dormitories. Even the old hospital beds were painted brighter shades. James Waters was given the boys' housemaster's job. He had a real talent for relating to boys. To balance his rather blokey approach, William appointed the new RE and junior English teacher as his deputy.

This chap, Evelyn Morley, was a gentle, warm, profoundly religious fellow who William believed would have a natural affinity with the more sensitive and vulnerable boys. The girls were housed in an attractive room next to William and Mary's flat. Until numbers grew, William and Mary would look after them.

William's plan was to convert the old stables into a self-contained girls' boarding house when numbers justified and funds could be found. The immediate consequence of all these changes and improvements was a significant increase in boarding numbers. It was clear that the girl boarders would soon outgrow their very limited accommodation.

William and Mary had supposed that their family was complete. Mary would have loved a daughter, but as one didn't appear she had over time reluctantly accepted this. Later in the spring term Mary announced that she was pregnant. This was a huge surprise to both of them, but nevertheless an exciting prospect.

William remembered that when they were first married and Mary was expecting their first child, who turned out to be Francis Gethin, his father had announced at the supper table that he did not expect a grandson. "After all," he opined, "the sex of the child is always determined by the stronger partner. Mary obviously wears the trousers, so your baby will be a girl". Three boys appeared in quick succession. Gethin was rather put out! As he said to Dilys after the birth of Charlie, the youngest of them, "William cannot even follow the basic gender rules: he seems to have even in this a tendency to be bloody-minded."

The other thought that amused William and Mary was the tongue-in-cheek observations of an old Catholic friend. "Being a Catholic schoolmaster means you must have four children to be above suspicion." 'Suspicion of what?" William and Mary laughingly enquired. Now of course they were likely soon to find out!

Chapter Sixteen

RUSSIAN ADVENTURES

The new deputy head, Brian Varga, arrived that September driving his new acquired Lada estate car. If nothing else, William thought this mode of transportation was a statement. This was not to be missed by a few of the more intransigent governors and parents.

He was accompanied by his Ukrainian partner, Ludmila. Brian, as expected, took a lot of the strain off William. He was efficient and organised and was able to develop systems that had quite eluded the more chaotic headmaster. Ludmila swiftly became a friend and helpmate to Mary. She was, William considered, an unusual wife for an English prep school master – exotic in looks, jet-black hair, shapely figure and an exquisite taste in clothes. She did not dress expensively but she had a talent for making modestly priced clothes look like a million dollars.

Her Jewish roots were firmly affiliated to what in the Soviet Union approximated to a kind of aristocracy. Her grandfather was the youngest general shot in Stalin's purges of the 1930s.

This was a fact that had rather, albeit temporarily, lowered their status, and for a few years meant they were actively persecuted.

Unbeknown to the Joneses, Ludmila still retained family and wider links with a few lesser figures within the floundering Soviet elite.

For William in many ways Brian became a surrogate for his more distant friend Alan. They, he reflected, had much in common. William and Brian were, Father O'Rourke observed, rather similar characters: "two peas in the same pod," he commented after the first staff social of the autumn term. William thought that Brian was one of the few people he knew who really seemed to understand what was going on in the independent school world or indeed in society beyond.

Neither of them accepted the conventional wisdom that permeated the thinking of most of their contemporaries. This was because one way or another they were outsiders looking in, rather than being fully immersed in the system.

Both men were not especially sanguine about the future of boarding as it currently stood. Despite a temporary improvement in St Dogmael's situation it was getting more difficult to attract children as boarders. It was clear that two things were happening simultaneously.

Firstly, fewer, and fewer children arrived to board at seven or eight. The second related phenomenon was that less children came from overseas or, more critically, for Parkies, from London or the armed forces. The future therefore seemed to be in persuading parents of day children to allow their offspring to convert to boarders later on. It was essential therefore to make the experience of boarding a really enjoyable one.

That required investment in more committed staff and an improved ambiance, as well as better facilities. They also needed to provide lots of enjoyable evening activities. Cynically Brian once commented, "We really should be running an amusement park, rather than a school." Yet both men understood that precisely what was needed. "Alton Towers in Suffolk," Brian commented in a dry, tongue-in-cheek way.

What also brought them together was a mutual fascination by the unfolding developments in Eastern Europe. William had organised in his previous school two trips to the Soviet Union so he shared Brian's interest, although not his depth of knowledge.

Ludmila was obviously very worried, as well as being rather excited by the extraordinary events of that autumn. She had a much more realistic feel for what was really going on than, both men believed, most Western commentators.

She feared that this presaged chaos and dissolution rather than the democratic nirvana that was then generally assumed in the West. When one BBC commentator was spouting some particularly ridiculous, optimistic nonsense, Ludmila was so irritated that she threw her shoe at the television. Much, it has to be said, to both Brian and William's amusement.

She didn't care for Gorbachev. She thought he was a dangerous chancer. This was not a popular view in England at the time so she kept it to herself and developed a truly spectacular ability to manage to say nothing whilst appearing to say everything when asked about the situation in her homeland.

Within weeks the Berlin Wall was down and the various Communist regimes of Central and Eastern Europe had clearly collapsed or were about to. What Ludmila feared most of all was the likely economic meltdown that would follow. In this, too, she was proved to be entirely prescient.

Early in the spring term of 1990, Brian approached William with an astonishing proposal. Ludmila's mother was a senior teacher at the technical school in her home city of Donetsk. She had suggested an exchange of pupils that summer between Parkies and the Donetsk Secondary School 48. This all seemed a very unrealistic, fantastical pipe dream.

Then out of the blue an official letter arrived from Donetsk proposing exactly such an arrangement. Clearly Ludmila's family had lost nothing of their former influence. William promised Brian and Ludmila that he would at least put the proposal to the governors at their next meeting. He emphasised, however, that there was little chance of it being agreed. William put this, as his promised, to the board of governors at the next meeting. He assumed the suggestion would be immediately vetoed or even worse laughed out of court. He also imagined that most of the governors would think he was going entirely loopy.

Others than those who thought he had already, Mrs McKenzie and Gerald Grimes were predictably entirely opposed to the idea. "Never heard of such a load of bloody nonsense. No surprise to me that Jones and that new bloke Varga have finally gone off their heads," commented Grimes when he talked to Margaret McKenzie before the meeting. Both were therefore implacably opposed to the proposal. Gerald Grimes led the opposition, enthusiastically endorsed by Margaret McKenzie who was vigorously nodding her head in support.

To be fair they both argued that they could see no way that such an exchange could possibly benefit St Dogmael's. Even William had to concede that they had a point. This looked like the end of this. William was about to shrug his shoulders in resignation when he noticed to his surprise that the suggestion had the warm backing from a very unlikely source.

Lord Robert Castle, unbeknown to William or indeed Brian, had a sister who had married a Russian, back at the very end of the war. His brother-in-law Sasha had been a prisoner of war. He had been forced into slave labour and finally to fight for the Germans when they had occupied his hometown of Belgorod in 1941. They had met on the Castle family estate at Haddon where his sister Clementine was working as a Land Girl and he was labouring as a prisoner of war.

They had fallen in love. At the end of the war Sasha had barely avoided being sent back to one of Stalin's gulags or worse. The couple were fortunate and for a few years they had lain low, therefore escaping the general round-up of anti-Stalinist Russians resident in Britain following Germany's surrender. Sasha didn't much care for Stalin. He hated the oppressive terrorism that he had brought to his beloved country. He still remained an enthusiastic, if rather naive, Communist.

After Stalin's death both Sasha and his wife Clementine returned to the USSR. Two decades later the Honourable Clementine Volkov after the death of her husband returned home to Suffolk. "Amazing," Brian commented when William related this story to him. "Who would have guessed that that curmudgeonly old toff has a Commie sister."

Lord Castle yearned for the whole Soviet authoritarian system to crumble. He had served in the Guards Armoured Division in Normandy and later in the terrible bloody push into Germany. He had seen harrowing things. He had for example been one of the first British officers into Belsen. It had left him with an intense dislike of all authoritarianism, firstly the Nazis and later the Communists.

They both summarised everything he detested and loathed. It was certainly true: Lord Robert had entirely disapproved of Sasha. He tried very hard to stop him marrying his sister. He thought of him as an impractical fantasist. He admired his principles however misguided he considered them to be and felt sorry for his awful situation.

He remembered, too, how many of his friends in Oxford in the 1930s had been so attracted to these soviet socialist ideals, many of whom had followed him into the Army and had eventually paid the ultimate price. For all his faults the old peer disliked bullies and tyrants. These fat, pig-faced fellows who stood on these various fancy podiums pretentiously directing their massed ranks of thuggy leathernecks rather reminded him in more recent times of the atrocious Grimes.

This was yet another reason to oppose any suggestion Grimes made. His elderly sister still lived with him in Haddon Park. Her husband Sasha was now long deceased. She, however, was still very much alive and still retained elements of her former romantic Russian Communist enthusiasms. This one wouldn't have vaguely imagined seeing her totter round the Haddon estate in her garb of headscarf, tartan skirt, and green wellies.

For quite different reasons both Prior Anselm and Father O'Rourke favoured the proposal. Both men were genuinely excited by the turn of events of that autumn. Prior Anselm saw it as the resurrection of Christian Europe, a portent of a new age of a glorious and long-delayed religious revival. Parkies could be, he visualised in moments of extreme nonsensical fantasy, the progenitor of a new Christian eastern crusade. When he expanded on these thoughts at the meeting, even the likes of Thomas Brown and Jonathan Carpenter shuffled in their seats rather uncomfortably.

Mrs McKenzie's expression was one of staggering incredulity. She obviously thought the old boy had finally gone off his head. For once even Jonathan and Thomas were inclined to agree with her. Gerald Grimes crossed his arms in a pose of belligerent boredom. As the old monk got more and more enthused by his theme, his eyes were raised in his classical gesture of contempt.

Father O'Rourke more prosaically viewed it as all about the hopeful if not very likely restoration of the rights of the poor, oppressed people of Eastern Europe. "So typical of these bloody milksop priests to rabbit on about freedom," later observed the cynical Gerald Grimes.

For all Brendan's kindly ways he truly hated and detested injustice and political persecution. Mary suspected lurking within him somewhere was a secret Fenian. Imperialism in any form was pretty obnoxious in Brendan's opinion.

Jonathan thought the whole notion of this school exchange was entirely potty. However, it was going to cost little and was potentially a great PR coup. It might even convince a few that St Dogmael's was finally becoming reasonably progressive. That in itself would be a first!

Perhaps most of all it would keep William happy. He recognised in his new man a certain Celtic volatility. He was, however, impressed with what he had achieved so far and at least for the moment he wanted to keep him on an emotional even keel. If that required this little Russian adventure, so be it!

So it all went ahead. Technically of course they were Ukrainians, but Donetsk was in that province's eastern marches. Ludmila explained that the people there spoke Russian and it was important to understand that was how they viewed themselves.

Ironically, too, from William's point of view, Donetsk owed its former prosperity to its steelworks which had been built back in 1869 by a Welshman called John Hughes. This seemed to make the whole venture even more appropriate and even rather blessed.

The fifteen children together with Irina Ludmila's formidable mother, another lady representing the local university, and a rather lugubrious fellow who claimed to be a local government official, were to arrive in mid-June.

Brian suspected he was in reality a functionary of the KGB. He was certainly very secretive, even furtive, and certainly not at all forthcoming. It amused William that Brian always referred to this secret malign organisation as the 'Kingston Gas Board'. He did not think that this humourless functionary would see the joke. It seemed, however, that Irina was a person of some influence. Even that could not secure her any air tickets.

Extraordinarily this party travelled by train all the way across Europe. This was a feat that would not have been possible literally weeks before. Their journey, it subsequently emerged, required a change of trains in Berlin.

They had to walk from Potsdamer Platz station across the old Berlin Wall, all carrying their little brown parcels and cardboard suitcases. They must have been amongst the first Russian schoolchildren ever to do so.

Then they entrained all the way to Calais crossing the Channel and finally arriving in London. They had no money and relied entirely on the food they brought with them. It was an extraordinarily brave, or perhaps also foolhardy thing to do. As most of the party were children of only eleven and twelve years of age it certainly displayed that grit the Russians were justly famous for.

They arrived at Victoria station on a typically rain-soaked English summer evening. They were laden with the remains of the food that had sustained them on this marathon journey, as well those roughly parcelled brown packages which contained numerous gifts. These were mainly of variations of highly coloured Russian wooden plates and spoons.

William and Brian escorted the group around the sights of London. They were assisted in this endeavour by the various London independent schools that William had known in his time at St Oliver Plunkett's. William had shamelessly called in old favours.

The Russian children were even given free accommodation in the dormitories of one of the leading London public schools. This must have been a culture shock. They probably only knew about such places from the pages of *Tom Brown's School Days*, if at all.

The group attended a West End show, the then incredibly popular *Starlight Express*. William watched the rather pinched faces of these wide-eyed Russian children. They had obviously never experienced anything like this before. They sat totally mesmerised by the experience. Given the fact they had just travelled hundreds of miles by train, the theme of the musical seemed absolutely appropriate.

The Honourable Clementine Volkov had persuaded her initially very reluctant brother to sponsor this. Given what they had been doing for the previous week, Brian wondered if they might even be just a touch 'over-railwayed'.

In complete contrast they were taken around Whitechapel on a 'Jack the Ripper' tour organised by another London independent school which Brian knew well. The run-down, litter-strewn streets of the East End were probably a useful contrast to the obvious prosperity of Kensington and Pall Mall where they spent most of the rest of their time.

William thought they had probably imagined the streets of London were paved with gold. Whitechapel gave them a different, perhaps more rounded, perspective. Whilst in the East End they were given a splendid kosher lunch in a Jewish soup kitchen. As most of the children were Jewish, this seemed especially appropriate.

On their second evening they caught a tube to Whitehall and attended a beating the retreat ceremony in Horse Guards. These tickets had been acquired and donated by Jonathan. Irina commented when they viewed the impressively colourful and beautifully drilled massed ranks of pipers parading into Horse Guards from The Mall that she had never before been to a military parade where there was no evidence of military hardware. She added, "That is why I like England so much: you love the pomp and the ridiculous uniforms, but the military strutting we are so used to is quite beyond you."

The most moving experience, from William's perspective, was when the group were taken shopping at a Tesco store in the Edgware Road. Irina was so overwhelmed and upset by the cornucopia of plenty she witnessed that Brian found her crying in one of the supermarket aisles: "I have never seen so much food, our shops contain virtually nothing," she wailed.

The local MP arranged for them to meet the then Minister of Education. They all trooped into Smith Square to have tea with this gentleman. The main purpose of the exercise seemed to be to allow him to have numerous photo opportunities with this group. Irina was not, however, impressed. "He reminds me too much of the apparatchiks in my own country." It was obvious that she found him as insincere, self-obsessed, and superficial as similar characters she had met in Russia.

Back in Suffolk the Russian students soon took an active part in the life of the school. They boarded with local families who, William hoped, would be a less traumatic experience for children who knew so little of boarding schools.

There was of course the additional problem that there was not a great deal of extra room. Most of them had passable English and being with English families massively and quickly improved their language skills. Quite quickly friendships developed. Some of them outlasted the exchange.

The Soviet boys enjoyed all the school activities. Their performance in athletics generally outshone their British hosts. Cricket was not quite so successful. All the Russian lads nevertheless made a gallant effort.

It was obvious and entirely to be expected that few had the remotest idea of the rules. They almost seemed to regard the game as another expression of weird English eccentricity.

Ludmila then unexpectedly discovered that she knew a middle-ranking official in the Soviet Embassy in London; William even wondered if the chap was a distant relative. In this period of perestroika the Embassy were very open to any suggestions of developing British contacts beyond London.

They had already organised an exhibition of Soviet paintings at one of the local country houses. Ludmila's proposal was therefore pushing at an open door. She suggested that whilst the Soviet children were at Parkies the deputy ambassador came as the special guest to Prize-Giving. Out of the blue, against all expectations the invitation was accepted. It was also arranged as a *quid pro quo* that two boys from the Soviet Embassy would be offered a free place at the school for the following term.

Lord Castle proffered an invitation on the evening of Prize-Giving to the deputy ambassador and his party to a formal dinner at Haddon Park without, it should be stressed, any trapdoors in evidence!

It was not just Lord Castle who immersed himself wholly into the experience. Many other parents got enthusiastically involved. Even the McKenzies were reluctantly persuaded to board one of the pupils in their house. Not an experience that they and this young lad especially enjoyed!

Thomas Brown invited all the Russian and English children and their hosts to a grand barbecue in his huge gardens. The Donetsk children all seemed to have lovely voices. Whilst there they gave an impromptu concert of Russian folk songs.

This was a magical moment when, for an instant, anything seemed possible. Out of the corner of his eye William noticed that Ludmila was quietly crying. Whether it was from joy or sadness he could not say. For this part of Suffolk at least the Cold War seemed finally over.

William together with the three Russian adult guests gathered for dinner with Jonathan and Celia Carpenter at Walton Hall. As he drove them up the long, beautifully manicured, tree-lined drive the dour official enquired whether this was a museum.

When they were welcomed at the front door by Jonathan's butler he seemed to think he was some kind of state official. The poor chap was much disconcerted and slightly offended by this suggestion.

They sat drinking wine in the beautiful, book-lined library overlooking the spectacular formal terraces and gardens of the Walton

Estate. Irina thought she was in a place that she could only previously have imagined in the novels of Austen, Trollope, Wodehouse, and E. M. Forster, some of the few English authors that were then approved in the Soviet Union.

She said to Jonathan, "I don't know why but I keep expecting Mr Darcy to ride up the drive." He replied rather modestly, "I think my house is more Bennet than Darcy." Irina wasn't sure she agreed.

Jonathan with his typical generosity asked the three whether they had any personal computers in Donetsk. When they replied that they did not, he then immediately generously offered them one complete with printer and all the gizmos that were then available. This gesture caused unexpected complications.

The question then arose: who owned the computer? Was it the school, university or the Soviet? The only solution eventually was for William to visit a notary in Bury St Edmunds and draw up a document giving it to the school. This did not make him popular with Irina's two colleagues.

Prize Day arrived and with it a large Russian ZiL limousine. It looked almost as if St Dogmael's had been converted into an adjunct of Red Square. The school was festooned with red flags. A huge one flew from the tower and smaller ones were planted all up the drive.

As the deputy ambassador got out of his vehicle, the combined choir of English and Russian children sang the Soviet national anthem in Russian. Ludmila had coached the English children in the necessary rudimentary Russian language. She never actually explained what the words meant. Their revolutionary import would, William believed, if understood, certainly have given half the parents a seizure. It amused him even more that this had preceded the Prize Day Mass. Father

Brendan then commented: "Not sure what St Paul would have made of this, William. I suspect Vladimir Lenin would have liked it even less?"

Alan was invited for the day. This was an occasion he simply couldn't resist. He even wore a smartish suit. His tie was a revelation. Large, pink elephants on a blue background. Mary assumed there was a message here somewhere. Everything went very well. The Soviet party were so utterly charming to everyone; there were no incidents of Russophobic rudeness which Brian feared.

The deputy ambassador even volunteered for the 'Wash the Beak'. He got awfully wet but was determined to get totally involved. There was nothing of that stand-offishness that was once so associated with Soviet officials. He ended his ordeal by laughingly throwing the final sponge at William. It was a fabulously accurate shot. One parent suggested, tongue in cheek, that he might wish to volunteer for the Stowmarket cricket team!

Later in the day William was showing one of the deputy ambassador's aides around the school. He stopped and then said with immense sadness, "I was once so proud of Soviet achievements. Now I am not sure what country I live in." William genuinely empathised with this expression of sad, frustrated, forlorn patriotism.

What had happened that day was so improbable and extraordinary, and perhaps also a momentary, unique junction between two incompatible worlds. William was sure that they were in their different ways in the process of dissolution.

That evening Brian, Ludmila, Mary and William and the three Russian adults, as well as Alan, for whom William had been able to scrounge an invitation, made their way to Haddon Park. Despite being

July it was one of those summer days familiar to Suffolk people where the north-easterly wind was very chilly.

Lord Castle had made quite an effort to tidy up the environs of his stately pad. The deputy ambassador turned up in one of those peculiarly shiny Russian suits which in itself rather marked him out from most of the other guests who were mostly kitted out in the penguin suited formality of the traditional English dinner party, the exception being William's friend Alan who plumped for a less formal attire of a slightly crumpled lounge suit. They all eventually sat down around a huge table in a gorgeous if rather shabby Adam dining room.

William and his party all soon appreciated that virtually everyone else in the room was made up of the great and the good of Suffolk society. In fact the only guests who did not possess a title were the Jones party, Jonathan, and Celia Carpenter, and the rather jaundiced, sour-faced Mr and Mrs McKenzie.

The Earl of Faversham was one of the few English guests not dressed formally, at least not in the conventional sense. He turned up attired from head to foot in authentic Indian gear. The Earl was an elderly, slightly built man who was magnificently dressed in a brightly coloured Achkan coat with white, tightly fitting Churidar trousers. He also sported a copiously impressive, droopy moustache. He looked for all the world as though he had just walked out of a durbar in Lucknow.

William asked Clementine Volkov why the Earl dressed as he did. Mrs Volkov laughed as she then remarked. "Didn't you know that he is descended from one of the most notorious nabobs, a chap called William Hickey, a robber baron who made a fortune robbing the Bengalis rotten? He half-imagines himself as his reincarnation. Certainly, he is more Hindu than anything else," she continued. "By the way, don't be fooled by the title: it was awarded to his disreputable war profiteering grandfather by that terrible scoundrel Lloyd George."

As he walked away William was amused to reflect that even the most socialist of the county set could be remarkably snooty. They sat down to dinner. The lukewarm Brown Windsor Soup was served by an elderly, shuffling retainer. William looked at the Soviet ambassador who sat uncomfortably perched next to Lord Castle. He was peering down the table at the extraordinary collection of mostly elderly, titled English aristocrats and he looked totally confused. Did he fancy that he had entered some bizarre English film set?

Perhaps William thought he might even have imagined they had entered a madhouse of English re-enactors attempting to re-create early 1917 Petrograd. There was definitely here a more than slightly Chekhov feel of a declining gentry world which William felt sure the Russians would have understood and appreciated.

Worse still, Haddon Park on this chilly evening possessed absolutely no heating. The Russian party looked quite soon as if they were in the early stages of hypothermia. This was evidenced by the slightly bluey tinge around some of their lips. Each course, roast beef followed by apple pie, seemed to take an age to be served and was lukewarm when it appeared. At one point it seemed the elderly servant was about to have a seizure as he staggered slowly from guest to guest.

On the way back to St Dogmael's Alan and Brian were laughing so heartily that at one point they both had tears running down their cheeks. Alan commented that only in England could such a bash occur. "No wonder," he opined, "the rest of the world think we English are all bonkers. If they had only spent an evening at Haddon Park that view would be totally confirmed."

"By the way, did you see Roland McKenzie's face when he saw you?" Mary observed more seriously. "He must have thought he had seen a particularly malignant sprite. He clearly could not fathom how you got invited." Alan then replied, "Nor can I."

"You know on the face of it that group of has-been old farts seem harmless but the deputy ambassador knew differently. In crumbling old houses like Haddon the future of England is still largely decided."

"I think you are getting a bit carried away, Alan," observed Brian. "If the Soviet system is collapsing we are not far behind." Alan's parting shot was: "If I thought Parkies was peculiar I take it all back. I have just witnessed the Oscars of oddity." He added, "Do you think anyone in Watford will believe me when I tell them this story?" Probably not, William thought.

The end of term came. The returning Parkies party made their way to Donetsk. The hospitality they received was overwhelming. The generosity of their Russian friends who possessed so little was breathtaking. If nothing else, this experience might have shaken the patronising sense of moral superiority to which so many of the English are so prone.

William hoped that the lucky children would return with a new appreciation of Russia and its culture. Perhaps, too, an understanding of how privileged their own lifestyle was. They certainly should have become more culturally aware with their trips to Kiev, Moscow, and Leningrad.

For William and Mary there were more pressing concerns. A few weeks later their baby Flo was born in Bury St Edmunds Maternity Hospital. They finally had a daughter. Every dream seemed to have suddenly come true. Gethin was right in the end: Flo was the absolute proof that Mary was really the boss.

This was something William was happy to accept and indeed treasure. The two of them not only had now survived the Suffolk experience but also seemed, for the moment at least, to have even triumphed beyond their wildest expectations. With this slight feeling of hubris they prepared for their next year with a renewed confidence they had not felt since they had first come to Parkies.

Chapter Seventeen

TRAGEDY AND COMEDY

Martin Pugh had health problems. In reality, of course, it was his alcoholism getting worse. It was no longer possible safely for him to attend parents' evenings. Martin always wanted to go but was often far too sloshed to cope.

William had increasingly dealt with this problem by inventing stories about Martin being ill. He often proposed that parents meet him at an alternative time, hopefully during the day when he was fairly sure he would still be sober.

However, on one such evening Martin sneaked through without being noticed. He sat in his usual place in the school hall where this event always took place. Whilst technically Martin was correctly attired in tie and jacket, his clothes, however, had that unwashed, crumpled look that had come to increasingly define Martin's appearance.

William was shocked to see him talking animatedly to a smartly dressed couple who, he was anxious to note, were amongst the most important of his parents.

Their heads were pushed forward as though listening with a very focussed, rapt attention and interest. It was as though they were determined to glean every morsel of Martin's wisdom. In reality of course, they were simply attempting to decipher some of the garbled gobbledygook they were actually hearing. It was as though William resignedly reflected that Stanley Unwin the comedian had slipped through the doors. It sounded as though what he said should make sense but was nevertheless completely unintelligible.

No doubt, too, these parents would have smelt the repellent odour of rancid alcohol and stale tobacco that always pervaded Martin's person. William knew that he would have to be more attentive in ensuring Martin was absent from such events in future.

For the same reason, Martin could no longer be trusted to direct the school plays. Some of his earlier productions had been extraordinary. The year before William's arrival he had directed *Journey's End*, R. C. Sherriff's masterpiece. The fact that he was able to get twelve-year-old boys to convincingly play young British officers was in itself an amazing triumph. Later he went for even more adventurous options like *Flowers for Algernon* by Daniel Keyes. These very demanding roles were played by children as young as ten years old.

These were achievements that were exceptionally enterprising as well as illustrative of Martin's prodigious talents and the ambitions he had for his pupils. Yet despite this stellar record, William could not escape Martin's growing and now critical problems with alcohol.

Martin, he knew, remained a very gentle, likeable, and sensitive character. However, when drunk he could sometimes furiously verbally lash out. One evening at the end of the play rehearsals which were going on rather longer than anticipated, a number of day parents started to become agitated and annoyed about their lengthy wait for their children. Eventually, Martin raised himself from his Director's chair and walked to the door of hall. With great clarity and, it has to be admitted, a tone of real command and authority he solemnly announced. "Why don't you all fuck off?"

Some governors would have liked him to have dismissed Martin. William wouldn't do that. Perhaps in strictly self-interested terms he should have. Possibly it was another example of his neurotic desire to please everyone, combined with a real difficulty and reluctance to wield the knife. What was it William believed Macmillan had said? "A Prime Minister needs to be a good butcher." Perhaps it was just as true of a headmaster! William always found these brutal and painful decisions difficult.

The central problem was that William liked Martin as well as recognising his real, prodigious talents and the many years of service he had already given to Parkies. These considerations made this decision even more difficult.

Mary and William had sometimes been invited to supper in Martin's pretty Georgian cottage in Lavenham. On the last such occasion Martin became so drunk that he had opened a bedroom window at midnight and announced to the quiet, sleeping streets of this village: "Fuck off, you bastards." As the lights in many houses were turned on they thought that it was time to make a rapid, strategic retreat. What this and many other incidents had made crystal-clear to both of them was that Martin's problems could no longer safely be ignored.

However, it was also true that William had had his fill of being hated. Martin was deservedly an extremely popular man in the Common Room. He always showed consideration and generosity to other members of staff. Interestingly, too, it later transpired in his own perhaps rather ineffective way he had recognised and even tried to support some of the boys who had been so cruelly abused. Martin always exuded an air of genuine compassion for others. William, with a rather less creditable motivation, had no desire to push further a stick into the Common Room hornets' nest.

Martin remained a fine History and English teacher. Provided his classes took place before 4:00 pm all remained tolerably well. In the end William went for a compromise. He secured for him early retirement and re-employed him as a part-time teacher responsible only for scholarship English and History, which were where his particular talents lay. In addition he looked after the school library.

The school plays now became the responsibility of Evelyn Morley. William knew that Martin would not now be sober enough to supervise most evening rehearsals. This was something, however much he regretted, that simply had to be faced. Evelyn was anyway an extraordinarily gifted drama teacher. He started to produce the most lavish musical productions. The first one, *Camelot*, was a huge success. So much so that even little Flo became obsessed with the characters and the vibrant colours of the set.

Two of the Jones boys played leading parts which added further to her enjoyment. For some reason she came to imagine her father's name was really Guinevere. She was perhaps encouraged in this by the mischievousness of the Jones boys who rather enjoyed the prospect of making fun of their dad.

This revelation was the source of some surprise and hilarity when halfway through the rather lengthy and perhaps rather boring, from

Flo's perspective at least, discourse from the monk headmaster of Ampleforth during Prize Day in 1993, she pointed at William who was seated next to the speaker and shouted, "That's my daddy, Guinevere!" This rather spoilt the chap's flow! The whole hall burst into laughter which was not the reaction the guest speaker expected from his profoundly serious comments on the fundamental principles of Catholic pedagogy.

William had increased his teaching commitment and taken over responsibility for most History classes. This was no great chore. William loved this subject. His classes were fun as one pupil later commented years after William had left the school: "It was all sex, blood and rock and roll."

It also allowed him to load onto Brian Varga the more onerous tasks of day-to-day administration which he hated. Martin was understandably not happy with this situation. He was unable or unwilling to accept the seriousness of his problems. Perhaps not untypical of many alcoholics, he never really recognised or accepted that he even had a problem.

He was too decent a man to become a centre of staff antagonism and angst or indeed complain to any significant degree. The warmth of their previous relationship did cool. He was at the beginning of a tragic descent which in a few short years would see the end of his career and quite soon afterwards of his life.

Another difficulty that had been bequeathed by the former regime was a land dispute. In the days of the Victorian industrialist the Parklands Estate had been over 3,000 acres. The property had been broken up after the war when Canon Paine had bought the mansion and the immediate park.

The various boundaries, as was often the case in these situations, had been poorly drawn. The former Home Farm had been purchased by the tenant farmer; a chap called Sam Netherton. Ever since the purchase there had been rumblings from the Netherton family that the boundaries had been drawn unfairly and should be reviewed. Sam's son Johnny reopened the issue a few years before Lancelot Waters retired.

Johnny was an interesting man. He reminded William of the character Ted Burgess in L. P. Hartley's novel *The Go-Between*. Johnny was a person with a reputation. He was a ladies' man and a hard drinker, and possessed a wild, devil-may-care approach to rural conventions.

When he was young in a kind of Hardyesque way he had been devastatingly handsome. Even in middle age he was a sinewy, powerfully built man. It was reputed that many of the young domestics working in the school were rather more closely related to him that either he or they would care to admit. Johnny referred to the school as "them buggers up at the hall". He had an ingrained dislike for all the 'gentry', as he saw them.

Nor did he care for the way that Lancelot Waters treated him. On their few encounters on the boundary Waters was rather sniffy and superior, often referring to him curtly as Netherton, and even when he had inexplicably forgotten his name, as "my man".

It seemed to Johnny that those 'snobby bastards' were worse than the former lot. They still saw him and his family as little more than serfs. His lad Jacob had even been threatened with prosecution for trespass just for daring to take a shortcut across the school park some years before.

Waters had approached the boy with a peremptory, "What the hell are you doing on my land, boy? If I see you trespassing again the police will be informed."

What enraged Johnny even more than Waters's bloody-minded attitude was the land wasn't even his. For all Waters's pretentiousness and arrogance, he was just an employee, whereas the Nethertons actually owned their farm.

Then four years before, Jacob had been tragically killed in a motorcycle accident near Lavenham. Johnny had taken to drink, in a cataclysm of grief, anguish and despair. After a time, his long-suffering wife could stand it no more and left him. He had by then lost interest in his farm as well as virtually everything else in what he now considered an increasingly pointless, meaningless existence. He spent most of his time in a maudlin rumination of the unfairness of his fate.

Home Farm became run-down and many of the barns ruinous. Fences remained unrepaired, grass uncut, paintwork chipped and uncared for. To make matters worse in a desperate attempt to stave off his creditors and avoid bankruptcy, Johnny had taken to defrauding the Revenue.

He had an illegal still and sold copious amount of rough cider, wheat wine, poteen, and other even more lethal concoctions, on none of which he paid any of the required excise duty. Not surprisingly some of this illicit booze even found its way into the Parkies' Common Room bar.

Eventually the Revenue men caught up with him. His position was made even worse when it was discovered that he was using red diesel in his Land Rover, another serious Revenue offence. He stupidly in a drunken rage pointed his shotgun at two of the Customs officers when they challenged him at his farm. He only marginally avoided jail but ended up having to pay a substantial fine, having the removal of his shotgun licence, and being bound over to keep the peace. This all added to his sense of victimhood which in some strange, irrational way he associated with "those buggers up at the hall".

At this point he thus renewed his land claim against the school. This became the new focus of his increasingly deranged, obsessive life. The claim consisted of two acres of former pasture, which had subsequently become the school's hockey pitch.

Waters had reacted to this by making a counterclaim to three acres of Netherton's land for which the school had not the remotest right. All this, of course, did was to provoke the enraged Netherton still further. For some reason, which William couldn't fathom, the governors had allowed this potentially expensive, time-consuming, and absurd legal case to rumble on for years. By this stage, it was clear that neither side could win.

The stakes were further raised when Johnny started a campaign of nuisance and harassment. Using the school fixture list as his bible, he would ensure that the most foul-smelling chicken manure would be spread the evening before important matches.

William for the rest of his life was always to associate this noxious smell with hockey, possibly one reason he never enjoyed watching it. When this didn't work he upped the stakes still higher when he loaded tons of this horrid stuff directly on top of the hockey pitch the day before Prize-Giving. He then lined the boundary with every derelict vehicle he could lay his hands on. As Jonathan Carpenter once commented, "The view from the school is a bit like that over a war zone or a gypsy encampment or perhaps both."

Ironically, there was a very easy solution which Lancelot Waters or the governors had never even been prepared to consider. The school had title to two acres of derelict scrubland physically separated from the rest of the estate. This was a remnant of what had once been the grand house's septic tank. It was now in the middle of one of Netherton's overgrown cornfields. Parkies had no conceivable use for this piece of shrub. All that needed to be done was to swap this land in exchange for the disputed hockey pitch. However, things had reached such a pass that in Johnny's mind this had developed into a mini-revolution.

He seemed to view it as a kind of Suffolk peasants' revolt! He perhaps saw himself as a kind of latter-day Wat Tyler. Worst of all, these legal fees had already reached a five-figure sum.

Luckily, Johnny didn't seem to mind William too much, perhaps because he avoided patronising him. It was pretty obvious even to Johnny that there was nothing about William that was vaguely gentrified.

For this reason amongst others the headmaster was therefore given the rather unappealing task of trying to negotiate with him. Quite early in September 1991 the two men agreed to meet on the boundary near the old horse chestnut tree.

It was still quite light in the evening when the meeting took place and Johnny arrived with a two-litre plastic bottle of his wheat wine. Johnny offered the headmaster a swig. "My God, that is powerful stuff," William sputtered. "Not to us real Suffolk men."

It had then become almost a question of masculine honour for William Jones. Every time Johnny took a gulp William did likewise. To begin with, it had little effect. However, firstly slowly and then more rapidly William felt increasingly light-headed. The deal was finally done.

To the delight of Johnny Netherton it was clear that the headmaster was now totally inebriated. "I don't think I can walk," slurred the very tipsy William. Johnny grabbed him by the waist and the two of them swayed back towards the front of the school building. The burly Netherton was effectively carrying the entirely sloshed, helpless Jones.

Mary saw them coming and ran down to open the front door. She then helped Johnny get William, now virtually a dead weight, up the main stairs into their flat. It was the first time that Johnny had ever been allowed, much less welcomed, into the building. Mary put William to bed and then offered the still relatively sober Netherton a coffee.

Johnny was certainly not impressed by William's inability to hold his liquor. He still thought the Joneses were basically all right. Still in his opinion he was still on the wrong side of the rural divide. William definitely was not a real Suffolk man! They were, however, not like the snobby, stuck-up people he had dealt with before. He had been treated properly and Mary's ultimate courtesy ensured that finally this particular war was over.

The school was lucky to possess a two-acre lake. William owned a small motor dinghy which the family took on camping trips and down to their house in Southwold. The rest of the time the boat was kept beside the lake.

He then acquired eight rather shabby canoes together with life jackets from a defunct outward-bound education centre. On summer and autumn evenings William took as many boarders who wanted on the lake for giant water fights. Everyone was equipped with a large, empty ice cream tub. The object of the exercise at least in the minds of the children was to soak the headmaster as much as they could.

He responded in kind. Frequently the canoes would tip over. The motorboat would then zoom up to the marooned canoeists and drag them out of the water.

At the end of these sessions a gaggle of happy children would process back to the school for a hot shower, cocoa, and biscuits. This was perhaps when William was at his happiest. He often thought that he was really a frustrated housemaster or maybe even a junior matron! On bleaker days he wondered whether that is what he should be doing. He loved this side of schoolmastering. Sometimes this activity would take place on Wednesday afternoons when there were no cricket or netball fixtures.

One day a big, twelve-year-old boy, Mark, who suffered with Asperger syndrome joined in. Possibly as a result of this condition he had no understanding of personal modesty. He then decided that he didn't like wet clothes. At the end of the activity he took every stitch of clothing off and walked entirely naked back to the school changing rooms.

He was, it has to be said, rather physically well developed for his age. This certainly surprised some of the mothers who were walking along the same path in the process of picking up their infant children from the pre-prep. William wasn't sure whether they were appalled or impressed! Certainly, Mark was entirely oblivious of their attentions.

The same lad was often bullied by the younger Grimes. Mark was a rather gentle, naive, sensitive fellow. He simply did not understand the nuances of much social intercourse. The issue which the bullying focussed on was Mark's physical maturity.

Mark was incredibly innocent and found this lewd, unpleasant ragging both inexplicable and very upsetting. Nevertheless Mark did not lack the courage or perhaps recklessness to try and address this. One summer afternoon when the school was playing cricket against a local rival – this was a school whose parents were noted for their effortless sense of condescending superiority – this lad decided that this was the time to finally deal with this. He then approached the table groaning with the 'posh' cricket tea for both Parkies parents and guests.

There must have been at least thirty guests from the other school as well as the usual smattering of Parkies parents. The visitors as usual were exuding the impression that they were slightly slumming it.

They stood chatting together in their usual haughty, patronising sense of disapproving antipathy. This was despite the fact that Parkies cricket teas were legendary. Far better incidentally than those offered by this or any rival. The fact remained that this crowd thought they were a cut above Parkies and couldn't resist any opportunity to hammer the point home.

The children were provided with a far less ostentatious feast. Jam rather than cream, orange juice rather than tea. There was a strict rule that children were never allowed to be anywhere near this parental beano.

Despite this, or perhaps because of it, Mark marched fearlessly up to Mrs Grimes. He then announced to the assembled body in a voice you could probably hear half a mile away. "I have a much bigger penis than your son and he has the smallest in the school." This statement was greeted initially with a hushed, rather shocked silence.

One Parkies mother, a rather stout, ruddy-faced wife of a local farmer, then exploded with mirth, the remains of her half-swallowed tea smattering the rather expensive summer dress of a visiting parent. "Really, that is bloody marvellous," she laughingly roared out to the entire company. Not a sentiment many of the other po-faced visitors seemed to share!

Matters were not helped by the fact that Margaret McKenzie was also present. William supposed correctly that she did little to calm the situation. In reality of course she was absolutely delighted to witness what was in her opinion another example of the malign influence of the Jones clique.

Soon after she went into a huddle with the incandescently furious Mrs Grimes. One of the young matrons managed to steer Mark back towards the school. It has to be said that her attempt to contain her own amusement, by furiously biting her lower lip, did not add a great deal of gravitas to the situation.

Half an hour later a fuming Gerald Grimes followed by an embarrassed Tracey stormed into William's study. They demanded immediate restitution. The headmaster wasn't quite clear what that might be. The real problem was that William could hardly keep a straight face. Grimes noticed that and it provided yet another reason for him to dislike this ghastly, smirking, obnoxious Welshman.

A rather attractive, young lady from *The Good Schools Guide* arrived to interview William during this summer of 1992. She had clearly not been listening to Lady Grey or for that matter Gerald Grimes and their companions' opinion of the headmaster.

To be considered for a mention in this publication was something of a feather in one's cap. Every school was desperate to be included. Parkies was of course no exception.

William and this lady immediately struck up a good rapport. William was rather enjoying escorting this pretty, very attractive young lady down the slope towards the lake on this beautiful, balmy summer evening. He was in a typically especially expansive mood as he outlined the many beauties of the school's location. This steep slope was constructed from the remains of the old ha-ha. Mid-sentence William unexpectedly slipped then rolled down the bank. He ended up on the ground clutching his ankle. He thought he had broken it. The pain was absolutely excruciating. His language was atrocious. This was much to the delight of the little boys who were still in the grounds playing French cricket.

This lady very kindly and solicitously helped him back to his study, and then the two of them consumed some large gins. As it turned out, of course, this was merely a sprain, if quite a severe one. Mary later observed to one of her friends. "Typical man, making such a terrible fuss just to get himself noticed by a pretty girl." It did seem to work. This lady then wrote in her guide that he was "charming". Perhaps William imagined if he hadn't sworn so disgracefully he might have been described as "exceptionally charming"!

Another visit from the editor of the same publication a year later portrayed him as: "Immensely reassuring to the dyslexic and uncoordinated but adds a magic to the school". William didn't know about the magic. He liked however to imagine that his somewhat manicured eccentricity was actually no bad thing as a marketing tool for the school.

William and Mary really felt that Parklands had finally become their home and as such their true milieu. They even imagined they were beginning to make a difference. Predictably there were a few parents and governors who didn't agree. "Uncoordinated and dyslexic:

perhaps they should have added half-witted and fatuous," an acerbic Roland McKenzie grumbled when he read the article.

William started to feel a kind of proprietorial pride when he walked around the grounds and entered the new, rather swishily equipped classrooms. He had even acquired two nearly new terrapin buildings at a knock-down price from a closing school. Brightly painted and filled with attractive furniture they did much to improve the previously somewhat limited teaching facilities.

The children had little of that worldly-wise, false sophistication he had sometimes met in his London school. They often looked rather scruffy with their ragged jumpers, dirty knees, and unkempt hair.

A few parents criticised that. William didn't much care about whether a child's knees were a bit grubby. Most parents, it seemed, agreed with him, and were well disposed to the school. This fact could be easily forgotten by William when the headmaster's job seemed to be mostly about dealing with the discontented and difficult. William needed to remind himself of that. These were only a small minority of parents. This was difficult to remember when one was often faced with a queue of particularly irrational complainants.

Some awkward situations could even be funny. One rather pompous dad did not like the way that Mary had handled a somewhat trivial domestic situation. So one Sunday afternoon he asked William to walk around the grounds with him. A long, rather superficially matey chat then ensued where he offered sage advice on how William should control his 'difficult' wife. "Women," he suggested, "much prefer clear instructions and firm guidance."

He obviously thought that William was entirely under Mary's

thumb. In that opinion he would have found a firm ally in William's father Gethin. He was struck, too, by the way this chap seemed to expect women to behave in much the way he might require Labradors: biddable and easy to control.

William nodded sagely, realising that he was being given a masterclass in misogyny. It was therefore a conversation he thought it would be unwise to share with Mary. This man was entirely mistaken if he thought William took him seriously. He simply went through the motions of nodding in apparent agreement.

William and Mary hoped, even sometimes believed, they were giving Parkies their own special brand. It seemed to be working. Although the school was no longer growing in numbers, these had now stabilised at 60% higher than it had been when William was appointed.

Neither William nor Mary really understood the power dynamics of schools which somewhat detracted from this optimistic assessment. They were wholly unaware that whilst most parents and governors didn't much care about their welfare, a minority were more focussed on a more malign intent. They were soon to appreciate that in any contest between indifference and malice it was usually the latter that won out.

Chapter Eighteen

THE GATHERING OF THE CLANS

Lady Agnes Grey Viscountess St Edmunds was the wife of the Earl of Faversham's heir, Lord St Edmund. She was the acknowledged head of the most prestigious clique, the only really important one within Suffolk's social scene.

Together with her husband and four children she occupied the Dower House on the Ashley Estate. Everyone who thought they were somebody yearned to be part of the St Edmunds set. That was at least what Lady Grey told herself. Whether or not it was true, it was a proposition no one, certainly in her social circle, dared to gainsay.

Lady Grey's background was not quite as smart as she liked to propagate. Quite apart from the fairly recent ennoblement of her husband's family, she was the daughter of a London surgeon. This was hardly one of centuries of breeding and long-established ownership of a landed estate she hoped everyone assumed was the case. Her clipped vowels and natural patrician air were, however, quite genuine. This was the result of years at Wycombe Abbey, followed by Swiss finishing school.

It was true, too, that her father Sir Reginald Godwin had been knighted for services to his profession, as well as being Serjeant

Surgeon to the former King. He was hardly a typical example of this particular species. Professional eminence aside, he was by no means as blue-blooded or patrician as his daughter Agnes often tried to pretend.

Parkies did not feature very highly on Lady Grey's social radar. It was true that two of her children attended the place. Under normal circumstances they would never have darkened the doors of such a second-rate papist establishment.

Lady Grey did not wish her children to board at least until the boys moved to Rugby, their father's *alma mater*, at the age of thirteen. Her boys were therefore day children. She knew that there was no other realistic alternative in that part of Suffolk, whatever her considerable reservations. In the case of her oldest daughter Emily these issues were no longer relevant as she was now firmly ensconced at North Foreland Lodge after a short spell at the little local primary school.

Her youngest child Persephone had just entered Parkies' pre-prep. Sooner or later she would have to make a decision about her future.

However, the prospect of boarding under the tutelage of the – she was reliably informed – soon-to-be newly appointed Daltons would not seem to be too bad a prospect.

The St Edmunds set was in part so small and exclusive because of the shortage of potential members. Celia Carpenter was not interested in joining. She considered most of the women associated with it, as she once said to Jonathan, "Snobby and malicious, stupefyingly boring women, so much so that when one goes to lunch with any of them one virtually falls asleep before the end of the second course."

Celia also considered that it was the ideal venue for initiating the numerous fumblings and sexual encounters which had become the *raison d'être* and focus of much local gossip. Despite the shortage of potential inductees, certain ladies were definitely not welcome. Amongst those were Tracey, the generally considered irredeemably common buxom partner of Gerald Grimes.

Margaret McKenzie was, however, very firmly ensconced within the group. Whilst she was not particularly popular, she was certainly feared for her biting wit and vicious, unbridled tongue.

Most of all she was a wonderful, indeed essential, source of much gossip and tittle-tattle which after all was the meat and drink of most of their gatherings.

The goings-on at Parkies had always been the fount of some of the juiciest and most enjoyable stories at these rendezvouses. The events of recent years were truly delicious. They were all eagerly awaiting Margaret McKenzie's most recent update. She was an exceptionally good raconteur as well as particularly well-informed. Whether or not her stories were strictly accurate was of less interest.

The ladies on that particular September Monday lunchtime were all meeting at their favourite restaurant, La Grande Maison, in Lavenham. Their date was rather spoilt by the unwelcome appearance of Calvin E. Bauer, formerly a colonel in the USAF.

Recently Colonel Bauer and William had struck up a friendship after being introduced by a mutual friend. They both shared a keen interest in history. Calvin didn't entirely buy into William's more fantastical historical notions. He did find him unusually open to alternative ideas, at least for an Englishman.

On a few occasions they would sneak off for a day looking at some of the remarkable historical remains of East Anglia. Calvin and his wife

Jenny had even joined the Joneses for supper, and once Calvin had been persuaded reluctantly to come and talk to the children about the USAF's connection with Suffolk and specifically Parklands House.

Calvin remained an enthusiastic flier. He had even taken William on trips in his small, two-seater aircraft. On one occasion William had accompanied Calvin on a flight from Suffolk to York.

This aircraft had been built by Colonel Bauer to his own design and was reputed to be the fastest single-engined aircraft in private ownership in the country. On the flight home William suddenly felt extraordinarily ill. It later transpired that the engine had caught fire and had melted the fibreglass engine cowl. The noxious carbon dioxide fumes had then entered the cabin mostly on William's side. By the time they returned to Suffolk he was suffering from pretty advanced carbon monoxide poisoning. As Mary pointed out rather anxiously, this incident could have severely shortened William's career as well as much else.

Occasionally William helped Calvin with the maintenance of his machine, effectively handing him his tools whilst he lay head-first in the cabin.

This had cemented a pretty close and affectionate friendship. Calvin now worked as a psychotherapist since leaving the Air Force and was able over the previous year or so to give some informal advice to William to help him deal with his growing difficulties with stress and anxiety. From this initial friendship a more formal professional relationship developed in future years as William's mental health problems got worse.

Calvin had retired to Suffolk when he retired from the Air Force where he served as a pilot and squadron commander latterly at Lakenheath. He was a large, sun bronzed, loose-limbed man with a rugged, lived-in face. Although perhaps not especially handsome, he maintained the honed body of a disciplined serviceman.

The ladies of Lady Grey's set may not have been especially attracted to him, but they would not as one of the mischievous women once observed, "Have thrown him out on a dark night." He affected a vaguely Southern drawl. It gave him, as it was intended to, the superficial impression that he was rather slow-witted and irredeemably coarse and uneducated.

In reality he had a doctorate from Chicago. His forebears were respectable South Carolinian old money.

He rather enjoyed the fiction. It added a frisson to the games he liked playing with these strange, puffed-up, showy, supposedly English blue bloods. The way these pretentious ladies bought fully into his fable reinforced his conviction that they were in reality the unsophisticated bumpkins rather than him.

It often occurred to him that it wasn't the truth that these silly people wanted. It was rather to find further 'facts' to reinforce their well-established and fully embedded prejudices. He was always perfectly happy to oblige.

He had then married a rather personable, pretty English girl who for a time Agnes thought might be recruited into their coven. After one lunch party Jennifer Bauer, having been genuinely shocked as well as absolutely detesting the nasty, malicious gossip and the appallingly patronising tone the group took to all Americans and her husband and his Air Force comrades especially, decided that she wanted nothing more to do with them. One of the comments that most upset her was when Lady Grey haughtily observed, "The trouble with living in Suffolk is one is surrounded by all these awful American bases and their dreadful fast-food joints."

She acerbically added, "All these McDonald's and Kentucky Fried Chicken diners: it is like living amongst the hillbillies or Hottentots."

Jennifer was so upset and angry when she returned home she immediately shared these nasty, racist remarks with her husband Calvin. He had exploded with fury. Sometimes the ridiculous stupidity of these people upset even him.

He was not good at the nuanced, understated, malicious vexation of the English shires. It was possibly more about his belief acquired over many years in the military that direct assault rapidly initiated was usually the best policy. He stormed out of their house and thus arrived uninvited at the front door of Ashley Dower House.

He had then announced in his best Tennessean drawl that the obnoxious Lady Grey could fuck off and take her loathsome hags with her. In her whole life no one, least of all one of these dreadful American hillbillies, had ever talked to her like this. Worst of all, however, much as she might wish, she could do absolutely nothing to harm him. Unusually for the residents of Suffolk he didn't, as he would say, "give a shit".

On that September day as he unexpectedly walked past the ladies at the door of the restaurant the loud, piercing, refined voice of Agnes Grey piped out. "Look, ladies, there is that dreadful, ghastly, common American." Calvin hadn't expected to meet what he now considered was a little better than a witches' coven.

Using his slow, languid, Tennessean drawl and relying on his bumpkin appearance he therefore responded calmly and clearly. "The trouble with you stuck-up Brits is you can't even spell the fucking word guillotine." It provoked a stunned, shocked silence as Calvin had clearly intended. It even rather spoilt the ladies' lunch at least for a short time. Lady Grey and her party grumpily made their way to their restaurant table with even less courtesy and consideration for the somewhat desperately obsequious Sicilian waiter than was usual.

Calvin Bauer's intervention did not diminish the expected, blabby, delicious pleasures for long. There was too much of an excited frisson about what was after all the greatly anticipated feast of Parkies tittle-tattle. No one wished to introduce the subject for fear of appearing a gossipmonger. Finally, during pudding Lady Grey could no longer restrain her inquisitiveness and enquired in her most lustrous tone: "So tell us, Margaret, what is the recent news from Parklands?"

It was as though she had fired the starting pistol. Margaret stuck out her copious bosom and talked. This diatribe went on for ages. Even the expectant blabbering of the assembled ladies was not quite prepared for the monotone, repetitive invective that was the essence of Margaret McKenzie's obloquy.

At this stage, the ladies were unaware of William's friendship with Calvin. If they had known it would certainly have further soured their feelings towards him.

The substance of Margaret's report was in part to remind the group of the shabby treatment meted out to poor Lipman a few years ago. "My dears, there are no decent teachers left at the place: the staff now consists of Jones's creatures, particularly that Communist Varga and his Bolshevik wife. You can see how many fewer scholarships the school now secures. The thought of a respectable Suffolk prep school entertaining a group of snivelling Russian brats and even inviting that Soviet functionary as guest of honour is an outrage." She then added, "Did you see that huge, bloody red flag over Parklands? Dear old Canon Paine will be rolling in his grave. Roland says, too, that that awful revolutionary friend of Jones's was up again for Prize-Giving and as usual he resembled an anarchist tramp."

She sucked in her breath pushed out her bosom and then continued. "Roland was so understandably concerned by his presence that he even checked criminal records." Margaret did not think it was wise to reveal that this act in itself was a serious professional lapse on her husband's part and could cause him major difficulties. "You therefore won't be surprised to know that he has one." There was a sharp intake of breath. "What kind of record?" one of the ladies hesitantly enquired. "The usual delinquent stuff: vandalism, affray, shoplifting, that sort of thing."

Mrs McKenzie savoured the moment and sat back in evidently replete satisfaction. She had rather exaggerated Alan's less than salubrious past. Shoplifting and vandalism had never been on his charge sheet. However, it made a much better story. "It is entirely unacceptable that our headmaster should have such dubious acquaintanceships," Lady Grey rather piously asserted. She said this with just a touch of exquisite gratification that this display of her own undeniable moral superiority afforded.

Roland McKenzie had as he had promised done some further digging about the relationship of Alan Howarth and William Jones. Margaret McKenzie was of course delighted to announce the fruits of that investigation.

Margaret loved to luxuriate in the sense of self-importance and secret influence that arose from this lavish display of her access to such juicy information.

She was not yet finished as she was so enjoying the sense of power these revelations produced. "They were at some second-rate teacher training college together." She paused to add a further dramatic frisson to her narrative and then continued. "Not, you will notice, even a decent university, just a glorified FE college." This she asserted with just the right imputation of a monumental personal discernment. Mrs McKenzie was incidentally someone who had never even darkened the doors of any further education college, second-rate or not.

She continued. "You will not be surprised to learn they were both involved in student politics of the most virulent left-wing variety." The other women were by now hanging on her every word. "There is even a suggestion that Howarth may have been into drugs at one stage." This was of course yet another dramatic invention.

"Both of them were threatened with rustication for a political prank of stealing the ballot boxes in a student election they apparently stupidly thought was fixed."

She luxuriated for another moment in the look of a stunned, shocked as well as delighted satisfaction on the faces of her fellow diners.

Some of the ladies in the group still found it difficult to imagine this lanky, rather ingratiatingly sports-jacketed, somewhat self-effacing fellow Jones as the dangerous political radical that Margaret was painting. Nor did they all believe that this prank seemed quite as dangerously revolutionary as Margaret implied.

Margaret was now on a roll and to hammer home her point she

added with just a little bit of additional relish, "I truly believe Howarth is still a Trotskyist and I would not be at all surprised if Jones was an active sympathiser." This narrative containing a smidgeon of truth had been spun so outrageously and skilfully to give the entirely false impression that William Jones was some kind of a Guy Burgess of the prep school world. He was a person, it was suggested, who was deliberately subverting their values from the inside. The central message had struck home. They already believed he was irredeemably common and entirely unsuitable to be headmaster.

Now as these ladies left the restaurant they were half-convinced William was a dangerous radical to boot. This sense of contrived moral outrage gave a kind of luscious justification to their malice.

Lady Grey and her cronies only half-understood the significance of this meeting. They were certainly not yet quite able to fully appreciate what had happened. The die, however, was cast: this group had implicitly agreed that they were now categorically opposed to William Jones not so much for what he did, but much more for what they perceived he was.

What had really most amazed all these women was that Lord Castle and his extraordinary sister seemed to have been largely responsible for bringing about this Russian Communist nonsense. Agnes Grey then acidly remarked. "We were at Haddon Park for that awful Russian shindig in the summer, as indeed were most of you. The sight of that old fool Castle bowing and scraping to those dreadful Bolshevik subversives was truly humiliating."

With just the right mixture of genuine concern and aristocratic hauteur she added, "Jones and his common little clique of lefty social workers and political miscreants and undesirables seem to be corrupting everybody. It is really quite beyond the pale."

Then Margaret made an interesting suggestion. "The governing board has some vacancies if anyone is interested. We do need to fight this man and his clique from the inside." Her expression contained that element of reluctant virtue which set the right tone to her righteous moral indignation.

This was not an impromptu idea. She had discussed it previously with her friend Agnes Grey. To her immense satisfaction it was clear that at least one of the women was interested. Margaret promised to mention this to Jonathan Carpenter. She now contentedly considered at last here was the start of the fightback.

William was still blissfully unaware of the extent he had offended the county set, not least this particular faction. Naivety and an overtrusting nature, were as Jonathan Carpenter had identified four years before, perhaps his greatest weakness. It was a character trait that Margaret McKenzie and her ilk were now to ruthlessly exploit in whatever way they could.

From William's perspective things seemed to be going pretty well. Francis was off to public school. There wasn't a great deal of choice of where.

The Jones family needed a significant bursary to make this practicable. In addition William felt that, given the religious tradition of Parklands, it should be a Catholic school.

In the end they had plumped for the Benedictine College of Downside in Somerset. This was a very long way from Suffolk but it was close to his mother. Francis would not, he hoped, be bereft then with lots of visits from a devoted grandmother. Nevertheless, he was afflicted with a horrid sense of guilt. Not for the first time he thought that just maybe he had put the interests of the school and his own career ahead of those of his family and especially Francis.

He hoped this was not true. When he left Francis as he walked into the vast Gothic extravaganza of Downside and witnessed his wan, anxious face he feared it might be so. With baby Flo as an addition to the family Mary was even busier than before.

It hadn't really occurred to either of them that with the arrival of the new baby, being sent away to school would be doubly worse for Francis and would deepen further his sense of rejection and feeling of isolation.

There were now sufficient girl boarders to justify the conversion of the stables. New house-parents were needed for the twenty new girls who had arrived that September. Part of the conversion included a small, two-bedroom flat, designated as their accommodation. This left William with a real problem. The obvious and only really very keen internal candidates for the post were Isabelle and Piers Dalton There were no funds available to appoint additional staff.

William wasn't yet aware that the Daltons were assiduously canvassing their case amongst many of the more significant members of local county society. This was of course the main reason why Agnes Grey was already so convinced they would be appointed.

Piers had been largely silent in the year or so since Lipman and de Vere's departure. Whilst he was not exactly friendly to William he seemed to have lost the openly hostile manner of former days. Indeed, both of them had been quite cooperative during the Russian exchange.

In the general reform of staff remuneration that Jones had initiated a year before the unqualified Daltons were now paid at qualified teacher rate. This had nearly doubled their salary. They had, Jones reasoned, many motives for gratitude.

He even imagined that he might have done enough to secure a measure of loyalty. Isabelle was remarkably good at her job teaching French. She had also enthusiastically supported the move to coeducation. It was also true that many of the new young girl boarders were instinctively drawn to her warm and ebullient Gallic personality.

Piers and Isabelle with their slightly down-at-heel social pretensions and long-standing county connections might, William thought, be an asset in attracting more girl boarders to St Dogmael's. William reasoned that it would be in the interests of the school and might even heal former wounds if he appointed them. In the end this is what he decided to do. He was of course under considerable pressure from governors and influential parents to precisely do this.

Isabelle predictably, as it turned out, was a great success. William had not anticipated that many of the girls came from local, rather socially smarter families who would never consider sending their boys to Parklands but were perfectly happy to allow their girls to attend.

The Daltons had a real eye for the marketing opportunities this could provide. With Isabelle's effortless style the dormitories became wonderlands of girly kitsch, beloved by the children and their parents alike.

They were able to oil and grease themselves into the good graces of all these often influential, or, more often, those who thought themselves influential families. It later occurred to William that Lancelot Waters would have been proud of them.

Brian and Ludmila Varga were genuinely concerned by this decision. They thought William was quite potty to have made it. Ludmila had developed a profound instinctive distrust for Isabelle Dalton.

Perhaps this was a consequence of a long experience of life in the Soviet system where she had become something of an aficionado in understanding devious dangerous insincerity. This meant that she knew that there was something profoundly inauthentic about this woman.

The extraordinarily contradictory mixture of French anarchist and British snob didn't convince her of Isabelle's basic integrity. When she and Brian had first arrived at Parkies the Dalton had tried to absorb them into their set. The Vargas had quickly recognised Pier's limitations. Ludmila considered that he was little more than a buffoon as well as being exceedingly self-obsessed and snobby together with a truly awesome line in malice. Isabelle was certainly more interesting and intelligent, but she had this overwhelming resentment resulting largely from her husband not being properly appreciated by anyone in authority, the present leading villain being of course William Jones. Unfortunately, Ludmila realised Isabelle had little understanding or perhaps more accurately any willingness to recognise the lacklustre talents of her preening peacock of a husband.

The further difficulty was that she had seen numerous examples of the deeply held, visceral dislike the Daltons had for William and Mary. Ludmila and Brian were amazed that William didn't seem to appreciate or understand this. Brian said to him when William raised the topic of the Daltons' promotion to girls' house-parents, "In my opinion this is an absolutely catastrophic decision, William. Don't you understand these people really hate you?"

William had already made up his mind and once this was done he rarely changed. However, Brian and Ludmila's perceptions certainly worried him. Somehow he still believed that this couple could be brought around. Surely, he reasoned, we are all on the same side: we all want Parkies to prosper.

This decision was nevertheless very popular and was supported by most of the governors. The only two to seriously question it were Father Brendan and Thomas Brown.

Father O'Rourke commented after the meeting, "I do hope you are right, William, but in my opinion neither Piers nor Isabelle have forgiven or forgotten the events of the last four years. There is a serious danger that you are letting a rather angry wolf into your gentle, undefended sheep pen."

Thomas Brown fully concurred. "In my view leopards never change their spots. These particular leopards have and are still displaying their claws. This is a bad decision and in my opinion you will live to regret it." Most of the governors thought it was just the right thing to do. Mrs McKenzie, as she left the governors' meeting, was heard to whisper to the beaming Prior Anselm, "At least there is a bit of class back in the place, don't you think, Father?" Prior Anselm nodded reassuringly.

As the months passed it became increasingly clear that Isabelle especially liked her own way. William was finding it difficult to manage her. If she disliked any decision or indeed perceived any faint criticism of her or her husband she would swiftly retreat into a sulk.

This all further reinforced Brian Varga's perception that despite her many social pretensions she was at root an old-fashioned French anarchist. The only rules she seemed inclined to obey were her own.

Mary found her impossible. Matroning and domestic arrangements were increasingly organised entirely for the convenience of the Daltons. The stables were effectively becoming a separate institution.

Yet in the eyes of the St Edmunds set the Daltons offered a much more socially acceptable milieu for their girls. Piers and Isabelle's status therefore grew apace. Part of this may have been associated with Isabelle's continental background. This was generally considered *déclassé* and as such much more socially agreeable. This was in contrast to the plebeian tone of the rest of the school and the Joneses in particular.

Piers Dalton's background was on the margins of smart county Catholicism. His father had been the estate manager at Saxon Hall, the Despenser country seat. As such Piers had grown up on the edge of this rather rarified world of decaying aristocratic privilege and expectations.

He had attended the former, now defunct Brentwood diocesan boarding school and junior seminary. For a time he had thought he had a vocation to the priesthood. This had not materialised and after a year at Allen Hall the senior seminary, he had decided to leave.

St Joseph's in Brentwood was not a public school, but it had quite a few of the pretensions associated with being so. There were prefects' houses, rugby, rowing, and a uniform of sports jacket and grey flannels which rather aped grander establishments.

Allen Hall was then an integral part of St Edmund's College, an ancient Catholic public school which had recently rather fallen on hard times. Yet it was situated in a complex of buildings that in design and layout deliberately aped the grander Anglican establishments.

All this had left Piers with a sense of being nearly patrician but not quite so. Robert Despenser, his contemporary, and former playmate, had attended the rather grander Jesuit establishment of Beaumont College. Afterwards he had studied at King's in Cambridge.

Despite Piers calculated pose of indifference he was embittered and resentful at what he considered was the sparsity of opportunity compared to his contemporaries.

This was directed above all at Robert Despenser, whom he considered far less able and much less deserving. This was made worse by the fact that after Allen Hall he had drifted and had never secured any formal qualifications.

Somehow Piers had reasoned that this, too, was all the fault of others. No one, least of all William Jones, had really understood or appreciated his latent talents. This had therefore become the core of his most recent anguish and resentments.

Therefore his failure to obtain a degree or any other qualifications was not, in Piers's opinion, his fault. Rather it was the consequence of deeply maligned, ill-fated malevolence, the result of being under-appreciated and unfairly done down. Piers was not a very self-reflective person. William Jones was merely the most current example of those who he believed had maliciously underestimated his extraordinary unrecognised talents.

He had spent a few years as an assistant in an English language school, in Tours. It was there he had met Isabelle. Even he in his rare moments of clarity and self-awareness had come sometimes to understand his real situation.

William sometimes thought he was in reality a kind of prep school parody of the down-at-heel gent with social pretensions and little else to offer. William considered that Piers was something of an Evelyn

Waugh character, more *Decline and Fall* than *Brideshead*.

He was what Gethin, William's father, sometimes described when referring to some of his hard-up, more puffed-up customers, "All fur coat and no knickers".

Piers had certainly not come to terms with the appointment of William Jones. Initially he had even hoped that he might be an improvement on the equally disagreeable Lancelot Waters. However, there was something ingratiating and weak about Jones. It was obvious that he simply didn't appreciate how Piers really felt. "Does he really imagine," Piers once sneeringly observed, "that I have simply put the past behind me?"

Dalton was not foolish enough to suppose he would ever have been appointed headmaster. He was however sure he could do a better job than William Jones. To have a man so obviously socially unsuited for Parkies was a disaster and could surely not last. It would not be long, in Piers's estimation, before the governors would appreciate this and appoint someone with real talent and connections: someone like de Vere or at least a person less like Jones. In the end Piers was very willing to do all that he could to undermine the head. He was not, however, foolish enough to expose himself to any risk in doing so.

Despite these numerous undertones this was for William and Mary a very happy time. The school seemed to be thriving: the new girls boarding house was up and running, William had found a real friend in Brian and more recently his pilot buddy Calvin. Both William and Brian were still basking in the aftermath of their Russian triumph.

Francis seemed much happier. They hoped he would be less lonely now that James was about to join him at Downside. Flo now aged two was a delight. Her mischievous, lively charm had won the hearts of most of the children and half the staff. There was a procession of little girl boarders always knocking on their door asking to take her out in her pushchair.

Sometimes she even escaped the confines of their flat. She could be seen toddling through the dining rooms with what Mary thought was a rather proprietorial air. Mary had made a few particularly good friends amongst the less pretentious parents and was developing a happy, if modest, social life.

There were large clouds on the horizon. An economic recession had started in London. By the summer of 1992 it was beginning to affect Suffolk.

Some children had been removed for obviously financial reasons as early as the Christmas of 1991. Many parents in the tightly knit social world of Suffolk found it difficult to admit the real reason for this.

Quite quickly the word was out that the school was 'going to the dogs'. Easier to claim this, William thought, than to admit that the bailiffs were about to turn up at your front door. By the summer term William realised that the days of rising numbers were well and truly over. The school roll was about to drop significantly. Initially it was not clear how significantly.

It became slowly and agonisingly apparent that boarding numbers were likely to drop by as much as a third and the overall school roll by one-quarter. Without energetic action the school was facing potential insolvency. There would have to be significant and very painful cutbacks. It was in this frame of mind that William was to enter the bearpit of a governors' meeting on one especially lovely summer's afternoon in June 1992.

That summer, too, a new governor, Mrs Barbara Watson, was appointed. She was the wife of an apparently successful London accountant who had recently relocated to a former rectory near Bury St Edmunds.

She was the mother of two children. Her son had been a day pupil at Parkies for three years. Her daughter had just started. Her children were academically able. It was also very well known that she was extremely ambitious for them.

What was not so well known was that she was not at all enthusiastic about the direction of travel of the school since the Joneses had arrived. She didn't believe Parkies was sufficiently focussed on scholarship success, and given her ambitions for her children, this represented a real problem for her.

David, her handsome, urbane husband, appeared on the face of it to be a successful businessman. David had, however, been rather unlucky in recent years. This centred around him being somewhat overexposed by being a Lloyd's name as well as some unwise speculation on the stock exchange. He had his hands burnt in the great crash of 1987. In short, David was nowhere near as financially secure as he appeared.

Scholarships were not just a question of ambition and prestige for the Watson family. They had become an absolute economic necessity. Without this, their children would simply not be going to any public school. This would be an absolute social catastrophe from the perspective of the ambitious and unexpectedly somewhat needy Watson family.

None of the governors had the remotest notion of the fragility of Mrs Watson's financial situation. Jonathan Carpenter just assumed that she was a rather attractive, possibly too affected for his taste, bright, prosperous, well-educated, underemployed patrician wife.

She had the additional advantage of serving as Chair of the District Council, as well as being leader of the Conservative group. As such she seemed an ideal choice. She might as well even be a possible future chair. Despite her potentially rather shameful secret she had become an enthusiastic as well as leading member of the St Edmunds set. Unbeknown to William and Mary she had developed an especially close relationship with Margaret McKenzie. This had helped reinforce her view that the Joneses were not a couple she greatly cared for. Barbara Watson was much more perceptive than Margaret. She was far brighter and more hard-headed than her friend.

She possessed many of the same prejudices and expectations as the McKenzies. It was for these reasons that she believed that the Joneses could not or should not have a long-term future at the school. Barbara Watson was a consummate politician illustrated by her many years in a leading role as a Conservative councillor in the county council. These thoughts would remain hidden for the time being. However, this lady was not someone who easily changed her mind.

Chapter Nineteen

PARKIES AT BAY

This critical governors' meeting took place in the more formal surroundings of the library at the end of June 1992. This choice of venue perhaps betokened the seriousness of the situation. There were a lot of the old stager governors present. There were new ones, too, who Jonathan was aware could and probably would change the entire dynamics of the group.

Things had, he considered, been going pretty well for a few years. Jonathan had not really expected that. It turned out against all his expectations that this fellow William Jones seemed more effective – or was it luckier? – than he had initially supposed. However, the crisis had finally come as he knew it eventually would. The question now was how could Parkies survive it? If indeed it could!

Prior Anselm had resigned. He was suffering from some severe bouts of poor health, as well as a growing realisation at least in the deeper recesses of his mind of how outdated his attitudes had become. He had started to really understand that his world was in the process of dissolution. This was the only reality he really knew or indeed cared about.

This had ensured that, in addition to his physical woes, he was increasingly afflicted by an ennui he seemed unable to shake off. His community in Ipswich had a decade before contained over forty monks. Now it was less than twenty. They couldn't seem to attract novices. There had not been one that had stayed for more than a few months for over seven years.

Anselm was seventy-three and yet was by no means the oldest in the monastery. Indeed more than half those who remained were more elderly than him. He said mournfully when chatting to Jonathan just before his final decision: "I feel more and more as though I am living in an old people's home. Nowadays there seem to be more nurses and carers wandering around than postulants or even worshippers."

His cosmos was disintegrating. Whilst Anselm didn't like it, it was a fact he couldn't anymore ignore. Spending time as a governor of a school he considered hardly recognisably Catholic was not the best use of his remaining time. In addition to this there were all those curious female pupils around. Prior Anselm had spent most of his time in all-male establishments. The only woman he had ever known was his mother. Girls were not only unfamiliar, but to him also profoundly disturbing.

Since the retirement of Major George Hardy a year before, a new bursar had been appointed. He like his predecessor acted as clerk to the governors. This new man, Graham Warner, a former local government accountant, was not everyone's cup of tea. "Too much like Jones for my taste," commented Grimes, a view that was held by some others including, predictably, Margaret McKenzie. Graham was a grammar schoolboy, red-brick university, and had a former career in the public service.

These facts did not go down well with the diehards. When he was appointed many would have preferred a military prefix like the retiring George Hardy. The title 'Major' seemed so much more appropriate than a mere 'Mister'. In the opinion of many it gave the school a touch of class, albeit specious.

Like William he knew that things must change. Much of what he saw at Parkies appalled him. The casual and ill-defined sense of superiority was especially annoying and he thought entirely unjustifiable. Some of the governors and indeed parents were extraordinarily patronising. He felt sure that some of them saw him as little more than a senior servant. This was epitomised for him in the way Lord Castle always addressed him as 'Warner'.

He hated dealing with these antediluvian dinosaurs and having to listen to their anarchic and often frankly unpleasant views. He associated them with a distant and unmourned past which was for him entirely unknown and thankfully unexperienced.

Graham was fundamentally a technocrat, a pragmatist whose mantra was "if it doesn't work get rid of it". Ironically, this marked him out from William whom he considered in most ways irredeemably romantic, even sometimes delusional.

The notion of Parkies as a Catholic educational community of shared values and mutual Christian endeavour was in Graham's opinion a fantasy. In trying to achieve it William was pursuing an impossible dream. Graham seriously doubted whether such a community had ever existed in the first place. This idealistic streak he would concede was one of the most lovable sides of William. At the same time it was also his most irritating.

Graham found William's very limited understanding of finance and balance sheets almost as frustrating. William was deeply impracticable and, worse still, rather overtrusting. This made him vulnerable in Graham's opinion to every huckster and deceitful villain around. The as yet relatively modest list of bad debts was an ample testament to this.

He knew that William disliked, as much as he did, the narrow snobberies and silly status games that seemed to define so much of life in rural Suffolk. He was also convinced that William didn't understand the basic economic realities. Profit and loss accounts often appeared as incomprehensible to the headmaster much as epicurean philosophy might to the average bus driver. Today, he felt sure, William was going to experience a steep learning curve.

The two new board members were Barbara Watson and Nigel Denton, both very much an unknown quantity. All that William knew for sure was Mrs Watson was a friend of Margaret McKenzie's. How close a friend he didn't yet know. This was a fact that did not fill him with much confidence. She was a middle-aged, rather attractive woman dressed in the classically English summer wear of the status-conscious metropolitan escapees who now seemed to increasingly dominate Suffolk society.

Her colourful, flowing skirt, decorated with a floral pattern reminiscent of William Morris, was clearly expensive, as were her fashionably costly leather pumps. Her modest cream blouse finished off an outfit which, whilst understated, was redolent of taste and effortless confidence. Her husband David still commuted twice a week to his plush offices in Bayswater.

Living as they now were in a former Georgian rectory they were now apparently able to fully partake of their rural dream. Yet, despite her colourful, summery appearance, there was about her facial expression a decidedly wintry sense of latent disapproval and irritated exasperation.

Her two children were now settled into Parkies as day pupils. She was, as both William and Graham knew, not enthusiastic about some of the academic standards or facilities within the school. Nor was she at all bashful about expressing those concerns. Mrs Watson was a fairly frequent visitor to William's study. These were not occasions he generally looked forward to.

She expected her eldest son to move on to Eton with a scholarship, and her younger daughter to the nearly as fashionable St Mary's Ascot on similar terms. She was not at all convinced that Parkies had the wherewithal to achieve this, especially under the rather easy-going and in her view socially inept leadership of Jones.

William knew that Brian Varga labelled such parents as "The old vicarage, Chelsea tractor brigade". This particular epithet in her case seemed entirely merited. She had retained a strong metropolitan air of ruthless entitlement.

Her move to the country had not in any way softened her focussed, unscrupulous ambition. What was not yet known was Barbara Watson's dark secret of financial precariousness. She had managed to keep it entirely hidden from her set. It was to her a furtive, shameful fact that could, if generally known, have torpedoed any realistic chance of maintaining her vision of the rural, gentrified dream.

The other new governor was a former pupil Nigel Denton, currently a solicitor in Cambridge. He was a chap no one knew anything about other than he was a friend of Jonathan Carpenter who had persuaded him to join the board. He was slightly younger than Jonathan. Rather rotund, personal trainers and riding to hounds were not part of his lifestyle or expectations. Like Jonathan he had been educated at Oxford. Whilst Jonathan's Pembroke was by no means one of the most fashionable of colleges, Nigel Denton's alma mater at St Benet's Hall was far less so. He had been at the school during the time that Lancelot Waters had replaced Canon Paine. He had then moved on to Downside.

As he had just completed his second divorce and was currently living with his much younger former secretary in a small apartment in Kings Road, Cambridge, his Catholic credentials looked perilously thin.

The costs of these proceedings had rather diminished his already rather modest wealth. They also meant that one way or another he was responsible for the upbringing and education of six children and stepchildren.

School fees, certainly of the size of Parkies, were well beyond his means. His legal speciality was property law. Much of his professional life was dominated by the search for appropriate development opportunities. He was still rather unclear why he had been invited to join the Parkies board other than some pleasant memories of the very different school world of more than thirty years before. Jonathan Carpenter's reasons for inviting him onto the board were eventually to become crystal-clear.

There was only one important item on the agenda. Numbers were expected to slip from the current 280 to 206, a drop of over a quarter. The boarding numbers were set to decline from 118 to 80, a fall of nearly a third. Graham had estimated that the school needed to save in excess of three hundred thousand pounds a year to break even. This was a catastrophe and everyone knew it. Jonathan had trusted that the meeting would not descend into acrimonious incriminations. It quickly transpired that that was a very faint hope.

"Well, this is a bloody disaster." Gerald Grimes kicked off the meeting by framing the situation in the worst possible and obvious light. This was a comment that Jonathan thought rather articulated the self-evident and, as such, was not at all helpful. There was a rather satisfied smirk on his face. This rather contradicted his later, apparently well-manicured, woebegone expressions of anxiety and concern.

Jonathan noticed this and bore it in mind. William then tried to place what was happening in some kind of context. Before he commenced his report he looked around the table at the assembled group. This was in itself, he thought, remarkably illuminating. Jonathan had that serious look of focussed, businesslike apprehension. He had seen things like this before. He was not one to make light of it but was not panicked either. A similar attitude of pragmatic realism and a willingness to find a way through was etched on Thomas Brown's features.

The new man Denton was more difficult to read. His face had that bland detachment which William recognised was characteristic of the typical shrewd, legal mindset. Lord Castle appeared to be suffering the consequences of a rather over lavish luncheon. His eyes were bleary and he looked much of the time as though he was on the edge of slumber.

Mrs McKenzie's face, on the other hand, betrayed a sense of eager, cheerful, delighted anticipation. Her cheeks were red, her plump lips seemed ready at any moment, it seemed to William in a momentary, fantastical diversion, to burst out into a tuneful ditty, rather an odd expression, William mused, for such a serious debate. Gerald Grimes, having dispensed with his initial imprudent, unintentional flash of relish, had reverted to his usual expression of surly discontent.

William was especially disconcerted by the way he kept clenching and unclenching his ham-like fists, rather in the mode of someone preparing for a prizefight than any constructive discussion, he thought.

Father O'Rourke sat in his standard mode when facing some difficulty or was annoyed or irritated by the proceedings. In this instance his irritation was directed at some of the individuals rather than any process. He looked at Mrs McKenzie and Gerald Grimes with an air of a growing, exasperated annoyance. He placed his hands in his trademark steeple, an image he stared at with apparently endless fascination.

His expression was unreadable yet it seemed the kind of serenity William abstractly imagined in another kind of fanciful mental reverie he often failed to control. A similar pose might have been employed by the samurai in the moments before conflict.

Father O'Rourke, William knew, for such a gentle unassuming sort of chap had hidden depths of irascibility few amongst the governors even suspected. At least William now realised he had one staunch ally amongst this motley crew.

Mrs Watson just now seemed uncomfortable. She shuffled around her chair in the attitude of someone who either had an embarrassing itch or more likely would prefer to be anywhere provided it was not in this room.

William's report referred to what was happening throughout the independent school market. He mentioned the two relatively local prep schools that had closed in the last few months. He talked about the national picture where boarding in all schools, but especially in prep schools, was sliding alarmingly. He referred to the terrifying statistic that there were now only a quarter of the boarding numbers in English prep schools compared with the 1960s.

As his peroration continued he was increasingly aware of the looks of frustrated irritation, annoyance and even anger on the faces of some of the more belligerent board members.

Predictably it was Grimes who interrupted with the comment: "This is all very well, but we didn't come here for a history lesson. What are you proposing we do about this, Mr Jones?" This seemed to release the floodgates of recrimination that Jonathan had always feared.

"My cousin sends her boys to Sunningdale: they are not suffering as we are," commented a rather self-satisfied Margaret McKenzie. "In my opinion, and I believe of many others on this board, the reason our numbers are so drastically down is entirely because of your imprudent actions, Headmaster."

Somehow William thought she even made the word 'headmaster' sound like an ominous threat. Jonathan stepped in. "In what way precisely, Margaret, do you believe this is William's fault?" Mrs McKenzie launched into her long-prepared denunciation. "This man," she combatively seethed, "engineered the departure or dismissal of some of the best staff. He has replaced them with the second-rate and inadequate."

Her tone reached a crescendo of fury when she added, "He has spent money as though it grew on trees and he even made this school the favoured stopping-off place for every indigent vagrant Communist and trendy ne'er-do-well." Her face by this point had developed a hue of deep crimson. Her bosoms heaved with an alarming independent motion.

It looked almost that the violence of this motion would soon pop the buttons on her straining, somewhat overtight blouse. Indeed in another moment of imaginative reverie it seemed to William she might take off from her chair rather like the scene in Roald Dahl's book *Matilda*, when Miss Trunchbull does precisely this.

William assumed accurately that her comments concerning 'vagrants and Communists' were a scurrilous, nasty, and somewhat exaggerated reference to his friends Alan and Brian. "Look how we wasted all that money and time on a load of Russian factory fodder two years ago. Do I need to say more?" Obviously judging from the faces of Mrs Watson and Mr Grimes, it seemed she didn't.

Thomas Brown now spoke. "It maybe that William has made mistakes." "MAYBE!?" Grimes loudly erupted. "I said maybe because I don't think he has or at least only a few. When he arrived here five years ago, I believe I am right in saying, but am happy to be corrected, the school consisted of a mere 184 children. You mentioned Sunningdale, Margaret, which as you must know is one of the most fashionable prep schools anywhere in the kingdom. It is located incidentally on the edge of Windsor Great Park, not in the back of beyond in Suffolk as we are. The point is, Mrs McKenzie, let us remember why we are here. We have to find a realistic solution unless of course yours is to merely dismiss the headmaster?" Judging from the facial expressions of Gerald Grimes and Margaret McKenzie, William supposed that was exactly what they wished to do!

William then nervously carried on. "The solutions are obvious, much better marketing and some cuts. The trouble with just focussing on the latter is we cannot just dismiss staff willy-nilly. Ignoring, for a moment, the redundancy costs we have to have sufficient people to teach the whole curriculum, look after the boarders and provide enough activities." It was then that William presented his plan which he had been working on with Graham for some weeks. In essence this involved the redundancies of a number of cleaners, gardeners, handymen and junior matrons. In addition, there would be a complete halt on all maintenance beyond the absolutely essential."

"All these savings are peanuts," interjected an aggressive Grimes. "I agree," confirmed William. "Brian Varga has just accepted a post at Haileybury. He will be, as I am sure you all agree, hugely missed." "Not by me, he won't," an increasingly belligerent Grimes spluttered. William took a deep breath and continued as calmly as he could. "This frees up one of our biggest salaries. I would also suggest that we freeze all other salaries, and to show willing, Mary and I are willing to take a 20% pay cut. I will also make redundant two of the junior teaching staff. I think you will find the total saving amounts to £280,000."

With this William paused. "Not the £300,000 needed," Mrs Watson rather caustically remarked. Graham then intervened. "Our plan cuts the staff to the bone. If we go any further we will have to reduce the number of subjects on offer. The first to go would have to be Classics."

Barbara Watson was acutely aware that an Eton scholarship required both Latin and Greek. "I take your point," she mumbled. William then talked about the marketing opportunities. "The pre-prep is doing well. I suggest this is the moment to start to take two-year-olds and extend our Nursery." "I thought you said we are saving money: that will cost," glared a growingly intransigent Grimes.

"Yes, it will, but not much," replied William. "On that theme, I want to send our minibuses to Bury and Lavenham to pick up potential day children and use our spare boarding areas for 'bed and breakfast' boarding." "Another bloody cost," interjected an increasingly exasperated Grimes.

William tried to ignore him and continued. "We know that parents of day children even now sometimes ask for occasional boarding which at the moment we offer free of charge. Indeed, I think you yourself did a few weeks ago, Mr Grimes."

Grimes flashed a look of unmitigated detestation in William's direction at this rather obvious dig. "What we now do is offer it more systematically and with much more enthusiasm and really market it. Very critically we charge for this. A kind of smart babysitting service," William added with a reluctant smile.

William's exposition ended. The room was now totally silent. Father Brendan, who so far had appeared to be in a kind of trance, finally perked up. "William has had no pay increase for five years. I know he is struggling to send Francis and now James to Downside. This extra salary cut will be a real problem for him. I think we owe him and Mary a debt of gratitude for willing to make this extra sacrifice." Jonathan, Thomas, and Lord Castle nodded their heads in supportive agreement.

At this point the board voted on whether to accept William and Graham's plan. Grimes and McKenzie were reluctant at this stage to appear overly obstructive and merely abstained. All the rest voted in favour. There were other matters of less import and the meeting finally broke up at 4:30 pm. The group then retreated to William's sitting room for a Parkies tea.

Jonathan seemed relieved that the whole thing hadn't gone too badly. Thomas Brown and Lord Robert shook William's hand. Robert Castle even said, "William, it is well known I didn't want you as head of this school. Truthfully, I don't always understand or indeed necessarily agree with some of your decisions. However, I want you to know I believe essentially you are doing the right thing. I for one wish to offer my total support for what you proposed today."

The ladies and Gerald Grimes left without a word. William was sure that Margaret McKenzie shot Lord Castle a dispirited, puzzled, somewhat annoyed even perturbed look. Had he disappointed her? William wondered. He was quite sure he knew the answer to that.

Father Brendan stayed behind. "I need a Jameson, Will." When they sat down, he continued. "Well, my lad, you stuffed them that time but it was a close-run thing. It was that bloody Irishman Wellesley who said that, by the way. You have won the skirmish but not the war. Have you thought how you are going to manage without Brian? No deputy and no friend either. It will be bloody difficult, old fella."

However, much Father Brendan might have considered this a victory albeit a close one. That was not the opinion of either Margaret McKenzie or Gerald Grimes. Despite themselves they were reluctantly impressed that, yet again, William had apparently been able to pull his chestnuts out of the fire. Neither of them believed that Jones's plans were practicable or attainable. "This is mostly wishful thinking: it won't work, Barbara, you know that." Margaret McKenzie gleefully confided to her friend. They were both sure that unless there was a significant change of direction. The future of the school was still under serious threat. The problem was that they had no practicable alternative strategy, at least at this stage.

Margaret McKenzie and Barbara Watson genuinely believed that if Parkies imitated schools like Sunningdale, all would eventually be well. However, neither had any real idea how to bring this about.

The Watsons and the McKenzies were sure that the central problem was William Jones, a man who had none of the class contacts or even the right attitude to achieve such a positive outcome.

Gerald Grimes's position was both simpler and predictably more brutal. He simply detested the Joneses and wanted them gone. He didn't imagine that their departure would significantly influence the future of the school. It might even improve it. In the end he didn't much care.

He expressed his view succinctly to his wife Tracey later that evening. "Parkies doesn't need William Jones: he has achieved bugger all over his time here. We need to get rid of him and his coterie of lefties and closet Communists as soon as we can. At least Varga is going, which is something. The only thing that amazes me is that a respectable place like Haileybury is taking him. The whole bloody world is going to the dogs!"

Tracey rarely, nor even dared, to see the funny side to anything her burly, bullying, rather frightening husband said. For a moment, the reference to 'dogs' seemed terribly funny. She had a difficult job to avoid smiling.

Chapter Twenty

A CHALLENGING YEAR

The summer holidays William often found were a gruelling, challenging time: Mary quite enjoyed the peace and quiet when the children weren't around. She felt that at last they had the place to themselves. William, on the other hand, thought the school buildings were like a wasteland where there were no chirping voices of children to be heard.

The mansion echoed to empty footsteps, and the sterile dust sheets covering the furniture were like shrouds on a still warm corpse. William predictably in these circumstances had another, rather worse attack of anxiety and depression. This was becoming a common feature of William's holidays and of increasing concern to Mary. It was mitigated a bit when they decamped to their cottage in Southwold. William's duties, however, required that he spend most of the school holidays in Parklands.

She knew that anxiety had been a problem for William long before they had met. Until recently she assumed that this had gone away. She was also now quite settled in Suffolk.

She realised that the stresses and strains of William's job were the core reason why he was suffering a reappearance of these difficulties.

In the end she might have to start to think the unthinkable. They might, she reluctantly conceded, ultimately have to leave Parkies to ensure William's future well-being. She hated the thought of this and earnestly hoped that finally things would start to get a bit easier.

So worried was she on this occasion that Mary finally insisted William visit a psychotherapist: Calvin Bauer, who was already aware of William's situation, was the obvious choice. They had been good friends for a little while, and Calvin had sometimes listened to William's increasing woes. Mary now insisted that William needed to have a proper, professional course of therapy which by definition would be quite expensive: "Another bloody expense," as Brendan would no doubt have said if he had known.

Unexpectedly this therapy became for William's potential future career at Parkies an additional threat. These consultations would turn out to be yet another weapon in the hands of the St Edmunds set. The visits were theoretically confidential but it was not long before it was common knowledge that he was seeing a "trick cyclist".

The belligerent way Calvin was viewed by the St Edmunds group just added to their antagonistic outrage. Not only was William bad and common, but now he was also obviously mad. Later, William would remember the aphorism about Lord Byron: "mad, bad and dangerous to know".

Whilst he could never claim the slightest resemblance or connection to Bryon, it amused him to discover later that Lady Agnes Grey's husband was a distant descendant of Lady Caroline Lamb, the lady responsible for that quotation.

For William at least his weekly appointments with Calvin were of enormous help. Ironically, Calvin's oblique if toxic relationship with so many of the St Edmunds set ensured he had a clear understanding of the pressures that were contributing to William's psychological difficulties. At the very least he offered a supportive and perceptive perspective which helped his patient, and increasingly his friend, find a route through these more and more trying times.

The following twelve months were what might sometimes be described as 'difficult'. This euphemism did not in any real way adequately describe the events of those dreadful few months that were to follow.

In September William heard the devastating news that his dear, much-beloved, closest friend Alan Howarth was dead. Alan had been organising a football tournament, the first session of the season when he had played soccer with the lads for about an hour. He had walked home to his flat in Watford. En route he appeared to have lit a cigarette. As he smoked it he suffered a massive heart attack. His body was found by a jogger the following morning. It seemed that the remains of the cigarette were still between his fingers, so unexpected and catastrophic was the event. Alan was only forty-five.

More tragically perhaps he had recently met a lovely girl called Gloria, and three days before his death he had asked her to marry him and she had accepted. Alan used to joke that he always played the field and had never been caught. At the very moment of a loving entrapment he had tragically died.

Alan had always regretted not having children. William knew he would have been a fantastic dad. A few weeks after his funeral Gloria announced she was pregnant. Alan had written to William days before his death telling him of the joyful news of his intended nuptials. It was a lovely, affectionate missive.

There was even an unintentional sense of goodbye in his words. The sentence that stuck out as William reread it was: "Will, I know you are in many ways a naive idiot, as of course I am, too. It is so wonderful to have met Gloria. I hope she will become to me what Mary is to you. The point is, Will, you and Mary are two of the people I most love. Don't get too bound up with all those posh tossers. In the end I don't believe that you belong with them and remember you and Mary are immeasurably better." William didn't imagine that the compliment was deserved but he would miss so much the one who made it.

William and Mary travelled to Chalfont for Alan's funeral. It was a lovely Norman church abutting the council estate where Alan was born. His parents were still alive. Alan was their only child. It was a devastatingly sad service in every sense of the word. The church was packed.

At the back were a group of boys who had travelled from the youth club in Watford. They were all dressed in black. The difference was it was black leathers and their motorbikes were neatly parked outside the church. Their boots were all polished; some of them even wore black ties. This was truly a mark of real respect. Mary noticed that a few of these large, rather intimidating-looking boys were actually crying. It genuinely moved her.

What also impressed both Mary and William was the extraordinary dignity of the distraught parents and devastated fiancée Gloria. This display of courage and fortitude from modest and impecunious people seemed to William to have more class, in the real sense, than all Mrs McKenzie's and her cronies blatherings.

William so missed the regular telephone calls to his friend. Mary thought that Alan's common sense often helped him navigate the various, more difficult situations he faced and didn't always handle terribly well. Now that neither he nor Brian Varga were around she thought that William often cut an increasingly rather lonely, isolated figure.

A week or so later Mary had a telephone call from her sister Samantha. Her father had just been diagnosed with terminal liver cancer. Within a few weeks he, too, had died. Mary, who had lost her mother fifteen years before, was bereft. She said to William, "Now you see I am an orphan."

Mary was incredibly close to her father. To her his death was the final irrevocable end of her childhood world. She mourned for a long time but, as always with her, she kept her feelings largely private and discreetly hidden. William and Mary remembered all the many lovely times in the family council house in Goring.

Even after the death of her mother their visits had been frequent. Ernest had regularly visited Parkies, although, like Dilys, he regarded this peculiar world as largely inaccessible. On the last time he had met Dilys the Christmas before he even commented, "Some of these people up here remind me of a few of the customers at the garage: noses stuck so far in the air they don't notice the dog shit that they so regularly step into."

Mary's dad was the very essence of old-fashioned, decent English virtue. He never imagined he was other than just an ordinary, unexceptional kind of bloke. He died as he had lived, with an understated, modest discretion. The same courage, William thought, he had displayed in the eleven months he had fought his way through

Europe from Normandy to Berlin, securing on the way his much-prized Military Medal.

In the end it was only the children, and especially Charlie and Flo, who kept Mary going. Flo was a lovely little three-year-old. She ran around the flat giggling away and charming everyone. All the girls were desperate to take her for walks, a privilege that was sometimes granted. Flo definitely had a mind of her own.

On one terrifying occasion when Mary was dealing with a sick boarder, she climbed out onto the balcony outside the Joneses' flat.

Luckily one of the young matrons rang Mary and enquired, "Did you know Flo is out on the balcony?" She didn't and was quickly able to gather her up. It was rather too close a call. Luckily, there were no further incidents.

A marketing man visited. He announced that Flo was one of the best marketing tools the school possessed. It struck William, in one of his bleaker reveries that this probably said it all. His family had been reduced to marketing jargon in the interests of the school. Alan, he thought, might have described it as a kind of congenial serfdom. Perhaps William considered it really was. Another reason to feel guilty – career ahead of his family yet again!

At the beginning of the spring term William and Graham were called to Walton House for a meeting with Jonathan. In a way his demeanour was quite positive. This had itself surprised both men. They had assumed he would be much more downbeat. The reason for this might have been that numbers that September were marginally better than had been anticipated at 212, and there were 83 boarders.

However, it was clear from Jonathan's developing narrative that he was not as optimistic as he had at first appeared.

With him was his friend Nigel Denton. Neither William nor Graham was quite sure why he was there. The essential point of the meeting was to hear Jonathan's own reflections on the likely future of Parkies.

As the chairman saw it, the central difficulty, as he was sure it was with similar schools, was that it occupied a large site with many buildings that needed to be fully used and maintained. To do this it needed to secure the kind of fee income only boarders could provide. If boarding was in free fall, as William's analysis suggested last July, then the likely future was very bleak indeed.

The chair thought there were only three possible solutions. The school could combine with another local prep school. Or get taken over by a senior school. Or finally it sold up and found a smaller site appropriate as a day school.

If none of this occurred Jonathan believed that Parkies had no real, sustainable future. He gave it at most three years. The reason for Nigel Denton's presence was at least now pretty clear. He had the wherewithal to offer advice should the school wish to relocate, or more likely close completely. William and Graham shouldn't probably have been surprised by Jonathan's bleak appraisal.

At least for William it was yet a further reason for his growing demoralisation. He had that sense perhaps common to men of his age that the possibilities that once seemed endless were closing down. He firmly believed he had done everything he could to save the school. Mary and the children had given up so much and now it looked like they had no real future either. Graham and he returned to Parkies in a mood of gloom and despondency.

Brian and Ludmila had gone and this, too, was a kind of bereavement. It was like the first year again. Without a deputy William's workload shot up. Mary no longer enjoyed the friendship and help of Ludmila. William especially missed having such a close confidant.

The Daltons were becoming even more obstructive. It seemed to the Joneses pretty obvious that they were encouraged and supported by Mrs McKenzie. Margaret McKenzie and Isabelle Dalton seemed always to be in close, labyrinthine conversation. These kinds of secretive tête-à-têtes seemed most ominous perhaps than anything else more concrete. Mary, with her small coterie of well-informed friends, was rather more aware than William of what those conversations might consist. They were certainly not complimentary to either William or her.

The boys' housemaster James Waters was in love with a junior female teacher, and his interest and commitment to the job had largely dissipated. The combined effect of all this was to convince both of them that they must at least reluctantly consider the possibility of moving elsewhere, probably in the fairly near future. Not something they remotely wanted to do.

It might be the only way of securing the future for themselves and their family. Brian was now firmly ensconced in Haileybury but it was close enough for them to have quite regular contact. Eventually William asked his friend for his advice. "In my opinion the future for schools like St Dogmael's is pretty iffy. If you want to stay in boarding prep schools you need to look for one that is supported by a strong senior school." This was helpful guidance and it encouraged William to define his search for future employment if the need arose.

Luckily for the besieged Jones family, help was on the horizon.

The previous summer the less than effective head of pre-prep had resigned. Extraordinarily fortuitously a mother of two Parkies pupils applied for the post. Her experience was a bit dated, although before she was married she had once held a senior post in a primary school. Ordinarily she would not have been the first choice. However, in these circumstances she was the only possible option.

It turned out to be an inspired choice. Kate Bell within months transformed the pre-prep. She then reorganised and extended the Nursery. This instantly became a roaring success. Her industry, enthusiasm, and talent somehow galvanised what had formerly been a rather mediocre staff. Within a year the numbers in this part of the school had doubled. She was, too, incredibly loyal to William. He had at last found someone else he could totally trust.

William's idea of using the minibuses was also unexpectedly much more successful than he might have imagined. By the end of the year minibuses were picking up children as far afield as Stowmarket and Ipswich. Boarding still remained a problem. However, numbers did stabilise even if they didn't increase as William had hoped.

'Bed and breakfast' demand rocketed. It still meant that many beds remained empty for much of the week, but this cheap form of babysitting was incredibly popular on Friday and Saturday evenings. Even the Watson, McKenzie and Grimes families took full advantage of this service.

Within a year numbers in the school had increased by over 20%. They were running at 253 by the following summer: this was nowhere near the pre-1992 levels. Parkies had nevertheless somehow survived.

There were problems still with the Daltons, and James Waters, the lovelorn housemaster, had now married his girl. The trouble was this did little to improve his or her performance. As he was the nephew of a former head and had lived his entire life except for a short interlude at Downside within the portals of St Dogmael's, dealing with this performance issue created some further challenges. Not least of these was the result of his somewhat entitled attitude which never really allowed him to accept or understand his obvious limitations. He was, however, a superb games coach. Parkies' enviable games record was largely the result of his expertise. Most of the house duties were, however, now taken by Evelyn Morley. He was another excellent find of recent years. The problem was therefore contained if not yet resolved.

Evelyn's plays just got better and better. At the end of the summer term the whole school were involved as actors, musicians, stagehands, craftsmen, and women. Everyone had their place. There could be rather unexpected dramas in the school hall, as well as on the stage. The visitor benches were raised up by means of large blocks. This made a pretty useable auditorium. This also meant that at the back there could be potentially a big drop off the side.

One rather tipsy mum had been rather overindulging on the sherry during the intermission and was sitting on one of these. At a quieter moment in the raucous *Guys and Dolls* musical she got really excited by the fine performance of her thirteen-year-old son.

She then managed to slip off the side. The "Oh fuck" comment she inadvertently, slurringly ejaculated whilst she fell amidst the tumble of benches and chairs rather detracted from the dramatic effect of the romantic proposal her son was in the process of making on the stage. "Best bloody moment of the play," the irreverent Lord Castle was heard to chortle afterwards.

Evelyn was also enthusiastically religious and took over as head sacristan in the chapel. There was something slightly camp about this gentle, very serious young man. His artistic, sensitive temperament, William thought, might explain his fascination with every detail of religious ritual. Father Brendan did not always feel so wholeheartedly committed to some of Evelyn's more unrestrained religious extravaganzas.

On Corpus Christi the whole school following the monstrance paraded through the grounds to the Grotto of Our Lady, another one of Evelyn's very gimmicky Catholic innovations.

They were all singing the Latin anthem, the *Panis Angelicus*. Father Brendan found this hugely amusing. He acerbically commented, "I believe that every former Cromwellian Congregationalist family in East Anglia is there happily singing a Latin motet. That old bastard Oliver must be rolling in his grave."

Evelyn flooded the small school chapel with so much incense you could not see from one side to the other and with half the congregation almost suffocating in the smoky haze. Brendan was less amused: "These bloody English ritualists are always trying to outdo Rome," was his cynical observation. This kind of London Oratory pageant of bells, books, ornate vestments, and clouds of smoke was neither Brendan's nor William's particular thing.

William thought there was more than a touch of the Welsh Puritan still left in him. Perhaps, he sometimes fantasised one of those Cromwellians when rampaging around Ireland had once sneaked into the bed of one of the O'Rourke ancestors! This might explain the good priest's surprisingly Protestant attitude.

Both Francis and James were now both at Downside. The arrival of his younger brother had done much to improve Francis's morale. Charlie, their youngest boy, was left alone at Parkies.

He often felt a bit isolated despite his close relationship with his baby sister. Francis and James's school life was, however, further improved by the numerous, much-anticipated visits of their grandmother Dilys. She was always sure to take them to the local supermarket in Radstock for supplies. Such was her generosity, William supposed that both Francis and James must have had the best-stocked tuck boxes in the whole school.

A special highlight of their spring term was a visit from Glynis and her new Australian boyfriend Tom Bruce. Tom, who had attended the famous Australian public school of Knox Grammar School in Sydney, was mesmerised by Downside and especially all the black-clad monks that seemed to be everywhere. His one memorable droll comment was, "Those black-gowned buggers would be too bloody warm in that get-up in Sydney. Do you think they have designed a lightweight miniskirt version for down-under?" Tom had clearly not yet grasped the English notion of understatement!

After his sister married him a few months later, where William was privileged to give her away, Glynis moved to Sydney. Although they kept in regular contact it was not the same. He missed her terribly.

Mary especially regretted that she hardly saw the boys. It was simply too far for a day trip. Another factor was her commitments to Flo and Charlie, as well as all the other increasing school duties which often seemed totally overwhelming. The distancing of the relationship between mother and sons was a price that Mary found increasingly difficult to bear.

Mary was, however, extremely talented in developing a bridge between William and the staff. He could be rather abrupt, especially when under pressure. Sometimes he could give ill-considered, peremptory instructions which Mary was often able to soften. She could even on occasion persuade William to change his mind.

Her efforts, however, remained wholly ineffective with the Daltons. Every issue for them became a drama. It was almost as though they were looking for reasons to be offended.

At the end of that year Richard Perry, a senior adviser and former chair of the prep school organisation IAPS, came to advise the school on a future management structure. As a result of his advice Kate Bell became deputy head and head of the Lower School. This was the new designation for the pre-prep and the junior part of the prep school.

Richard Perry was extremely impressive. He oozed charm and bonhomie. A former head of a rather grander prep school, he managed to secure the trust and confidence of nearly everyone he met. For once the governors and the headmaster were at one about this man's virtues. It would turn out later that William had been again too easily taken in by his smooth charm and high status.

The governors decided, enthusiastically supported by William that he was just the chap to approach for future advice. He became the school's informal mentor. William was especially delighted to have a senior and respected figure available who also seemed to quite like what he saw.

At about that time William was invited to apply for a post in a Gloucestershire prep school. This was the junior school linked to local Catholic senior school. As such it seemed the perfect solution to ensuring for the Jones family a more secure future. It was exactly the kind of arrangement that Brian had thought might work when William had sought out his advice some months before.

It seemed to him and Mary a very agreeable possible solution to their numerous and growing predicaments. They would be closer to Downside and to Monmouthshire.

Most of all they might even escape from a gnawing sense that their position at Parkies was entirely conditional on people who didn't much care for them. To Mary what made it especially attractive was it would also ensure they were much closer to their boys whom Mary was still missing with an increasingly painful and intense poignancy. Therefore some weeks later they made the long journey to Gloucestershire for the interview.

They both knew immediately it wasn't for them. The school was centred on a manor house that was even more run-down and down-at-heel than Parkies. It felt, Mary thought, rather coldly institutional, more reform school than preparatory school. Nor did it possess those wide acres that were the real attraction of St Dogmael's. Rather it was on a cramped site in the middle of a less than attractive village.

It was clear, too, that if appointed, William would be even more boxed in than he was at Parkies. The governors there seemed to be looking for someone to maintain their rather old-fashioned, tired authoritarian, Catholic ethos. Innovation was clearly not on their agenda. Indeed, William was sure his own brand of somewhat disruptive, chaotic creativity was one which would appeal about as much as John Calvin on steroids in this deeply clerical institution. He was sure too if he secured this position he would be jumping out of the frying pan directly into the fire.

Perhaps the denouement arrived when the rather haughty,

somewhat remote, detached, unsympathetic priest who was a senior functionary of the diocese was escorting them around the campus. He was incidentally at great pains to ensure that everyone knew his elevated status.

He was also Chairman of the Board which William felt was a very bad omen. As they accompanied this clerical poohbah the only issue he seemed really particularly exercised about was when he asked William and Mary their feelings about what they had already come to judge as the obviously inadequate, very small and badly located, isolated headmaster's house.

Mary simply commented, "It is rather too small for all of us, Father." This was an observation that clearly annoyed the overbearing priest. The clerical indignation was reinforced when William, who had previously spied a much more appropriate, larger building in the middle of the school campus, enquired, "Who lives there?" "The senior matron," the priest replied with obvious irritation at again being so impertinently challenged. He then pompously announced, "She has convinced me that it is absolutely essential she remains there." William perhaps unwisely, but pertinently, responded: "Who do you care most about, Father: the matron or the headmaster?"

The answer to that question came in a telephone call the following day when their application was rather haughtily rejected. This adventure had not improved their situation at Parkies. It seemed even to those well-disposed to the Joneses that they had shown that they were not fully committed. This had caused considerable damage to their situation and reputation, as William was to increasingly discover the following year.

Chapter Twenty-One

THE BEGINNING OF THE END

William made some approaches to a neighbouring prep school suggesting a possible merger. These proposals did not in the end go anywhere. As Kate Bell's successes multiplied and numbers of both the Lower School and Nursery grew apace, the urgency or indeed need for examining any merger or a takeover by a senior school somewhat diminished. The 'bed and breakfast' boarding also grew like Topsy.

The numbers of day children increased to such an extent that by 1997 a survey that William had commissioned suggested that Parkies was attracting nearly 70% of the potential market within a ten-mile radius of the school. This success seemed to be a factor in the closure of a smaller rival which in itself further increased the numbers.

By that year, the school had grown to over 300 pupils. It had even finally become genuinely coeducational with over one-third of its pupils being female.

This meant that William needed to develop relationships with girls' senior schools which for him was an entirely new experience. Early on quite soon after girls started to appear, two pupils were entered for a scholarship at one of these grander establishments. The recently appointed Director of Studies, whose job it was to organise these things, had not appreciated that this establishment had a unique system of a pre-scholarship examinations.

The intention of this arrangement was quite reasonably to weed out the weaker candidates. Almost certainly that would include these two. On the morning that this was supposed to happen, William realised with horror that the girls had not taken this examination. He knew that if he simply telephoned the school to ask if they could take it the following day he would be pointed to the rules and that would be that.

With relatively few girls yet in the school he had virtually no leverage, as both these children were from significant local families. One, for example, was Lord Castle's granddaughter. This would have been a potential public relations disaster. William therefore got in his car and drove the hundred or so miles to beg for mercy. He got to the entrance of this imposing place just before lunch. This was after three hours of growing panic as he contemplated the likely consequences if they refused.

The delightfully charming Irish lady registrar was very sympathetic. Faced with this trembling, obviously very anxious, shambling individual, she organised a coffee and sandwiches whilst he sat down to await the verdict.

The Vice-Principal was not so sympathetic. She was a grey-haired, scholarly-looking lady sporting half-moon glasses. William's dishevelled, chaotic appearance seemed to confirm to her the fundamental incompetence of all men and this one in particular. She peered at him as though he was of another exotic, as well as a wholly inexplicable, uniquely strange, new species. He knew he was being closely examined by her frighteningly razor-sharp, analytical mind. It was obvious to him that she did not approve in any way of what she had seen of this shambolic individual standing in front of her.

Finally the ultimate decision was to be taken by the Principal. William had never met her before. He was aware nevertheless of her formidable reputation. He was then called to her study. He entered with some trepidation. She looked at him with a withering disdain, but he noticed just a touch of a twinkle in her eyes. She handed him the papers and said, "You are absolutely hopeless, Mr Jones, but" she added with a smile, "you have just twenty-four hours."

He had this overwhelming desire to kiss her, but he thankfully resisted the impulse and sped back to Suffolk with the vital documents. As he predicted, the girls didn't get any further. A few years later when William had become a friend of this lady's she was heard to say, "Such a charming man, William Jones, but the most disorganised fellow I have ever known."

Not all William's relationships with senior girls' schools were quite so friendly or ultimately so fruitful. The headmistress of a prestigious, at least in its own lights, local girls' day school was someone he found especially challenging.

As was normal with such contacts William and Mary were invited to look around the school followed by lunch. When they arrived at the front door the rather short, prim headmistress immediately sniffly observed with a cross, irritated scowl. "You must be a joint headship!" She had clearly not expected Mary to be present. The chill that this lady exuded was positively Arctic.

They were marched around the establishment. The girls pressed themselves against the walls in what William imagined was absolute terror. This pint-size martinet glared malignantly in every possible direction. It felt more like a concentration camp than a school.

William disliked her. Indeed his feelings were rather stronger than that! Courtesy of course demanded he did his best to hide this. Her feelings for him were obviously just as antagonistic. The trouble was the more William concentrated on hiding his growingly hostile agitation, the clumsier he seemed to become.

He tripped on stairs and he bumped into walls. Finally there was a truly uncongenial lunch where the other guest was a local archdeacon. He droned on about every tiny detail of his recent holiday to Chile. The topic could have been fascinating but this man, William thought, has a monotone voice and prodigious memory for every detail of each meal they had ever eaten, as well as an obsessive partiality for name-dropping every important Chilean he had ever met. Not one of these people William had ever remotely heard of. This made his exposition turgid and more boring than watching the grass grow.

The headmistress was obviously very captivated by the topic or perhaps, more likely, the clergyman. Then the denouement together with the coffee arrived. This was served in those tiny cups which were really too small for William's large, clumsy hands. He dropped the scalding liquid down the front of his trousers and inadvertently let out a very rude oath. Needless to say they were never invited again.

Rather unkindly, this lady was always subsequently privately referred to by William and Mary as "the poisoned dwarf". Mary commented when they were later talking about the archdeacon. "Sometimes there seem few good reasons to be Catholic but avoiding the terrible tedium of that man's sermons must be high amongst them!"

On the face of this the growth in numbers and the success of coeducation was excellent news. Unfortunately boarding continued to slip. By that year 1996 only seventy children could be so described. The occasional boarders slightly confused the issue. On some nights there were up to 120 children sleeping in the school. However, the fees one could charge for children sleeping for one or two nights a week hardly made a dent in the subsequent reduction of income. The Nursery and pre-prep, now called the Lower School, required a higher staff ratio, and could only attract smaller fees.

So whilst on the face of things there was some most gratifying progress, the school could rarely make a surplus. Without a surplus there was little chance of significantly improving school facilities. This was therefore the continuing conundrum that William and Graham Warner faced. Jonathan Carpenter incidentally was not at all happy that the school's financial situation was not improving as quickly as he thought it should.

The other related issue was that many families who were now attracted to the school could barely afford it. As Parkies lost its wealthy, faraway market it needed to dig deeper into the generally less prosperous, local potential clientele.

Quite frequently such families ran into financial problems. William understood that independent school headmasters expected some latitude in awarding bursaries in the case of hardship. There was, he thought, a generally accepted convention in prep schools that these bursaries should never exceed 5% of the gross fee income.

This was not a principle that many governors accepted or were willing to countenance. In the view of most of them William tended to be far too generous in his treatment of impecunious families.

Graham had recognised a few years before that William was too easily influenced and sometimes made awards which were somewhat dubious and had limited justification. In short, William was inclined sometimes to be a bit of a soft touch. Graham felt therefore that this criticism wasn't entirely unjustified.

Part of William's motivation was extremely hard-headed. There was no waiting list. Few prep schools whatever they said, could claim to have one. If children left they could not usually be replaced. William was also conscious from his previous experience that families forced to take their children away for financial reasons often invented other excuses that could be very harmful to the school's local reputation. His view was it was better to secure part of the fee than lose it altogether.

This issue of the award of bursaries became a central controversy in most governors' meetings during that period. The monk headmaster of Downside, Dom Osmund Ward, had joined the board. This was a generous thing on his part to agree to. Parkies no longer sent many boys to his school and it was a horrendous journey, as William well knew, from Somerset to Suffolk.

The good news, from William's perspective, was that he saw in Father Ward a natural ally. A man who understood the basics of how independent schools operated or at least should do. After these meetings Dom Osmund stayed overnight. It was a good opportunity to chat things over. If Father Brendan was available they would, as he put it, have "a really good crack".

Father Ward was quite supportive of William over the issue of bursaries. He, too, recognised, as did Brendan and Graham, that William was often rather too easily conned. However, he also understood that in the minds of some of the board this question was less about the loss of revenue but a malicious power play.

The other linked issue at least in William's mind was the question of his salary. There had been no attempt to restore the cuts that he and Mary had voluntarily taken back in 1992. By 1996 he was only earning two-thirds of the average salary for the sector. With Charlie now at Downside the Jones family finances were seriously stretched. As it turned out, this issue was never resolved.

William's determination to continue to offer generous help to struggling families was in the view of even his closest friends on the board a great tactical error. Everyone else seemed to see this but William was blind to the dangers that were obvious in his uncompromising attitude.

This was a sign, Mary knew, of one of William's bouts of extreme foolishness. She would admit this sometimes verged on arrogant stubbornness. The trouble was William didn't see the school as first and foremost a business. Nor did he want it to become over socially exclusive.

He wished to attract families who would not normally have considered a prep school education for their children. He didn't believe that it was possible or desirable to maintain this narrow social exclusivity anyway. Most of the smarter, wealthier families had originated from London. That market was disappearing fast. When William had arrived in 1987 the school had provided a 52-seater coach to ferry children from the metropolis. By 1996 all that was needed was a single taxi.

William also understood like Dom Osmund that the campaign to curtail his power in this area was being orchestrated by governors whose concern was mostly about hobbling his power and undermining his authority. For this reason, more than any other, William was determined to resist.

William's attitude to bursaries was the perfect issue for his enemies to focus upon. This was made worse by his recent unsuccessful application to the Gloucestershire school. William now looked irrationally stubborn and at the same time not really fully committed to Parkies. This was a potentially fatally damaging combination.

If William might not appreciate it, his enemies certainly did. Because most of the neutral and even friendly members of the board thought he was mistaken about this, it ensured that their support was usually rather muted at best.

Finally it was Gerald Grimes who brought matters to a head. "I demand," he announced, "that in future all bursaries are only awarded when all the facts are presented to a subcommittee of the board. The decision should be entirely theirs, not the headmasters."

William was now at his most obdurate. He refused to accept any diminution in what he thought was his legitimate authority. Whilst Dom Osmund largely agreed with him. He remarked in some frustration after one difficult meeting, "I do understand your position, William, but by being so pig-headed and by refusing to compromise, the majority of the board will impose a diktat that you will not like. If you compromise now you might be allowed some leeway."

Of course William should have compromised. Later even he could see that. Yet, he had at this stage become obsessed about the question.

It had become an issue of principle. It was in the end an expression of what he believed was what the school was all about.

Brendan understood. When chatting to Osmund at a meeting at his presbytery the day after a particularly unpleasant governor session he commented, "He is a strange one, William. It is this romantic thing again. For all the faults he knows more than anyone that Parkies possesses. He has a ludicrous, naive dream. It reminds me of that quotation from Isaiah, the one about the Lord's temple being established on the mountains and all nations streaming to it. Part of him sees or wants to believe this very ordinary little school is the Lord's temple. I still see him as the utopian, starry-eyed dreamer he was when he went on all those student marches years ago. I think that sums up this fellow. He wants to change the world and is arrogant or bone headed enough to think he still can. He even imagines Parkies is his flawed instrument for doing so."

Father Osmund then observed. "I like your analogy, Brendan, but I think to William it is much more like a Sir Percival looking for his Holy Grail. For some bizarre reason he seems to believe he has found it in Parkies. Whilst we both basically agree there is more than a touch of the utopian dreamer in him, the problem is there are a lot of people around here who are determined to destroy him. I don't think he really understands that. I also believe he is simply giving them the perfect weapon to use." They decided to chat to him. In the end, as they suspected, their efforts were in vain.

Whilst this issue bubbled away, William was still not really conscious of its importance at least as far as his own future was concerned. The most immediate and difficult problem for him was the Daltons.

Isabelle's talents ensured that the girl boarding numbers in the Stables House held up better than the boys'.

This was a fact that she exploited with considerable zest. The social status of many of the girls' parents remained rather more exclusive than the rest of the school. Isabelle Dalton was increasingly aware that the St Edmunds set much preferred her to Jones and his menagerie, something she also exploited with absolute glee. Whilst Piers's limitations were known, he still possessed the easy charm that went down much better with this clique than the less obsequious, stiffer, more formal attitude of the headmaster and his wife.

Isabelle was now a regular attender at the St Edmunds lunches. She rather enjoyed the status this gave her. Lady Agnes Grey even seemed to treat her as a near equal. This was done as it was intended to flatter Isabelle's fragile ego. Mrs McKenzie had appeared to become a bosom friend for similar reasons.

Roland and Margaret had even been to dinner in their flat. Barbara Watson's youngest daughter was an occasional boarder in the stables. Piers and Isabelle were now frequent guests at Watson family barbecues. She had been able to pass on school gossip that this group would not have generally been aware. This made her a hugely valuable asset in what, in the view of many, was developing into an attritional war with the Joneses.

Whether it gave her any real access into this county set was rather more questionable. To Agnes Grey, Isabelle was little more than a kind of superior servant. Her use was purely an instrumental one. This was not of course Isabelle's understanding of her role. She maintained the illusion that in some sense she was seen as a genuine equal in this prestigious clique. Ultimately this misunderstanding was to be a tragedy that would ultimately destroy the Daltons just as comprehensively as it was intended to ruin William and Mary.

It was Isabelle Dalton who had first mentioned William's visits to the psychotherapist Calvin Bauer. "Delicious," Mrs McKenzie gloated. "This man is a lunatic, as well as being a malignant little oik."

The fact that the group so detested Bauer added a frisson to their outrage. "Why," Agnes Grey commented acidly, "of all the psychotherapists he could have chosen he plumped for that appalling American clodhopper? Perhaps," she added sardonically, "like meets like."

In return for these juicy morsels, Mrs McKenzie was able to share with Isabelle and Piers the problems over bursaries. "But didn't you know?" Isabelle smirked. "The most impoverished family you mentioned are close personal friends of the Joneses."

This was true. Mary's closest friend was someone who had asked for and been given help. That request, in the mind of William and Mary was entirely unconnected to their friendship.

This was not how their enemies saw or chose to see it. When Mrs McKenzie passed this little nugget onto Grimes, his normally grumpy demeanour was transformed immediately. "I think we have got this bugger giving school funds to his mates: now that is very serious indeed." He walked away from this conversation almost chortling with delight.

Finally Thomas Brown came to see Graham in the autumn term of 1997. It was just after the whole country had suffered a kind of mass community nervous breakdown after the sudden death of Princess Diana. They sat down in Graham's little, cramped office. It was Thomas who introduced the topic he wished to discuss. "How do you think it is going, Graham?" he enquired. "Quite well," Graham confidently replied. He then added, "We started this term with 335 children, not including the Nursery. Boarding is a smidgen down at 68. It looks, Tom, as though we will make a small profit for once." "A different story is being told in the wild blue yonder; at least that is what I understand, or to be more precise what Sarah has been hearing." Graham listened intently to Thomas's increasingly alarming narrative.

"Look, we have been hearing for months, perhaps years, that William doesn't get along with the Daltons. Recently, the word is that things have got worse." "In what way?" "Isabelle Dalton is claiming she is being intimidated and bullied by Jones and to a lesser extent by Kate Bell. She further says that despite repeated requests, William has refused to do anything to resolve their cramped living conditions.

She claims that things are often so bad that the only way she can protect herself from his continuous, nasty, vicious coercion is by avoiding Jones completely, and that he is now even making an issue of this." Graham was bemused. "I don't deny that relationships are strained. In my opinion the intimidation is largely the other way round."

"The worst is yet to come. The rumour is being put about, I am not sure by whom, but I can guess that William is literally going off his head and has sought psychiatric help. It is said he is giving special fee discounts to his particular friends. It is even alleged that he has his favourites on the staff, especially this young fellow Evelyn Morley. As a result he is turning a blind eye to some dodgy, inappropriate relationships between him and some of the boys."

Graham was obviously shocked and outraged by these revelations. "This is all a tissue of lies and innuendo," he angrily exclaimed. "The trouble," Thomas Brown added, "is that there is just enough truth in them to allow the most sinister and malign interpretation."

Graham felt all these vicious rumours were so nasty and unfair that to tell William the unvarnished truth would perhaps have provoked a meltdown in what he knew was the fragile morale of the headmaster. This was something the Daltons and their allies anyway seemed to be determined to engineer.

He decided to approach Mary. He swiftly came to understand that she understood exactly what was going on. This rather surprised him, but it shouldn't have. Ever since she and William had met nearly thirty years before she had always understood about the failures of judgment her husband was prone to.

She recognised it was part of the man she loved and had married. She remembered, for example, on the very day before their wedding in 1973 when one of William's then Trotskyist friends had almost persuaded him to sign on the dotted line and join the Socialist Workers Party. She had barely been able to stop him.

She remembered, too, his fantasy at the time they met about whether or not he should try what he mistakenly imagined was a vocation for the priesthood. She knew better than anyone that this was all nonsense. It took some time for William to accept this. There was a childlike, trusting quality to William which probably made him a good teacher, but hugely detracted from his capabilities as a headmaster or leader.

This of course was not helped by his being prone to the most irrational, illogical moments of extreme stubbornness. He would get an idea and would not let it go. She had witnessed this years before when he had a terrible row with the clerical headmaster of the boarding school in which he had served as housemaster. She couldn't even remember now what the issue was all about. On reflection, it now seemed a storm in a teacup. The problem was that he had pushed the issue way beyond what it warranted.

Graham's confirmation of what she already suspected filled her with a sense of righteous rage. For all his faults, William didn't deserve this character assassination. The problem was she did not know how she could save him from these ghastly people and even more so from himself. His increasing bouts of melancholy were also of great and growing concern to her. She recognised that Calvin's help was extremely valuable. However, it worried her that he was so detested by many of the county set.

She feared that this cure might turn out to be worse than the initial disease for William's diminishing status. For the first time she felt a genuine panic.

Her first port of call was to go and see Father Brendan. He in his turn had telephoned Dom Osmund. The further difficulty was, she now discovered, the appalling intelligence that Brendan was being moved. The bishop, who didn't much care for his rather radical interpretation of Church doctrine and discipline, had decided that a parish in a run-down part of Walthamstow was a much more appropriate venue for his talents.

Brendan was, she knew, an unusual priest. He had always found authority a problem and had never tolerated fools for long. In his mind most bishops were fools, and Bishop Hart his diocesan leader was perhaps the biggest fool of all. Many years before Brendan had taught this now rather pompous, self-regarding prelate in the seminary when he was just a humble seminarian.

On the last of the many occasions he was called to Bishop's House for yet another dressing-down. In great frustration and annoyance he had unwisely observed, "You weren't very bright when I taught you, my Lord, and you haven't improved much!"

This was probably one of many reasons for provoking the Bishop into moving him. He wished to make sure that Brendan ended up as far away from his presence as possible.

With his departure, Mary knew that William's closest friend and ally on the board of governors would soon disappear. She increasingly feared that William would be hung out to dry. Frustratingly she had absolutely no idea what to do to prevent this.

Dom Osmund's problem was that not only had he a school to run with plenty of problems of its own, but also that he was over 150 miles away. Mary therefore did not find the visit to Brendan helpful or in any way reassuring.

Brendan through no fault of his own could offer her little reassurance. In her heart she recognised that he was equally frustrated as her by some of William's odd behaviour. She could see that he, too, knew precisely where this malice and vengeance flowed.

The trouble now was not merely that he was going as a result of this, but that Brendan's already small influence was waning still more.

Later that autumn term William was forced reluctantly to accept that all bursaries would be handled by a subcommittee of the board. Because he had ultimately been effectively routed over this issue, he did not have sufficient remaining credibility even to influence who would sit on this panel. Thomas Brown, Dom Osmund, and Father O'Rourke all tried to ensure that the group were sensible and reasonably compassionate. William would have liked Thomas to be one of the members. He knew that Brendan could not be involved because of his role as parish priest as well as his recently announced departure. Dom Osmund was just too far away to make this practicable.

In the end it was decided that Barbara Watson, Nigel Denton, and Margaret McKenzie would sit as the final arbiters. Mrs Watson would act as chair. At least, William reflected, Grimes was not involved. What from his point of view made this whole situation worse was how detached and cold Jonathan Carpenter had become. It was as though he had rather lost interest, or worse still, had lost confidence in him.

A few weeks later a family with three children in the school applied for some help. They had been clients at the school for over six years and had always been supportive and were very involved in all aspects of school life.

These were people with whom William had a long-standing and warm relationship. In short, he liked them. Their children were bright with real potential. He very much wanted to keep them. They were, however, not part of the dominant county set.

Gary Simmonds was a man of humble background who was a very gifted potter running a local, bespoke pottery, a business which had recently hit rather hard times. They were very anxious about this new bureaucratic process and came to see William to discuss it and to air some of these anxieties. William tried to be reassuring. He believed they had an excellent case and were anyway asking only for relatively modest help.

One thing that Gary disliked was the requirement to provide a detailed description of the family finances. Understandably, William thought, they found this humiliating. Nor were they at all sure that their private affairs would not soon be common currency in the drawing rooms of Suffolk. They did, however, do as required.

This was partly because they were reassured by the head that this was going to be a relatively painless process which he was sure would have a positive outcome. As it turned out it all went quite differently from what William or they had supposed.

They were summoned to a meeting in the school library. They were questioned intimately about every detail of their income. It was soon clear to them they were not believed. The rudeness and dismissive attitude with which they were treated ensured that Sharon, Gary's wife, was in tears by the end of the session.

What had most upset them was when Mrs Watson peremptorily demanded why they should seriously expect any help when so many other parents were prepared to do the honourable thing and pay their share.

A few days later a cold and formal letter was sent to them refusing them any assistance. There was a clear implication within this letter that the panel considered that they were exaggerating the seriousness of their situation as a ploy to secure this help. Gary came to see William, his face a picture of disgust and distress. He felt betrayed, but not he believed just by this officious, nasty panel.

He also suspected that William had disregarded the warmth of their long relationship and had used this panel as a cynical ploy to avoid making the unpleasant decision himself. The result was that the children were immediately removed. They never talked to William again.

William was called to meet Jonathan at Walton House in the early months of 1998. Despite their occasional disagreements William always considered that his relationship with Jonathan Carpenter was a good one.

The recent renaissance in the fortunes of the school he assumed might even have raised his stock somewhat. William was greeted with an unexpected coldness which he had already started to perceive when he had met Jonathan in recent months.

Jonathan did not bother with any social niceties. "William," he said, "I am hearing the most concerning things about your performance." "What exactly are you hearing?" enquired William. "First you haven't got a grip of the staff. From what I understand they have lost respect for you. I believe that this is especially so with Isabelle Dalton. It is essential, in my opinion, that we keep her. She is, as I am sure you realise, one of your most talented members of staff. Secondly," Jonathan icily continued, "that your judgment is often very questionable indeed. Not only was there that brouhaha over bursaries, but I am also told that you are turning a blind eye to some pretty questionable behaviour on the part of young Evelyn Morley. Thirdly, that you are still giving away bursaries despite clear instructions to the contrary."

Jonathan made some other important, but probably less significant points about the recent fall in academic scholarships, the number of dyslexics and oddballs that William was accepting, together with his less than stellar relationship with some of the parents. Jonathan finished his peroration with two devastating revelations. Firstly he announced that as he had been chair for more than twenty years he felt it was time to give up. He now rather changed into a less confrontational tone. "Don't you think, William, you have done all you can at St Dogmael's?"

He then urged William to look for new employment: "I think maybe," he added in his kindest voice, "this role is becoming a bit too stressful for you."

When William arrived back he looked, Mary thought, as though he had seen a ghost. She sat him down and drew out of him a full description of the events at Walton Hall. As she listened she felt the gore rise. Mary rarely profaned, but she now ejaculated, "These people are such ungrateful, graceless shits."

They both decided they would immediately go and see Father Brendan at this presbytery. He was due to leave for Walthamstow in a few weeks. William repeated his story and Brendan took up his familiar pose of steepled hands. The odd thing, Mary thought, was he didn't look at all surprised or on this occasion especially sympathetic.

Then with much deliberation of speech he responded, "I think you know how very fond I am of both of you. I know this job has cost you both and your children a great deal, I know, too, you have done your absolute best and in many ways you have been a remarkable success." He went on. "In a way Jonathan is right although he put it very clumsily and rather cruelly in my opinion. You have been here too long. For all his strange ways Jonathan has protected you all these years. He never I think expected you to achieve what you have. He always assumed the place would fold. You have I am afraid rather ruined that expectation. I think you know that they underestimated you, Will."

Brendan allowed himself a wry smile, "That fellow Denton was brought in by him on the assumption the place would indeed fold. Don't you see he was preparing for the school's closure. Parkies after all sits on prime development land." "But why did Jonathan say all this now?" enquired Mary. "Partly," Brendan went on, "because he is tired he doesn't get anything out of this but all he seems to see is the place stagger from one crisis to the next. Secondly, Margaret Gerald and that new woman Barbara Watson have been bending his ear for years about your perceived deficiencies. I think you now know by playing hardball in that rather obstinate and silly fashion over bursaries you have rather played right into their hands. Worse, Will, you need to think who will take over as chair when Jonathan goes. The only person I believe you really trust other than me and Osmund is Thomas Brown. Take my word, even if I was still around which I won't be, Thomas hasn't a chance even if he wants it, which I don't think he does. You, old chap, are stuck with one of those women. Pray it is Barbara rather than Margaret."

Six months later, Jonathan resigned as Chairman but stayed on the board for a short period. The new chair was to be, as Brendan predicted, Barbara Watson. Jonathan hosted a lunch party at Walton Hall so as to oil a smooth transition. This was a surprisingly agreeable occasion. Barbara seemed to make a genuine effort to establish a good working relationship with the Joneses. At the end of this, William thought that just possibly he might be able to cope with this lady. Certainly, she seemed friendly and interested. Perhaps, he imagined, he had misjudged her. He was determined to give it a go at any rate.

Mary believed William was deluding himself that Barbara Watson's attitude had significantly altered. Her hostility to them, she initiatively understood, was so obviously deeply ingrained. Even at the lunch party Mary was not convinced that Barbara Watson's attitude was really genuinely friendly. She was sure that this was largely a front designed to impress Jonathan Carpenter.

Mary was certain that trouble was on the horizon. She wished not for the first time that William was not quite so forgiving and credulous. He seemed always to take all situations at face value when he should be far more wary and suspicious.

She even noticed at the end of the party that William had buttonholed Barbara Watson and was passionately outlining his many future dreams for the school. Extraordinarily he seemed not to have noticed the bored, hostile, disengaged look in Mrs Watson's eyes masked as always by her charming flirtatious rather pretty smile. It amazed Mary that men so often failed to discern the threat behind a pretty face. Even worse in his open, enthusiastic peroration he was giving to someone who Mary increasingly believed was his enemy, further ammunition. The stupidity of her husband often totally annoyed and frustrated her.

By now dear Brendan had gone. The new, rather coldly disapproving, somewhat humourless parish priest was not interested in replacing him as a governor. Another one of the St Edmunds set was thus slipped onto the board. Things, Mary considered, did not look at all good. Mary was settled into her life at Parkies. She had now got used to Suffolk. Flo was happy Francis and James were now both at university. They needed a home base and William and they were still paying for Charlie at Downside.

Mary did not wish to move. Even if they could, she doubted whether they could find a similar job. In the end they absolutely needed Parkies. She imagined that without it her carefully constructed family dynamic would simply collapse. She would do all she could to avoid this. Somehow, she had to get William to understand the real peril he was in.

It was the summer of William's fiftieth birthday. They had a big party at the beginning of the holidays. They had combined it with Francis's twenty-first. The most moving moment for Mary was the Mass they had in the school chapel. They had been married for twenty-five years and Father Brendan travelled up from Walthamstow to officiate. When they renewed their vows he gave them his blessing.

Even in these difficult times she thanked God for the blessings that her marriage to William had brought. Mary had also arranged a really special holiday in America. When they returned home she hoped that they would have at last managed to get things into perspective and truly address what was really happening.

Chapter Twenty-Two

TARUN

Returning much refreshed from their American interlude both William and Mary had a much more positive frame of mind. The new term seemed to promise much. Kate Bell's amazing efforts had ensured that the Lower School was thriving as never before. Funds had even been found to extend this area and add two new classrooms. She had a wonderful eye for detail and had laid a beautiful flower garden and children's adventure area. Boarding numbers remained a problem and both the girls' and boys' boarding houses were short of pupils. William knew, however, that compared to many competitor schools Parkies was doing remarkably well. Many governors were not interested in comparative statistics. They just focussed on the decline of boarding in St Dogmael's which for many was yet another sign of William's failure.

He for many years now had been undertaking the lion's share of History teaching. This is something he genuinely loved. It allowed him to further augment his natural, perhaps, if he was truly honest, somewhat simulated eccentricity. He was in his professional dreamworld working away in his History room.

He had built up a large archive of material. It became a bit of a hobby for him to look for books, pamphlets, posters, postcards and historical films and audiotapes with which he adorned his room. He also developed and wrote his own rather basic textbooks. The costs of all this came out of his own pocket.

There was such a demand to spend money on other subject areas, he didn't think he could justify more expenditure on what was after all his pet project. William basically self-financed his passion. It was worth every penny from his point of view where he could spend many happy evenings beautifying his little private empire.

When describing the various battles such as Hastings or Bosworth he was inclined to charge up and down between the children's desks waving an imaginary sword rather in the mode of his hero, the indomitable Mr Evans. He delighted in the reaction of bemused glee on the faces of most of his pupils.

He much preferred teaching about wars and battles than the more mundane issues of everyday life. In truth, his lessons were not always very well prepared.

He relied rather too much on the violent and scandalous aspects of these historical stories. He didn't much enjoy teaching that important aspect of the subject, 'sources'. He did so, but without much enthusiasm.

Most of all he wanted the children to enjoy their experience of the subject. On the whole, he considered, they mostly did. He was reassured, too, by the fact that in Common Entrance and Scholarship History secured some of the best examination performances.

Mary, Kate, and Graham, too, thought that in his increasing obsession with his History teaching, he was using it to escape the many problems he knew were rapidly building up. It was easier to focus on these narrower academic and pastoral sides of his job, rather than the really critical management and strategic issues which he felt increasingly powerless to address.

William was developing a remarkable capacity for ignoring things he didn't want to face. Mary did not possess this dubious talent or at least to the same degree as her husband. It was clear to her that the apparently placid and calm atmosphere that seemed now to pervade the school was a mirage. In a sense she believed that William was also just starting to perceive this, too.

Mary understood with a growing understanding and increasing alarm that their position was becoming more and more tenuous. She kept noticing gaggles of known, ill-disposed governors in intense conversations both between themselves and with the Daltons and various discontented mothers, most of whom she knew were linked in some way or another to the St Edmunds set.

These conversations, she noticed, ominously ceased whenever she approached. This merely adding further to her growing apprehension. For the time being, superficially at least, things seemed to going on much as before. Not a situation Mary thought would last for long.

William had a new idea. He was now focussing once more on the core issue of numbers which as far as boarding was concerned was a continuing headache. He was also considering ways to improve the academic profile of the school. He knew that many children were enrolled because they found maintained schools difficult to cope with.

With closer pastoral care and smaller classes parents imagined this would resolve the problems their child had previously suffered from. This often worked. A higher proportion of the pupils arriving also had learning difficulties of one kind or another.

By now, Parkies had a full-blown 'special needs' department and had developed quite a lot of expertise in many of the expanding list of acronym-defined special educational conditions. There wasn't in the end much choice anyway and most similar schools were travelling in the same direction. This was a marketing fact of life that many Parkies governors did not fully understand. In some cases they simply wished to ignore this.

William had always rather liked oddballs. Maybe many thought it was a form of transference on his part. It was perhaps this welcoming, accepting attitude that persuaded some parents of such children to choose the school. Some of the governors, predictably Gerald Grimes and Margaret McKenzie, were constantly expressing hostility to these developments. Grimes was particularly virulent; he once commented: "This is supposed to be a school for normal children, why do we have to fill it with all these freaks?" Some governors were quite supportive or at least recognised this as the way the market was developing.

Lord Castle, who was nearing the end of his time, increasingly surprised William with some of his more enlightened, humane observations. "I wish we had something like this when I was a boy. When I got things wrong, as I did all the time, I got thrashed. Well done, William, for trying to do something different."

Many of these children were extremely able and Parkies did especially well with them. This was not the judgment of some of the irreconcilable governors and staff. The previous year, one such boy got a scholarship to Winchester and another secured a place at Eton. These were facts that could not be gainsaid, although they were entirely ignored by his critics.

One lad with Asperger's was a special fan of his History classes. This boy's knowledge and grasp of detail were remarkable. This of course was a feature of his condition. He was obsessive in finding out every single fact, however inconsequential it seemed to others.

Every morning in chapel the head would tell the children a story with a religious or moral theme. Many of these were drawn from his extensive historical repertoire. This young fellow would frequently interrupt his flow to point out some small, or even sometimes larger, error. William always gave the floor to him. Apart from anything else he knew he was always right. He thought this was great for this boy's confidence and was anyway an amusing interlude.

Because he judged that the school was especially effective with dealing with such children, William decided on a new initiative.

On Saturday mornings twice a term the school offered special free extension classes for gifted children from the locale. He swiftly realised that whilst many of these children were very able, the 'gifted' epithet often said more about the parents than the children. He started to think of the National Association for Gifted Children as more aptly named the National Society of Neurotic Mothers.

Whilst a few children enrolled in the school as a result of this, it did not in any way justify the expense and time involved. After a term or so this initiative was abandoned.

One afternoon early in the spring term of 1999 he received a telephone call from the Director of Social Services from a neighbouring county. After some initial pleasantries he quickly moved on to the meat of what he wanted to say.

"We have got a ten-year-old boy who needs a boarding school

education. This boy, whose name is Tarun, is an extremely able little person with an IQ in excess of 150. He is simply not coping in the maintained system. The name of your school has been given us by the National Association for Gifted Children as a place with the expertise to cope with such children and indeed really transform this little fellow's life chances."

William suggested they meet. The Director was invited to Parkies for lunch. William was very flattered. He was proud that he was helping to forge a new, interesting path for the school. This important chap, he told himself, was travelling sixty miles because they had heard of Parkies. This seemed too good to be true. As it turned out it was!

Tarun was apparently very disruptive because he was bored and frustrated. In the right environment of small classes and high expectations he was convinced he would thrive. William was anxious about only one thing. "Is he violent?" he asked. "No no, Heaven forbid," the Director expounded, "Just a wee bit lively, that's all!" On that assurance Tarun was accepted.

An important part of the deal was that the county would pay full boarding fees with a generous supplement that might be required for any extra help. This, William was sure, would be the start of a flood of applications from similar children who would transform Parkies' flagging academic reputation.

Tarun arrived accompanied by his mum and dad as well as a designated social worker. This lady did not approve of William's school. She sat in the drawing room with a facial expression that suggested she had just smelt something especially noxious. The shabby elegance of this room, the country house setting and the sight of lots of relatively smartly dressed children politely standing aside as adults walked through seemed to epitomise for this lady all that she disliked about this ghastly, elitist world.

She simply couldn't understand why the Director had taken leave of his senses and even considered a place like this. Despite her antipathy to the institution she found herself quite liking the slightly shambolic headteacher, she recognised that William was well intentioned and kindly.

She didn't believe that he had any of the skills necessary to deal with a disturbed little boy like Tarun. She also recognised that this man had no real idea of the nature of Tarun's difficulties. The Director had, moreover, been less than frank. She knew that there was something going on of which she didn't approve. It was not her place to say anything.

This ten-year-old was small for his age. To William he looked totally terrified. It even seemed from the look in his eyes as though he expected an immediate and painful execution. His eyes flicked from person to person in what seemed total terror. The hostility and angst that they expressed was both pitiful and unsettling.

His parents were not much less anxious either. His father was a tall, thin Scotsman. He had that typical broad, open Celtic face typical of Western Scotland, and spoke with an attractive, soft Ayrshire brogue. His head was topped with an untidy thatch of red hair. His mother was tiny, not much taller than her son.

She was an Indian lady and her face had those sharp features so redolent of the subcontinent. William thought she seemed more uncomfortable even than her husband. Yet her dark eyes sparkled with intelligent concern, as well as interest in – or was it bemusement of? –

this strange new environment.

Her jet-black hair was tied tightly in a bun. She looked like a schoolteacher. He quickly established that this was actually so. This lady taught Science in a London grammar school.

It was agreed that the Joneses' sitting room would be Tarun's "place of safety", a rather odd piece of Social Services jargon. If Tarun was anxious or worried he was to feel free to come to this room. William tried to emphasise the informal atmosphere of the school. This seemed to please the parents if not necessarily the scowling social worker.

She increasingly felt that this was yet another reflection of the hubristic pretensions of this middle-class domain of naive do-gooders. It was further agreed that the school would make a weekly report to both the Social Services and the parents. For the first week or so William promised he would telephone the parents daily. When all these arrangements were in place a boy was summoned to take Tarun on a tour of the school and help to settle him in these new, strange surroundings.

To begin with, everything seemed to be going pretty well. Tarun was certainly tense and quiet but he seemed to be coping. The evening of his second day William had a chat with him. He felt very sorry for this little waif. He looked lost and confused. It seemed that, as yet, he had made no friends.

William tried to reassure him this would happen soon. Tarun didn't appear convinced or indeed particularly interested in the prospect. William asked him whether he would like to talk to his parents.

Tarun eagerly agreed. William sat Tarun down on his chair in front of his newly acquired, much-prized antique Georgian desk. This was a gift from his mother on the occasion of his fiftieth birthday.

He rang the parents' number and then gave the telephone receiver to Tarun and proceeded to tiptoe out of his sitting room. Just before he got to the door Tarun's voice shouted out with ear-shattering venom, "Get me out of this fucking shithole! I hate this horrible school; how could you do this to me? I hate you!" He then started to hammer the receiver down on the shiny, polished, expensive surface of William's prized desk. Tarun was certainly not behaving as William had hoped or indeed expected. The message he had expected Tarun to convey to his parents was the exact opposite of what had happened.

Somehow he decided he needed to retrieve the situation. He feared that Tarun's parents would be mortified. This was notwithstanding his anxiety about the damage that was being done to his cherished new possession. So he decided to turn around and tiptoed back towards Tarun.

He then carefully knelt down onto the floor beside this piece of furniture. His intention was to pull the telephone wire out. This would terminate this unfortunate outburst. He then intended to try and calm Tarun down before he contacted his parents again.

He imagined that he might telephone Tarun's parents later to reassure them and explain what had happened. He leaned over and started to pull out the telephone cord.

Tarun then directed his tight little fist with incredible force firmly into William's nose. William didn't realise that such a little instrument could cause such acute pain. The blood streamed down his face, splashing onto his shirt and suit. Tarun's blow was accompanied by a very curt: "Fuck off."

Mary rushed in and tried to calm down the little boy as well as patch up her blood-spattered husband. She rang the parents to reassure them that most things, if not quite all, were well. William disappeared to change and effect what repairs he could on his swollen and throbbing beak.

Later when he thought about this he decided that he hadn't handled things well. Having inadvertently surprised the boy, Tarun was understandably stressed and had lashed out without thinking. He telephoned the social worker to explain what had happened. She was happy to go along with this convenient fiction, although it has to be said, she did not believe a word of it.

Within days it was clear that William's trite evaluation was wishful thinking even to him. Very quickly Tarun was engaged in thumping quite a few of his dorm and classmates.

The other children now avoided him like the plague. Even much bigger children would step aside when Tarun appeared in the corridor. It was as though the seas parted when he appeared.

It was almost as though this evidence of the fear he engendered in others somehow actually increased in him a malign self-confidence. This seemed to increase the incidents of his antisocial violent behaviour.

William decided that the best appropriate action would be when these situations occurred for Tarun to be sent to the flat and isolated in one of his son's empty bedrooms until he had calmed down.

Francis was in his final year at university, James in his first and Charlie was away in Downside's sixth form. This room was where Mary kept some of the dormitory linen, as well as being used as an overflow sickbay during term-time. One day when Tarun was sitting on Charlie's bed following the most recent violent outburst, Mary said to him, in what she hoped was her best, firm but kindly, Mummy voice, "Come on, Tarun, you don't need to keep hitting people, do you? They would really like you if you let them."

She then turned away to carry on with her various domestic tasks, and Tarun, who had found Charlie's old toy pistol down the side of the bed, suddenly leaped towards her. Before she understood what was happening, Tarun had pistol-whipped her. This had temporarily rendered her unconscious, as well as leaving her with a large cut and even bigger bruise on her forehead.

William telephoned the Director of Social Services. His former urbane attitude of polite courtesy had radically changed. He was not at all sympathetic. He now made it perfectly clear that in his view it was entirely the school's fault and especially William's responsibility that these incidents had occurred. This attitude was in William's opinion dismissive and very arrogant.

The Director was most unwilling to accept even a smidgeon of responsibility. He even denied that he had ever claimed that Tarun was not violent. When William suggested that, given Tarun's aggressive behaviour, it was likely that he might ask him to leave, the Director then angrily asserted that Tarun was not being given a fair chance and William was clearly breaking the promises he had made a few days earlier. The conversation did not end on a friendly note!

Tarun's parents were distraught with what had happened and begged William to give Tarun another chance. It was for this reason that William and Mary decided to try again. His proviso was that they would expect the Social Services to fund the employment of someone to mind him during his free time. This was when most of these incidents took place.

Very reluctantly the Director agreed to this at least for a limited period. The only person available or interested in the depths of rural Suffolk was a charming old fellow who lived in the local village. He was known to be a very well-meaning chap with some experience of dealing with difficult situations. He was, after all, a decorated retired lieutenant-commander. William reasoned a stroppy ten-year-old would be nothing to him after his experience of the Arctic convoys. He did his best, but it was not a success. This was mainly because Tarun kept running away from him and he simply couldn't keep up.

At least it meant that some of the more unpleasant incidents didn't take place because Tarun was more interested in escaping from the elderly lieutenant-commander than assaulting his next victim. By this stage, the parents of many of the other children were lining up outside William's study in ever-increasing numbers.

The final straw came a week later when one of the most gentle final-year boys approached him at breakfast. Tarun looked more morose and unhappy than usual.

The older boy seemed to feel really sorry for him and said sympathetically, "Are you all right, Tarun?" The response was a vicious punch into this lad's nose. As a consequence a fountain of blood erupted. Tarun then shouted, "Fuck off, you c..t!"

It has to be said this was not usual language in any educational institution, least of all in a smart prep school. William, who was supervising the meal, immediately intervened; Tarun then turned on him with the identical comment. William lifted him up, an action which in itself broke the protocol he had previous agreed with Tarun's social worker. He carried him to his flat.

He had missed a basic biological and mathematical fact that Tarun's manically kicking feet were directly in line with his groin. When contact finally occurred William thought he was going to die, the pain was excruciating. With much difficulty William eventually was able to deposit him in Charlie's room. Mary and William locked the door and rang the Social Services demanding his immediate removal.

Reluctantly this was agreed with, it has to be said, the minimum of courtesy. He then had a more difficult conversation with Tarun's father, a man he had come to like and respect. Whilst he was entirely distraught William quickly realised he was not particularly surprised.

Later, William wrote a report to the Social Services Department describing the various events that led to this situation. Tarun was transferred into locked psychiatric care.

It was obvious to William that he and the school had been cynically used to provide the evidence necessary to ensure this satisfactory outcome at least from the perspective of Social Services. One result was that the reports of these incidents at St Dogmael's finally gave Tarun's mum the courage to admit that she had been regularly assaulted by her son. She was quite literally terrified of him and overwhelmed with guilt for feeling so.

The predominant feeling William had was he felt he had been used. The combination of his naivety and hubris had been again successfully exploited. His pride and stupidity had ensured that he fell for it. He was also wholly aware that this was a truly terrible tragic situation.

William wondered whether there was any real hope for this little boy in the long term. His sympathy for the family in many ways deflected his anger at being exploited and lied to by people who should and did known better.

This incident was of course used by many of the governors, enthusiastically aided and abetted by the Daltons, to suggest that this was yet another example of William's lack of judgment, an observation that William painfully realised was certainly true.

The various stories Isabelle Dalton was able to recount of Tarun's vicious exploits described in the most vivid and often distorted detail enlivened many of the St Edmunds set's lunch parties. They vicariously enjoyed her account of the numerous injuries that William and Mary had sustained. Sympathy was entirely absent. Indeed, the more painful and serious the damage done, the more relish with which it was recounted. These ladies were quite simply delighted by William Jones's difficult predicament.

Unbeknown to the Joneses, Mrs Watson, now the chair-elect of the governors, was now yet more convinced than ever that William and Mary should not be any part of the future of the school. William didn't know what the social worker really thought. If he had he would probably have agreed with her.

He realised throughout this he had behaved with palpable, conceited arrogance. This was something he now reluctantly accepted. Worst of all he now knew this, as, of course, did his enemies and even his friends.

What effectively was happening, a fact now very obvious to Mary, Kate, and Graham, was the slow drip, drip of subversion and criticism which was gradually disempowering him. This was crucially undermining William's diminishing self-confidence which Mary supposed might even be his enemies' principle objective.

It was therefore becoming more and more difficult for him to assert his authority. Concepts of confidentiality did not seem to exist in the minds of many governors. His apparent limitations and failings were regularly discussed, dissected, and laughed at by both selected parents and staff. Some governors were actively encouraging this. They were at the forefront of promoting the worst and most damaging gossip.

Chapter Twenty-Three

STAFFING ISSUES

The issue of appraisal was at the core of the next developing crisis. William had for some time been trying to introduce a more robust system of staff appraisal. Most staff were happy to accept this. Kate Bell had largely already achieved this in the Lower School. However, the core problem in the rest of the school was Piers Dalton.

He was now in William's view by far Parkies' weakest teacher. Unfortunately, even the mildest criticism of his performance provoked apparent mystification and a theatrical display of angry resentment on his part, as well as, more ominously, fury from his wife Isabelle. Quite often she then went into purdah and refused to talk to either Mary or William for weeks on end. This made the effective management of the school virtually impossible.

Over the years William had been able to replace or reassign all the other poor teachers who were in situ when he had first arrived. He had even managed to persuade James Waters, the one 'O' level Geography teacher, that grounds work in another school might be a more appropriate career choice.

Every attempt by William to address the Piers issue was scuppered by a combination of his wife Isabelle's influence supported by a growing number of sympathetic school governors. Crucially, over the last few years that seemed now to have become the majority.

To try to minimise the worst consequences of Piers Dalton's inadequate performance William had timetabled him to teach junior French and Geography to the younger, less able children. These seemed to be areas in which he could do less damage to the school's reputation.

William knew in his heart, of course, that it was a betrayal of those children assigned to him. Their interests were being sacrificed for the greater good of appeasing the Daltons. It was interesting to note that all the children of the St Edmunds set were all placed automatically by Isabelle in the more able groups whatever their actual capability. These parents were therefore largely unaware of Piers's huge limitations.

That these children were being taught by her and definitely not by him obviously further masked any unfortunate perceptions of his incompetence to anyone who was in any way influential. These parents and their children were thus spared the experience of Piers Dalton's laminable teaching performance. It was increasingly obvious this was not a sustainable situation and William knew it.

Even to William it was becoming more and more obvious the detestation with which Piers regarded him. One afternoon he decided to confront him with this. "What is this all about, Piers? What have I done to so offend you?" Piers had not expected this and was therefore rather taken aback. He seemed to have no obvious reply so he simply spluttered what must have been the first thing that entered his mind. "Some years ago you showed the film *The Lion in Winter* to a group of eleven-year-olds. It was rated as a 15 and you totally ignored me when I pointed that out."

William was amazed. "Are you seriously saying that all the unpleasantness of all these years is simply and only about me showing the children a slightly inappropriate film?" Piers didn't reply and merely slunk away. William realised this could not be the real source of all this angst. If it was, either he or Piers or perhaps both were clearly totally mad.

In an attempt to find a resolution to this problem in the spring term governors' meeting William proposed that they ask Richard Perry to advise. He had been so helpful for years. He further suggested as a sweetener that he should be the guinea pig in a new appraisal structure. Perry, he submitted, could appraise him and that could act as a template for a whole school policy.

William was somewhat surprised that the governors accepted this so readily. Even Grimes thought it was a good idea. He supposed that they had not appreciated that his main target was bound to be Piers Dalton. Any half-decent process would in his opinion quickly expose Piers's total and obvious incompetence.

What William had not appreciated was the critical significance that governors' input would have on the outcome of any headmaster's appraisal. This was not a consideration that had been missed by his enemies. A week or so after the decision to proceed had been taken, the McKenzies and Watsons were sitting around the dining table at one of their regular dinner parties.

On this occasion the venue was the rather smart McKenzie manor house. During coffee, the topic of Richard Perry's future visit was introduced by Barbara Watson. "What do you make of this recent appraisal proposal from Jones?" she asked them all. Roland McKenzie who of course had been kept fully informed of what was going on immediately intervened. "As I see it, Jones is trying to be rather too clever. He believes that if he can start this ball rolling the most likely victim is going to be Piers Dalton. We all know that Piers is useless. Any half-decent process will expose that."

"What about Jones's own appraisal?" Margaret McKenzie anxiously enquired. "We know, don't we, that when this fellow Perry came four years ago he was quite polite about him. He is hardly likely to change his mind in so short a time, is he?" "You are going to help him to do exactly that," observed David Watson. "Have you not considered that a key, perhaps the most important, component of Richard Perry's judgment will be based on the views of governors. All you need to tell him is that you have lost confidence in Jones. Make sure that he talks to the right people of course. If enough of you say this, he is truly finished."

So the plan was laid. No one cared much about Piers Dalton. He was, after all, collateral damage. They seemed to have found a rather elegant solution for William Jones. "One other thing," Roland added, "I believe that Perry is supposed to seek the opinion of a few parents, too. I am sure you, Barbara, can ensure they are just the right ones."

This seemed to amuse the newly knighted Judge Roland McKenzie. After the Watsons left he turned to his wife, smiled and for the first time for many months put his arm around her shoulder and gently and meaningfully said, "See you upstairs, my love."

William had come to rely more and more on Evelyn Morley. Not only did he produce the extraordinarily impressive plays, but he had also effectively run the boys' boarding house for many years. Ideally William had hoped to find a married couple to undertake this task.

Such was Evelyn's commitment and care as well as having no funds to further increase staffing that William ultimately gave him control as well as the title of housemaster and the small extra allowance that went with this.

Evelyn always assiduously avoided the various politics of the Common Room. He was a deeply moral man, and gossip and mud-slinging were not things he ever indulged in. This young man was of course deeply religious in a slightly agonised Catholic kind of way. Whilst he was generally popular with the rest of the Common Room he was not naturally clubbable.

William noted that he was usually on his own. He often saw him returning from long, solitary walks. His dramatic flair continued to enhance the liturgy within the chapel. With Brendan's departure and a successor priest who was not vaguely interested in the school other than simply saying Mass on Sunday evening and pocketing the small stipend that came with this. Evelyn's role in this area thus became even more crucial. By this stage Evelyn quite literally personally embodied Parkies' Catholic heritage.

Not all parents were happy with him. The core of this discontent was his rather camp style. Whilst he hailed from a respectable, Catholic, upper-middle-class background, and had attended Ampleforth, the famous Catholic public school, he made no real attempt to ingratiate himself with any of the influential parents. Because he was inclined to avoid any social contact he cut rather an isolated figure. It probably helped fuel rumours that spread widely and remarkably quickly. These were that he was both gay and a potential if not actually a paedophile.

It was unfortunately true that Evelyn on occasion was rather too close to some of his charges. This was in part William knew because a few of the more insecure boys rather pestered him. Evelyn was just too kind to reject them. On a few occasions William had to have a word with him to warn him of the dangers this posed.

He had taken these observations on-board and William was pleased to notice that this was a much-diminished problem. There was no evidence whatsoever of any inappropriate behaviour. Indeed, quite to the contrary. If a boy was unhappy Evelyn was the first to notice and attempted to address it. Evelyn had secured William's total trust and confidence. He was, it seemed to him, a good man whose reputation was being unfairly trounced.

None of this satisfied his most obdurate critics. Unsurprisingly the most persistent, although certainly not the only one, was Gerald Grimes. The issue came fully to a head when on one occasion he had insisted on seeing William to discuss his concerns about Evelyn. His opening observation was, "Look, William, this fellow Morley is obviously queer. What the hell do you think you are doing putting him in charge of boys?" William responded more calmly than he actually felt. "What evidence have you that Evelyn is homosexual? I don't believe he is. For what it is worth, even if he were, that doesn't make him a paedophile."

Gerald Grimes on another occasion got so annoyed about William's refusal to take his observations and complaints seriously enough, he exploded with fury. He approached the headmaster's desk thus invading William's personal space in the most intimidatory, alarming way.

He then peered into his face his rather beery, foul-smelling breath intermingled with copious spittle. He came within inches of William's face. "Look here, Jones, you have employed a queer who is an obvious danger to little boys. You have put him in a position of trust so that he has *carte blanche* to fiddle with them to his heart's content." He added, with an air of further menace. "If I ever discover evidence that he is what I think he is, not only will I chop his balls off, but yours, too."

Grimes was not the only parent who was worried by Evelyn, although their concerns tended to be much more moderately expressed. William conceded privately that Evelyn might possibly have homosexual inclinations. However, there was absolutely no solid evidence whatsoever of that.

It was worth remembering, he thought, that for many years Evelyn had a girlfriend. He therefore robustly defended him whenever he was attacked. Indeed he saw it as his clear and moral duty to do so. He was upset and outraged that this good man's reputation could be so fragrantly assailed without any right of reply. Mary and Graham were more aware of the additional even more damaging rumours.

"Of course," Isabelle Dalton disingenuously opined at one of her frequent luncheons with Lady Grey, Mrs Barbara Watson and the now Lady Margaret McKenzie. Roland's appointment had now finally been confirmed to the judicial bench. "William Jones rather likes Evelyn," she added meaningfully. "Who can say why. He is one of the few members of staff he trusts. He therefore allows him total unrestrained and, in my opinion, dangerous freedoms. All that lavish expenditure on his plays, for example."

"Quite different," she quickly and deviously added, "from the way he treats my poor Piers." Evelyn was then a homosexual and a paedophile and William his protector, Mary thought when she heard this rumour almost as his pimp. Nothing was ceasing to surprise her of the depth of malice and vicious maleficence that some people at Parklands were capable.

Chapter Twenty-Four

POWERLESSNESS

Early in the summer term of 1999, William received a telephone call from a Chief Inspector Patton of Suffolk Police. He asked for an urgent meeting. The Chief Inspector then arrived at the school later that day. He was a large man, dressed in a rather baggy, creased suit which had clearly seen rather better times. His face gave away nothing.

This intrigued William, partly because Detective Chief Inspectors were not frequent visitors at Parkies. Indeed as he considered it, he thought this might be entirely unique. After he had sat down with a cup of tea in William's study and they had completed the initial courtesies, it transpired that he was the senior officer in the county Child Protection Squad. From being initially curious about his unusual visitor William's emotions were rapidly being transformed into something akin to panic. What could be happening, William imagined, that could possibly explain or justify the presence in his study of such a senior police officer?

Chief Inspector Patton then explained that he had received an anonymous note a few days before containing a cryptic message: "I think that Mr Morley is overly interested in little boys: you should investigate it."

Mr Patton then asked, "What job does this fellow Morley do?" William described Evelyn's duties. He wondered as he did so whether he imagined a fleeting flash of satisfied, justified triumph cross the policeman's face. What William was saying seemed to confirm Mr Patton's worst suspicions. "Do you think there is any truth in this?" giving the clear impression that he thought there was. William replied, "Chief Inspector, obviously not otherwise he would not have been employed at this school for eight years."

William's original, fearful response was turning to anger and outrage. He wanted to try and explain to the policeman what he thought was really going on. "There has never been the slightest suggestion of anything of this kind." Continuing on this theme, he observed. "It is true that a few parents dislike him and there has been some very malicious, unfounded gossip." "Are you really sure this gossip is malicious, Mr Jones?" There followed a somewhat ominous pregnant pause.

It was difficult for William to respond adequately to any of this. He was quite sure that the accusations were spiteful nonsense. To try and explain in detail the kind of nastiness that was almost certainly behind it might have seemed like special pleading. This would reinforce the suspicions that were in the Chief Inspector's mind.

William decided to dissemble. He realised that to do otherwise might further damage Evelyn. Most of all he needed to play for time to think of the best way to deal with this.

"How do you intend to proceed?" William nervously enquired. "We would like to talk to him and, if he agrees, search his rooms." Chief Inspector Patton would have quite liked to have searched Evelyn's rooms immediately. He grudgingly recognised that such a non-specific, unproven accusation like this gave him precious little authority to do so.

William then confessed, "Evelyn is away with other members of staff on a junior camp. At the moment he is in Barmouth in Wales and therefore is difficult to contact." Whilst Mr Patton was not at all sure whether he believed this, he reluctantly agreed that this could wait until he returned. The policeman then commented, "Tell Mr Morley, headmaster, there may be nothing in this. He will of course know if there is or isn't. It would be much better for everyone perhaps for him to have a chat with us as soon as possible and sort it all out."

William didn't think for one minute that the policeman believed there was nothing in it. He believed more than a hint of threat in the Chief Inspector's last observation.

"One other thing, Mr Patton, can I see this note?" The Chief Inspector was initially a bit reluctant. Eventually he agreed. He produced a scrappy piece of paper out of the file he was holding. William studied it for a minute or two then handed it back. A feeling of cold terror then gripped his heart.

William called an urgent meeting with Mary, Graham and Kate. "What do we do?" William asked rather plaintively. He then shared with them his shocking suspicions about the handwriting on the note. He described in some detail the particular features of the script that had convinced him of the authorship. "What are you saying?" Graham sceptically observed. "I am saying," William asserted more strongly and irritably, "that I think I recognise the handwriting. I cannot be absolutely sure but I believe it is young Grimes's. I know he left the school four years ago. His script is very distinctive. I did, after all, have to read rather a lot of his nonsense in the past."

"Somehow," Kate anxiously observed, "you have got to see Evelyn before you talk to the governors." Graham observed, "If Grimes is involved, I would not be at all surprised if others might be, too. There are only two governors you can really trust, Dom Osmund and Thomas Brown."

"I am going to see Thomas this evening. I have already rung him. First thing tomorrow I am driving to Barmouth on the pretext of paying a headmasterly visitation to the camp. That will give me a chance to talk to Evelyn. Finally, I will come back via Downside and see Father Osmund."

He added with a wan smile, "I can even visit Charlie at the same time." "That is a four hundred-mile round trip, William." Mary anxiously expostulated. "It will give me plenty of time to think," her husband firmly replied.

William arrived at the Brown's beautiful Georgian former vicarage in a small coastal village north of Ipswich at 7:00 that evening. Sarah opened the door. She was Thomas's wife of over twenty years. She was still a very handsome woman. William had long appreciated she must have been absolutely stunningly beautiful when she was young.

She welcomed him with her usual unaffected, kindly smile. "Tom is in his office, I thought you might need a long talk. I have laid out some sandwiches in preparation." The two men thus sat down in an untidy room full of various detritus, evidence of Thomas's many varied, eclectic interests. His desk was bestrewn with stacks of papers held down with paperweights acquired on family holidays.

There was even one emblazoned with the logo 'Welcome to Wales', rather appropriate in these circumstances. Thomas could see immediately how upset William was. He even had a passing impression that he might break down in tears.

"I know you are very busy; the trouble is I desperately need your advice." "Fire away, old chap." William then recounted the dreadful story of the policeman's visit. At the end of it he also shared his suspicions about Grimes's son.

Thomas was getting used to horrors going on at Parkies. It seemed that every day one or another new, damaging, and vicious rumour was being assiduously promulgated. Often he had considered resignation. In the end it was only his affection for William and Mary that really stopped him. If what William thought was true or even partly so, this malice had reached a wholly new dimension of spite.

A thought entered in his mind. It was a comment made by the chief American prosecutor Robert Jackson at the Nuremberg trials. Someone had asked him what was the nature of evil and Jackson had replied, "The absence of empathy."

This, he thought, was what had been happening for some time at Parkies. These dreadful, egotistical people had ceased to view William or anyone associated with him as persons. They had become merely pawns in some awful demonic game. There was absolutely no empathy. Just a cold, vicious, nasty calculation. Thomas agreed that William should see Evelyn as soon as possible.

Thomas didn't entirely approve of Evelyn himself. To be honest he thought Evelyn was just a touch fey for his taste. Thomas wasn't a Catholic and he had to admit that he hadn't quite escaped the prejudices of his austere Methodist grandfather.

He had rather liked Father Brendan and his down-to-earth, unvarnished, non-sentimental, kindly vision of the world. However,

Evelyn's clouds of incense, lace cotters, gold-trimmed chasubles, and Latin chant were definitely not his cup of tea. He recognised all Evelyn's hard work, his many exceptional talents, as well as his considerable and continuing positive contribution to the life of the school.

The terrible calumny that this accusation represented, especially if it was the work of fellow governors, offended his strong sense of justice, what he thought was fair and decent. It was these principles of justice and fairness that ultimately defined Thomas's world.

It was why, despite his great wealth and prosperous, bourgeois lifestyle, he remained an enthusiastic member of the Labour Party. He couldn't even claim to be New Labour. Tony Blair was yet another politician he loathed and distrusted. He imagined that if most of the other governors knew of his political inclinations it would only add further to the suspicions most of them entertained about him already. William left happy that at least Thomas was in support of his approach.

Thomas Brown had become increasingly fond of William and Mary Jones over the years. However, he had also become more and more frustrated by what he saw as William's complete lack of political nous. He was also irritated by his frequent lapses in judgment. He simply couldn't understand why William had not appreciated long ago the danger he was in.

He felt sure that this attack on Evelyn was in reality actually a diversionary assault on William himself. He recognised that at last William was finally starting to grasp what was really going on. It was rather too late, he feared. Indeed he had discerned a clear element of panic in William's attitude that evening. That in itself might make matters yet worse.

Later he was chatting to his wife Sarah. "You know, darling, I have been thinking about William and his love for all things Russian. I think there is a touch of Dostoyevsky's Idiot about him. I am increasingly sure, darling, that we are witnessing the end of William's career, at least at Parkies. I can see no way out for him."

Sarah replied sadly, "These are principled people who simply don't deserve this awful viciousness. The Indians are circling: surely we can provide some cavalry support?" Thomas knew that, however quixotic it might appear, he would do his best to defend William.

He was often insufferable, sometimes chaotic, but still a fundamentally decent man. However, in his heart Thomas realised that it was a lost cause.

Early the following morning William started his long drive to Barmouth. There were miles of boring motorways until he finally stopped for coffee near Shrewsbury. As he drove he listened to his favourite audiotape. It was of course Thomas Malory. He didn't really see himself as Arthur or even less so as Guinevere Flo's wonderful conceit of a few years back.

He thought he might have a few potential candidates for Mordred, yet more for Morgan le Fay. Perhaps he considered the noble Percival as the closest to Evelyn. His final reflection was who he considered he might end up most like. He thought of Bedivere, the last of the Knights. He was pretty sure it wasn't going to be him!

The last part of the journey seemed to take forever. He was driving through the mountains of mid-Wales, places he remembered from his childhood. In a strange way their looming presence reassured him. The glowering menace of these austere peaks put in mind those images of

Camlann, Arthur's last battle, wonderfully and evocatively described all those years ago by his teacher Owen Evans.

He wondered whether he was facing his own private Camlann. This ancient landscape of an immovable enduring age-old permanence helped to get things into some kind of perspective.

In the end, he realised all things came to an end. Even trivial matters like his own career at Parkies. There were also those words of Malory which described Arthur's last dream the night before the battle. This somehow seemed to encapsulate William's thoughts, even his present situation:

'There in were all manner of serpents, and worms, and wild beasts, foul and horrible; and suddenly the king thought the wheel turned up-so-down, and he fell among the serpents, and every beast took him by a limb.'

It was partly, William thought, of deciding who precisely were those serpents, worms and wild beasts that were gnawing at his and now Evelyn's entrails. This of course wasn't a very difficult question. He knew who they were. It was so exceedingly difficult to actually prove their culpability. He had never until now had the courage to fully admit the seriousness of his situation; more importantly, to attempt to address it. The trouble was he had not the remotest idea how to. It was this sense of frustrated impotence which was now at the core of his present dilemma.

Finally at lunchtime he arrived at the campsite. The group were having a typical Parkies picnic. This consisted of a number of pieces of buttered bread loaded with delightful goodies: ham, beef, hard-boiled eggs, potato salad and a smidgeon of something green. This, William always imagined, was there to satisfy some of the younger, health-conscious female teachers.

All this was being organised by the redoubtable Noah Bradley. He wandered around the scene supervising everything like a gentle, over-affectionate, if now greying, old sheepdog.

Noah always kept his own counsel. He had a fairly good idea of what was going on. Noah had been at Parkies for over twenty years. Typical of his intense sense of personal loyalty, he remained a close friend of John Lipman's.

He had not abandoned him after his disgrace. Occasionally he visited him in his new home in Leicestershire. John was a sad shadow of what he had once been. These visits had become more challenging, especially as he was no longer employed as a teacher and had to settle instead for poorly paid part-time clerical work. John was increasingly immersed in a growing sense of self-pitying victimhood. Noah, however, never judged him. He was filled with compassion and pity for his sad situation.

Noah did not blame William Jones for John's fate. This made him virtually unique amongst the more long-serving Parkies staff. He recognised that what had happened was mostly the fault of his friend John. Nor did he consider that many others at Parkies had covered themselves with much glory. Many people he felt had behaved abominably. Nor had they paid a price for their behaviour in the way that his friend John had. In the end he felt that John Lipman had become a patsy for other people's malign agendas.

Noah belonged to an independent Baptist congregation in Bury St Edmunds. This in itself was extraordinary in a man who had served in a Catholic school for most of his career. He possessed a simple, sincere, unadorned religious faith which remained entirely uncontaminated by the Catholic practice he had witnessed at Parkies.

He had rather liked Father Brendan and had often chatted to him about religion. He thought they had a great deal in common, not least their mutual sympathy for John Lipman. Both Father Brendan and Noah tried to live the simple faith of Jesus, not something that Noah had recently witnessed often within the portals of St Dogmael's.

To the uncomplicated Noah the gap between the religious practice and the moral turpitude he had so often observed in Parkies increasingly shocked and appalled him.

There was no point in proclaiming Christian principles when one's behaviour so often was entirely contrary to them. He wasn't at all sure whether he liked William. He found his tendency to be a little preachy on occasion somewhat trying. He did recognise him as basically a good man.

He hated the nasty gossip he could not always avoid. Nor did he think the behaviour of the Daltons and their allies was in any sense moral or decent. In the end Noah needed this job. He had no choice but to avoid taking sides if he possibly could. An unworthy thought had also increasingly occurred to him. He was sure that William Jones's star was quickly fading.

He could not hitch his wagon to the side he was sure were going to lose. He was not fooled by the insinuated reason for this visit. Men do not drive 400 miles for a spot of lunch, he reasoned. He knew that there was a crisis brewing and in some way it involved Evelyn. On past performance he was sure that something unpleasant was about to occur.

William was eventually able to beard Evelyn, and together they walked along the nearby beach. William told the story. Poor Evelyn looked as though he had been run over by a bus.

After a long silence William asked, "What do you want to do, old chap?" Evelyn responded, "What do you think are my options, William?" "In my opinion you have two. Firstly you could contact Chief Inspector Patton, agree to see him, and allow him to search your room. Or you could play hardball, see a lawyer, and refuse to cooperate. Look, for what it is worth, I know, as you do, there is nothing in it. If it were me I would cooperate. Although I would chat to a lawyer before doing so. It would, at the very least, give the police a sense of your good faith. In the end, Evelyn, I will support you whatever you decide." Later that afternoon he made his farewells to the party.

They were all somewhat confused by his reason for visiting. As one of the young matrons observed, "It is a hell of long way to drive for a Parkies picnic." They were still scratching their heads for any believable reason for his visit as he drove away into the looming Welsh landscape.

He continued his journey to Somerset. He decided not to go via Usk. He would have loved to have visited his mother Dilys. This issue was rather too closely related to the one that had involved Gethin all those years ago. He didn't wish to reopen that unpleasant can of worms. After a night in the Travelodge in Bath he travelled on to Downside.

Charlie was in his final year. He was by far the most able of William's children. His very laid-back, almost horizontal attitude to life was ensuring that he wasn't making the progress William had hoped. William thought he was happy, which was of course the most important thing. There were, he knew, hidden depths to his youngest son.

He was only able to see Charlie for an hour or so. This included the obligatory trip to the supermarket to pick up the necessary goodies.

Charlie was surprised to see him. He didn't ask him why he had travelled so far. By the worried and distracted look on his father's face he didn't for one moment believe it was an entirely social call.

William took Dom Osmund to lunch at The Talbot in Mells. They sat in the pretty, oak-beamed bar and William again outlined Evelyn's story. Osmund listened carefully. No headmaster of any boarding school could be indifferent to accusations of this kind. He would admit that he, too, had some concerns about some aspects of Evelyn's eccentric behaviour. Like William he was also convinced that the whole business was a tissue of lies occasioned by the growing atmosphere of malicious tittle-tattle which seemed to be overwhelming St Dogmael's.

Dom Osmund made the obvious observation that William had no choice but to inform Mrs Watson and the rest of the board. "I understand your reluctance but the longer you delay, the more ammunition you give them." Osmund also shared the news that he was giving up as headmaster of Downside. He was off to run one of the monastery parishes at the end of that term. He was clearly hugely relieved and pleased by this.

If running a dysfunctional prep school was challenging, to have these problems multiplied in a much larger public school was even worse. In the nitty-gritty of the educational world of curriculum issues, finance, public relations and all the other myriad demands of a public school headship, Osmund needed to remind himself sometimes that he was still a monk. That vocation was what he mostly really cared about. It was the reason he had sacrificed his life to it. The power games, politics and exploding quantity of largely meaningless administration that he was now required to undertake were a total anathema to him.

Nor did he even have someone like Mary to share his worries. His role of lonely remote authority meant that he was isolated from his sadly reduced elderly monastic community. Sometimes he felt like Prometheus chained to his rock in splendid lonely solitude. However much he sympathised with William's predicament, his main focus was on the imminent changes that were about to take place in his own life.

William now grimly realised that his future and that of Evelyn were entirely dependent on the hostile St Edmunds set who now so dominated the board of governors. Other than Thomas Brown, and the soon-to-retire Lord Robert Castle, he would soon not have a single friend or supporter. This was not a cheery thought as he drove home to Suffolk in the darkening dusk.

A few days later Evelyn returned from Wales. He and William then arranged to meet Mrs Watson. She was at her most imperious. "Why?" she coldly declared. "Why was I not informed immediately?" Her eyes were flashing with irritation and William suspected something worse.

He had until then not really apprehended so clearly and undeniably how much this woman disliked him. Being so fully in her power was not a comfortable feeling. By this stage Evelyn and William had both decided that their preferred approach was for Evelyn to meet Chief Inspector Patton and allow the police to search his room. William suspected that, given Mrs Watson's initial reaction, it was highly unlikely that she would concur with this suggestion.

He sensed that she was bound to automatically reject any idea emulating from him. William continued to explain as best he could that Evelyn had nothing to hide. Why not, he suggested, be as open and transparent as possible?

William was not oblivious of the fact that over the years he had built up a good relationship with the local constabulary. He wasn't keen to impair this. They had always in his experience behaved with tact and consideration. Some years before they had intervened when a wife's husband and lover had threatened violence within the school grounds.

They had even helped out when a drunken friend of Johnny Netherton's had decided to shoot Canada geese over the school lake, barely missing the heads of a number of children on a nature ramble. They had spent hours looking for a runaway boy after his parents had telephoned him to announce their divorce. There was no reason that this sensitive, reasonable attitude would not be their approach on this occasion, too.

William thought it was not yet tactful to mention his suspicions about Grimes. William's misgivings about Mrs Watson's likely attitude were confirmed when she stated. "That really won't do at all," in her coldest, most disdainful tone.

"I will contact Sir Roland and seek his opinion." The two men were then summarily dismissed rather like the footmen he had amusingly compared himself to all those years ago to the headmaster of Eton.

A few days later a criminal law barrister friend of the McKenzies' had been engaged. He arrived at the school to give William and Evelyn the benefit of his wisdom. He advised that Evelyn and the school must under all circumstances refuse to cooperate with the police in any way whatsoever. William tried to challenge this. His point of view was brusquely brushed aside. The barrister appeared to consider the headmaster's observations as mere irritants best to be ignored.

William was truly coming to understand why his long-deceased friend Alan had so detested these kinds of people. He could imagine Alan saying, "You are so bloody naive, Will, those bastards don't care for the likes of you or me. Your problem is that you think because you suck up to them and creep around them, they take you seriously: they fucking don't!"

Everything about this man displayed an insufferable self-conceit. William supposed that he had been briefed by Sir Roland. He didn't imagine that Roland McKenzie had very sympathetically portrayed him or indeed Evelyn.

Evelyn was too cowed by the sight of such a self-important QC to even question him. It seemed obvious to William that this charade had little to do with defending his interests. William was sure that Evelyn was the last person these people were interested in. The poor chap was simply the patsy in some kind of vicious, demonic power game.

At the next governors' meeting a few days later, William's judgment was openly and hostilely lambasted. Lady McKenzie summed up the view of the majority when she opined. "Why, Mr Jones, should you imagine that you understand more about the law than my husband and his colleagues?"

William noted with some alarm, but little surprise, that she now referred to him as Mr Jones rather than William. He was being put firmly in his place. Lady McKenzie was truly savouring this long-anticipated rout of the Joneses. Her rotund, meaty chops were diffused in an aura of delighted gratification. It was almost William rudely thought as though she was achieving a long desired, if rarely achieved, sexual climax.

William's point of view was supported, but then only momentarily, by Dom Osmund, Lord Castle and Thomas Brown. Even they could barely resist the overwhelming palpable antagonism displayed by the rest of the board.

Grimes was predictably boorish, rudely, and ostentatiously playing with one of his rings. At the same time he lifted his eyebrows sarcastically whenever William spoke. Giving at the same time meaningfully sneering side glances in the direction of Mrs Watson and Lady McKenzie. A hunched and dejected William slunk defeated out of the room.

He was also given the unappealing task of contacting Chief Inspector Patton and conveying to him the governors' decision. This policeman was, not surprisingly, very unhappy as well as astonished by this development, whilst he didn't mind the lanky and well-meaning headmaster. This decision provided further evidence that St Dogmael's and schools like it were nests of insufferable, arrogant snobs. He would not be surprised if that included pederasts and perverts, too.

Amongst the consequences of these decisions was that the local police never trusted the school again. Evelyn, who was innocent, was now assumed by the constabulary to be hiding something and was thus guilty. Chief Inspector Patton was even more convinced by the truth of his initial suspicions. What was left of William's authority had been publicly and humiliatingly trounced. Grimes's perfidy was of course left entirely unexposed.

Most of the governors were happy to promulgate and rejoice in this intelligence which was thus spread far and wide. The image of the headmaster's increasingly depressed and dismal demeanour reinforced the widely perceived sense amongst both staff and parents that his authority was on the wane.

Even poor Evelyn didn't have the opportunity to clear his name. There were plenty of people who were delighted to broadcast their suspicions of him, usually employing the false hypocritical guise of moral outrage.

He was thus effectively tried and condemned on what amounted to a ghastly fraud that was perpetrated by individuals who were simply using him as a means to an end.

William couldn't help reflecting how often evil intent was so frequently masked by such high-sounding, virtuous imperatives. The Daltons were of course cock-a-hoop as well as being further emboldened to defy William on every single issue in the certain knowledge that they were absolutely fireproof.

Chapter Twenty-Five

THE APPRAISAL

The time thus arrived for Richard Perry's visit. A few weeks before, a large pack of forms and questionnaires appeared which William was required to fill in. They were similar to the ones he had completed four years before. William could see no point in going through this process unless he was entirely honest. This was exactly the approach he had taken previously.

He was probably over-self-critical more so than he should be. He hoped and believed that Richard Perry's professional wisdom would help him navigate a way through his present difficulties.

Four years before he had found that Richard Perry had responded to his honesty and self-criticism in a positive and helpful way. He had no reason to suppose that it would be any different this time. This man was one of the most senior, respected persons within the whole prep school world. William was slightly in awe of him. He had even, after all, received an OBE for services to children. William had thought on his previous visit that Richard Perry had liked him.

These facts alone persuaded him that all would be well. He was confident that he would be judged fairly and his anxieties would be listened to and even, given the status of his appraiser, perhaps even addressed. He reasoned there might be hope after all and he might even recover from recent defeats. What he didn't know of course was his enemies: now they saw him on the run and were determined to convert this retreat into a total rout.

Richard Perry was in the school for two days. During that time he talked to some of the senior staff, three governors, one who was the chair, and some selected parents. On the first morning of his visit, William's secretary Janet Chester and his deputy Kate Bell came to see him. "We are really worried," announced Janet, his ever-loyal secretary. "All he seems to be interested in is what happens after you have left." Kate confirmed this. "William, there is something seriously nasty going on, I don't know what. I am like, Janet, very worried." These declarations left William feeling somewhat queasy and Mary even more so. It certainly added a further dimension to his growing apocalyptic sense of foreboding.

What of course William didn't know was that Richard Perry had already received a pretty damning report from Barbara Watson, Margaret McKenzie, and Gerald Grimes.

As David Watson had suggested, the governors he had consulted had been carefully selected by the chair. Worse still, all the parents he had questioned were all part of the St Edmunds set, a fact that William was blissfully unaware. The vast majority of the 'evidence' that Richard Perry had accumulated was entirely negative about William's performance.

There was absolutely nothing William could do about any of this. He just hoped that his two friends were mistaken. He had not remotely appreciated yet how conclusively Perry had been manipulated. He still reasoned that Richard was clearly a fair and honourable man: surely he wouldn't have prejudged matters. It was with this optimistic rumination that he awaited the appraisal's conclusion.

On the afternoon of the second day Richard Perry asked to see William and Mary. They brought him into their dining room and sat down opposite him across the large table. The formality of the situation rather disturbed William. There was none of the former *bonhomie* he had received when they had last met.

Richard Perry sat with a notebook and bundle of papers laid out before him. His face was sternly set and difficult to read. It was not an expression that filled either of them with much confidence.

He then sternly started. "I have spent the last two days observing the school and talking to many people." He then coughed meaningfully. "I have some rather bad news for both of you." He then listed a series of devastating criticisms. The Joneses were not given the opportunity to put their side. To be frank, both were so shocked and upset they would at this point have been barely able to articulate an adequate defence.

He ended his peroration with: "It is clear to me that you have in effect two choices: either you resign, or the governors will dismiss you." Both William and Mary looked at this man in blank dismay. For some silly reason William remembered the last word Tsar Nicholas has uttered before his Bolshevik executioners shot him: "What?" It seemed about the only word he could think of saying. Perry continued: "You are, in my opinion and many of those I have talked to, no longer up to the job. Most of the day-to-day running of the school now falls to Kate Bell. You have become effectively irrelevant to the functioning of the school. Most of all," he added with a short, pregnant pause, "you have entirely lost the confidence of the governors."

Mary looked at this snappily dressed, self-confident, well-groomed man and understood in a sudden, clear flash of insight that he was rather enjoying this.

True, his face presented a mask of concerned commiseration, but his eyes betrayed a real delight in the power and self-importance of his position. He reminded Mary of one of those insincere clergyman epitomised for her in the character of Obadiah Slope in *Barchester Towers* who so enjoyed character assassination whilst pretending regret and pious concern. She now understood that this man was the hypocrite personified.

Rather lamely, a shocked and clearly devastated William enquired in a rather bewildered, quivering, cracking voice why his opinion had changed so radically in the last few years. He went as far as to remind Richard Perry that on that occasion he had even credited William with saving the school. How, he pleaded, could this opinion have so totally changed within such a short period?

Perry did not appreciate or value this line of questioning. It was far too close to a challenge of his Olympian judgments. "When I write my report," he impatiently asserted in a patrician tone intended to intimidate as well as terminate this line of questioning, "you will have a full explanation of the rationale behind my judgments. Unfortunately, you will have to wait until then."

As a sort of afterthought Perry observed that if the Joneses cooperated the governors might be prepared to offer a generous settlement of perhaps £100,000. He referred to William's enjoyment of boating. "Think how much time you will be able to spend pursuing this hobby," he seductively suggested. Finally he observed, "You do have one great strength, William: you are good with the children. He then added in a surprisingly fraternal tone, "Rather like I was when I ran my school."

The final part of the conversation consisted of Perry's rather hectoring demand that he expected that William and Mary would resign quickly. "Delay in doing this," he averred, "would be fatal. It would mean that you might not secure any settlement at all." He finished by informing William and Mary that an appraisal report would be sent to the chair and to him within a week. Included with it would be a specimen resignation letter.

Immediately after Richard Perry's departure William had to attend the weekly school assembly. He stood at the front of the hall and looked at the faces of all the familiar children in front of him. He realised that the events of the last few minutes had essentially annihilated his career and, he feared, his life, too.

He couldn't imagine what else he could do. It felt so odd that in these transformational moments everything seemed so ordinary and unexceptional at the moment they happened. His legs felt wobbly and his tummy liquid. He looked fearfully around the hall with an irrational and humiliating anxiety that everyone already knew. It was as though he was in a bad dream. None of it seemed real. He wasn't even absolutely sure that it could really be true. He imagined this is what was sometimes called denial. The truth was of course that his whole world in one single instant had fallen apart.

William's most overwhelming emotion was intense, debilitating shame. He had been judged and found wanting. He didn't at this stage question any of Richard Perry's judgments. He assumed that these must be accurate given the eminent status of the man who was making them. William thought of the comment his brother had made all those years ago in Usk. Yes, he thought he was a piece of Welsh rarebit who should never have imagined that he was remotely competent to do this job.

Perry, he reasoned, had simply found him out. Mary was desperately upset herself but she was primarily concerned for William. He seemed to be awfully close to the edge. Actually she reflected that had been so for months. This, she feared, might finally tip him over. She knew that she was not the only one to make this judgment.

Some she knew were also genuinely concerned by this. Others she knew were earnestly wishing that it was so. When he returned from the assembly William sat in their dining room and simply sobbed. She now realised that William was in free fall. If she didn't do something he might simply crash into utter catastrophe.

Mary then sent William off to see Calvin, his psychotherapist; together they arranged for the school doctor to see him. He promptly prescribed a hefty dose of antidepressants.

As soon as William had left the flat she then asked to see Graham, Kate, and Janet to discuss the possible options. They trooped into the Joneses' dining room rather, Mary considered, as though they were arriving at a wake. Janet was tearful and extremely upset. "The injustice of this is awful," she wailed. Kate Bell and Graham Warner were more practical and hard-headed. "Wandering around as though the sky has just fallen in will just fuel rumour and make matters worse," commented the tough-minded Kate. "Where can he go?" she asked Mary. Mary thought for a moment. "Well, there is always Father Brendan in Walthamstow," she suggested. "Not sure about that," commented Graham. "I think he needs to get away from anyone associated with the school." Sadly, they no longer had a bolt-hole in Southwold. It had been sold a year before to help finance the burden of school and university fees. This was therefore no longer an option.

"What about Usk?" Kate proposed. The further difficulty, Mary pointed out, was Calvin had just telephoned her to say William was now on very powerful antidepressants. This would make driving impossible.

After this meeting it was agreed that Graham would drive her to Calvin's place and pick up William and the car. It was finally agreed that Janet would take him to Paddington the following morning. He would then catch a train to Newport. Mary telephoned Dilys to make the necessary arrangements.

After Graham had left her with Calvin she had the opportunity to have a quick word with him. William sat beside her on Calvin's sofa whilst he explained what he believed was the import of the present situation. "Jenny and I have been hearing the most appalling things for many months." He then listed a few of the people he suspected were involved in this farrago. Most of them were people that she knew or already judged likely.

Some of the names of parents he mentioned who might be obliquely involved were a bit of a surprise even to the grounded, level-headed Mary. "What is clearly going on is in my opinion a very British coup. Remember, both of you," he added, "your first and only objective now is to protect yourselves and your family. You know I will be doing all I can to help." Unexpectedly he finished with an explosive, angry oath: "What total fucking shits so many people associated with your school really are!"

From Mary's perspective that night was especially difficult. Soon after Richard Perry had first left, William had certainly broken down. He had always been an emotional man: that might therefore be expected. Mary had only witnessed this on such a devastating scale once before when he had lost his closest friend Alan.

When they returned to school after his therapy he was almost catatonic. This Mary found far worse. He didn't speak and just stared unfocussedly ahead. He reminded her of a cat in a car headlights. They could at least now more clearly perceive, especially after her conversation with Calvin, which particular car headlights were bearing down. There were an awful lot of them!

Mary knew she would have to fight with all her might and courage but no longer now for their jobs and way of life. This now seemed, she painfully realised, to be an entirely lost cause. More important still was to shore up the crumbling sanity of her husband.

The following morning William's secretary drove William to London. Janet had worked for him for seven years. Normally she was bubbly and talkative. On this occasion she had absolutely nothing to say. They drove in ominous silence. Janet knew of William's numerous failings but she also appreciated his strengths. The school that presently existed, she believed, was largely a reflection of William's vision.

Over the years she had also gleaned something of the forces that had been arrayed against him. The growing atmosphere of vicious gossip and malice convinced her that the only real option for her was to look for a job elsewhere. She simply couldn't bear the kind of Borgia world Parkies had descending into. The bell might this time be tolling for William and Mary. She did not imagine that it would not soon be tolling for her, too.

That night she thus prepared her own curriculum vitae. William caught the train to Newport. For the first time he didn't even notice the sign 'Welcome to Wales'. He simply sat huddled up in a bubble of his own intense, isolated misery. At the station he was picked up by a surprisingly solicitous Carwyn. They motored in silence to Dilys's house in Usk.

Now that the immediate crisis was over Mary decided the time had come to confront Mrs Watson. If this were a coup she thought that Barbara Wilson was the most significant instigator. She had wanted to do this for some time. She was also fairly sure what Barbara Watson really thought of her.

She also knew that the Watsons and their ilk had underestimated her. Perhaps as a result of Barbara Watson's basic sense that there was something Olympian about her own judgments. She never imagined that those she considered beneath her and especially women like Mary had either the intelligence or the wit to have valid alternative, worthwhile opinions.

Mary was thus absolutely sure that Barbara Watson had judged her as someone whose views were of absolutely no value. She did not imagine Barbara yet realised that Mary did precisely know the contempt in which she was held. This was of course entirely mutual! Such was Barbara Watson's scorn for the Jones family she probably didn't care much anyway. This, Mary considered, might be ultimately his woman's Achilles heel.

Mary was going to take some pleasure in disabusing her of all these notions. Until now she was worried that such an approach might further damage William. She understood that they were now well beyond such considerations.

Nagging at the back of her mind was the suspicion that there was something slightly fishy about Perry's judgments. It all seemed too convenient given her experience of William's disintegrating relationships with the governors and Barbara Watson in particular. She increasingly felt that the whole thing was a fix. It was an ambush that her unsuspecting naive husband had walked innocently into. She remembered the emphasis that Perry had put on William having lost the confidence of the governors. Which governors she wondered and were they the only ones that Perry had talked to?

At the very least this was an opportunity to express to this woman her own intense anger. She was determined that these awful people, and Barbara Watson in particular, should at least be aware of the damage their spite was doing to her family. She didn't imagine any of them would really care about that.

She would, however, ensure that this woman would know that her hateful feelings were fully reciprocated. Barbara Watson would at least realise that she would not be trampled upon.

She thus drove to Barbara Watson's house, rang the doorbell, and was then ushered into the drawing room. Mary could not help reflecting that until she had arrived in this strange Suffolk world she had always called such places a lounge.

Mrs Watson walked in. She stood in the doorway, clearly expecting and ready for trouble. She had half-expected this visitation. She was determined to ensure that if nothing else was achieved Mary Jones would know exactly her place. She didn't suppose that would be a difficult objective to achieve. Her hands were firmly placed on her hips and her face wore that hard, supercilious expression that she composed especially when she had to confront one of these lesser mortals. She immediately dispensed with any conviviality. "What do you want, Mrs Jones?" she intoned in her most unwelcoming, coldest tone.

It was as though she was about to address an errant maid, Mary reflected. She noted the formal title: no more Mary, she observed. "I want an explanation concerning your behaviour to my husband and my family," Mary calmly and purposely replied. "Whatever do you mean?" Mrs Watson sneered. The two women faced each other down. It was clear that this was going to be a thoroughgoing stand-off. Barbara Watson had expected Mary to slink away when faced down. She was surprised and a little disconcerted that she had not.

Mary continued with a growing conviction and rage, "I have watched the disgusting and vicious way you and your friends have consistently and deliberately undermined my husband for years." Mrs Watson was not used to being challenged, certainly not in her own house. Nor by someone she considered her inferior in every possible way.

"I don't think I like your tone, Mrs Jones." Mary was not going to be cowed by Barbara Watson's dismissive, arrogant, and barely civil responses. She looked directly at her, making no attempt to pander to what she increasingly regarded as Mrs Watson's insufferable conceit. Looking directly into her eyes, Mary then calmly outlined what she knew of the various unofficial meetings Mrs Watson had held with other like-minded governors. She referred to the numerous contacts she had evidence of that existed between governors and the Daltons.

All the while Barbara stood, her face betrayed a growing attitude of exasperated, frustrated irritation and even an increasingly, if contained, feeling of mounting fury. Despite this she was intrigued to know how this ghastly woman was so well informed. Mary left her nuclear detonation to the end. "I know that the letter that was sent to the police about Evelyn Morley was written by Gerald Grimes's son. I think you know that, too.

This means, Mrs Watson, that a governor who I believe is a friend of yours was fully complicit in besmirching the reputation of a member of Parkies' teaching staff. That, in case you need reminding, is serious stuff. It might even be criminal." Actually, Mary could not be absolutely sure that this was true or not. However, she was in no real doubt of its essential veracity. She wanted, most of all, to test Mrs Watson's reaction.

Mrs Watson reddened alarmingly. "How dare you make that suggestion, Mrs Jones!?" Barbara Watson spluttered. She was rattled, Mary knew. "I dare because it is true. I will not allow you to destroy William: you had better understand that I will use anything and anybody I can to protect my family." With that, she turned on her heel and walked out.

Barbara Watson sat down on the sofa exhausted by this tiresome tirade of plebeian outrage she had just received from that dreadfully common, uppity woman Mary Jones. She had been rather pleased and even quietly gratified with the way the fatuous Jones had fallen into every trap she and her group had designated for him. He had amusingly even added a few of his own.

She had always assumed that Mary Jones was merely a not very bright, simpering wife of her dullard, callow and foolish husband.

Everything about Mary offended Barbara's sense of what she considered proper, appropriate decorum. It started with her slight

Berkshire vocal intonation, her awful, suburban taste in clothes, and her unwillingness ever to show the right attitude of seemly deference to her betters. After all, she considered, this woman was merely a functionary and seemed in some way to assume arrogantly a status of something more. That was laughably ludicrous.

It was clear to Barbara Watson, if not, it seemed, yet to Mary Jones, that simply refusing to accept that her common housemaid looks and mundane proletarian demeanour entirely disqualified her from being taken seriously in Suffolk society. It didn't change the essential indisputable facts. The Joneses were simply toast; it was now a matter of clearing them away.

Barbara Watson recognised that Mary's display this morning revealed her as something more and therefore of infinitely greater danger. She had displayed a feisty, courageous, articulate defence of her husband which at one level Barbara rather admired. Barbara Watson anxiously considered that she might have even underestimated that woman. She was not, however, seriously concerned: there was, she realised, absolutely nothing Mary Jones could do to save her foolish spouse.

Nevertheless, it was clearly necessary to concede that this woman seemed to have more perception and intelligence than she had ever remotely imagined. The revelation about Grimes's son she didn't know whether it was true or not. However, she suspected it probably was. Mrs Watson had few illusions about anyone or anything. She knew what a deeply unpleasant man Grimes was. This made Mary Jones's assertion that he was in some sense a friend utterly laughable. He was, from her perspective, merely a useful tool. If he was in any way responsible for the note that would certainly need very careful handling. At the very least she would have to ensure that she personally could maintain a plausible deniability.

Mary Jones had also entirely misunderstood Barbara Watson's relationship with the Daltons. Yes, Barbara recognised that Isabelle was a fine teacher and excellent house-parent. She had not, however, been taken in by the seedy and insincere charms of Piers. She reckoned that William's judgment of him was about right. They were merely convenient. Once Jones was out of the way they would soon follow him swiftly to the door.

As far as William Jones was concerned she would even reluctantly concede that he had, as that bog Irish priest O'Rourke, once rather emotionally asserted, probably saved the school in his early years.

However, he had long since become a liability and anyway did not fit into her determination to have a rather more socially elite and sophisticated vision for the place.

His rather archaic notion of an informal, friendly, chaotic, rural school, and his attempts to satisfy the needs of the odd mad and the peculiar clientele he encouraged to join simply didn't figure in her future plans. If Parkies were to survive it needed to model itself on one of those socially exclusive successful prep boarding schools of Berkshire, Hampshire, Surrey, and Sussex. That meant special education bursaries for the socially contemptible, bog Irish religion, and most of all the Joneses had to disappear and very quickly.

Mary then returned to Parkies and telephoned firstly Thomas Brown and then Father Brendan. They listened in silence to her litany of woe. By now, Mary's armour of indignation was rapidly disintegrating. As she talked to Brendan she could hear her voice cracking and the tears were just starting to well up in her eyes.

She had expected that both men would express the surprised indignation that she felt. She then realised neither was in anyway discomposed. They both agreed to meet her the following morning at the Station Hotel in Ipswich.

At 10:00 am she arrived at the venue. Thomas and Brendan were already waiting for her. Thomas had already solicited a great deal of further information from Graham and Kate. He had arranged to meet Brendan a little earlier so as to bring him fully up to speed. Whilst surprise was not something they both felt, anger and disgust were. Mary tearfully started: "I think William is on the edge of a breakdown: what am I going to do?"

Mary was so wound up she suddenly started to sob. She hated herself for this display of contemptible weakness. Thomas Brown was the first to react. He placed his hand solicitously on Mary's shoulder and growled. "What is going on is monstrous. The trouble is that this fellow Perry who William thought was his saviour has turned out to be his nemesis." "I accept that," Mary reluctantly conceded. "This is not just about what Richard Perry said. It is about a long, well-thought-out process of personal and professional annihilation which preceded his visit. It was organised essentially by these two women, McKenzie, and Watson, as well as of course Grimes and the Daltons and perhaps others, too. I don't believe incidentally that Perry's report was impartial or fair. Remember also I watched his face when he delivered his judgment. He was really enjoying it. I actually believe that it was giving him some kind of vicarious pleasure. Do you think he had been got at?"

"Probably," Thomas conceded. This understated Thomas Brown's actual suspicions. He knew enough of the nefarious goings-on of the business world to understand that such an ambush was easy to organise if one had a mind to do so.

Brendan had been silently considering matters. "I know that Jonathan is no longer chair. I also know that you, Thomas, and he do not always see eye-to-eye. If they are going to give you a package, Mary, he will end up footing the bill. Jonathan is basically a fair man. He won't be party to any of this. I think someone has to see him and put him fully in the picture. If you like I will do that." Thomas added, "You will need legal advice, Mary, and it will have to be the best. I don't think you can't afford that. I will with pleasure pay. I will give it some thought; I have someone in mind. I just need to see if he is available. One point," Thomas continued. "We will need to see a copy of Perry's appraisal, preferably before the rest of the board and certainly before the Daltons." At the end of the meeting Mary felt a bit calmer as she drove back to Parklands.

That evening she rang Dilys in Usk. William had gone for a long walk, and both women were able to talk freely. "I have never seen him like this before," Dilys confided. "He doesn't seem interested in anything. To be frank he spends most of the time sleeping." Mary gave her a fuller account of what had been going on.

Dilys then shared. "All William has said to me is that he finished. I know he is very down." "To be frank, Dilys, we probably are 'finished' in the sense that Parkies is over." Mary sighed. "There is so much we can still do and we have to remember we are so lucky with what we have got. I have been thinking if we are forced to leave here at the end of term can we move in with you for a time." "If it comes to that, of course," Dilys generously replied.

Three days later, William returned. He still looked haunted, Mary thought, but he seemed calmer and not quite so downbeat about everything. Richard Perry's report had arrived. It was of course devastating as they had both expected. It was essentially a brutal litany of William's deficiencies. It ended with an expression of regret for fulfilling what Perry described as "his painful duty". Richard Perry had again referred to William's good relationships with the children.

Apart from this throwaway comment there was absolutely nothing positive in the report whatsoever. Interestingly, nothing was mentioned about any settlement. Least of all the £100,000 Perry had suggested a few days before. As she had promised, Mary made sure that Thomas Brown and Father Brendan had a copy of the report immediately.

However, she recognised, this wouldn't probably stop Mrs Watson who had also received a copy at the same time sharing it with her cronies and probably the Daltons, too. In this she was largely, if not entirely, accurate. Whilst the flags were not exactly flying yet outside the Watson, McKenzie, and Grimes households, they were fully aware of its contents within a few hours. As it turned out, the Daltons were not sufficiently trusted as yet to be given a copy. Margaret McKenzie very quickly ensured they both knew the gist of what it contained.

Brendan had telephoned and explained that he had contacted Jonathan. He had been invited for supper the following day. His parting shot was: "I am sorry but I am not optimistic, Mary. I think all we are likely to achieve from this is a reasonable settlement. My main objective is to open his eyes to what is really going on. I have real faith in his basic decency."

The lawyers Thomas Brown had instructed also rang. They were based in Holborn in London. This meant Mary knew that they were bound to be expensive. They had asked to see William and Mary later that week.

Finally Mrs Watson had also telephoned. "I would like to see you at my house tomorrow," she peremptorily demanded.

William replied, "I am sorry, Mrs Watson, that really isn't convenient." There was he thought a sharp intake of breath at the other end of the line. "We have as you must understand many important matters to discuss," came the chilly, soulless reply.

"That is obviously true," William responded. "However, before I talk to you, I need to discuss things with others." Mrs Watson's voice was becoming increasingly tense and annoyed. "What matters do you need to discuss and with whom?" William finished the exchange with: "My lawyers, for one: even you cannot expect me to meet you without having taken proper legal advice. By the way all future meetings between us will take place here at school and will of course be fully minuted." Before Mrs Watson could frame a suitable reply, William said: "Goodnight, Mrs Watson." He was actually following through what his lawyers had told him to say. He realised now that the game was up, but he was determined, if he could, to draw some blood before he was finally banished.

Chapter Twenty-Six

DENOUEMENT

Father Brendan had recently decided to invest in a new car. In truth this was not much of an improvement on the old one. He had acquired a second-hand Lada. It was decked out in a kind of sick-green paint. This was perhaps one reason that Brendan had bought it so cheaply.

The other problem at least from Brendan's perspective was that it was difficult to drive. Power steering was clearly an alien concept to the Russian automotive industry. It was built like a small tank and the physical effort of turning the enormous steering wheel had exhausted the elderly priest on his over sixty-mile journey from Walthamstow to Walton House. He wasn't getting any younger he told himself.

This business with William and Mary had quite discomposed him. It wasn't that it was entirely unexpected. In his heart he had known it was coming for a few years now. It was, however, the brutality and viciousness of the Joneses' demise that most disturbed him. Brendan had always believed in the fundamental goodness of the humankind.

He thought probably that such a view of human nature was unorthodox and probably heretical. He laughed to himself when he considered what the Bishop would say if he knew he was a secret follower of Pegalius, who of course was a 5th-century heretic, who believed that human nature is perfectible without Divine Grace.

The events at Parkies had rather disabused him of this notion. He was coming to accept that there was such a thing as evil, which he now realised could only be resisted with God's Grace. For a supposedly Christian foundation. Parkies seemed somewhat deficient in that most essential Christian virtue of charity, the nastiness and malice that were so evident there seemingly now to pervade the very atmosphere, even the walls and fabric of the place.

He had come to reluctantly accept that something demonic was going on in that school. This was profoundly disturbing. He felt this most because his association with the place was more than a decade long. What, he asked himself, had he achieved? The truthful reply was very little indeed.

Brendan tried to understand why it had all gone so horribly wrong. However much he liked and respected William, he had to accept that a large part of the cause was him. William had never really understood what was really on offer at Parkies.

From the very beginning, he had assumed that the radical changes he thought necessary were so obvious that everyone else would simply fall in line. There was a kind of breathtaking arrogance in this attitude as well as a somewhat insensitive dismissal of every other opinion. These were by no means all as entirely mistaken as he supposed. That was, Brendan thought, the nub of what had happened.

William was the consummate outsider. He was never going to be accepted by most of movers and shakers of the Suffolk county world. The trouble was he rarely understood this. Everything he seemed to do in one way or another offended this clique. Brendan didn't think this was done deliberately. However, it did suggest at the very least together with his lofty hubris a certain lack of sensible, rational self-interest. Sometimes he had showed little real empathy for those he had already written off.

Perhaps most of all was his lack of basic common sense that had made this fall inevitable. He thought of the interview twelve years before and reflected that he now genuinely considered it would certainly have been better for William and his family if he hadn't been appointed. Perhaps, he now believed, it might have been better for everyone else, too. He accepted that if it hadn't been for William and Mary in those early years the school would have probably gone under. Then, he thought bitterly, it certainly deserved to.

The curious idea crossed his mind that Parkies was a kind of microcosm of England. He knew that that was in most ways a silly, irrational notion. Yet the more he thought about it, the more he believed it might have an element of truth. Schools like St Dogmael's had originally been founded for primarily ethical and religious reasons. He had once met the elderly Canon Paine. To be honest, his rather sniffy English ways had not especially endeared him. Brendan knew that he had a real Christian vision which wasn't primarily about privilege. His school had he believed, lost its way when Paine's vision had been effectively discarded by Lancelot Waters.

Parkies had become in the eyes of most of its governors and parents essentially a snob factory. It was about providing privilege and a dubious, exclusive status to people whom Brendan considered didn't usually deserve or appreciate it. The new shibboleths of independent schools were now sports halls, astroturfs and all the accruements of prestige-driven amenities. This had become what was really important. It amused him to reflect that Parkies could never quite afford any of these. The only thing it had recently managed to erect was a glorified cowshed which the school insisted on calling a sports hall.

William had in his own often inept way held out for the older, less fashionable principles of community shared values and religious formation.

These principles were always going to place him in conflict with the current prevailing ethos of the selfish individual at the expense of the many. This was the notion that wealth was entirely about personal enhancement and status-grabbing. In other words, he thought, the ethos of the new, materialistic, mean-spirited, money-obsessed England.

Years before Brendan had met Father Sean O'Connor William and Mary's former parish priest. Father Sean had also observed that there was more than a touch of the gullible crusader in William. Sean had remembered the way that William had been so naive about diocesan intentions when he was in London. He simply didn't understand the vicious menagerie that was diocesan politics. Perhaps the priest suggested all politics.

He assumed that when something was promised it would happen. It didn't in London, and such notions of chivalry and keeping one's word seemed even less honoured in Suffolk. Brendan had to concede that William had been initially mesmerised by this snooty county world. Snobbery was not merely the failing of the rich and powerful. Those far less elevated like Lancelot Waters and sadly even William, too, were not immune. Yet what made William different and to Brendan rather special was that he had despite all of this still retained something of the genuine idealist.

To illustrate this point Father Sean recounted a conversation he once had where William had suggested that it was actually right that independent schools should aspire to be ivory towers, a term which critics used often to characterise negatively their elitist ways.

William had propounded the slightly dubious sophistical notion that the great thing about towers was you could ride out from them and conquer the world. Education, in the truest, fullest sense William had proposed, should be as ambitious as that. He had never for one moment considered what would happen if the ivory tower had already been seized by the forces they were supposed to oppose. In the end Brendan thought the situation of Parkies was precisely this.

Meanness, snobbery, malice, and enmity had already taken possession of the place. It would have been better, he now thought, to have left the school to die. Indeed he even wondered whether that might have been the really moral thing to do. All that the naive crusader William had ever really achieved was to have delayed the inevitable for a few extra years. The cost of that fruitless endeavour was now plain to see.

He remembered his chat with William all those years ago at that Prize-Giving. He had then suggested that he could be ruthless. In a sense, he thought, he was still right.

Perhaps he now thought it was more an intractable mulishness than anything else. Both William and Mary could certainly be single-minded and stubborn. Even in William's case sometimes petulant and irrational. However, he had never found them malicious. He thought that William didn't really understand the spiteful nature of so much of the discourse at Parklands. He naively assumed that other people were basically decent with honest if misguided opposing notions. Until recently, Brendan was sure he had not the remotest idea of the overwhelming forces lined up against him.

Brendan had once met William's friend Alan. He had really liked him. He felt Alan had a real integrity, if one that was rather blunt and uncompromising. Alan, Brendan thought, had been one of the few people who had really understood William. Father Brendan wished he was still around. He was probably the only person who could have got his friend to understand the error of his ways and inject a bit of sensible realism into his mind.

Alan he was sure would have persuaded William to have left Parkies long before the present debacle. At least he thought he would have turned William away from the self-destruct mode in which he seemed to be presently drowning.

Truly Brendan thought William was the innocent abroad. The image of Holman Hunt's painting 'The Scapegoat' came to mind. It seemed the perfect analogy to explain William Jones's present terrible situation.

He had telephoned Jonathan two days before. He had not been at home. This had given him an unexpected opportunity to talk to Celia Carpenter. Until then he had never understood how wise and perspicacious she was. It was now obvious that she knew exactly why he was coming. Not because he had yet told them, but because she knew him too well. It was entirely in character for this elderly priest, she considered, to be trying to protect a beloved friend.

She knew how close William and Brendan had become. Her dear

Father Brendan, for all the world resembled a reborn Don Quixote tilting at windmills, not on his donkey but in a bright green Lada. The idea was oddly enough hugely funny. Brendan's skinny frame and intense soft, brown eyes also gave him a slight resemblance to those images she remembered on her convent school walls of the austere St John of the Cross the famous Spanish mystic. Father Brendan retained something of that other-worldly optimistic vision of the possibility of Christian salvation. It was what made him such a wonderful man.

However, much as it amused her, she respected and applauded Father Brendan's passion. Eccentric and quixotic as it sometimes was, it was always about doing the right thing.

She was fully aware of the situation at Parkies and was equally appalled as Brendan by the shabby treatment that was being dished out to William and Mary. She had spent her formative years at the convent school of St Mary's Shaftesbury and Brendan reminded her of the best of those nuns. It was priests like him and the memory of some of those IBVM Sisters that kept her hanging on in the Catholic Church.

There were moments when she wondered what still held her. Today seeing again this shabby, unsophisticated, elderly cleric riding out to do justice and right, she thought she understood what it might be essentially all about.

She had grown to detest these bored and diabolical women, optimised in her mind by the awful Margaret McKenzie who seemed to regard the destruction of other people's lives as mere sport and entertainment. Distractions from the ennui and pointlessness of their daily lives. It delighted her to momentarily consider she wouldn't mind acting as Sancho Panza to Father Brendan's Don Quixote.

It was partly the difficulty of being a celibate, Brendan supposed, that made it so hard for him to understand women. This was to some extent because he hardly knew any other than a few elderly penitents and his pious and kindly housekeeper. He hadn't even had any sisters and had been plucked from the loving embrace of his warm, courageous, deeply pious mother at the tender age of eight to attend the brutal junior seminary a few miles from his country home in County Cork.

He thought that for most of his life women had rather frightened him. At any rate this meant he didn't think he understood or appreciated the female capacity for wisdom and good sense he now understood so often outshone those of men. Mary and now Celia were changing and challenging those old prejudices. He had to admit to being glad of this. He could hear his beloved, long-dead mother saying, "About bloody time, too, Brendan."

Jonathan met him at the door of Walton House. Somehow Brendan's bright green Lada looked especially incongruous parked in a line-up of Jaguars, BMWs, and Range Rovers. Jonathan was genuinely amused by the contrast. He was delighted to see again the dear old priest and appreciated how much he had missed him in the year he had been living in Walthamstow. He realised again how much he liked this eccentric, kindly old man.

Brendan had already requested that Celia join them. He felt they were sorely in need of her calm insight. They sat in Jonathan's sumptuous study so they could chat comfortably. Celia had provided a buffet of cold meats, Coronation chicken, potato salad and quiche Lorraine. From previous visits to their house she knew these to be amongst his favourites. For pudding there were strawberries, ice cream and Irish coffee cake which she appreciated was his special delight. She didn't think it was just his Irish charm when he said her efforts were almost as good as his dear old mother's.

There was no need to go through the bones of the situation. They were all fully aware of what had been and was happening. Brendan thought that the Carpenters were less mindful of the backstory that had led to this situation. In this, too, he was largely mistaken. Early on Celia piped up, "I know these people who are so assiduously engaged in destroying the Joneses. The focus of all this is Margaret McKenzie." Father Brendan noticed she did not grace this woman with her newly acquired title.

Jonathan then proceeded to make what the priest thought were some interesting and very honest observations. "I have assumed that Parkies had no future. Perhaps rather cynically I believed that William would not make a go of it. You must remember how reluctant we were to give him the job back in 1987. I thought the school might last, at most, five years.

"He was younger then. I suppose that if the school had collapsed when he was in his early forties it wouldn't have done a great deal of harm to him or to his career. Although to be frank I didn't give it much thought. I hadn't realised or even imagined that he would achieve so much. That was a real revelation: I had clearly underestimated him.

"Worse still, I didn't for one moment imagine that he would make Parkies his own personal crusade. You must have realised when I persuaded Nigel Denton to join us on the board that I had some ulterior motives. He is a property man and in 1992 when he joined us I assumed we would be selling the Parklands Estate pretty soon. You must remember how dire things were then. If the school had gone under, if that had happened and the land was sold for agriculture, the school would have been unable to cover its debts.

"If, on the other hand, we got planning permission for houses on at least part of the land there would have been plenty of funds to do this and more. I have been financially propping up this school for over twenty years. There is a limit to what I am prepared to do and incidentally what I can afford." Father Brendan, always direct, asked, "Do you think you always acted in total good faith in all this?" "Probably not," conceded Jonathan.

The discussion developed into an examination of the present situation. Celia was vitriolic about the St Edmunds set. She repeated to the two men the thoughts she had expressed some years ago and felt increasingly passionate now. "If I thought those dreadful women were the future of England I would bloody well decamp to Outer Mongolia," she angrily announced. "We all know that these bored, vitriolic women's only real interest in life is to destroy other people. It was just unfortunate that they decided to target William. He was of course their obvious prey."

Jonathan was more circumspect, even defensive. "Look, darling, I have always known that that woman McKenzie was a total nightmare. Her ghastly, pretentious husband is not much better, but I thought Barbara Watson was made of different stuff. For God's sake she is chair of the local party. David and her are regular guests here. I had no idea that Barbara was going to go bloody native with the likes of Grimes and McKenzie."

He then continued. "The problem is I believe the Joneses have brought this situation largely on themselves. William especially has been an arrogant, bloody silly fool. He gets ideas into his head and won't ever let go. You remember his insufferable attitude to the bursaries, don't you? We also have to remember that a highly respected member of IAPS has made the same assessment of his performance, as did much of the board. Everyone cannot be wrong!" Father Brendan very largely, if somewhat reluctantly, had to accept this.

The elderly priest felt he did need to go into more background detail about the reasons for much of the board's hostile attitude to Evelyn Morley, William's arguably not unreasonable position on the question of bursaries and what had caused the disaster with Tarun.

He emphasised the clear evidence of malicious vicious gossiping and Machiavellian plotting, as well as the malevolent involvement of the Daltons. "Can you imagine, Jonathan, what it must have been like for William and Mary to live for years in the knowledge that the slightest error they made would be used as ammunition in a campaign of increasing spitefulness?" Whilst much of this was already known the details of Brendan's narrative and the passion with which he expressed it seemed to genuinely impress the Carpenters.

Brendan ended by saying, "All this illustrates some of William's mistakes but you know as much as I do he always acted in good faith, bloody-minded perhaps, but always motivated by what he thought was in the interests of the school. I don't believe many of the others have behaved half so well. I think he needs at the very least to know you are not party to this. Talk to him." "I agree," Jonathan conceded. "I will go and see him as soon as I can." With that assurance Brendan drove back to Walthamstow.

Lady McKenzie was restless with excitement. She was desperate to know what was really going on. It was true that Barbara Watson was providing her with some basic information. She had a strong presentment that for some reason Barbara was holding back. She could not be seen with Piers or Isabelle. Even she recognised that was a bit obvious. She certainly didn't want the whole world to know what the real game was.

Whilst she had made an ally of Gerald Grimes she couldn't really pretend that she found him other than truly odious. She didn't want him or his dreadfully common wife Tracey to imagine that any real friendship existed. That ruled him out as a confidant. She assumed anyway he probably knew as little as her. She decided therefore to drive to St Dogmael's and try by subtle means to elicit some information from William's secretary Janet Chester.

The trouble was that anyone who knew Margaret McKenzie was very aware that subtlety was not her forte. She bowled into Janet's office and thus played what she hoped was convincingly the role of the concerned, caring and interested governor.

Janet was not fooled. She understood exactly the kind of woman Lady McKenzie was. She also suspected that she would not be giving her the time of day unless there was an ulterior motive. Nevertheless, at one level, she was still quite flattered that this rather grand lady wished to talk to her.

They then promenaded around the gardens. Margaret oily enquired in her most unctuous tone, "How are poor William and Mary coping?" "Not well, Lady McKenzie," replied a surprised Janet who didn't believe this woman cared one jot. This one-sided conversation veered into what Janet knew was the entirely fantastical when Lady McKenzie opined, "They have done so much for the school, don't you think, Janet?" This was obviously breathtakingly false.

Janet could not believe she was hearing it. Lady McKenzie then elaborated this obvious falsehood when she pouted, "Oh how they will be so sorely missed: my husband Sir Roland and I are so fond of the Jones family." Janet knew enough of past relationships to appreciate that this was a further outrageous tissue of deceit and fabrication. She could not understand why Lady McKenzie was bothering to include her in this charade. Yet she knew her place and simply smiled sweetly and kept absolutely silent.

Lady McKenzie was very frustrated and getting more so. She wasn't succeeding in achieving anything with this plain, frumpy, and excruciatingly boring woman. However, she persisted. "What do you think of Kate Bell?" she enquired. Janet offered the comment. "She is very loyal and efficient, I like her enormously," to this surprising question.

"It is so unfortunate," Margaret McKenzie then confidentially opined. "I am sure you will agree with me that she isn't quite right socially. She is absolutely wonderful of course but she does still have that dreadful Suffolk accent." Janet again didn't comment. "I know," an increasingly desperate Lady McKenzie confided, "that the board want the school to attract the very best sort of people. I am sure you will agree she is not really quite suitable for that."

Margaret had failed to elicit a single piece of useful information from this infuriating woman. Janet, on the other hand, had made a mental note of all that had been said. As soon as a somewhat frustrated, annoyed Margaret McKenzie had left her office she rang through on the school internal telephone to Kate. Janet recounted the conversation to an increasingly incandescent Kate.

What neither Janet nor Margaret McKenzie knew was that whilst Kate was married to a local if substantial farmer her background was in reality firmly gentry. She was far more socially secure than the parvenu McKenzies. Her grandfather had been High Sheriff of Norfolk, and an uncle was a senior officer in the Grenadier Guards.

Whilst Lord Castle, or Jonathan Carpenter, would not be seen dead inviting the McKenzies anywhere near their dinner table, the Bells were regular guests. They were equally welcome in many of the genuinely smarter houses of Suffolk. Kate considered her Suffolk accent irrelevant and regarded it as insulting and offensive for this awful woman to even mention it.

That evening after talking to her equally irate husband, Kate telephoned Jonathan Carpenter. It is interesting, Jonathan was to note later, that she did not attempt at this stage to contact Barbara Watson. When Jonathan answered the telephone it was less than twenty-four hours since Father Brendan had left. That conversation had left him feeling very uneasy as well as somewhat guilty about the whole situation.

He recognised that he had not played matters as openly as he should. In fact he sometimes worried that he might even sometimes have behaved badly.

He had, he thought on consideration, been blindsided by Barbara Watson's appearance of ladylike decorum, a pretty face and terrifying efficiency. What he had imagined was her intelligent, reasonable, and well-judged approach to problems seemed increasingly to be something else. Celia more cynically assumed that he had just been duped by her pretty looks and simpering smile.

Now he was talking to an obviously furious Kate Bell. She was someone whom he truly admired. This revelation confirmed his growing and niggling doubts about the whole situation. This was a development he had not expected and certainly did not welcome.

Kate, although fifteen years his junior, had been a family acquaintance for decades. Her husband Robin was a long-standing friend of his cousin Rupert's. In short, they were at least obliquely part of the same social and familial network. As he listened to her, he found himself in a growing quandary. He knew that Kate should have reported this first to Barbara Watson. He probably should not even be talking to her. The fact that she had not done this spoke volumes. Now he was no longer a member of the board, he had no authority to do anything. His long-standing relationship with the school and his well-known generosity to it afforded him immense influence. He determined now that it was high time to use it.

After he had ended the conversation with Kate he sat down and chatted to Celia. He needed her natural wisdom. Oddly enough she had just returned from a district council meeting where both she and Barbara Wilson served as Conservative members.

"What do you think, darling?" enquired a hesitant, irresolute Jonathan after he had anxiously recounted Kate's conversation. "I have just spent two hours with Barbara Watson in the chamber," recalled Celia. "She couldn't even look at me. I have never seen her so flustered before. Tonight she was all over the place. When we were discussing that building application in Wetherden she was totally unlike her usual self. You know how so coldly efficient and well prepared she usually is. Just now she was thoroughly chaotic, papers all over the place and not really concentrating on the matter in hand. I don't think she had even read the stuff beforehand. She is usually so meticulous about this. Someone I thought with things on her mind. She was certainly under great pressure. Jonathan, I think this thing is getting out of hand. If it all goes belly up as it looks as if it will this will impact on our reputation whether you like it or not." Following what from Jonathan's perspective was a rather inconclusive and somewhat disturbing conversation, they both agreed that Jonathan would have to talk to Barbara.

He needed her to agree to remove McKenzie and probably Grimes, too, from the board. Whatever happened to the Joneses it needed to be done with decorum. Certainly not the hatchet job it was currently becoming.

Barbara Watson was by now rather regretting her decision to take over the Parkies chair. She had just been telephoned by Jonathan with the news of the McKenzie debacle. Nor was he very polite about her role in the affair. In fact as she reflected about it later she thought he was rather blunt if not actually rude. "Look, Barbara," Jonathan announced exasperatedly. "This bloody woman McKenzie is out of control. She has to go and you need to wield the axe. This situation is becoming unmanageable. This is not great news for you or for that matter me either." His implied suggestion that somehow she was involved more intimately than she cared to admit seriously annoyed and upset her. She realised that this implication was entirely accurate. This was something she could hardly dare admit even fully to herself. Most of all she did not wish to fall out with the Carpenters. They were far too influential to risk that.

She hadn't yet been able to meet Jones largely because of his new, irritatingly stand-offish, hoity-toity attitude. She noticed in the first solicitor's letter she had received that morning that the firm he was employing were one of the most expensive in London. She knew Jones couldn't afford them. It followed that someone rich and probably important was bankrolling them. She had a pretty good idea who that was. Her enemies seemed to be circling.

Thomas Brown was the likely candidate as the money man. She believed but also couldn't prove he was also attempting assiduously to build up parental support for the Joneses. She even gathered that that dreadful bog Irish priest O'Rourke was somehow also involved. There was even talk of that geriatric old fool Strange riding into the fray, and he was definitely not on her side!

Margaret's stupidity took the biscuit. How could she not have imagined that comments made to Janet would not get out? Janet was after all a fully paid-up member of the Jones fan club, and now it seemed that Bell was one, too. She agreed reluctantly with Jonathan: Margaret would have to go. Her task now was to persuade her to fall on her sword. If she forced her dismissal that might get horribly messy. This was clearly the last thing she wanted at this moment.

Lady McKenzie felt rather uneasy about her conversation with Janet. She feared she might have gone too far. As she haltingly and rather diffidently commented to her husband Roland at supper that night, "I think I may have been a little unwise in a comment I made the other day to that Janet Chester woman up at the school." Sir Roland was only half-listening. It was a tactic he often used when forced to listen to the witterings of his increasingly irritating, irrational wife.

His reverie rather was on the smallest details of the many physical charms of the delectable Marcia and the prospects of examining these more thoroughly the following evening at a tryst at Roland's little *pied-à-terre* in West Hampstead. His mind jolted back to his wife's disclosure. "What were you saying, dear?" he responded in a rather detached and uninterested tone. Margaret replied with more than a hint of irritation. "I was saying, my dear, that I may have been somewhat indiscreet about that Bell woman at Parkies." Roland was confused. He was finding this all rather irksome. "I thought it was Jones and his coterie that you were targeting." "I was, I mean, we are, but Kate Bell is only marginally more acceptable, don't you think?" "In my professional opinion," an exasperated Roland replied, "you must only concentrate on one target at a time. If you don't you may miss your main prey and end up with more enemies than friends."

Barbara Watson invited Margaret to her house for coffee the following morning. Margaret was certainly insensitive and foolish. She was not entirely stupid and she had guessed what this was likely to be about. Barbara did not beat around the bush. "How could you have been so foolish, Margaret? The comments you made to Janet Chester were crass, to put it mildly." "I was only telling the truth," a rather woeful, browbeaten Lady McKenzie lamely replied. "I am not sure I would agree," snapped Barbara Watson.

"Even if that was true, you have just provided a great proverbial sledgehammer for Jones and his friends to use. Can't you imagine how this will be exploited by that dreadful man Thomas Brown, for example?" "Surely he doesn't matter, Barbara? After all he is just a glorified tradesman." "Yes, he does!" Barbara exploded. "He may be a tradesman but he is a very influential and rich one and, moreover, he is batting full-time for the Joneses. Who the hell do you think is paying for those expensive London solicitors, for example?" she added with a wry, if sour humour. "Well, it certainly isn't Roger Rabbit!"

She then continued with mounting fury and increasingly irritation. "Kate Bell telephoned Jonathan Carpenter the night before last. He is absolutely furious." "Carpenter isn't even on the board anymore, what can he possibly do?" "Quite a lot, Margaret."

She then went on to point out his influence in the county. She referred to all the money he had poured into the school and the high regard he was held in by many parents staff and old boys. "I am sorry, Margaret, but you must resign from the board immediately."

At this point Barbara abruptly ended her peroration. Margaret was shattered, upset and angry. Her initial inclination was to stick to her guns and battle it out. After all, she reasoned, most of the board probably agreed with her about Kate Bell. They certainly did about William Jones.

Barbara Watson was not in the mood for prevarication. She thus outlined in the most direct and brutal terms the social importance of the Bell family. She rammed home the relationship between the Bells and the Carpenters. Finally she painted in the most apocalyptic terms a vision of the social annihilation the McKenzies were imminently facing.

Finally Lady McKenzie reluctantly realised she had no choice but to resign. She even thought somewhat encouraged by an insincerely, momentarily conciliatory Barbara that by a timely departure she might even retain her membership of the St Edmunds set. Barbara Watson, on the other hand, privately believed this was highly unlikely!

The only issue that still remained, at least for Mrs Watson, was the combined and linked questions of when the Jones went and how much it might cost. The simple answer to these were very soon and as cheaply as possible. It now became Barbara Watson's chief focus to ensure that these objectives were achieved. The key point in her mind was that whatever Jones's supporters might try to do they couldn't escape the fact that he had been found wanting by one of his own. She chuckled merrily as she remembered with what subtle skullduggery this had been achieved.

Chapter Twenty-Seven

COMPROMISE AGREEMENT

The next most immediate issue was to address the question of the Joneses' compromise settlement. William's lawyer pointed out that the £100,000 mentioned by Perry was at best merely speculation on his part and did not in any way form a contract. He further mused that this was the line which would certainly be taken by the Parkies board.

As far as the lawyers were concerned, the only issue remaining was for William and Mary to secure the largest possible payment they could. It was, they believed, unlikely to be anything remotely comparable to Perry's proposal. Any attempt by them to stay at the school and fight it out they considered pointless. It was, as their solicitor strenuously asserted, a lost cause. "It might even mean that you will get nothing. In our experience," the lawyer stated, "in these situations, employers eventually discover something they can spin as Gross Misconduct. If they achieved that, you might leave with nothing."

As Jonathan Carpenter had promised Father Brendan, he came to see William. His difficulty was that as matters were still in the process of negotiation, he was unable to say much of real interest.

His purpose was to reassure William that he would be fairly treated.

By implication he wished also to distance himself from the worst of the nastiness. Something of which he was intensely embarrassed. William trusted Jonathan and believed he would behave as he had always in a reasonable, fair and honourable way.

However, he knew, as of course did Jonathan, that he was not an entirely free agent in all of this. Later, William remembered his last words as he departed. "William, all careers end in failure. You have done a good job but perhaps the challenge was too much in the end."

This was meant kindly and may well have been accurate. Unintentionally Jonathan's words were ambiguous. The implication that in the end William was not up to the challenge of headmaster was not something he needed to hear.

William earnestly hoped that Jonathan's obvious good faith would still protect him from the worst of his enemies. When he recounted this conversation to his solicitor, he was not at all convinced that Jonathan was still in a position to make a real difference. "William, you must understand we are talking about hard-headed business decisions. Whatever you think you deserve or whatever you imagine you have done for this school is irrelevant. You don't seem to have fully grasped that," the exasperated lawyer announced. It was true William after all the woes of the last few months still trustingly believed that the board would finally recognise his contribution. He assumed that the severance agreement would reflect that.

That summer William and Mary were booked to spend a few weeks in Australia with his sister Glynis. The senior partner also commented to William, "I am concerned that whilst you are away they might turf your belongings out of your flat. Change the locks and make your dismissal a *fait accompli."* He advised them to cancel the trip. Mary said, "Even these people could not behave like that, surely." The lawyer quizzically replied, "Based on their past performance I judge them capable of absolutely anything. If you do go, try and ensure that at least one of your boys continues to occupy the flat whilst you are away."

This presentment of further unpleasantness despite William's continuing optimistic belief in the basic decency of most of the board would be duly confirmed at a meeting the governors had agreed to hold with William to discuss the settlement the following Thursday. Early on Monday morning, Gerald Grimes arrived at Graham Warner's little office. There was hardly room for his large bulk in this tiny space after squeezing himself in.

This alone made the encounter an intimidating one. He came quickly to the point. "I happen to know, Mr Warner, that the headmaster continues to award bursaries without the consent of the governors." Graham knew this to be true, at least in a technical sense.

Since the embargo two years before William covertly supported by Graham had given help to a few very needy cases. This was only done occasionally when valued families faced particularly challenging financial circumstances.

If such a family came to see him he encouraged them to remain by sometimes putting the child on the wrong fee band. A few boarders were designated as day children and senior children as junior children, thus reducing their fees. The whole lot amounted to £15,000 on a gross annual fee income of nearly £2,000,000. Grimes continued: "If you provide a complete disclosure of every arrangement I will persuade the other governors to overlook your part in all of this." With a smirk of vindictive pleasure Grimes added, "If on the other hand you do not cooperate fully I will ensure you lose your job together with Jones."

Grimes retreated from Graham's office with an air of perfect contentment. He was truly savouring the realisation of his final, long-desired revenge on Jones and his pathetic crew. Gerald Grimes liked power.

There was nothing better than seeing worms like Warner and Jones snivelling away at his feet. Grimes seemed always to love hurting people, especially if it enhanced his own status. This had been a truly delectable experience. Grimes felt wholly indestructible. He had a feeling of potency which he now so rarely experienced. In this moment he had entirely fulfilled all he wanted. Gerald Grimes considered after this very satisfactory interview all was well with the world. Things could not be going any better.

Graham was in a dreadful dilemma. If he didn't disclose he was sure it was curtains for him, too. He thought anyway that Grimes could probably find the evidence for himself. If he did disclose he believed it to be the most appalling act of betrayal on his part. That evening he returned home in something of a funk and talked to his wife. "We need this job," she pleaded. "William and I did this together; it is unfair just to blame him."

She firmly and vigorously replied, "Without this job we will be on Carey Street. William and Mary are finished anyway. You can do nothing to prevent that. You absolutely have to save your own family." After much hesitation Graham reluctantly and shamefacedly telephoned Gerald Grimes and agreed to his demands.

Graham had never felt worse about anything. He knew he had no other realistic choice. "One other thing," Grimes now insisted. "I want these figures in my hand by Wednesday evening ready for the meeting on Thursday. If Jones finds out the deal is off. So remember, Warner, to keep your bloody mouth shut. If you don't, I will make sure you will go with him. Is that clearly understood?"

This plot – elegant, malicious, and potentially devastating for Jones – had this been organised almost entirely by Grimes? He told himself that this was necessary to protect the school from an overgenerous settlement to the Jones family. This was something he was sure was felt by many governors.

Few would have sunk to Grimes's level to achieve this. Grimes in his mind was doing nothing wrong other than devising a means of achieving this. In effect he thought, as he was protecting the interests of the school, that justified everything. It might be brutal but it was necessary and was therefore, in his mind, wholly commendable.

Margaret McKenzie, although no longer on the board, had been fully consulted. She was absolutely delighted by the scheme. She was still feeling more than a little bruised by her treatment by Barbara Watson.

When Gerald Grimes told her of what he intended to do she felt again triumphant. This was the very epitome of her revenge on this odious man who in a rather peculiar way she irrationally blamed for her fall from grace. Barbara Watson was informed later by Grimes on Wednesday evening. Whilst even she would not have initiated such a brutal plan, she was quite heartened by the evidence that had been accrued. As such it further weakened William Jones's fragile position.

It might even mean that they could summarily dismiss him. Most of the board were entirely ignorant of these machinations until they arrived in Parkies' library the following Thursday. Margaret McKenzie, even with her excited anticipation, had with difficulty avoided mentioning it at her lunch party on Tuesday. Lady Grey was surprised to have noticed her flushed and excited demeanour which, given what she understood to be the very difficult events of the past few weeks had therefore rather puzzled and confused her.

On Thursday afternoon William entered the library to attend the meeting. He was not looking forward to this but at least it would bring things to an end. He thought that to finally know what he would eventually receive would be a kind of closure.

He had accepted finally that there was no other alternative but to give up. It felt of course as though he was running away from his life's work. This was a thought that did nothing to improve his overall morale.

He thus walked into the library and sat at the end of the table. All the governors were present as well as Jonathan Carpenter, who as he was likely to be the money man, was invited, too. William noticed three new faces that he hardly knew. The new headmaster of Haverhill College was attending his first meeting. He had only been in situ for less than a year.

He was, William reckoned, firmly in the new tradition of the well-dressed handsome, rather smooth, youngish men in their early thirties who seemed to be securing recent public school headships. In a few years he would no doubt decamp to somewhere rather smarter and grander.

The two others were women whom William knew lunched with Mrs Watson. William didn't think they were yet fully paid-up members of the St Edmunds set. They both had children in the Lower School. They were two typical examples of what Noah Bradley amusingly referred to as "the yummy mummies."

William spitefully thought in a momentary diversion that being invited onto the Parkies board was part of a strange initiation ceremony before they became fully fledged members of the Suffolk elite, as if they were in the Freemasons. The idea impishly occurred to him that they might bare their left breast as he believed his father and brothers had done in their initiation ceremony in their lodge in Usk.

No one looked at him. Even Thomas Brown and Jonathan Carpenter were firmly avoiding his gaze, staring fixedly at a thin pile of papers neatly stacked before each one of them. Mrs Watson in her coldest, most austere tone started the meeting by announcing: "In front of you, Mr Jones, there are a number of papers on which we would like you to comment." It was immediately obvious what they were. There were a list of figures with the names of various parents attached.

She then continued. "We believe this is a list of unauthorised bursaries you have awarded over the last two years in direct contradiction of governors' instructions." Her tone became even more intransigent when she intoned the words, "What have you to say?"

William looked at Graham at the other end of the table. He knew that this information could have only come from him. He was clearly struggling with himself.

William thought that he detected a tremor in his hand and a slight tick in his face. He imagined that the sheen of sweat glistening on his face was further evidence of his acute mental anguish. He thought for both of them this must be like the experience of facing the Inquisition. The only thing missing was the threat of physical torture and the presence of a Jesuit priest.

He couldn't yet imagine the awful pressure that must have been put on his friend to reveal these details, although he had a pretty fair idea.

He was not surprised or especially upset by this ambush. It was not wholly unexpected.

William in rather a defeatist way had recently come not to be surprised anymore by further catastrophe. He now had come to accept that the worst was likely to happen. This situation merely confirmed his growing cynicism and paranoia.

Ironically, he felt none of the anxiety and fear he had at the interview with Richard Perry a few weeks before. Indeed he was now peculiarly detached. It was similar to the emotion he had experienced in the school assembly just after Richard Perry had left. He felt as though he wasn't really there.

He of course knew what this meeting was about. If they could sack him for 'Gross Misconduct', a settlement would be entirely unnecessary. It was as his lawyers had feared and what he had so foolishly previously pooh-poohed. He further supposed that the idea that he had dishonestly obtained school funds could be spun to parents as a justification for his dismissal.

At one level he did still care. To be sacked without a penny with his reputation in tatters would have been a disaster for his family as well as him personally. At another level he felt he knew he now had absolutely nothing to lose. It provoked in him a reckless courage. The only thing that did still unsettle him was that Jonathan and Thomas seemed to be at one with the rest of the board. They were certainly avoiding any eye contact with him.

Predictably it was Gerald Grimes who then rounded on William. "You do realise that this is fraud, don't you, Headmaster? This is a dismissal issue and I for one think you should be sacked without a penny." The one thing about Grimes, William thought, was that his nastiness was always open and above board. There was never any artifice masking his malice.

He was a man when, in hurting others, he did it with such relish. He reminded him of the boy who he now suddenly remembered was called Gavin Cronin at his grammar school who was responsible for putting him into the imaginary scrum. He was one of the few other people he had ever known who so luxuriated in nastiness in the way Grimes clearly did.

William looked around the table. Most of the board members simply looked embarrassed. There was absolutely no sign of any support. The headmaster of Haverhill said absolutely nothing. William knew that this struggling, minor public school almost bribed parents with bursaries. He suspected that the sums involved were many multiples more than he could ever dream of awarding.

Yet, he offered not a smidgeon of support. Or even a friendly or supportive glance. This man merely looked down at his papers in a fudge of discomfort and embarrassment. William realised he increasingly felt a swelling, angry contempt for this craven attitude. It reinforced a growing disgust for so many of his colleagues. This man represented in his mind the new management guru, PR-obsessed breed of heads he so detested. It was all about spreadsheets and balance sheets.

Schools seemed to them to have become businesses where the individual pupil had about the same status as each unit leaving the assembly line. He wondered why so many such heads believed in nothing other than providing numerous astroturfs, theatres and hotel-type facilities so as to attract rich foreigners.

The days of Arnold, Thring, Sanderson and the visionary headmasters of the past were truly long gone. He thought that his friend Alan was right after all. It was all a massive con. Alan would, he suspected, have laughed at his present predicament. "You have brought this on yourself, you silly old bugger, Will," he heard him saying.

He knew that Graham had been cajoled into revealing these details. He also knew he was a decent man who would have never provided these willingly. He didn't yet appreciate the full extent of the brutal pressure that had been put upon his friend. He thought he could detect a smirk of consummated satisfaction on Barbara Watson's face; but wasn't quite sure. Grimes's features glowed with an intense satisfaction. He looked, as William imagined Napoleon might have done after Austerlitz. He was savouring the potent fulfilment of his absolute victory. There was literally nothing William could say or do to change the likely outcome.

He therefore stood up and announced with as much dignity as he could muster: "Ladies and gentlemen, I have served this school with some distinction for twelve years. The amounts involved are trivial. Much more has been gained in fee income from those children who have been enabled to stay. I have never claimed expenses and not a penny of this £15,000 has ever entered my pocket. If you want to sack me go ahead, feel free." He ended with: "Good afternoon, ladies and gentlemen. If you wish to speak to me, I will be elsewhere." With as much dignity and aplomb as he could muster he then walked slowly out of the room.

He plodded up the stairs to his study opened the door and flopped onto a sofa. It was a strange feeling, this one of complete detachment. It wasn't exactly that he didn't feel anything. It simply required too much energy to respond to any emotion. All he really wanted to do was crawl into the nearest hole and pretend it wasn't happening.

He assumed that any moment the triumphant Mrs Watson would arrive with his final marching orders. However, inexplicably, nothing happened. About an hour later he heard a medley of Mary's, Thomas Brown's, and Jonathan Carpenter's voices outside the door. Mary was saying, "I don't know where he has gone, Jonathan. Perhaps he is in his study." The door opened and the three figures entered.

They all seemed very anxious and even somewhat perturbed. William didn't quite understand or care why. He just felt calm, detached, and totally disassociated . Whatever the reason was for their arrival he simply didn't really want to know. He had come to the point where he assumed that any news was likely to be very bad. Better, a subconscious voice seemed to be saying, to simply pretend he wasn't really there.

Their voices felt far away as though they weren't in the room. Jonathan spoke first. "Are you all right, old chap?" It seemed such a ridiculous question that William could not find the energy to answer it. Mary's voice was more forceful, "Snap out of it, William, there is some good news." Jonathan then continued. "Walking out of a meeting like that is not generally a good tactic, old man. I wouldn't advise doing it again." His face then softened. "You must believe me when I say that Thomas and I and most of the other governors had no idea this was coming."

Thomas then added, "We have spent the last half an hour with a very distressed Graham Warner. He believes he has betrayed you and is absolutely mortified. He has, however, told us the whole story." "It has to be said it was not a good idea to ignore governor edicts, even if you thought they were ridiculous," Jonathan quietly and quite gently asserted.

Thomas then outlined the narrative of Grimes's threats, Graham's capitulation, and the final events in the library after William had left. Jonathan added, in rather a shamefaced way, "I had no idea of the sheer nastiness of what has been going on. The last few weeks have truly opened my eyes."

"It is an odd thing, William. It was Robert Strange who I thought had never really cared much for you who started the fightback. Your dramatic exit provoked his lordship beyond endurance. He turned on Grimes and used language I didn't know the old boy knew."

William's face became a little more animated. He felt for the first time that afternoon just a smidgeon of hope. "This is the old boy's last meeting, you know. It was a hell of an exit." Thomas then interjected, "The old fellow obviously has been keeping a closer interest in recent goings-on that we gave him credit for." Jonathan then observed: "The point is that finally the board has stood up to this awful culture of bullying and intimidation. After his outburst and having made a few pertinent observations on what had been happening, Robert Strange demanded Grimes's immediate resignation, and except for him and Barbara Watson it was carried unanimously."

He carried on more sagely. "This doesn't mean you have been saved, William. Sadly, Richard Perry's damning report has done for you. I think you know that. However, it does mean that there is no question of you being sacked. You will be given a year to leave and find another job. I give you my word I will ensure you get a decent settlement, although it won't be quite the £100,000 that Perry appears to have suggested." Mary looked relieved: it wasn't all they had hoped for. It was definitely something.

Two days later, Barbara Watson arrived in William's sitting room. She behaved reasonably gracefully and no longer seemed to be insisting on immediate letters of resignations. Now that William knew the extent of her dislike of him, he allowed himself to feel the same. There was no altercation, but the coldness between them was Arctic.

William thought someone had talked to her. There were of course no prizes for guessing who. It didn't really change things, but at least it meant that Mrs Watson would have to treat him with a little more care in future. The trouble was William could not escape from the extremely critical judgments of Richard Perry. He had to believe the gist of his report as accurate. He wasn't up to the job, and perhaps never had been.

This was the core of his distress, and whatever little victories he could secure over the likes of Mrs Watson he was left with this crushing sense of his own inadequacy and failure.

In a small way salvation was at hand. Just before the end of term there was a report on the front page of the *Telegraph*, with more salacious details on page three. It seemed that the egotistical Richard Perry could not resist a self-advertising interview on the BBC.

This had provoked nine former pupils, seven girls and two boys, to approach the police with a long list of sexual abuse allegations. The case would go to court in September after William, Mary, Dilys, Flo and Charlie arrived back from Australia. This might not entirely invalidate Perry's judgments of William. Yet it, he supposed, would certainly undermine them.

This man was supposed to represent the integrity and good faith of the whole prep school system. William had trusted him and like many others had been duped by him. Whatever this man had done to him in no way compared with the damage he had obviously caused to so many children's lives. William reflected that such a man had been allowed to hold such sway over the world of English prep schools for two decades or more.

He wondered what future such schools could really expect or deserve if they had allowed that. "So much for my good relationships with children just like him," laughed William as they drove to Heathrow. Things were certainly improving, but there was still Mrs Watson and of course the Daltons to worry about when they returned from Australia.

Chapter Twenty-Eight

GOODBYE, PARKIES

Australia was to be the final seminal moment in William and Mary's relationship with Parkies. Glynis, William's younger sister, had laid on a wonderful trip. A week on the Great Barrier Reef in a glorious little town called Port Douglas in North Queensland as well as a visit to Brisbane.

Most of their time was spent in Sydney with trips to the Blue Mountains, Richmond, and Canberra. Glynis had noticed an alarming change in William, and to a lesser extent in Mary. When she chatted to her blunt, but kindly Australian husband one evening she shared these anxieties with him: "William has aged ten years since we last saw him three years ago. He looks totally downcast and defeated. Mary, too, looks terribly stressed and neither of them is at all happy."

The problem was that other than moral support there was little they could do. Whilst Glynis loved her wayward elder brother, she had never really understood his strange enthusiasms. The most impenetrable of these were his religion and the prep school world he had long ago drifted into.

This further reduced the effective support she could offer. It didn't reduce her natural sympathy. She just couldn't fully imagine worlds she knew so little about.

Glynis talked to Dilys and discovered there was a meeting of minds. Dilys was in some ways relieved. The treatment William was receiving rather confirmed her natural distrust for the posh, perfidious English. She had even less of a grasp than her daughter of the various nuances of William's world.

Fantastically she also had the delusory idea that this might mean that he would eventually return home to work in Monmouthshire. Dilys always hoped for the best, and deep in her heart she still half-hoped that William would return to the family ironmonger business.

Tom agreed with Glynis with similarly only a slight understanding the world William still inhabited. His commented to Glynis soon after they arrived: "I was chatting to Will about the situation at his school. To be frank it looks pretty bloody awful." His Australian candour and his basic Antipodean sense that the best way to deal with bloody-minded people, especially if they were uppity Brits, was either to thump them or tell them to piss off came fully into play.

He recognised the first option was not practicable or probably desirable. He therefore suggested the latter to William. As with most of his observations this was made very tongue-in-cheek. As he said later to Glynis, "The poor bugger is absolutely stuffed. What else can he do when this is all over?" "I don't know," she somewhat disconsolately replied.

Glynis was not unaware of William's failings. As a small girl she had witnessed some of the awful rows that had occurred between William and his father. She knew in her heart that the fault was largely Gethin's. She was also very conscious of William's tendency to be bull-headed, opinionated, and tactless. She supposed that some of his difficulties at Parkies were in part the consequence of these failings.

Her expertise in recent years in HR, which the irredeemably old-fashioned William still insisted on calling Personnel Management, meant that as William described his problems with the Daltons in particular, she realised that he had not handled these well. Indeed his handling of these situations had often been totally crass and pathetic. He probably had tended to be too amenable when he should have been firm, and too confrontational when he should have compromised. If William had known of these observations he would surely have agreed.

William and Mary, now they were halfway round the world, were able to view their situation in a more detached, relaxed way. The truth slowly further dawned on Mary that Jonathan's intervention and Richard Perry's disgrace at the end of the previous term did not in any way signify deliverance. It was merely the stay of execution that Jonathan had outlined a few weeks earlier.

In the first few weeks of the holiday William regained something of his old optimism. Occasionally he came to half-believe that it might still be possible to stay at Parkies. This was a delusion, as of course Mary and Glynis knew. The forces arrayed against them were still absolutely overwhelming.

More important from Mary's perspective was her growing awareness of the collapse in William's self-confidence. Some of the criticisms made by Richard Perry she knew were self-evidently accurate. The fact that William knew this, too, had eaten into his fragile sense of self-worth. He had, as Perry had said, increasingly given more and more authority to Kate Bell who was immensely competent. The problem was that her proliferating poise and confidence had inadvertently further exposed William's growing despondency and weakness. There was, she considered, no way back from this.

They talked about their options. William at fifty-one was too old to be a serious contender for another prep school headship. His problems at St Dogmael's were anyway too well known in this rather small, incestuous, gossipy prep school world. He would therefore be unlikely even to secure an interview.

In the pressures of the last few years he had failed to develop the kind of network that might just have helped. He rarely attended prep school headmaster meetings, for example. In truth he didn't much care for some of the new model heads. Too smooth, insincere and patronising for his taste!

He also felt that these events were more usually about self-promotion than any educational value they might have. He also recognised that to go back as an ordinary History teacher when you had once been a headmaster was very difficult. William's opinionated, rather stroppy nature meant it would probably make this impossible. Few heads he knew would be willing to take the risk.

They knew that as William's real love was history this might be the route for his future career. The heritage industry or maybe museum work would seem to be a possibility. These dreams were in part predicated on getting a good report in the following term's School inspection.

If this happened he could leave Parkies on a high note. His future career prospects might even have survived the events of the previous term. This inspection was what worried Mary most. She judged that whilst he was a talented teacher he wasn't well organised. The stresses and strains of the last year or so had not helped him develop adequately the skills necessary for the growing administrative burdens of his job.

The final and most concerning aspect of the situation was his increasing difficulties with frequent and ever more crushing bouts of depression. On the whole he was fine in Australia. The cajoling, loving approach of Glynis helped, together with the fact that he was so far away from Suffolk. Even there he would suffer dark days evidenced by his tendency to go for long walks through the streets of Sydney on his own.

When they returned home the problems immediately built up. Evelyn had been so upset and hurt by the events of the previous year that he decided on the spur of the moment to resign. William was pleased that he secured a post as Head of Drama in a leading girls' public school. It was good that Grimes's malice seemed to have done his career no permanent damage.

Janet Chester, William's long-serving secretary, had also left for similar reasons. This was a particularly serious loss as her impressive administrative talents were often able to mask William's lack of them. She used to laugh that when she carefully neatly organised William's tasks in order of priority, he would simply scrabble through the lot and choose the ones that most interested him.

It frustrated her but didn't detract from her affection for him. Nor truthfully was it just about losing Janet's administrative abilities. She was a trusted confidante and there were fewer and fewer people whom he could totally trust. Most of all both William and Mary were very fond of her. Her departure left a considerable hole in both of their lives.

One interesting piece of news was that Richard Perry's case finally went to court. He was convicted on two counts of sexual interference. To be fair to him, he then handed back his gong. The truth is he probably had little choice.

Before sentencing many of the great and the good wrote to the court. This included a former Cabinet minister. They claimed that all these charges amounted to a relatively small lapse in a very distinguished career.

Leaving aside his almost certain guilt in the seven "unproved allegations", extraordinarily the judge accepted these pleadings with alacrity and gave him what seemed to Mary especially the derisory penalty of a suspended prison sentence. The justifiable anger expressed by many of his victims was splashed all over the popular press. Not of course that it did them any good. At the very least, William and Mary realised, this perfectly illustrated the continuing overwhelming power of the establishment. The children he had damaged seemed hardly to matter. Perry's distinguished career and reputation of course did!

William had also lost his last consistently reliable, friendly governor. Thomas Brown wrote to Mrs Watson during William and Mary's sojourn in Australia, accusing her of organising the previous term's plot and demanding her resignation. He was of course quite right about this. It was not something Barbara Watson was ever going to admit, even probably to herself. When her resignation was not forthcoming he decided himself to resign.

He said to William a few weeks afterwards, "At least McKenzie and Grimes are very obviously nasty and unpleasant people. Watson is, I think, worse still because she looks as though butter wouldn't melt in her mouth whilst wielding her large battleaxe and exposing her long, vicious talons.

Look, William," he added more seriously. "Sorry but you have got to go please don't delude yourself that you can stay. You know in your heart that it will only get worse. In the end it comes down to your personal survival and that of your family." His final observation was perhaps his most prescient. "In the end this is only a job: you must remember that your family and your own well-being are much more important."

Whilst Lady McKenzie had left the board she was still a malign influence. Her gossiping skills were unabated. These even ensured together with her new title her continuing membership of the St Edmunds circle. However, she never fully regained the trust of Barbara Watson and therefore Lady Grey, too. It was true that all the set treated her with a growing wariness. She seemed hardly aware of that. Margaret McKenzie's regularly meetings with Isabelle Dalton reinforced her continuing if now increasingly futile obstructiveness.

Gerald Grimes remained his normal obnoxious self. As he was no longer a governor his power to cause mischief was therefore much curtailed. The new issue he and his wife obsessed about were lost socks. Specifically those of his second son Henry, now in his final year. His wife Tracey hounded Mary continuously about various missing rugby or school socks.

"It really isn't good enough, Mrs Jones. We pay an awful lot of money to send him here and even his possessions aren't adequately looked after," she angrily opined. But the fact that he had been forced to resign in that traumatic meeting much reduced his power and authority. Most people knew now of the depths of his malice and nastiness. He certainly remained a pain but it was now merely an irritant rather than a cancerous growth.

Barbara Watson might have lost her battles of the previous term but not, in her opinion, the war. She would bide her time but in the end William Jones would most certainly go. This expectation of the board of governors that William would soon be gone meant William quickly realised that he had virtually no influence on policy or the future direction of the institution. This merely added to his frustration and a growing sense of ennui. Brian Varga his friend and former colleague came for a visit. He wasn't the first person to share his concerns with Mary. "He is all over the place, Mary, he really doesn't have a grip."

The inspection occurred and as expected the team were justifiably very complimentary about Kate Bell's role; less so about William. They were devastating about Piers Dalton's capabilities, rating all his classroom performance as inadequate in every category. William had expected this.

What he didn't expect was that they rated one-third of his classes as inadequate, too. In some ways this was a greater blow to his morale than Richard Perry's earlier observations.

For months, perhaps longer, William had prided himself mostly on his teaching. Whilst it was clear even to him that he was no longer doing an effective job as headmaster, the quality of his teaching had become the very core of his sense of self-worth and value. He knew that he didn't prepare sufficiently. This was related to teaching virtually a full timetable with the additional tasks, if somewhat diminished, associated with his other duties.

He was arrogant enough to imagine that his natural talents would see him through. Throughout a career of nearly thirty years no inspector had ever been other than very complimentary about his teaching performance. He reluctantly recognised again that he was guilty of appalling hubris. This fact further depressed his morale. Their criticism, however justified, he might recognise in his more tranquil moments but it hurt him profoundly.

This judgment simply broke William's back. He descended into a mood of bleak despair. Even his regular visits to Calvin, his psychotherapist and friend, no longer seemed to help much.

Mary and William finally decided that the time had come to resign. This was made more difficult because neither had the remotest idea of what future job prospects, if any, they could expect.

Mary was especially worried about Flo who was already so clearly distressed by her father's moody introspection. The uncertainty of her own future now also weighed heavily upon her. They drove to the coast on a windy December day to help them come to this final decision. Both of them had come to love Suffolk. They knew they would miss its now familiar landscape. They came slowly, if reluctantly, to fully understand what had to be done as they walked hand in hand along the beach at Southwold. They finally and belatedly realised that they had no real choice.

William tendered his resignation to Barbara Watson the day before the start of the spring term in 2000. He brought the letter to her house. There were few courtesies observed. He had telephoned to say he was coming. She opened the letter whilst William explained his decision. He stood in her hallway. He was not invited into her drawing room.

She coldly, if politely, thanked him for coming and William was then quickly and summarily dismissed. He supposed that by this stage he was so finely attuned to the slightest negative nuance of others' behaviour that these impressions might have been pure imagination.

He couldn't dismiss the idea of a rather skipping motion in her step as she left him. There was certainly no expression of regret or kind consolation in her expression. Merely he thought he saw the consummated realisation of a long desired triumph.

Mrs Watson called a special meeting of the governors to decide upon a job description for the new head. They also called William and Mary in to discuss their severance deal. As one might predict, Mrs Watson was determined to be as obstructive as possible. This attitude was best expressed by her when she observed, "Richard Perry's criticisms were about William, not Mary. Why should we offer compensation to Mary? Surely she would be welcome to stay on without him."

This suggestion, so apparently reasonably expressed, was in reality another ploy to reduce the value of any settlement. It was also in William's opinion about maliciously trying to split up his family. Barbara Watson had the rare capability of wielding the proverbial cleaver of retribution whilst smiling in her most charming beatific way. It was, as Thomas Brown had said, as though butter wouldn't melt in her mouth. In the end it was Jonathan Carpenter who finally saw through the deliberate nastiness of Mrs Watson's suggestion and put his foot down. The settlement was agreed, although it was barely half that initially proposed by Richard Perry.

By now, at the beginning of the spring term, William was little more than a figurehead. He taught and he became a regular minibus driver for school trips and took on more boarding duties. As he was leaving in a few months it was no longer seen as appropriate for him to see any prospective parents. He felt too humiliated and ashamed to attend headmaster meetings out of school. In teaching the stories of the English

Kings he had never before appreciated what Henry VI must have felt like during these years of captivity in the Tower during Edward IV's reign. Now he thought he knew. In reality of course the school was now being run by Kate and Graham. The fact that they did such a good job had the unintended effect of further demoralising him.

Unbeknown to William and probably almost everybody else involved in the recruitment process, Barbara Watson had a favoured candidate. Robert Crawford was a friend of a distant cousin. However, more importantly he had many of the attributes that Mrs Watson felt were essential for the future welfare of the school. He was an Etonian. His family were minor Northumberland gentry. He had even served a few years in the Grenadier Guards. He had also worked for a number of years as a housemaster at Harrow. The only slight drawback was that he had run a rather grander prep school for a few years. It appeared not to have not been a great success.

Gossip had even suggested that he had jumped from this post before he was pushed. Nor was he a Catholic. That, however, was seen as less and less important. In the wash-up meeting after the interviews Barbara Watson confidently asserted, "This seems just the chap we need. He will ensure with all his contacts that St Dogmael's will again be recognised nationally as a serious prep school."

There were no governors left who were prepared to disagree with her analysis. Like the time all those years before when William was appointed, there was a great sparsity of candidates. It was of no surprise when this man was eventually chosen. In the days that followed Mrs Watson looked like the cat who had got the cream.

William found the process more difficult and painful than he had ever imagined. His overwhelming sense was still that of shame. He was prostrated by a feeling that he had let everyone down, most especially Mary and the children.

Flo was devastated: her whole life had been at Parkies. All her friends were in the school, and now at the age of ten she would lose everything that was familiar and safe. She now had to move into an unknown and uncertain future. It took her years to fully forgive her dad for this.

When William escorted the candidates around the school, he had this extraordinary sense, rather like Huckleberry Finn, of being present at his own funeral. This was reinforced when he inadvertently overheard a conversation between Barbara Watson and the newly appointed headmaster elect. "You do understand that this is a failing school, don't you Robert?" she confided. "William Jones has lost the plot: you will therefore have to pick up the pieces." William recognised that whilst this was cruel and insensitive these comments did contain much essential truth. This made it all seem even worse to bear.

By the end of that spring term William was spending more and more of his time sitting in his study playing an especially mindless computer game. Somehow by focussing on this meaningless activity he felt he could escape his increasing disconsolateness, and a growing sense of despair.

Then his old friend Brian Varga came to stay. After a number of drinks one night in his sitting room William confessed. "Brian, I know what a pretty useless fellow I am, but I am having these really terrible thoughts." "What thoughts, William?" Brian asked rather anxiously. "I am embarrassed to mention it, but I keep obsessively thinking of ways to do myself in." William realising he had said too much and added, "Don't say anything to Mary: they are after all just silly fancies."

Brian was so worried he talked later that night to Ludmila. "What should I do?" he pleaded. "I seriously think that William is going to top himself. I have promised him I will not talk to Mary." "You must," Ludmila forcibly reacted. "If something happens you will never forgive yourself." Brian then did approach Mary, despite William's firm injunction not to do so.

Things then developed very quickly. Mary took charge. She together with the school doctor and Calvin, William's friend, and psychotherapist, insisted he urgently visited a consultant psychiatrist. This man then required that he was signed off work for the rest of his time at Parkies. The doctor described William's condition in indecipherable medical gobbledygook which William didn't really understand. It amounted apparently in layman's language to the fact that William's illness constituted a serious nervous breakdown from which the consultant believed it might take him years to recover.

For the next four months William became a kind of prisoner in his own flat. He did occasionally go away. He visited Downside. He stayed in Usk with Dilys and even saw Father Brendan in Walthamstow. During these weeks he sometimes remembered the Catholic doctrine of Limbo. He sometimes thought that in living through this experience trapped in his flat he might be personally encountering that.

This situation was made bearable for him because as part of his treatment he was prescribed quite strong antidepressants. For Mary and Flo the situation was increasingly unbearable. Mary felt that they were in a nightmare goldfish bowl where they had to try and keep a calm exterior when both were fighting to avoid uncontrollable panic. Flo was simply watching her world disintegrate.

For William and Mary their life at Parkies ended with Prize-Giving. William sat quietly, and he hoped unobtrusively, at the back of the hall. When the parents saw him the vast majority spontaneously stood in a standing ovation. He was overwhelmed with emotion, especially when he saw Mary wiping her eyes on the edge of weeping on the other side of the hall.

He stood in front of them all and he stupidly couldn't stop the tears streaming down his face. He was so embarrassed by this display of weak emotionality that he retired as quickly and discreetly as he could. William also couldn't help guiltily and furtively observing that the Watson, Grimes, McKenzie and Dalton families ostentatiously didn't join in. Mary pointed out later that ovation was worth so much more than all the malice and gracelessness of this tiny minority of horrid people. William wasn't sure he believed her, but he appreciated and loved her for saying it.

They left Parkies and Dilys generously split her house to make room for her son and his family. The conditions were very cramped especially when all the boys came to stay. One even had to sleep in the kitchen. It was slightly easier than it might have been because for most of the time James was at Sandhurst and Charlie was away at university.

William's brothers seemed slightly too solicitous for his welfare. Perhaps it was the result of his strange mental state, but William even thought they might be gleaning some satisfaction from his and Mary's fall from grace. Later, William and Mary, with Dilys's help, bought a little cottage in Ledbury. This pretty little town was close enough to Usk to keep in contact with Dilys but far enough away to develop their own independence. As it turned out, William was to live there for the rest of his life.

Robert Crawford took over as head of Parkies. Mrs Watson should have noted more closely the reasons for Robert Crawford's problems at his previous school. He and especially his rather snooty, distant wife did not much care for Parkies' core market of farmers, local professionals and prosperous tradesmen. Rather unwisely they often patently showed it. Many of these parents reacted in kind by removing their children in copious numbers.

At the time of William's departure the school role stood at 345. Within two years it had dropped to below 200. The consequence of this catastrophic fall of over 40% meant that within two years Parkies went steeply into unsustainable debt. Finally even Mrs Watson had to accept that the game was up. When the Crawfords were finally dismissed in 2002 she resigned the chair and left the board of governors.

The damage to the school had been irreversible. Kate Bell made a valiant effort to reverse things. In 2004, despite her and Graham Warner's best efforts, Parkies finally closed its doors. Jonathan Carpenter then arranged for Nigel Denton to sell the estate for housing development.

At about this time, too, Martin Pugh's life ended. He was someone whom William thought of as ultimately the saddest casualty of the school. For nearly ten years before his death he had ceased full-time teaching. In the end his problems were so acute that he left the school completely.

This quite literally broke his heart. He retreated more and more into the solace of drink. Finally his marriage broke up and he ended his life in a shabby bedsit in the grubbier end of Ipswich. On a night of copious drinking his heart finally gave out.

A man who had started life as prosperous member of the Welsh gentry ended it as little more than a drunken derelict. A sad end to a disappointing life. Yet William knew that Martin was a much better person than he ever really believed he was. Part of his problem, perhaps most of it, was his overwhelming sense of Catholic guilt and unworthiness. William often wondered whether he would have been happier if he had never darkened Parkies' doors. On balance, William thought that he probably would have been.

Gerald Grimes, too, ran into some difficulties. His taste for questionable deals eventually brought him to the notice of HMRC. The subsequent fines, obloquy, and social humiliation, as well as a massive reduction in his wealth, ensured that the family decamped from their grand house in Suffolk to a more modest abode near Walthamstow.

He was too late to have met Father Brendan again who had died of cancer six months before. In his last few months Brendan wrote little notes to William with profoundly moving contemplations about his own approaching demise. They were full of reflections about his profound religious faith and what William knew was his essential holiness. When he finally went to his Maker, both William and Mary missed his benevolent wisdom.

His last comment to them when they visited him a month or so before the end was: "I know it is difficult to believe, Will, but there really is a God. I feel His presence more and more each day." Brendan, they came to believe, was perhaps the one truly good person who had made their sojourn at Parkies really worthwhile.

Mrs Watson's children never did get the scholarships she yearned for, and the great dream of Eton, or indeed any public school education, eluded them. Eventually her family's money problems were exposed in a widely publicised bankruptcy. The McKenzies eventually split up. Marcia finally got her man, a fact she was swiftly to deeply regret. These well-publicised scandals as well as others less well aired ensured that the St Edmunds set soon disintegrated. Perhaps the one success that Robert Crawford did achieve was something that had always eluded him. Within a year of his removal the Daltons, too, were forced out. So, William reflected maliciously, there was sometimes a silver lining!

Throughout this period William was rather poorly. He suffered with the severe depression the consultant had diagnosed at the end of his Parkies career. Such attacks in the past had normally passed on quite quickly. Living so far away he could no longer often employ the wise counsel of his friend Calvin. Quite frequent telephone calls were however of enormous help.

These problems stayed with him for a few pretty dreadful years. It was, he reflected, like one of those weather patterns which gets stuck over a particular location. There were moments when Mary feared for his sanity. Slowly things got better, especially after they moved to Ledbury. He undertook an external MA, which gave him another real interest and allowed him to make some really good new friends as well as a chance to avoid introspection. As it turned out, no future career opportunities appeared. Mary thrived, becoming eventually a much-respected deputy head of a local primary school.

William tried assiduously to avoid news of Parkies. Many of these developments therefore largely passed him by. The closure shocked but didn't really surprise him. He sympathised with those like Graham and Kate who had tried so hard and valiantly to keep it going. If, he reflected, they had not been so hobbled by Barbara Watson's blind arrogance and stupidity, and if Kate had immediately taken over from him as head, she would have definitely succeeded.

William and Mary came to increasingly believe that the boarding prep school world they had entered in 1987 was truly the fag end of an educational experiment two hundred years old. It was, they now realised, inevitable that Parkies would close, as, they came to understand, would most other schools of its type.

William would never have recognised that he was the true heir of the charismatic Canon Paine. Yet when Jonathan Carpenter thought about William's fate years later he remarked to his wife Celia, "Perhaps when I arranged William Jones's appointment I think I was trying at some strange subconscious level to re-create something of Father Paine's vision. I believe he would have rather liked William. A very different man but they sang from the same hymn sheet."

William didn't know of Jonathan's musings and would probably not have understood or recognised them even if he had. It amused him, though, when he thought of his great friend Alan who he knew would have been quite diverted. "You see, Will, it was all bollocks in the end."

William of course had always loved Thomas Malory's *Morte d'Arthur* possibly partly because of its associations with his beloved Monmouthshire and the nearby Roman towns of Caerleon and Caerwent. He delighted especially in the offshoot musical *Camelot*. In Evelyn Morley's last term in 1999 he for the second time decided on this as the school musical. He didn't then know that he would be leaving the school within a few weeks. A kind desire to respond to William's romantic inclinations as well as his well-known love for the Arthurian story had been important considerations in Evelyn's choice.

CAMELOT DEPARTED

Ironically in later years William thought in what he now considered was probably a rather silly, pretentious way that Parkies had been his own personal Camelot. He had simply tried to nurture the extraordinary idea that it might be possible to devise a kind of childhood paradise for the pupils in his care. It was a whimsical, nonsensical, unrealistic fantasy of course. In the happy children's faces William and Mary so often remembered in later years in the end it meant that in making that attempt it wasn't such an inconsequential achievement after all. "There was a spot for one brief, shining moment that was called Camelot" – that perhaps said it all.

Jonathan White
July 2020